THE CONTRACT

KT-177-050

Gerald Seymour comes from a strong writing
background: his father was Chairman of the
Poetry Society and a Fellow of the Royal
Society of Literature and his mother has
published more than thirty novels.

After taking a History degree at London
University, Gerald Seymour joined the
reporting team of Independent Television
News. Among his assignments were the
Vietnam War, the Indo-Pakistan conflict, the
Aden crisis, the Northern Ireland troubles, the
Yom Kippur War and the abduction and
murder of Aldo Moro in Italy. In between his
reporting jobs he wrote his first four novels,
Harry's Game, *The Glory Boys*, *Kingfisher* and
Red Fox.

He has now retired from active television
reporting and lives with his wife and two sons
in the hills south of Dublin.

GERALD SEYMOUR

The Contract

FONTANA/Collins

First published by William Collins Sons & Co. Ltd 1980
First issued in Fontana Paperbacks 1981
Third impression December 1986

Made and printed in Great Britain by
William Collins Sons & Co. Ltd, Glasgow

To Gillian, Nicholas and James

Chapter One

=

They were last off the aircraft.

The middle-aged man and the boy in his early twenties had not joined the queue of passengers who scrambled along the aisle towards the forward exit. The pilot shut down his engines and the music cascaded from the hidden loud-speakers in the ceiling. The man ignored the buffeting his elbow took on the arm rest of his seat as passengers' bags and belongings and Duty Free parcels pummelled against him. He was engrossed in his book, dog-eared and much consulted, a tome on European birds: his attention was held by the winter markings and juvenile colourings of the Golden, Grey, Ringed and Kentish plovers. There was nothing he could learn from text or illustrations, but he handled the pages as a widow will consult a much used family Bible. When he was jolted by a bulging plastic carrier boasting the name of a fur shop on the Rue du Mont Blanc, he looked up, just the once, in irritation. But it was momentary and replaced by the satisfaction of knowing that Heathrow's Customs and Excise staff reserved their closest scrutiny for travellers from Geneva.

They made strange and unlikely companions. The man was round-faced, bald-headed with untidy strands of wispy grey hair settling about his ears. The boy was striking in a muscular, lissom, empty fashion, good looking in an inade-quate way, with weather in his cheeks. The man wore a tired suit with a small tidy darn on the right elbow and his shoes were brilliantly polished. The boy was dressed in sports coat and slacks that made only a casual fit, too long at the sleeves, too short at the legs, a temporary and borrowed habit.

The boy shivered as he waited for the aisle to clear. It was more than five hours since he had been in the water, but the

7

cold still nestled close to his bones and the chill had settled on his skin beneath the singlet and underpants and socks that had been given to him. His hair was damp and slicked down by combing and his nostrils were filled with the static odour of the lake. They had said at the home of the British Consul that there was not time for him to have a bath, they had given him a towel only and told him to be quick, and his drying had been perfunctory because they had looked at their watches and shuffled their feet and talked of the departure time from the airport.

When the cabin behind them had emptied, the man pocketed his book reluctantly and reached between his feet and lifted his briefcase onto his lap and then twisted it about so that the gold indented E II R insignia was hidden against his chest. His hands rested protectively on the handle and he stared back at the stewardess who glanced frequently and nervously into his face and could not summon the courage to query him. The music was switched off. The cockpit door opened and the flight deck crew bowed their way out from the controls. The boy had his hands on the arm rests, ready.

The man bided his time. The stewardess whispered to the pilot, who made a brusque and quiet answer. She shrugged petulantly and opened a cupboard for her uniform coat and hat, and had her back to the door and so did not see the entrance of the British Airways ground crew official into the cabin.

'It's Mr Carter, isn't it?'

'That's right.'

'There's a car and a driver waiting.'

'Thank you.'

The man stood up, stretched his back slowly, wriggled his shoulders, reached up to the rack and pulled down an old fawn raincoat.

'You won't be needing that, sir, it's really been quite nice here the last couple of days.'

'I know that,' the man said quietly. 'I only flew out at lunchtime.' He wondered why he had taken the trouble to deflate the official. Unnecessary and uncalled for. The boy

8

was still in his seat as if requiring an instruction to move.

'A good flight, Mr Carter?'

'Very smooth, thank you. Come on, Willi, let's be on our way.'

The man led with his raincoat draped over his arm and his briefcase tight against his thigh, and the boy who had no bag and no case was close behind him with his head lowered and shielded as they passed the ground crew official and the stewardess who had her lipstick at her mouth and the pilot who gazed after them in curiosity. They stepped onto the platform that had been manoeuvred to hug the aircraft fuselage, but avoided the tunnel stretching ahead and went through the open doorway and out into the night air and down the steps to the apron. A light wind blustered off the concrete; the man's hair danced and the boy shuddered, and the engine sounds of taxiing aircraft bludgeoned their ears. The man looked around him until he saw the maroon Rover parked in the dense evening shadow of a petrol tanker. He looked back towards the open, lit doorway above the steps and saw the ground official watching them and nodded in gratitude, then walked quickly towards the car. A rear door was open, the engine was idling.

The man let the boy into the car first because that way he would be against the door which could not be opened from the inside. He waited while the boy slid across the back seat. Better safe. And the boy would be on the raw edge of his nerves and his strength and his control. They were all unreliable in the first few hours, those who had crossed the chasm, they were all unpredictable. Better safe, and this boy had been through more than most. The swim had exhausted him, the parting from the girl had bled him. He was docile enough at this moment, but his face was a mask suppressing his emotions. The man could only guess at the turmoil waging in the boy's mind, but he could guess well and his experience told him that the boy should be handled with care, with kid mittens. Whether they came from an outstation of Soviet intelligence or were junior interpreters attached to the permanent Moscow delegation to the Conference of the Committee on Disarmament at the Palais des Nations in Geneva, they all carried the same hallmark. They differed little, the defectors who came over.

'George, this is Mr Guttmann, Mr Willi Guttmann.' Henry Carter eased himself into the car, and circumspectly pulled the door shut beside him. 'Willi, this is George, he'll be helping to look after you over the next three or four weeks while we sort things out, get things into order.' A large fist snaked backwards from the front of the car and gripped Willi Guttmann's hand. The boy's eyes flickered upwards, but won no smile, no friendship.

'Pleased to meet you, Willi.' A watchful greeting.

'When we've been on the road a bit I'd like to make a phone call, George. When we're down by Cobham or Ripley, I'd like to ring the office.' Carter smoothed his hair into shape, pushed it back from his scalp.

'No problem, Mr Carter. They'll be pleased to hear from you.'

George's familiar bonhomie always annoyed Henry Carter, perpetually irritated him. But then George had been with the Service twenty years, on the payroll since a Cypriot gunman's bullet had put a stop to his Commando soldiering. He was part of the furniture, part of the trappings, part of the team that handled the 'runaways'.

The car pulled away, skirting the Terminal buildings, heading for the Underpass and the Staines Road. Beside him Henry Carter sensed Willi Guttmann's defiant stare through the window.

Four men had come down from the Residence on the hill above Lake Geneva and they stood in the dark on the shingle at the shore line, huddled together against the harsh spattering rain. With them was Geneva's Chief of Police.

Their shoes were soaked, their trousers below their coats were wet and wrapped to their shins. The wind squalls caught at their shoulders, bent their bodies, drilled at the skin on their cheek. A bitter, clouded April night. Their voices carried to the man who stood apart from them and stared out, expressionless, at the activity on the grey dark water a hundred metres from the narrow beach.

Valeri Sharygin was described on the personnel lists as First Attaché to the Secretary of the Soviet delegation to the Conference of the Committee on Disarmament. It was not an arduous post and one designed to consume little of the time of the principal security officer at the Residence. As a senior KGB officer, as a man noted for the penetration of his intellect and the gimlet sharpness of his suspicion, he was almost always alone, often on the outside of the group. He was feared, he was avoided, he was respected. Through narrow-rimmed and thick-lensed spectacles, over a close-cut brush of a moustache he watched the bobbing endeavours of the rubber dinghies that circled the short and white-painted hull of the capsised yacht.

Two searchlights that were powered by mobile throbbing generators played their beams from the shore onto the water where the frogmen dived and where the ropes with the grappling hooks were thrown. And they were futile, the efforts of these searchers, an obligatory show with very little prospect of success. Three hours since the angry keeper of the marina beside the Jardin Botanique had telephoned the Residence to ask how much longer was he supposed to wait for Monsieur Guttmann to bring back the yacht that was on permanent hire to the delegation. When anyone was late, missing, overdue at the Residence Sharygin went first to their sleeping quarters with his pass-key, sifted their possessions, and evaluated whether their tardiness was innocent or criminal. There had been clothes scattered on the floor, money and a half-written letter to his father on his desk, a bag of laundry by the door, an empty suitcase under his bed. One hour later the Second Secretary to the Permanent Mission had run into Guttmann's room, found Sharygin rifling a drawer, hesitated in an embarrassed silence and then blurted the information that the drifting boat had been sighted from the Coppett road. So Willi Guttmann, junior interpreter, had overturned a yacht on a foul afternoon when only an idiot would have put out from the marina.

11

Who knew how far the yacht had drifted since or how far the deep currents had transferred a water swollen corpse? Futile the efforts of the searchers. They should wait for daylight, they should wait for the body to be washed to the shore.

'Monsieur Foirot . . .' Sharygin shouted against the wind towards the group of his countrymen and the Chief of Police. He stood his ground, saw illuminated for a moment that glimpse of annoyance as the policeman detached himself and walked up to him. 'Monsieur Foirot, from your experience, please, when should we find him?'

'Difficult to be certain, the lake water has many vagaries . . .'

'Tomorrow, the day after?'

'I cannot tell you. He was not wearing a life jacket; we have recovered that. If he is far down then we have no method of measuring the patterns of the currents that will take him. Normally they surface within forty-eight hours, but I cannot tell you where that might be and there are relatively few craft on the lake before the season, it could be many days before the body is sighted if it is carried far out. And then again, Monsieur Sharygin, if he has tangled himself with a rope, if the rope has snagged on the lake bed . . . I cannot tell you.'

Sharygin looked away, back to the water, back to the divers and the dinghies and the yacht that was now righted and sluggish in her movements from the water she had taken on board.

'He was a lunatic to go out in such weather.' Sharygin stamped his feet against the cold.

'If you say so, Monsieur. What position does he hold with the delegation?'

'He is nobody. Twenty-four years old, an interpreter for us. This had been his first assignment outside the Foreign Ministry. He was due to return tomorrow, now that the conference session has ended. A fool.'

The Russian pounded away across the beach towards his car. A lunatic and a fool, that had been Willi Guttmann. But would Moscow have sent an idiot . . .? That was the missing segment of the circle. He might find the answer in the boy's personal file. He would find no answer here, not in the rain and the cold and the wind.

'Mr Mawby? . . . It's Carter.'

'Why didn't you call from Geneva?'

'Behind the clock there, he was running late. But I wanted to put you in the.picture as soon as possible, because it'll be another hour before we're at the house.'

'That's good for you, Henry. Home and dry are we?'

'We're home, the boy's not dry . . . He had a rough time in the water, Mr Mawby. When he turned her over I think he was trapped for a bit under the mainsail. Sounded a bit nightmarish, and the weather was ghastly, the swim would have taken a deal of pluck.'

'He chose the way, he made his bed.'

'It was the first thing he said to me, that his father had to be spared. Had to seem an accident, that's what he said, Mr Mawby.'

'So be it, and apart from a throat full of water, how is he?'

'A bit choked up about the girl not coming on the second leg. He's quiet and sullen most of the time, sort of bottling it.'

'That's damned stupid, not much point in going through with this charade and then having his girlfriend disappear on the same night. The boy has to see that.'

'I think it's the girl. Flood of tears at the parting, quite a scene really.'

'You're going soft in your dotage, Henry.'

'He said they'd kept it very secret, plugged the keyhole I suppose.'

'Chatter him through the Geneva end for a couple of days, then I'll send an armour king down to you.'

'Right, Mr Mawby. We'll be on our way again.'

'Good . . . oh, and Henry, it's been very well done. Very smooth.'

'Thank you very much, Mr Mawby.'

For a man of his build, Henry Carter had quite a sharp step as he returned to the car. At his position in the Service with a lowly plateau of advancement reached and little to look forward to bar the cut glass decanter and the hand-shakes and the good riddance and the bored smiles of the retirement party, praise was welcome. It was his talent that he sold himself short, that was what his wife said anyway, and he usually told her she was right.

Lying on the carpet in his small study, wearing the Guernsey knit sweater that provided him with a boyish sense of the outdoors, puffing at a cigarette that dropped from a monogrammed holder, Charles Mawby studied the mole hills of paperwork that he had dispersed across the floor. His wife never disturbed him while he was working, left his coffee and tea outside the door before going at tip-toe back to the living room of their Knightsbridge flat, and the con-solation of the portable television. Sometimes he wished that she would intrude so that she could flavour the concentra-tions of files and maps and photographs with their 'Secret' and 'Restricted' stamps, but the door stood as a barricade between his professional life and what private existence the Service permitted him. If she had come in then Charles Augustus Mawby, of good pedigree, good school, good Cambridge College, would have assumed irritation and made a show of covering typescripts and said something about 'Not really good for you to see this sort of stuff, darling', and wallowed secretly in a sort of pride. An Assistant Secretary nominally working at the Foreign and Commonwealth Office, Mawby was a career officer of the Secret Intelligence Service, climbing high and well. A bright future at every compass point in the offing.

The paper mounds represented the briefings he had received during the previous week. They concerned a success that was not spectacular but might be significant. A mite of triumph in the unending struggle for information and the placing of pieces in the jigsaw that had no horizon. Two years back Mawby and select colleagues had taken a private room at the Garrick Club and over champagne and lobster, and afterwards port and Stilton had celebrated the four hundredth anniversary of the Service. They had toasted their Elizabethan founder, Sir Francis Walsingham, who had created the principle that knowledge is never too dear, that no price could be set on intelligence material. For Mawby that evening had set the seal on his determination that within the confines of his influence the Service would remain a virile and lively agency. He munched at the sandwich he had retrieved from the doorway, scattered crumbs on the papers left by the Ministry of Defence (Intelligence) and the Service's Russian Desk/Military.

If the Service were to remain the vital agency that he conjured in his mind, stay free from the constraints of the 'parsimonious politicians' that the Deputy-Under-Secretary was for ever complaining of, then it must be alert to chance, responsive to good fortune. In the case of Willi Guttmann they had much with which to be satisfied.

An English girl of good county stock, employed by the World Health Organisation, leaning towards middle age and fear of the shelf, had plucked up the courage to jump from her virginal pedestal and launch herself into an affair with a junior Soviet diplomat. And managed to get herself pregnant for her pains.

A nice girl from a nice home and father doing well in the Inner Temple, and so, of course, the thought of termination was unthinkable. And Willi Guttmann, naïve and infatuated and far from home, had been persuaded that a baby needs a father, and wet little blighter that he was had agreed that Lizzie Forsyth should trip round to the British Consul in Geneva who would know what to do, what arrangements could be made.

The Consul had been quick and his telex had finished up on Charles Mawby's desk.

The German name and the Soviet background had nagged at Mawby, caused him to take the lift to the Library in Century House, caused him to smile sweetly at the wide-hipped ladies who could drop their hands on cross references, caused him an agreeable sting of pleasure when they reported back that the junior interpreter was the son of

15

Doctor Otto Guttmann. Mawby had glanced once at the files the ladies showed him and with rare excitement hurried to telephone the Consul.

He brushed the crumbs from the biography sheet, wondered why his wife needed the television's volume so high and glanced again at the typed detail.

Lizzie Forsyth's little indiscretion, her failure to get herself kitted up, had landed in their laps the son of the Director of Russian anti-tank missile research. There would be some pieces for the jigsaw out of that, could hardly be otherwise.

Sweet, wasn't it? And the Deputy-Under-Secretary had already offered his congratulations, and there would be something to go to the market place with, barter for the friends across the water, and you needed something strong to wring material in exchange out of Washington.

That evening Charles Mawby immersed himself in the technology of weapons code named Snapper, Swatter and Sagger that could destroy a NATO Main Battle Tank at a range of two thousand metres, and read the evaluations of the potential of its untried successor. He buried his mind in blueprint studies that showed skeleton mechanisms with appended titles for Hollow Charge Warhead, and Gyroscopic Controller, and Guidance Wire Spool. He assimilated a paper on the theory of the tactics that the Warsaw Pact would employ with infantry operated anti-tank-warheads to halt a NATO armoured counter-thrust. He browsed in a Central Intelligence Agency report that detailed the career of a young German scientist attached to rocketry in the Second World War who had not run fast enough to escape the advancing Russian invasion, who had been carried back to the Motherland as a spoil of war and put to work, who had married a local girl and risen through proven ability and intellect to the position of director (Technical Research) at Padolsk, fifty miles south of Moscow.

And Henry Carter was taking Otto Wilhelm Guttmann's son deep into the Surrey countryside, and they were going to start in the morning, gently to prize open the can that held the boy's knowledge of his father's work.

She'd done them well, very well, little Lizzie Forsyth. They'd probably have given her a medal if anyone could think up the wording of the citation.

No talking in the car. George following his headlights and concentrating because they had now left the main roads and were into the rabbit warren of lanes that threaded the Surrey hills. Carter resting and far into his seat and with his eyes closed and his breathing even. Willi Guttmann peered through the dirty glass of the side window and out into the night's blackness.

Willi thought of a girl called Lizzie. He thought of a bar called the Pickwick where the decor was English and where she sat at a stool and bought him drinks that were warm and unfamiliar and that burned his throat, and where her friends gathered and the talk was noisy and happy. He thought of visits to the cinema after Conference had finished in the afternoon and where moist fingers were held before the rush to be back inside the Residence doors before the last sitting for supper. He thought of the night after the girl who shared a one-bedroomed box of a flat with Lizzie had flown back to England for a job interview and he had been invited back for a toasted cheese sandwich and coffee. He thought of loving Lizzie through the snow carpeted months of February and March in a Swiss city where the idyll had lasted until the meeting when he had seen the strained eyes and the pale cheeks that warned of her day's weeping. He thought of her telling him she was late, had never been late before, and was he going to walk out on her, was he flying back to Moscow at the end of the month. He could not fight a girl in anguish, could not pull the wings off a fallen butterfly. And his father should not know. His father who was an old man and who had caused him no pain should hear only of an accident. Grief was less lasting than the shame of having reared a traitor. There was no retribution that they could bring against the father of a drowned son, no loss of privileges.

He thought of Lizzie with the soft, warm mouth. Lizzie with her arms around his neck in the sitting room of the home of the British Consul. Lizzie in tears as the Englishman had said that she could follow in three weeks or four to England. Gentle, darling, sweet Lizzie.

The car swung off the tarmac lane and the lights caught at high iron gates that had been opened and a squat lodge house, and the wheels ground on shallow gravel, and high trees dwarfed them, and thickset bushes spilled over the edge of the driveway. He saw the house, its pale stone bright in the lights, before George swung the wheel and braked viciously so that the man beside him started and grunted and was awake. Before Willi could feel for the handle, George was out and opening the door and after he had stood for a moment and tried to see about him there was a hand on his elbow and he was guided towards a porch where a dull lamp shone.

'Mrs Ferguson said she'd leave some cold cuts out, Mr Carter,' George said as he ferreted in his pocket for the front door key.

'You go along with George, Willi. There's something to eat for you, and he'll show you where you're sleeping. I expect you'll want a good hot bath too . . .'

The boy walked across the polished floor of the hall, past the painting of a stag at bay, past a wide table on which was set a vase of bright daffodils, past an oak staircase and a panelled wall. Behind him he heard a door close and when he turned he could no longer see Carter. George pushed him forward towards another door. He had lost something, felt bereft, because the last link with Geneva had been taken from him.

George sat him down at a table with a blue plastic cloth over it and took the metal cover off a plate displaying a yellowish piece of chicken and three curled slices of ham.

'I expect Mrs Ferguson didn't think we'd be so late,' George said.

Willi felt the tang of the lake water in his mouth, behind his teeth. He was very tired, his eyes hurt and his knees trembled, and a kaleidoscope of memories from far back and far away burned in his mind.

18

Chapter Two

=

The house, close to the village of Holmbury St Mary, was set in a wooded valley west of the Surrey county town of Guildford. It was used by the Secret Intelligence Service, and not infrequently, for the reception of east bloc defectors. Eight bedrooms, two bathrooms, six acres of grounds, a gargantuan annual heating bill, a formidable schedule of roof repairs. A defector with knowledge of the internal machinery of Defence, Foreign Affairs, the Politburo or Security in Moscow might expect to spend months here hidden from the scattered community that lived beyond the high fence and the thick encircling hedgerow. The accommodation and the matters of catering and cleaning were in the hands of Mrs Ferguson, an unobtrusive housekeeper who kept a myopic, shuttered mind on the events and personalities around her.

It was a warm, close evening, unseasonably so, but Carter had worn his raincoat and a woollen scarf for a walk around the lawn with Charles Mawby. The big man was down from London, and he'd been expected. Inevitable that he'd come himself after the low-key material that had been sent to the capital in transcript each evening. Mawby down from Century House to play the dragon and breathe some fire into the question and answer sessions of the debrief of Willi Guttmann.

'Putting it indelicately, Henry, he knows bugger all.'

'Barely worth the airfare, Mr Mawby,' Carter said mildly. He was aware that some of those in the Service who carried his own grading felt able to address the Assistant Secretary on first name terms. Sometimes it rankled that he had never received an invitation to do so.

'If we're lucky we get one of them a year. Either damned good or bloody useless.'

'I suppose we always hope for the platinum seam, what we're digging into here is barely fool's gold.' Carter often carried in his coat pocket a dried out crust taken surreptitiously from the kitchen. He ground a piece of bread to crumbs in his pocket and threw them discreetly in the direction of a pair of chaffinches, and saw with pleasure how their greed surpassed their caution.

'I'm supposed to report to Joint Intelligence Committee in the morning.'

'You'll not have much to tell them, Mr Mawby. I suppose his Foreign Ministry material is marginally interesting.'

'It's boring, uninformed and not new.'

'We were very thorough, the fellow you sent down here and me, the fellow with armour and missiles and warheads sprouting from eyes, ears, God knows where else. Very thorough, but the boy just stone-walled us. "My father doesn't talk about his work", that's the hub of it, and the boy's sticking to it.'

'I'm going to put the rod across his back, Henry.'

Carter sighed. It was against all the precepts of a debrief that you hurry. 'If that's what you think right, Mr Mawby.'

'The rod across his back.' The fleck of daisies in the lawn brought a tremor of irritation to Mawby's mouth. The weeds in the rose beds buckled his lips in annoyance. 'It's a damned shame they can't keep these places the way they used to be able to. When I first came here there were a couple of gardeners full time, absolute picture the place was, really rather a pleasure to be here for a few days. Bloody mess now ... Get him up, Henry, get him out of his bed, and we'll have another go.'

Mawby swung on his heel, gouged a muddy smear in the wet grass, flailed the insects besieging his face, frightened the chaffinches into flight.

'I'll do that, Mr Mawby,' said Carter.

From the darkened outline of the house a light burned in a window set under the eaves. That's where the boy would be, Carter thought, probably dressed, probably gazing at the wall, probably close to tears because of failure to please and win approval. He'd be sitting there moping the time away till he was ready for sleep. Even odds, if he could turn the clock back, he'd be heading for Geneva and then the Aeroflot to Moscow. But Willi Guttmann was wanted as a jewel for Charles Mawby and had been offered as a subject for consideration by the Joint Intelligence Committee in the morning.

'Bad luck, young Willi,' Carter said quietly to himself. 'I think you jumped the wrong way.'

The Ambassador who was the Permanent Representative of the Soviet Union at the Conference for the Committee on Disarmament sat in a comfortable chair close to the woodfire. He had not asked the KGB officer to be seated. As a career diplomat he had no love for the security man whose job entitled him to wander roughshod across the protocol and rank of the delegation.

'I cannot see any mystery in this matter,' the Ambassador said.

'I have not spoken of mystery,' Valeri Sharygin said. 'I have said only that it was extraordinary for Guttmann to go to the lake on such a night, in such weather. For an experienced sailor it was peculiar behaviour.'

'Perhaps he had been working hard, was taking what opportunity was presented to him.'

'His job was the least demanding of any here. You know the position of his father?'

'I have read Guttmann's file. I don't remember anything exceptional.'

'In the area of military technology, research and development, his father is a man of considerable stature, an Honoured Scientist of our country although of German origin.'

'Where are you taking me?'

'I don't know, Comrade Ambassador, but by now there

should have been a body. In two days I have to return to Moscow . . . I will be asked many questions . . .'

'Are you saying that the boy wasn't drowned?'

'Perhaps there was an accident. Perhaps the boy took his own life for reasons that we do not know. Perhaps we have been deceived.'

'The suspicion you can manufacture is a credit to you.'

'Thank you, Comrade Ambassador. I apologise for having disturbed you.'

Valeri Sharygin returned to his bedroom in the newly built annexe across the compound from the main building of the Residence. Beside his bed was the locked suitcase containing the wordly possessions of Willi Guttmann.

George had come for him. Willi had been sitting on his bed, shoes and socks off, shirt unbuttoned to the waist. No knock at the door, just the flooding impact of the frame of the minder in the doorway, and the summons for him to make himself decent again because he was wanted below. They had never called for him in the evening before. Always a morning session and another after lunch, and then supper with George watching over him and then his bedroom. George was perpetually with him in the house. When they walked in the corridors George was there. When he went to the lavatory George seemed to stop reluctantly at the door and when the business was finished and the bolt withdrawn he would be waiting. George was the one who brought him a mug of tea in the morning, and took him to his room in the evening and wished him good night and asked him whether he had everything, when he had nothing. George with his jacket buttoned and whose left breast pocket was bulged and distorted. He was a captive, and his freedom to be with Lizzie must be bartered. He knew that the currency he offered was stale and not valued.

George ushered the boy into the ground floor room that was bare of ornaments and pictures and comfort. Thin hair-cord carpet. Thin cotton curtains. One wooden table and half a dozen upright wooden chairs. Carter was sitting at the table, hands clasped, face impassive not meeting his eyes. There was another man there, shorter, younger in his shirt sleeves and with his tie loosened. Instantly menacing, wide and aggressive eyes.

'You'd better sit down, Guttmann. I've come from London because we're not happy with you, not happy at all with the help that you've given Mr Carter.'

'I've done my best. Mr Carter will tell you . . .'

'Then your best has got to get better.' Mawby had his elbows on the table, his full and close shaved chin in his hands.

'I have told you everything that I can.' Willi was defiant, surprised at his bravery. 'I told Mr Carter everything about the working of the delegation . . .'

'And for that do you think we sent a man to Geneva to help you? We've brought you to this place for that drivel, you believe that?'

'I want to be with Lizzie, that's why I came.'

A slow smile from Mawby. 'Lizzie's a long way off for you, Guttmann. She's light years distant, and unless you're talking to us the gap stays open.'

From an inside pocket Mawby took a postcard sized photograph, glanced at it and then tossed it onto the table where Willi could see it. The boy recoiled. The same picture that was in an album at home. Four men in a line together with their arms around each other's shoulders; one was taller than his companions and had a face wrapped in privacy, not wearing the bold grin of the others. 'Lübeck, January 1945. Your father making warheads for the Nazis. Otto Wilhelm Guttmann. Born in Magdeburg in 1912. Expert in short range missiles. Taken to the Soviet Union in 1945. Married Valentina Efremov Guttmann, killed in a car accident in 1968 . . .' Mawby reeled off the information, referred to no notes . . . 'One daughter, Erica. One son, Willi. Technical Director of Research at Padolsk for the last seven years. Expert now in MCLOS, that's Manual Controlled Line of Sight. Developing the successor to the AAICV, we call it Sagger over here. That's what we brought you here for,

Guttmann. That's what we've got to be talking about if you're to find yourself between Lizzie Forsyth's thighs again.'

'Bastard.'

'Good boy, Willi. Now you're understanding me,' Mawby chuckled with satisfaction.

For four hours, with Mawby wielding the pickaxe and Carter handling the scalpel, they kept at him, dogs in a pit with a dying bear. Willi shouting and Willi whimpering, alternating courage and submission. A bright light in his face, the rattle of the questions from behind its beam, and never the answer that they sought.

'My father didn't bring work home to the flat.'

'At home he hardly ever talked of Padolsk.'

'If he had to work then he had a room in the flat where he would go. Right from the time I was a child I was never invited into that room.'

'When I disturbed him and he was working, then he was angry. I didn't do it.'

'He never spoke of difficulties and solutions.'

'Maybe he talked with my sister. Erica is at Padolsk with him, she is his secretary there. He never talked with me.'

'I hardly saw him after I went to the Foreign Ministry. Before that I was at the University of Kiev. I have a room at home, but I was working or at night classes for languages.'

'When we went to Magdeburg, when he went home for his holiday in the summer, then we were close. Two weeks in the year, and then we did not speak of this AAICV that you talk of.'

'I don't know . . . I don't know about his work . . . believe me, I don't know.'

Mawby looked at his watch, rapped his fingers on the table. Willi heard the door open. He stood up and saw George standing inside the room. A pitiless, cold face, and there was the nod for him to follow. Surely now they would believe him? Surely they would realise the truth of his ignorance. He tried to remember Lizzie's face and could not,

24

tried to feel her hands on his skin and could not, tried to hear her words from the pillow and could not.

In his room after he had fallen onto the bed Willi heard the key turn softly in the lock and the diminishing footsteps of George. The tears welled in his eyes and dribbled on his cheeks. He was their prisoner and their pawn and he buried his head in the blankets.

The exalted company would have deterred a less confident man than Charles Mawby.

He stood at the end of the mahogany table in the third floor room of the Foreign and Commonwealth Office that overlooked Horseguards, and from his handwritten reminders told the story of the flight of Willi Guttmann and of the sparse information that the defection had provided. He was listened to patiently by the Deputy-Under-Secretary who headed the Service, by the Major General who commanded the Directorate of Service Intelligence and who took copious pencilled notes, by the Permanent-Under-Secretary who chaired the Joint Intelligence Committee and lit a chain of matches to fire his pipe, by the Director of the Security Service who gazed out of the window.

The Joint Intelligence Committee met every fortnight and it had been the opinion of the Deputy-Under-Secretary that the success in bringing over the Russian boy was a matter for moderate congratulation. As he heard Mawby out, he increasingly regretted his decision to offer Guttmann for the agenda.

'. . . so from our point of view it's been an interesting but frustrating start, the debrief. The boy is obviously extremely fond of his father, and says it's reciprocated. He may in his answers be trying to protect him in the same way that he sought to spare him from punishment through the planning of the escape. After personally questioning him last night I tend to regard his lack of knowledge as genuine. I think that's it, gentlemen.'

Mawby sat down.

'But we are hoping there will be more to come,' the

Deputy-Under-Secretary countered the tepid response to the Service's efforts. 'We're getting into a very sensitive area, close to a sensitive man.'

'Close to, but not up alongside,' murmured the Permanent-Under-Secretary.

'From our point of view it's pretty clear-cut.' The Director of the Security Service who had worked his apprenticeship with the Malayan and Kenyan colonial police, offered no concessions to the small room and the limited company. 'There'll be no difficulty giving the boy a new suit, a new identity when the time comes.'

'It's a bit of a strip show, isn't it? Plenty of fans and feathers.' The Major General grinned. 'It promises us the moon, gets us forward in our seats, and then it's lights out and the curtain's across. Do you suppose we'll be seeing any more flesh?'

The Deputy-Under-Secretary fidgeted, unhappy that he had over-priced his property. 'We haven't by any means exhausted the enquiries by which Guttmann may give us something of great value.'

The Permanent-Under-Secretary was shuffling his papers, the preparatory move for the agenda's next business. He said politely, 'Thank you for attending, Mr Mawby, you'll keep us posted I am sure.'

Mawby started to rise from his chair. He hadn't done well, and neither had the Service.

The Director's voice boomed out as if addressing a snatch squad about to launch a dawn raid into a tropical township. 'The old man, he goes to Magdeburg each year?'

Mawby stood by his chair. 'He apparently takes his holiday there.'

'Magdeburg in the German Democratic Republic?'

'Yes.'

'How far is Magdeburg from the border?'

'Between forty and fifty kilometres.'

The Permanent-Under-Secretary tugged his spectacles from his face and wiped them vigorously with his handkerchief. 'I'm not following your drift, Director.'

'Mr Mawby gave us two pieces of significant information. Guttmann senior is not a member of the Party, and is extremely fond of Guttmann junior. As I see it we have a tasty carrot and a non-ideological donkey. Couldn't our carrot be used to entice our donkey from one field to another? The fields would seem to be adjoining.'

'It's a very juicy thought,' the Major General chuckled. 'You'd have us queuing up to chat to him.'

'You've the sort of chaps on your books who could trek over there and proposition him, haven't you Deputy-Under-Secretary?' The Director beamed.

The Deputy-Under-Secretary held his head hidden in his hands, his voice was muffled through his fingers. 'Would it have to go to the politicians?'

The Permanent Under Secretary seemed pained. 'They're so dreadfully squeamish these days, aren't they? You'll bear that in mind when you judge the issue.'

They were on their way. Quick steps down the corridors and stairs and through the front door and towards the waiting cars. The lunch period had been eaten into and unless they scampered would be lost.

'Dig into the files, would you, Charles, for a suitable fellow. See if you can come up with a name for me by tomorrow evening,' the Deputy-Under-Secretary said over his shoulder.

Carter spoke from the dining room door. 'Willi, there's something they want to clarify in London. What are your father's holiday dates . . . in Magdeburg this summer?'

God Almighty, what were they thinking about in their ivory towers? What bloody scheme were they hatching up above the cloud level? They weren't going to try to bring the old man out, not through the minefields, not through the bloody fences. Remember the maxim of the Service, Henry; it exists for the gathering of information and how it is acquired is irrelevant. And it's what the old Service would have done. He curbed himself, doused the thought. They wouldn't be so bloody mad.

27

'From the first of June to the fifteenth . . .'

'Thanks, Willi.' Carter glanced at his watch face, read the date. A month till Otto Guttmann went on holiday. Six weeks till he left, that was more positive. What on earth were they playing at in London?

'Why do you need to know, Mr Carter?'

'Don't ask me, lad. Don't expect me to be told anything.'

They had been in the earth bunker at the edge of the Spellersieck wood for eight hours and the relief lorry to collect Ulf Becker and Heini Schalke was late.

The 0400-1200 duty, the killer time. The duty that started as the first birds broke the night silence and that ended at noon with the head pounding in pain, the legs stiffened, the eyes red rimmed from staring out in concentration over the cleared ground to the border fence.

There was no friendship between these two boys as they squatted in the half dark. Becker from Berlin, Schalke from Leipzig. No basis for mutual understanding or trust. The orders of the company commander insisted that sentries should talk together only on matters that affected their operational readiness. And if one spoke in the earth bunker or the watchtower or the patrol jeep then he must know first that his colleagues would not denounce him, and it was the skill of the officers and the NCOs and their rosters that the conscripts never knew with whom they were safe. The boys watched each other with lonely, hawk suspicion. Becker was close to the end of his eighteen month service in the Border Guard of the National Volks Armee of the German Democratic Republic, Schalke was new and raw and barely introduced to the barracks back in the farming village of Weferlingen.

The cold seeped inside the walls of the bunker, edged through their mudstained denims, caught at their ears and cheeks, and the hands that gripped their MPiKM automatic rifles. They must always be close to their rifles because the earth bunker had been dug one hundred and fifty metres from the border fence and this was the shooting zone where challenge was unnecessary. If there is a civilian close to the wire, shoot. That was the order given to the boys in the company at Weferlingen. Shoot to kill. Do not challenge and offer the fugitive the opportunity to run for the wire and try to climb. Shoot to prevent the fence being breached. For that duty they were armed with the MPiKM automatic rifle and two magazines of ammunition. Each time he lay in the bunker or climbed the watchtower or rode in the jeep, Becker posed for himself the same question. Why was it necessary more than thirty years after the founding of the state to maintain a wall of wire, to lay a field of mines, to build a line of watchtowers, why were there still young people prepared to challenge the barricade and the excellence of its defences. Schalke would have no answer, not this lout from the factories at Leipzig who never in his life had doubted the religion of the Party.

Becker had never spoken of the erosion of his faith.

From the far distance, muffled by the trees of Spellersieck came the drone of the lorry.

Becker grinned at the fatty, pallid face of Schalke. He had much to look forward to. From the lorry to Weferlingen. A shower to wash away the night dirt and a change into his best uniform. Transport to Haldensleben, a train to Magdeburg and a connection to Berlin. A 48 hour pass. There would be an obligatory visit to his parents' flat in the Pankow sector of the capital and then he would be away with the Freie Deutsche Jugend group to the camp site at Schwielowsee, 30 kilometres from the city; and in the party would be Jutte. For two days Heini Schalke could crawl into his bunker, or mount his watchtower, or freeze his arse, or learn his manual without Ulf Becker for company. It would be his last weekend pass before demobilisation in June. The lorry braked in front of the bunker.

They came out together, emerged into the daylight.

An officer jumped down from the driver's cab onto the patrol track, two guards from the back tailboard.

'Anything to report?'

'Nothing to report,' Becker said to the officer. He did not

salute: such mannerisms were not required in the National Volks Armee. He nodded without affection at the men who would replace him in the bunker and occupy the position till eight in the evening.

He was well built and finely muscled and he climbed easily onto the back of the lorry, Schalke, overweight, struggled to lever himself upwards with his pack and rifle and night-sight binoculars. He was offered no help.

On the pavement outside Century House the two men who had come from Charles Mawby's office reckoned themselves lucky to have flagged down a taxi. At that time, late in the afternoon, it could take more than half an hour to get from the north end of Westminster Bridge to Euston Station. Adrian Pierce checked the rail vouchers, first class return to Lancaster, and settled to the evening paper. Harry Smithson gazed sightlessly at the passing metropolis, his thoughts brooding on the file of a man called Johnny Donoghue.

Chapter Three

=

The clouds pushed hard down over the honeycomb of small streets between Willow Lane and the railway line and the River Lune. The slate roofs shone with a dull polish, the first fires of the day had been lit and thrust thin grey spirals into the early day. The brickwork of the houses, terraced and semi-detached in haphazard pattern, was weathered red, and solid. This was Lancaster, a county town rich with history, its castle a monument to the work of five centuries before, its prospects in decline, its usefulness outgrown. Not that there was such history in Cherry Road, but the houses had a steadfast, enduring appearance.

In the terraced homes the layout was uniform and identical for all.

A narrow hallway with a front sitting room leading off and behind it a parlour where the chairs were comfortable and the television stood in glossy splendour permitting the sitting room to be left for best. At the end of the hall and beyond the bent staircase was the kitchen with a back door into a stone flagged yard. Upstairs was one large front bedroom and then space only for one smaller bedroom, and the bathroom. Not a large house, but sufficient for the needs of Johnny Donoghue and his mother.

When he had first come home to live here, a year and a half ago, he had tried to freshen and brighten the old house, to warm its walls with colour, and for months he had busied himself with his paintbrush and his electric drill and the ladder he stored in the yard.

A little paradise, his mother called it, the nicest house in Cherry Road, and didn't the neighbours admire the effort he had put in? Nothing more to do now at the weekends, and so Johnny could lie in his bed, lie on his back and brood.

31

His mother had adapted well to the changes of fortune that had cudgelled Johnny Donoghue. Few enough mothers could have acted out the pretence that a catastrophe had not struck at their lives. A tiny nest-fledgeling of a woman but with strength, and the bitter disappointment at Johnny's plunging fall had been carried in her short, scurrying stride. Tough as a boot, he thought her, and it was right that he should have come back home to live and find himself again.

Born in 1945, the only son of Herbert and Charlotte Donoghue. The first six years of his life eked out in married quarters of the British Army of Occupation in Germany. His father had been an officer, but made up from the ranks, and was promoted to Captain when aged 43 and two decades older than most of the other men in the mess. Just a small gratuity had been paid him when he left the army and then there was a hardware shop that was open six days a week in the centre of Lancaster and behind the Town Hall. The King's Commission was exchanged for trade, Saturday night drinks in the mess for glasses of beer in the British Legion, card games for dominoes. And with his only child reaching for his ninth birthday, Herbert Donoghue had without warning or previous illness fallen dead across the wide counter of the shop. Hard times for a widow. The business was sold up, the house purchased outright because Charlotte Donoghue said the home was the bedrock of the family, four mornings a week cleaning for a family that lived in a big house out on the Heysham road.

When he lay in bed of a morning at the weekend and gazed at the flower print curtains, Johnny Donoghue thought often of his childhood.

Johnny at eleven winning a scholarship to the Royal Grammar School and being given a new shirt as a reward. At fifteen collecting a Modern Languages prize for his German and mother sitting in the Great Hall of the school and beaming her unashamed pride. At eighteen leaving school with a clutch of examination passes and a glowing testimonial from his headmaster. At nineteen getting a scholarship to the Royal Military Academy at Sandhurst and going away on the train from Lancaster station with his mother's waving handkerchief the last glimpse of home.

At twenty-two at Passing Out, and at the march past in front of the College, back straight, arms straight, and wondering how his mother was coping out there amongst all the other families who had come to watch their sons. A small woman in a green coat, with a hat she could not afford, and they had left The Academy by taxi queuing at the exit gate with the Daimlers and the Bentleys and the Jaguars.

With his knowledge of German, backed by good school French, he was just what they wanted, they said, in the Intelligence Corps. A fine future was predicted. Straight indulgence, that's what it was, even to think back, because those days were gone, obliterated.

Ten years after entering the army, ten years after winning his dress sword, Johnny Donoghue had walked from the station to Cherry Road, dressed in slacks and a sports jacket. Uniform sold, mess bill paid up, an engagement ring returned by a civil servant's daughter. An embarrassment to his friends, a wound to his mother. In his suitcase he brought his boots, and three plate silver mugs awarded for marksmanship the sole relics of a military career. Awkward in his disgrace, embittered by the treatment meted out to him, Johnny had come home.

After a full breakfast Adrian Pierce and Harry Smithson paid their bills and checked out of the Royal King's Arms Hotel. From the cut of their suits, the trim of their hair, the knot of their ties both were plainly southern creatures. Strangers in Castle Park and heading for Willow Lane.

'Do you think he'll be easy, Harry?'

'Not too easy I wouldn't have thought.'

'Not after what they did to him.'

'There are always casualties, bound to happen when you put troops in to do policemen's work.'

'A bit hard, to charge him with murder.'

'Bloody ridiculous.' They were crossing the railway bridge and Smithson paused to watch an express train rocketing beneath them.

'A dreadful place that Belfast. I go down on my knees each night and pray God I'm not sent there.'

'Keep your nose clean on the German Desk and the Lord will look pleasantly upon you. Not much of a place this, either.' Smithson sniffed unhappily at the air. They crossed Willow Lane and Smithson glanced at the scribbled directions given him by the hotel porter.

A damn good career officer, that's what Johnny Donoghue was in the mind of Adrian Pierce, damn good till they posted him to Army Headquarters at Lisburn, Northern Ireland. He'd taken the file from Smithson, read it in bed, tried to colour the portrait of the man they were sent to collect. A damn good career officer, a captain knocking on major. Expert on Germany, steady and reliable. But the great appetite of the Northern Ireland commitment for manpower meant that Intelligence Officers must be seconded from the main battle forces of northern Europe to the twilight of counter-insurgency just past the British back door.

It had been a surveillance stake out. Donoghue and two squaddies lying up in a hide for three days and nights to watch an explosives cache and a figure approaching it at night, trousers and anorak, and it was raining and there was something in the hand. Perhaps he should have challenged, that was procedure. But why the hell should he have done that with three hundred soldiers dead and buried and the police and reservists to keep them company? Why the hell should he? Fire first and ask questions later, that's what any other army does.

The poor bastard must have damned near died of shock when he found he'd hit a child, a fifteen-year-old girl . . . must have fetched his food up at the very least. Not Guilty, of course. Not Guilty of murder. But the stain was there, and the judge's sarcasm. Cutting words that read no less viciously on paper than they would have sounded in the

Belfast Crown Court. And nobody had wanted to know Johnny Donoghue afterwards. No celebration party back at Lisburn. Just a chilly goodbye and an escort to the RAF wing at Aldergrove Airport. Now he was back home with his mother. Now he was teaching German at night classes at the Technical College. And Smithson had said that Donoghue wouldn't be easy. Who'd blame him for that?

They walked into Cherry Road.

'Number 14,' said Smithson.

In the bathroom at the back of the house, standing at the basin in pyjama trousers, his face wet with shaving cream, Johnny Donoghue heard the beat of the knocker on the front door. Not Mrs Davies from next door because she'd know that his mother was at the shops, and she never came before eleven to share a pot of tea. Not the milk bill, not the paper bill because they came with the delivery. Who would come that early to Cherry Road? Not the meter reader, not on a Saturday morning. He cursed and scraped on with the plastic handled razor. Another knock. His mother always left the front sitting room window ajar, so they'd know there was someone in the house. And he'd left the curtains drawn. He sluiced the soap off his face. A fine sight he'd look, dark hair and therefore a dark beard and half of it scratched off and the other cheek set with bristles and alive. He pulled his dressing gown off the hook on the back of the door, slipped it on and tied the belt.

'Coming,' Johnny shouted.

There was an answering note. A high, clean call of thanks. No hurry. A voice of the middle class, of the south. Johnny paused a moment on the stair in indecision, and then opened the front door. The morning light struck him and he blinked. The two men were in shadow, their features indistinct.

'Mr Donoghue? Mr John Donoghue?' The older man spoke. Police? Army? London, anyway.

'That's me.'

'I'm Harry Smithson.'

'My name's Pierce.'

'Can we come in?' Smithson asked. Not happy at having to ask, not happy on the pavement.

'It depends what you want.'

Smithson looked around him, the automatic response. The glance over each shoulder as if in Cherry Road there might be a listener or an eavesdropper. His voice dropped. 'We were sent from London to see you, Mr Donoghue. It's a government matter.'

'Who sent you? What do they want?'

'It would be better inside . . . it's not trouble, Mr Donoghue, nothing like that.' Pierce seemed the same age as Johnny and better equipped to communicate.

He would have liked to send them away, liked to have spun them round and packed them away up the road, but they'd crucified him, hadn't they? A government matter, and that pricked his interest. He'd had his fill, the over-brimming cup, of men on government business. The army's Special Investigation Branch detectives who had taken his statement. The solicitor appointed to prepare his defence. The barrister paid out of public funds who represented him in court. The pin-striped suit who had come from Ministry of Defence and said that Guilty or Not Guilty there would be no place for him again in Intelligence Corps. But a government matter . . . and not trouble . . . his curiosity won through.

'You'd better come in.'

Strange how a house could quickly lose its warmth when outsiders came. Johnny apologised for the size of the living room, scuttered forward to retrieve his cigarettes and matches, to empty last night's ashtray into the grate, to gather up yesterday's newspaper, to smooth down the cushions on the sofa. And he hated himself for his concern.

'I'll go up and get dressed. Make yourself comfortable.'

'Thank you, Mr Donoghue.' Pierce was conciliatory. 'We're sorry to be barging in so early.'

Johnny nodded, then closed the door behind him and went up the stairs to his room. He dressed in the shirt hanging from his chair, the underclothes that were on the floor, searched for his shoes, took socks from the drawer. The shave would wait. Below him he heard a key in the door, the chatter of a farewell from his mother to a friend. He shoved the shirt-tail into his waist and went to the top of the stairs. The front door closed.

'Mum,' he called.

She stood small in the hallway, engulfed in her coat, wispy grey hair protected by a scarf, shopping bags around her. 'Have you done your breakfast, Johnny?'

'There's some men in the front, came to see me. I'm just dressing.'

'Would they like some tea?' The thin piping voice. After all that had happened this woman could not believe that men who came to the house could be unwelcome.

'They'll not be staying long enough for tea, don't bother, Mum.'

Not having any bastards in dark suits with the whiff of London on them make his mother fuss round to get the best china out and rinse the milk jug and flap herself as to whether the room's tidy enough. He heard her go to the kitchen, and he came down the stairs and into the front room. They were where he'd left them, close together on the sofa and they smiled as if in a chorus act and stood up.

'So how does a government matter affect me?' Straight into the eyes of Smithson, because he'd be the spokesman.

'Quite right, Mr Donoghue, we shouldn't waste time. We shouldn't beat about the bush . . .'

'Correct.'

'Mr Pierce and I work for that part of the Foreign Office that concerns itself with intelligence gathering . . .'

'Identity cards, I'd like to see them.' Johnny held out his hand, watched amused as the two dug in their wallets. He took the two plastic coated cards complete with the polaroid photographs. Access to Century House, London, W1. Good enough.

'Very wise, Donoghue,' Smithson said. 'With your background you will know of the work initiated at Century

37

House. We've been asked to offer you a job, Mr Donoghue.'

Johnny squinted across, slant-eyed, at the two men. Too bloody early in the morning to be concentrating.

'Why me?'

'In London they think you fit the scheme of things,' Pierce said quietly. 'This is nothing to do with Intelligence Corps. Fresh faces, fresh work.'

'What does it involve?'

'We haven't been briefed, not fully, only that it involves a show in Germany.'

'And that's all you're going to tell me?'

'That's all we *can* tell you,' Smithson said.

'When do I have to make my mind up, by what time?'

Smithson looked at his watch. 'We're taking the lunch-time train to London. It's our hope that you'll accompany us.'

Johnny slumped back in his chair, closed his eyes, blacked out the sight of the two men opposite him. Nothing more to be said was there? Couldn't be anything else. Of course they wouldn't travel north and march into the front room of a terraced home and then talk matters of National Security. All that would be in London, and there was no way of finding out more about what was asked of him without getting on the train to the big city. And the more they tell you the harder they'll make it for you to escape. Step onto that train, Johnny, and you're in, the clock hands will turn back ... and they're *asking for you,* all nice and polite and they're asking for you. Sent these men up to this God-forsaken town on a Saturday morning because it's Johnny Donoghue they want, because Monday's too late for them.

What to do, Johnny?

He sat a long time and the quiet burrowed through the room. He'd been kicked bloody hard in the teeth by the establishment. But now they wanted him back. They wanted the man from Cherry Road. He'd never live with himself if they walked back to the station empty-handed.

Johnny smiled, open and wide, the trace of a laugh.

'If I'm to go to London I'd better finish shaving,' he said.

The door was closed on the messenger and Doctor Otto Guttmann carried the suitcase back through the hall of the flat and into the small, pinched living room. He placed it on the floor, in the centre of the carpet and stood quite still and gazed down at the black leatherette case. He saw on its handle the baggage tag for Geneva, and attached by string was a cardboard label that carried the name and address written in a familiar and beloved hand. He looked up then at the plain wooden cross hung from the wall, contemplated it, as if it were a guarantor of strength.

Otto Guttmann was tall, well shouldered, a large and imposing figure, but the sight of the suitcase magnetised his eyes and bowed his body. The messenger had known what he brought, had hurried to deliver the case and be away.

Memories bounced into Otto Guttmann's mind. Memories of a small boy laughing and bickering with his father and mother on picnics on the Lenin Hills outside the city. Memories of a child dressed and scrubbed for school. Memories of a teenager complaining of lack of attention. Memories of the adulthood of his son and the pride of the boy that by his own efforts he had achieved selection to the interpreter school of the Foreign Ministry.

Such a short time ago, it seemed, since Otto Guttmann had seen the case open and the clothes and trivial possessions placed in it and then its top pushed down and zipped and the lock fastened, and he heard again the laughter and excitement before the departure to the airport. The first time that one of his children had left the nest that he had made of the flat after the death of their mother. He stared down at the bag and in his hand was the key that the messenger had given him and he knew that by himself he lacked the will to open the fastenings. Old men can cry, are permitted to weep, it is the young who must not demonstrate their feelings of sorrow at bereavement. The tears came slowly and then rained on and on.

Why had Willi been out on the lake in the darkness?

Why had he taken a boat when the harbours were deserted? Why could they not even produce a body for a father to bury?

His daughter had come into the room behind him, quiet as a gazelle, respectful of his mood. He started and shook himself as her hand linked under his arm and her fingers gripped at his elbow. A girl nearly as tall as himself. As the daughter of an old man should be, the prettiness of a picture, the strength of a buttress. She eased up on her toes and softly kissed his tearstained cheek.

'I heard the bell, but I didn't think it would be this, not so early.'

'They said that they would bring it today, they said that in the letter from the Ministry.'

The letter from the Ministry of Foreign Affairs had scarred him. Hand delivered as the telegram had been five days previously. The letter had been confirmation of the unthinkable and had irrevocably destroyed the chance that some terrible mistake had been woven around the family.

'You want to open the bag, Father?'

'We should.' His voice had a husked control.

'The car will be waiting . . .'

'This once let it wait.'

Erica Guttmann carried the suitcase to her brother's bedroom, and her father followed. It was a tiny cubicle of a room that Willi had used, but then there had been no complaints; a three-bedroomed flat was a rare privilege, was the evidence that Otto Guttmann had been accepted into the elite of the establishment. A poster from the Olympic Games took pride of place on the wall in front of them, the symbol of the yachting competitions fought out in the Baltic city of Tallin. On another wall was a large framed colour photograph of a crew at work in the interior of a Soyuz space craft. A desk that was bare and cleaned. A radio with chrome finish on a low table and the pile of cassettes neatly stacked beside it. Curtains that had been drawn in the awful moments after the telegram had arrived. The single bed with gaudy coverlet where Willi would have slept the last two nights if he had returned with the delegation from Geneva.

The room of Otto Guttmann's son, the room of Erica Guttmann's brother.

She lifted the bag onto the bed.

'It is best that it's done now,' she said.

The key turned smoothly in the lock. The top garments spilled out and across the bed cover and with a careful discipline she began to make piles around the suitcase. Trousers and jackets, shirts and vests and underpants, ties and handkerchiefs. The shoes she put on the floor. She felt the brooding, wretched presence of her father, but did not look round at him, continued with her task, and then she sighed as she reached the bottom of the bag and the thick, clear plastic sack in which her brother's personal possessions had been packed. She bit at her lip, and emptied the contents onto the bed. A wallet that had been his father's present for his eighteenth birthday. A silver ink pen that had been Erica's gift at the last Christmas. A photograph frame that held in its three compartments pictures of father and sister and the three together in the sunshine of the Archangelskoye Park with Willi shining in his happiness and rising half a head above those who looked down at the picture. The girl heard her father's choked breath and his hand came to rest on her shoulder.

'Go and get your work ready, Father. I will finish it.'

He obeyed and the door closed behind her. She slid the clothes into the drawers of a chest, shovelled the possessions back into the sack and found room for it under the bed, hidden by the fall of the coverlet. Time when she came home for her to be more thorough. It was horrible for her father that there was nothing tangible for him to fasten to. No funeral, no rites, no burial . . . and if at some future date the remains of Willi were recovered from the water and returned to them then the wound could only be reopened and the pain reawakened. The stupidity of the boy but she must not think ill of him, not now, not ever again.

She walked out into the hall, easy and graceful on her feet, swung back her head loosening the shoulder length of corn silk hair and pulled on her coat. Otto Guttmann waited by the door with his overcoat, gloves and scarf, and wearing on his face the conquering burden of age and extreme tiredness. For a moment they embraced, tight and clinging, arms close around each other, and then she had the key in her hand for the front door and they went out onto the landing and she shut the door of their home and locked it.

Henry Carter knocked tentatively at Mrs Ferguson's sitting room door, was told to enter, but stood in the doorway to deliver his message to the lady who rested her sewing across her lap to hear him out.

'Mr Mawby's just been on the telephone. There's going to be a bit of a party here for the next few days. He will be back himself and there's three more coming tonight, they'll all be in time for dinner . . . if that's possible? Mr Mawby asked me to apologise for not having given more notice.'

'It'll be no trouble.'

'Something a little unusual, I think,' Carter confided.

'I like the house full. It's such a waste when it's empty.'

'It'll be a bit like the old days.'

'And that'll be welcome,' she said placidly.

Carter closed the door on her privacy. He walked into the main sitting room and pondered his own instructions, changed again by London. The boy, Willi, was to talk about his father. His personality, not his research work. Everything about the man himself, his habits, his interests, his lifestyle. Another blow at the consistency that Carter had been trained to believe was the hallmark of the debrief.

Could they really be thinking of bringing Otto Guttmann out of East Germany? The repercussions if it went sour, by God. Carter felt his knees weaken and flopped into an armchair. Perhaps he was going too fast. Perhaps, but where else did the trickle of circumstantial information point?

Chapter Four

Because of the very stillness of the house Johnny woke early.

Noise didn't concern him, not after the dawn bustle of a day starting in Cherry Road and the grind of the buses in Willow Lane, and the farther thunder of the fast trains through the town. Not after the daily rumble of Mrs Davies forcing her man out of bed beyond the common wall, and his mother on the move for the first of the kettle boilings, and the children pitched on to the pavements because it was a long walk to the new comprehensive school. He could stomach that. But the quiet was a killer, a destroyer.

No one moved beneath him and he lay in his bed soaking up the silence, alert for any noise. An uncanny vacuum of sound, as if he were alone. But that couldn't be true because he'd seen a man who introduced himself as Henry Carter on his way to bed, and he'd climbed the stairs with Smithson and Pierce, and there was also the boy who was spoken of as Willi, and the shadow at his back, his minder. He hadn't actually seen the boy, but he had been told of him. And there was the housekeeper too. But none of them had stirred in Johnny's hearing that morning.

He had cantered out of Lancaster almost without a backward glance. He had kissed his mother firmly on both cheeks, told her that he had been offered something special, that he would be away for a while, that the money was going to be good and could she be sure to give this envelope to the Prentice boy to take to the Tech – that he was turning the corner on the past. He had left her confused and struggling for composure, standing on the front doorstep shyly waving as he walked away.

A couple of whiskys had been downed the previous night and there had been sporadic talk with Carter and Smithson and Pierce weighing him, and Johnny turning his concentration at them, evaluating their capabilities. But Johnny had it over them. He had the high ground. A contract man was only brought into the tight web structure of an operation to fulfil a pinnacle role. If it were too easy, too simple then one of the pension scheme men could have been recruited. When the going would be rough they looked for the contract man. Rough and dangerous, Johnny.

Abruptly he swung his legs out of the bed and padded across to his bag. No need to pack for a lifetime, Smithson had said. A few shirts and underclothes, a spare pair of shoes, his army boots, his washing bag. He'd turned himself out well enough when he was in uniform, but that was back in the dark ages. Who looked at him now? He put on a shirt and knotted the old boys tie of the Grammar School, pulled up the trousers that were creased at the back of the knees, eased into his shoes that he should have polished before leaving home. The clothes he would have worn to the Technical College to take the German class.

He let himself out of the bedroom and went carefully down the stairs. A wide, curved staircase with a polished wooden banister. He walked around the hall, and his feet sank into the pile of the carpet, his eyes on the pictures that were strewn over the timber panelling. They'd have plotted the subverting of the Bolshevik revolution in a place like this. Nothing would have changed. Extraordinary people, these hidden creatures of the Service. Perhaps the pond they now looked into was too filthy, too slimed for their own hands, and so they needed a contract man to do their work, they'd have an outsider in for the job. And afterwards they'd let him wash and perhaps they'd wave a polite farewell and perhaps they would say he had done well and let him stay for more.

'I hope you slept well, Mr Donoghue?'

Johnny spun round. Caught off balance, caught dreaming. Henry Carter was standing in the doorway that led to the dining room.

'Thank you, yes . . . I didn't know anyone else was up . . .'

'We didn't want to disturb you, we thought we'd let you wake in your own good time.'

Johnny looked at his watch. Twenty-five minutes to eight. He blushed.

'There's some breakfast in here, if you'd like it,' Carter said. 'We don't usually have much at lunchtime. It'll keep you going till the evening. Mr Mawby's coming down then.'

Carter showed Johnny into the dining room. They sat down by the window.

Of the four other tables only one was occupied. A boy with a face that once had known the sun and a man opposite him who toyed with his teacup, heavily built and expressionless. Neither spoke.

The housekeeper emerged from a far door, advanced across the linoleum floor.

'Eggs and bacon for Mr Donoghue, I should think, Mrs Ferguson,' Carter said.

Johnny agreed. That was the way it was going to be. He would be told his rest hours, told his work, told what to eat. Carter leaned forward, conspiratorial. 'Over there, that's the lad we're working on. Junior interpreter on the Soviet delegation of the disarmament chat in Geneva. Defected a bit over a week ago because the English girl he was taking out said she was pregnant and life couldn't go on without the two of them being together. It's not him that interests us. His father's the prime one. Dad was taken to the Soviet Union after the war along with a truckful of scientists and he's made his name there on the ATGW programme . . . you know what that is, Anti-Tank Guided Weapons.'

Memories for Johnny, memories of 'I' Corps days. 'I know.'

'He's specialised in MCLOS, you read that?'

Johnny nodded. 'I know what that is.'

'Well that's about all I can tell you.' Carter chuckled. 'Nothing changes in the Service. There are the princes, the God Almighties . . . that's Charles Mawby, and there are the carriers of pitchers of water. I lug buckets around and do

45

what I'm told and that way if it spills then I don't get it in the neck . . .' Carter paused, looked again at Johnny, and keenly. 'You were a German specialist in Intelligence?'

'Army Intelligence.'

'But a specialist in German theatre?'

'For seven years.'

'Fluent?'

'Grade five.'

'What does that mean?'

'Grade four and five classify you as having colloquial capability. It means you can pass as a citizen.'

There was a little gleam of understanding from Carter, as if another jigsaw piece had slid into place. The house-keeper carried in a laden plate for Johnny. Carter seemed not to notice, absorbed in what he had heard. Johnny began to eat, fast and without finesse.

'I was listening to what the two who brought you here last night were saying, you were upstairs unpacking your bag.' Carter was now companionable, sympathetic. 'They said that you had a bit of bother over in Ireland . . .'

'Right.' Johnny, mouth full and brusque.

'Well, that's all behind you.'

If it could ever be behind him, if it could ever be forgotten. Maeve O'Connor aged 15 years, not old enough to wear mascara, the girl blasted to death by the single shot from Johnny Donoghue's Armalite. It would never be forgotten.

Johnny finished his food, swilled the last of his coffee and stood up, Carter rising with him.

'Pierce and Smithson have gone for a walk. They're chalk and cheese. God knows what they find to talk about. Nothing really happens till Mr Mawby shows, he's the one that chose you.'

They went out through the door and Johnny said, 'I think I'll just stroll around a bit. Get my bearings.'

'Please yourself, but I'd rather you didn't leave the grounds.'

Carter called back into the dining room for Willi and together they set off for the interrogation room and the start of the morning session. Getting serious, weren't they, the big men in London? Had to be serious when they pulled Johnny Donoghue into the game. No longer just play-time out in the school yard for Henry Carter and Willi Guttmann, no longer sparring across the table in the hope of brightening a 'restricted' report. Could be a matter of life and death, couldn't it? Johnny Donoghue's life, Johnny Donoghue's death. And he seemed a nice chap, that was Carter's first impression anyway.

Because the message to the British Embassy in Bonn would be transmitted in cypher, Charles Mawby had come that Sunday morning to Century House. Amongst the security personnel on the door and the weekend rostered clerks there was little surprise at the sight of him striding purposefully through the front hallway and along the corridors of the near-deserted building. He was a workhorse, that one, they said. All hours the good Lord gave, and his wife must be a saint to put up with it, or a bitch to have driven him that far.

His communication was directed to the SIS officer working from the Embassy in the German Federal Republic's capital. An evaluation was to be made of the feasibility of bringing a Soviet citizen out of the German Democratic Republic. That person would come of his own volition, and the collection point would be in the vicinity of Magdeburg. The collection could be left to German nationals who dealt in such matters and the commercial rate would be paid for those services. Co-operation with the West German authorities was not to be sought. Mawby would be free to travel to Bonn in a few days' time if that were thought desirable by the field station.

The signal was marked priority, and called for a preliminary answer within two days.

The rain slapped into the roof of pine branches high above

Ulf Becker and Jutte Harnburg.

All of the group had been walking in the forest when the first heavy drops had fallen in unison with the shell crack of the thunder.

Some had run for the chalets on the shore of the Schwielowsee hard in the wake of the Freie Deutsche Jugend organiser. Others had scattered, allowed the volume of the rain beating on the path to provide the excuse that they were better sheltering and waiting for the storm to pass over.

Ulf and Jutte had stripped off their blouses and used them as protection against the floor of pine needles. Jutte underneath with her tight, small lemon breasts pushed up into Ulf's face. The boy with his hands groping at the waist of the girl's trousers. The girl with her hands pulling and gouging at the skin beside the boy's backbone. No words, no sentiments. Trousers slipping, elasticated pants stretching, fingers grasping, mouths meeting hot and wet and seeking each other. And the rain falling in a steady drip on the boy's back and him unaware, and she too uncaring that the water rivers ran on her face and savaged the hair that she had carefully combed that morning. No need for preparation, no vantage from ritual courtship. Her hands drifting beneath the cover of his trousers, and the boy arching and desperate and she wriggling her bottom upwards that he might draw her clothes down, that she should bare herself to him. Ulf panting. Jutte moaning, a sweet and soft treacle sound and the call for her boy. Ulf's trousers at his knees, and his face wrapped in the moment of annoyance as he must lose her and reach for his back pocket. Always when he was on leave from Weferlingen and he would see Jutte he went first to the chemist or the machine in the lavatory at Schöneweide railway station. And always at that time she helped him, he passing it to her, and she tearing the packet open. And always then the fast road to the glory and the escape and the fierce freedom. Rising and falling, the raw wind cutting against their nakedness, wrapped in arms, encircled in legs, till the shriek of pleasure burst in them and the strength failed and eventually crawled away. Hard together they lay, a long time, exposed only to each other, bewildered by the beauty.

'Sweet boy.'

'Darling Jutte, darling lovely Jutte.'

'So good.'

'Better than good.'

'Better than the best.' The girl's fingers reached to his neck, held his head close to her shoulder, wound the thin strands from his cropped hair between her nails under which had caught the earth from the forest carpet. 'You are a good son of the Fatherland, Ulf . . . always you get better, always your production is higher . . .' She giggled.

'Piss on the Fatherland.' The snarl exorcised the gentleness from his mouth.

'Piss on the Fatherland?' Jutte dreaming, eyes closed in safety. 'Piss on it? Even little Ulf, hero of output in the DDR, protector of its frontier . . . even he cannot drown it.'

'Does not even know how to fight it.'

Jutte opened her eyes, pushed his head back so that she could look into his face and the clean bones beneath his skin, and the downy blond hair on his upper lip, and his clean and even-set teeth. 'Does not know how to fight it? Ulf does not know how to fight the Fatherland?'

He rolled from her and hastened to pull up his underclothes and trousers. She made no move to follow and lay quite still on the two crumpled blouses.

'Ulf is a soldier, he should know how to fight the Fatherland . . . if that is his wish.'

'It is easy to talk of it.'

'Some boys were talking at the Humboldt . . .'

Ulf creased his lips, a swift spasm of rage. He hated, detested it when she spoke of life at the University in Berlin. Jutte the second year student of Mechanical Engineering. Ulf the second year border guard of the National Volks Armee. She the daughter of the Director of an industrial Kombinat. He the son of a lorry driver. Jutte the product of the Party elite. Ulf the product of the Party faithful.

'What did they say at the Humboldt?'

She grinned up at him, careless and happy in her power. 'They said there was only one way to fight them.'

'What way was that?' Hoarseness crawled into Ulf's voice.

'To run away from them . . .' Her laugh tinkled close to him. 'That they hate. That is why they have so many of you pretty boys on the border. The ones who run from them are the ones who fight them.'

He shrugged, uncertain. 'It is impossible.'

'Some do it,' she whispered. 'We see it on the television that comes over from the West. Two families and they made a balloon, they did it. The man with the glider, the man who swam with the air tanks, the man who pushed the boat with his wife and daughter across the Elbe . . .'

There was a nervousness now about the boy, and he bridled. 'You have not seen it.'

'It has been done so it must be possible.'

'If you saw it for yourself then you would not say that. There are automatic guns, there are mines, the wire is more than three metres high, there are dogs . . . vicious horrible things. If you had seen the frontier you would not say that it is possible.'

He pulled her upright, then bent to pick up her brassiere and to shake the pine needles from her blouse. She stood with her trousers at her ankles.

'Why do they go there, those who come to the frontier and face the gun that you hold?'

'We should get back, or we will be missed.'

'The boy who said piss on the Fatherland, that boy is afraid that the FDJ nursemaid will miss him?'

He knelt at her feet. A ridiculous posture, and his nose brushed against her upper legs and he kissed her and pulled at her trousers till they were at her waist. He flicked the mud from her blouse and pushed her hair back to its parting. 'What do you want of me, Jutte?'

She took his hand and they went slowly to the path. 'I want you to know that my father is going this afternoon to Dresden, some dreary meeting early tomorrow, and my

50

mother is going with him. I want you in their bed at home when these children's games are finished.'

'I have to get the train at midnight.'

'Piss on the Fatherland, the boy said. Silly boy, you'll get your train.'

He put his arm around her waist, squeezed her. The girl pressed her hips close to his as they went back towards the chalets. They would be in time for lunch. Lunch would be stew, that was usual for the Sunday meal at the Schwielowsee camp.

It had been a low, wearing day for Johnny. Marking time, treading water, waiting.

He had walked the grounds, mapped the geography of the small wood, and the orchard and the thick-grassed tennis court, and the lawns and the outbuildings, once stables. The place smacked of a lost grandeur, everything had slipped out of hand. Only the chain link fence topped with the single strand of barbed wire that ringed the boundary was new. They'd be bound to pick a house like this, he thought, with a warren of rooms and ivy clinging to the stonework and eating through the mortar, and the paint falling from the window frames. Crumble right into the bloody undergrowth if they weren't careful. Smithson and Pierce had brought the Sunday papers back with them. In the afternoon Johnny curled in a chair in the hall and read. It was a long wait before the car came, scraping on the gravel.

Charles Mawby came thrusting through the front door. Instinctively Johnny stood up. This was the power, the head of patronage.

George, the sheepdog, herded them into the living room while Mawby settled his bag in his bedroom. Carter brought from the interrogation room and holding his notepad. But not Willi. Smithson and Pierce roused from their siesta. And Johnny who was there to be told of a mission.

They stood, eyeing the chairs, as if even those on the team

51

were uncertain of the seating protocol. The fire was not lit, the curtains not drawn. A virile chill in the air.

Mawby came in, closed the door firmly behind him, took an armchair and waved them down. Johnny sat back a little way from the inner circle. He was not yet a part of their plan.

'We'll have some tea later. I don't want Mrs Ferguson fussing about us just as we get going,' Mawby said. There was a slim chorus of agreement.

'You've all met each other now,' Mawby said quietly. 'You've had the opportunity to see a bit of Mr Donoghue, though from this stage on I'm going to call him Johnny . . .' He smiled. 'For everyone's benefit,' Mawby continued, 'we'll take the history first and then the plan. Willi Guttmann, Soviet citizen, junior diplomat, defects from Geneva. He is of little value to us, but for the accident of his birth. Willi Guttmann is the son of Doctor Otto Guttmann who is as important to this country and her allies as the boy is unimportant. Otto Guttmann heads a major and highly specialised weapon research team that is currently working on the replacement for the Red Army of the MCLOS Sagger in the ATGW range . . .'

Mawby paused, let that sink in. Johnny looked across at Henry Carter and saw the trace of a wry smile.

'Otto Guttmann is now an old man, close to his seventieth birthday. We can assume that if the Soviets did not regard his work as of the foremost importance they would have pensioned him off. They have not done so, nor are there any signs that before this present programme is completed he will be permitted to retire. The British interest in Dr Guttmann is quite straightforward. We are about to launch the building programme for the new Main Battle Tank of the late eighties. It involves a minimum of a thousand vehicles, at an average cost per weapon of half a million pounds. Thousands of jobs are tied into the manufacture process. In the event of conventional hostilities in Europe that tank will have to face the weapon currently being prepared by Doctor Guttmann at Padolsk in the Soviet Union. I think I make myself clear.' It wasn't a question, but there was a faint mutter of assent from Smithson and a drawled acknowledgement from Pierce. Carter toyed with his wedding ring as if nothing had been said that was new to him. Johnny sat very still. It was coming closer to him, the tide on its way to his sand castle, sneaking nearer.

'Willi Guttmann managed his defection with a brilliance that those of us who have had dealings with him here find hard to credit. He sought to protect his father from having a son who had betrayed his adopted country, so for his escape the boy feigned a drowning accident. From what we have been able to discover subsequently the hoax was successful. Both his father and the Soviet authorities apparently believe that Willi Guttmann drowned in Lake Geneva. Willi Guttmann was close to his father, it was a loving parent and child relationship.

'Willi has told us that each year his father takes a two-week holiday in his former home city of Magdeburg in the German Democratic Republic. Magdeburg is 48 kilometres, that's 30 miles, from the Inner German Border. Half an hour's drive down the autobahn. Dr Guttmann will be staying at the International Hotel on Otto von Guericke Strasse from Sunday the first to June the 15th. It is our intention while he is in Magdeburg to persuade Otto Guttmann to take advantage of escape facilities that we shall provide and so follow his son to the West.'

A hundred questions, a thousand negatives, bounced in Johnny's mind. Only difficulties, only problems, only dangers. But that was the way of 'I' Corps; always to fling ice water over any new plan.

'We've read all we can about you, Johnny. On Friday afternoon I spoke to as many people as I could reach who had commanded you during your time in the army. The reports are very good, it's a series of commendations . . . We would like you, Johnny, to go to Magdeburg, to persuade Dr Guttmann to take the opportunity to rejoin his son, to deliver him to the pick-up. That's the proposition.'

Johnny sighed, drew the air deep into his lungs, wanted to look around him, but they would all be gazing at him, and he stared instead at the carpet, tried to concentrate on its pattern while his mind reeled and lurched and his heart thumped.

'You wouldn't be involved in the actual transfer, Johnny, you've no worries on that score, it'll be taken care of.'

Johnny Donoghue back on the inside, lining out on the team.

'Your job will be strictly the approach and persuasion in Magdeburg. It goes without saying that coercion is not involved.'

Almost a time for tears. Almost a time to leap up and grab these men, wrap his arms around them and hold them close to him and thank them, thank them from the deep depths.

'You'll learn more as the days pass, but that's the broad outline and there will be a big team working on the details. There'll be all the support you need.'

Too easy, wasn't it? Slow down, Johnny. It can't be that simple. Don't look up. If it looks easy, it isn't. The only piece of advice he ever had from his father. So where's the catch?

'We're reacting to events, Johnny. The authorisation for us to set this running came just 48 hours ago. That doesn't bother us, we have the capability, we have the expertise, and for a critical part of the plan we want you.'

Was this the time to remember that his country had kicked him . . . in the groin, in the crutch, kicked him bloody hard and bent him double? No, you have to forget that, Johnny, because if you don't forget it where is the future? Is it for ever Cherry Road and German classes at the Technical College?

'Whatever happened in Ulster, Johnny, doesn't matter. As far as every one of us here is concerned you start with a clean sheet and a damn fine record behind you.'

Turn your back now, Johnny, and you're away back to Cherry Road. Just as you were a year and a half ago. Home in the shame, back into the shadow.

'I'd like to give it a go.'

He lifted his head and Mawby was beaming at him, Pierce

shook his hand, Carter with evident pleasure and welcome on his face waited his turn and Smithson slapped him on the back. George, with an eye on Mawby, stayed still and distant.

Working from an office temporarily provided for him at headquarters on Dzerzhinsky Street, Valeri Sharygin wrote in longhand what he hoped would be his final report on the disappearance of Willi Guttmann. No, not the disappearance, the drowning . . . The KGB major frowned privately, his head turned away from the typist by the window. The absence of the interpreter's body irritated him, but he could wait no longer. Leave beckoned before the departure of the delegation to the United Nations in New York for the summer session of the Conference. Perhaps before he flew to the United States he would telephone Foirot in Geneva.

He had been thorough in the writing of the report. Thorough enough to have visited personally the messenger from the Foreign Ministry who had taken the Guttmann possessions to his father's flat. Thorough enough to have registered the bitter swell of bereavement that had greeted the messenger.

What could he achieve by further delay? He anticipated that while he took his fortnight at Sochi the corpse would drift to Lake Geneva's surface.

It was peculiar that it had not already done so.

Chapter Five

=

Lizzie Forsyth ran up the two flights of stairs to the flat of the British Consul. She rang the doorbell, and heard the muffled whisper of a door opening deep inside and the murmur of annoyed voices. Who came on Sunday evening to do business with the Consul? He'd be placating his wife, saying he wouldn't be long, wondering what matter could not wait till the morning. Lizzie reordered her hair, raised herself handsome on her heels and waited.

'Yes?'

Lizzie smiling. 'You remember me, Lizzie Forsyth?' Lizzie radiant, a grin and white teeth. 'I wanted to see you.'

He had started back, as if exposed to danger. The Consul remembered Lizzie Forsyth. Not every day that he played host to a Soviet defector, that he entertained a man from Intelligence in his drawing room. He would not forget Lizzie Forsyth and her shivering boy and the quiet competence of the man who had taken him away. Unhappily he gestured her inside and led the way to his office, calling to a closed door on the way that he would not be long.

'What can I do for you, Miss Forsyth?'

She spoke with the fervour of a gale at an open window.

'I've just had the most marvellous thing happen. Just like that and without warning . . . my period's come. I'd given up hope, resigned myself to it, having the baby, and now it's come. God knows why I was as late as that. Well, it's come now . . . so the problem's over.'

'You're not . . .'

'I'm not pregnant, isn't it marvellous? I want to tell Willi. I didn't know how to write to him. Where to send a letter.'

'You're not pregnant?'

'It's wonderful, I think it's the happiest thing that's ever happened to me.'

'And now you want to tell Willi?'

'He'll want to know. I'm a bit ashamed really . . . I sort of railroaded him.' She was quieter now, calmer, the flood tide running steadily. 'I don't know whether he ever specially wanted to marry me. Willi ought to know, oughtn't he? It'll make everything different . . .'

The Consul winced, pain clear on his face, and he held up his hand for her to stop.

'Pray, how does this make everything different?' He looked into her clear, azure eyes and watched the light run against them and heard her certainty and sureness.

'We don't have to get married, well not in a hurry anyway.'

He put his hands to his chin, rubbed at the skin. 'There was no more compelling reason for Willi Guttmann's defection than that you had told him you were pregnant and that he must stand by you?'

'About right, yes.'

'And now that you are no longer pregnant, what do you think should happen?'

'Well, he's free, isn't he?'

'Free to do what?'

'He can go home, if he wants to,' she blurted. 'He's under no obligation to me.'

'He's defected. For your sake he has made himself a traitor.' The Consul paused, sighed. 'There is no second chance, there is no change of mind. He came across and that's that. He is somebody that we are interested in, that his own side cares about . . . Willi Guttmann no longer has a home.

'It was as much his fault as mine.'

'Do you still want to marry Willi Guttmann, make the rest of your life with him?'

'I don't know.' The certainty was gone, the radiance had dripped away. Just a secretary, one of a hundred, and the prettiness trodden out of her.

'The relevant authorities will inform Guttmann of what you've told me.'

'It's not just me that's to blame . . .'

'Get out, Miss Forsyth. Get out of this office and never come near it again.'

She didn't understand, he knew that, and his anger was wasted on her. She hadn't the smallest comprehension of the squalid mess she had left behind her. He tried to recall the face of the boy under his wet and sleeked-down hair, and could remember only the way that he had stood beside the girl and held her hand and looked with love at her and trembled from the cold of the lake.

He walked to the door and opened it and then went across the hallway and unlocked the front door. She hurried past him and when she was gone he heard only the sharp clatter of her heels on the steps.

They stayed up late in the sitting room.

The terms of reference for the evening had been set by Mawby. No shop talk, no gossip about the Service. This was a night off for all concerned, the last they would have, Mawby had said, this was the team familiarising with its selection, learning the mannerisms and habits and peculiarities. There was a bottle of whisky on the table and crystal glasses and the level of the drink slipped as the tongues loosened and the laughter echoed from the walls. Mawby played host, his back to the fire, orchestrating the entertainment, involving the players, and did it skilfully.

Henry Carter talked of a strike-bound family hotel on the Costa del Sol with guests cooking and washing and making their beds, and a suspicion of cholera up the coast. Adrian Pierce recounted his Cambridge days and the homosexual don who took tutorials in a satin dressing gown and the chase around the table and the flight back to his room. Harry Smithson, a leer at his face and a grin at his mouth, told of the 19-year-old second lieutenant that was himself and the posting to occupation forces in Germany and the favours that could be gained for a pair of soft stockings and a bar of milk chocolate.

Happy, friendly, nonsense talk, and Mawby allowed

Johnny to remain on the fringe, to enjoy but not to contribute. Sizing them up, weighing them, and he could bide his time over the development of the relationships. No fool, Charles Augustus Mawby. Nobody's fool. Johnny basked in quiet pleasure because this was how it had been sometimes in the mess, and he was the moth drawn to an old flame. Johnny had laughed and chuckled at the private faces of the men in the room. Carter for whom nothing worked and the tale was of chaos and failure. Pierce, whose sarcasm was vital and cutting. Smithson the cynic, believing in nothing, trusting nobody.

Content to be in charge, giving them their heads and for a purpose, Mawby dispensed the whisky.

And it was good to be part of something again. The noise of the room highlighted the narrowness of the escape bolt that Johnny had chosen for himself in Cherry Road. Run away, hadn't he? Sprinted for cover after the awfulness of the trial. Shunned contact with the great outside and leaned on his frail mother for support. Not healthy, but inevitable. What would any of these men have done if they had sat in the wide dock of the Crown Court in Crumlin Road? Would they have bounced back and erased the memory of the military escort across the city each morning and afternoon, and the stern-lipped warders with the keys and chains and truncheons? The whisky helped the memories to run, and with the clock chimes Johnny's attention to the jokes and anecdotes became weaker, was replaced. What did these men know of trial for murder? Nothing, Johnny, but that's not their fault. And they were doing their best to make him forget. But they knew . . . of course they bloody knew.

The court of the Lord Chief Justice of Northern Ireland. A high and red-painted ceiling, ornate moulding, hanging lights, a garish wallpaper, layers of scrubbed duck green paint over the dock and the benches for the lawyers and the journalists and the public. The Lord Chief Justice, without hostility or kindness, asking and probing, writing his answers with a creaking pen. Counsel for the prosecution, the disbelief at his raised eyebrows and the voice that carried the quiet, incisive questions. The father of the girl and her brothers, all in a line, all hunched and staring at Johnny, their eyes never leaving him, all loathing him for the irreplaceable loss that he had brought to their home. Carter and Pierce and Smithson knew of it. Mawby would have read the file, read of the accusation and the defence before he sent his minions to bring Johnny to London. To bring the poor fool who would do what he was told so that he might regain his stature as a free man.

Pathetic and snivelling they seemed to him now, his courtroom explanations.

'It's different when you're sitting here, things don't happen the way you've put it, not when you're on the ground . . .'

'It happened very quickly. It's not like being sat in a cinema and watching it on a screen . . .'

'Yes I did think at the time that the person I fired on was holding a gun. I thought that my life was endangered, my life and those of the men who were with me . . .'

'I was confronting an armed terrorist, that's all I thought . . .'

And the deathly hush of disbelief. Always the unforgiving silence in the court and the wait for the Lord Chief Justice to look up from his ledger and for Counsel to frame his next question. A desperate quiet focused on the man who sat in the low witness box in a clean shirt and plain tie and a sports jacket.

Counsel turning the screw, driving it deeper. 'The suggestion I put to you, Captain Donoghue, is that you believed your military rank and the special nature of your duties put you above the law. I suggest that you wilfully ignored the standard procedure of issuing a challenge before opening fire. I suggest that you were prepared to shoot dead any person, terrorist or civilian who approached the cache.'

'It wasn't like that . . .'

What was it like, Johnny? Johnny still and damp in the

bracken and under the bramble of the hedge, and the figure bending at the fox hole, the flicker of the plastic fertiliser sack as it was drawn clear, the bag pushed back into the hole. The figure rising short and lightweight onto the feet and then the gun presented to him . . . not a gun, Johnny, a collapsible umbrella. One shot from the Armalite, half a scream and a tumbling shape. Got the fucking pig, the corporal behind him said. Radio for Quick Reaction Force. Land-Rover in the lane within ten minutes, and a voice calling from a farm house in the hill, calling a girl's name in panic and desperate fear.

Pierce drawled through his story, acting out the parts with his eyes and his hands. '. . . he liked the Grammar School boys best, reckoned he stood a better chance of buggering them, because they weren't part of the scene at Trinity, they'd be frightened of getting packed off home. He was a cheeky old turnip. One chap came along to read an essay when he'd a late date afterwards at the Nurses' Home, he was smothered in after shave and talc. The old fellow went quite bananas, hardly gave the lad time to get his script out of the bag . . .'

Maeve O'Connor shot through the right breast, stone dead. Johnny heaving his guts into the hedge. Why a girl, for the love of God? The corporal whimpering like a badger with a leg in a gin trap. The tongueless journey in the Land-Rover to Keady police station. The telephone message from Brigade headquarters; say nothing, sign nothing, name and rank and nothing more. The arrival of the Army Legal Service officer, and the men from Special Investigation Branch and the faces of contempt and disapproval and Johnny not shaved for three days and needing a hot meal and a clean bed.

Smithson shook his shoulders in laughter as he talked. '. . . for a pound of sausages you could find a biddy who would actually chuck her old man out of bed and send him to sit downstairs to wait till you'd finished. And when you came down the stairs then he'd thank you for coming and say that he hoped you'd call again. Bloody marvellous time we had . . .'

The girl's cousin had found the cache. A combat jacket, a black beret, a Luger pistol, a packet of industrial detonators. Found it when out with the farm dog that had sniffed at the hole. Reported it, and a Catholic too. Done his duty as a citizen. And the family had talked of it inside their home and Maeve O'Connor had heard the chat when she'd gone to her Auntie for supper, and she was a child and she was curious and no one had thought it necessary to warn the family to stay clear. Maeve O'Connor with a pale and pretty face and freckles and a smear of terror, shot and killed because Johnny Donoghue hadn't challenged, had believed he was fighting a war, had thought a teenage shadow was his enemy. On trial for murder, facing the full majesty of the law, with a life sentence to serve if the case went against him.

They don't care, these people. Charles Mawby and Henry Carter and Adrian Pierce and Harry Smithson, they don't give a shit. There's a job to be done in Germany, and Johnny's the one they want for it.

'You're very quiet, Johnny,' boomed Mawby.

'Don't expect him to compete with Harry,' said Carter.

'You'll have one for the stairs?' Mawby surged forward with the bottle.

'Just one more, a small one. Then it'll be my bedtime.'

'Quite right.' Mawby was filling Johnny's glass. 'A dose of Pierce and Smithson does more damage than a litre of this poison.'

They all laughed and Johnny with them. He had the right to join them, hadn't he? He was on the team, integral to it. And in the morning the work would start.

In his darkened bedroom Willi heard the feet on the staircase, and the voices that drifted through his door. He curled under his sheet and blankets to find warmth.

The changes in the household had not been explained to him. Carter had merely said that new men would meet him in the morning, bringing new questions, that he must answer them as best he could. Perhaps in the morning he would ask again when Lizzie and he would be reunited. But he asked that each day and the answer was always vague and no one would give him a definite date. Why did they want to know of his father? Why was his father the only subject that Carter had discussed for two days? What was their interest in an old man? The noise had died in the house, but the climb to bed by the company from below had wakened Willi, left his mind clear and alert. Sleep would come hard for him now.

He dressed fast, fingers fumbling with the buttons of his tunic. Frantic and quick and hurrying because he had looked at his watch and dived from the bed. And she had been faster, drawing on her pants and fastening her skirt, thrusting a sweater over her head, ignoring her tumbled hair.

'They'll kill me if I miss the train,' he muttered as if from her he might find relief from the punishment.

'Keep your feet still,' Jutte snapped, knotting his boot laces, catching the contagion of his fear.

Ulf Becker turned towards the bed, dishevelled and disturbed, creased and used. 'Will they come back?'

'Not till tomorrow, I told you. I'd do it later.'

'I'll get extra duties for a month.'

The girl grabbed at her small handbag. Together they flung themselves through the front door, Ulf stumbling with the weight of his canvas issue grip bag. Running down the stairs because it was always too long to wait for the lift, running and hoping that they met no one, running into the night air and feeling the draught of the wind catch at their faces. Hand in hand on the pavement and then the girl's hesitation, she pulling one way, he another.

'We should take the U-Bahn to Alexander Platz, then the S-Bahn . . .'

'We don't have time, we have to run to the S-Bahn.' Ulf's anger rose as the cool of the evening sobered him.

'It is quicker to go to Schilling Strasse and the U-Bahn.'

'We have to go direct to the S-Bahn.' Ulf shouting his argument and using his strength till the girl allowed herself to be pulled. Ulf sprinting and the bag handle cutting at his palm, its bulk banging against his knee. Jutte beside him with the long and sleek stride. Where did the girl find the speed? Where did she find it after what she had done to him on her mother's bed? Down Lichtenberge Strasse, past the great edifices of the blocks of flats, past the blank windows, past the drawn curtains, past the emptied play grounds with the children's apparatus. Feet hammering on the pavement, echoing and raucous. Down to Holzmark Strasse. No one on the street to impede them, cars only distant and no hazard. Running across the road where there were pedestrian crossing lights, running on the pavements. Heaving chests and her breasts bouncing in the movement, his hand aching at the weight of the bag.

Into the station of Jannowitzbrucke. Change hands. Diving down the wide staircase. Ulf bringing from his pocket a handful of coins, Jutte scratching in her purse. Two twenty-pfennig coins into the machine. More stairs and corridors that carried the heavy, uncleansed tunnel odour. What betting that the first would be on the Kopenick and Erkner line, not the Schöneweide track? The platform deserted. Only the two young people to make their own company. The tall boy in the uniform of the Border Guard of the National Volks Armee, the grey cloth fitting him well, the trousers hanging true to their creases, the sharp green of the epaulette and wrist ribbon. The clean-faced girl, athletic and slender, who hung on his arm and gazed up at his face and whose fair hair was long and loose and casual. Both pouring huge, heaving breaths into the cold night air.

Ulf looked again at his watch.

'Don't do it,' she said.

'Perhaps there is still a chance . . .'

'Perhaps . . .'

The train sounded its approach, deep in the black well of the tunnel, taunting them with the slowness of its approach. Coming slowly, coming at its appointed speed.

'Is there a chance?'

'Perhaps . . .' Her breathing had subsided and her breasts

were still and the nipples pushing at the wool of her sweater and the boy wanted nothing more than to bury his face against her and feel her warmth and the gentle scent of her body. 'I think it is not possible. But we will try, lover, we will try to send you back to Weferlingen.' She laughed lightly.

The train came slowly, steadily into the station. No one leaving, only the young couple joining. A stop of a few seconds and the doors were closing on them. Alone in the carriage with the wooden slat walls and the advertisements for mouth rinses and savings policies, into the tunnel darkness, the strangling tunnel, rocking and swaying. Jutte sat very close to her boy. Thigh to thigh, her hand linked under his arm and resting on his knee, her head at his shoulder. Out from the tunnel and into the night. The crisp rattle of the wheels on the rails. A drugging, soporific rhythm.

'Ulf.'

He was thinking only of how he would spend the time before the early morning train. 'Yes.'

'Did I tell you that I have an uncle that lives in Hamburg?'

'You told me.'

'Well it is not actually Hamburg, that is where his factory is. He lives in Pinneburg which is on the autobahn to Hamburg.'

'You told me.'

'He came to see us last summer.' The train crept into the pale-lit platforms of Treptower Park. 'He came with his Mercedes. When it was parked outside our flat many people came to look at it, not obviously, but they made the opportunity to admire it.'

'So?'

'Do you know his children did not come to see us because they said it was too tedious to come to the DDR, they said it was a waste of time. My uncle said that if ever I reached Hamburg then he would give me a job. Even a secretary, he said, is paid more than two thousand marks a month.'

'More than four times what my father takes.' Ulf could imagine it, Ulf could feel it. The pay of the NVA conscript was 44 marks a month, with food and accommodation and transport found. 'But there everything is expensive, you pay much for a flat.'

'But not for a car, not for a television, not for a pair of jeans. You see the advertisements on their television in the evening.'

Ulf sagged back, tired, in his seat. He was going back to Weferlingen, the boy who loved her and knew her, and she was talking about the price of a television set and the wage of a secretary in Hamburg. The train was edging clear of Planterwald. Still they were alone in the carriage.

'When we were in the Tierpark my uncle said that many young people were still able to leave, to go over there.'

'If someone pays then perhaps it is possible. There are criminals who will provide forged papers, will try to take people out. They charge thousands of marks, West marks, and many are caught. They are scum, filth, human traffickers.'

Jutte was close against him and her lips brushed against the lobe of his ear and her voice was as a light wind among leaves and her fingers traced patterns on the surface of his trousers. 'My uncle talked of that. He said what you have said. But he spoke about the border, Ulf. He said it could be crossed.'

He wanted only to love her and she had teased him into anger. 'It is one thing to talk of it, it is another to act. There is so much there, do you know that? The Restricted Zone, five kilometres deep. The Hinterland fence that is electrified. There are towers for observation, there are patrols, there are minefields, there are automatic guns. You cannot even climb the fence . . . It is easy to speak of it, easy only to talk of crossing.'

They passed through Baumschulenweg. No one boarded, no one left the train.

'My uncle said that it could be crossed, but that there was one requisite, one thing was necessary . . .'

'What was that?'

'One in the party that makes the attempt must know a

particular place. You cannot go as a blind man and hope to win through, but if you know the place . . . He had read it in *Stern* magazine, there are places . . .'

The train was slowing, the driver hard with the brakes, the wheels screaming on the rails, the illuminated sign flicking past the windows. Betr-Bahnhof Schöneweide. Thirty-four minutes past midnight. Departure time for Magdeburg was thirty minutes after midnight. Ulf was on his feet and waiting furiously impatient for the doors to open, Jutte gripping his hand in a vice of possession.

'You're going to run?'

He nodded.

The doors opened. They ran, legs stretched, boy and girl, stride matching stride. Along the platform, down the steps, along the corridor, up the steps. There were carriages beside the open, stark platform on the main station. Carriages that carried the routing 'Potsdam, Brandenburg, Genthin, Burg, Magdeburg, Halberstadt'. A whistle blowing, shrieking in his ears. The train sliding forward, crawling and restless. Ulf leapt for the nearest door, wrenched it open and jumped for the high step.

He heard her voice, firm against the gathering impetus of the train.

'Find me that place, lover. Find it for me.'

He shook his head as if trying to rid himself of a pain, and she was smiling and her face was burning beacon bright, and her eyes shone at him.

'Find it, and write to me.'

She turned and did not look for him again and was lost on the descending steps from the platform.

Ulf Becker began the hunt for a seat. On the night train it would be 4 hours to Magdeburg.

Erica Guttmann had changed to her nightdress and dressing gown, had done that before she carried a pot of tea to her father. She had read a book and listened to her radio, and could not find tiredness. The worry prevented that, the worry and hurt bred from watching his deteriorating efforts to maintain the close routine of their life since the telegram had come from Geneva. An old man, and ageing, and growing in his dependence on her as the days passed.

Renate was both a relative and a friend. A second cousin and a contemporary. They'd met in the town ever since she could remember the holidays in Magdeburg. Always Renate was there from the days of dressing up and playing skipping games and taking picnics, right through to adulthood and confidence. Renate the single girl like herself, and bubbling with a cheerfulness that was champagne to Erica after the long winter and slow spring of Moscow. Bewildering that such a lovely girl as Renate, pretty as a flower, had allowed herself to become the mistress of a policeman. A policeman called Gunther Spitzer. The two girls would be swept by gales of laughter when they spoke of the affair. But at least he was a senior officer, he was prominent in the Schutzpolizei. What a choice for her lovely friend to have made. But in less than a month they could talk of it. From the drawers of her table she took a writing pad and her pen.

My dear Renate,
You will have heard of the awful thing that happened to Willi in Geneva . . .

Chapter Six

=

There was pressure on the bathroom space on the Monday morning and on the days that followed. And at eight o'clock sharp Mrs Ferguson bustling into the dining room with her trays of fried food and jugs of coffee and pots of tea and racks of toast played to a full house.

The fierce jollity of the all-male working society. All together, lads, Mawby seemed to be saying, something for us all to have some pride in, and only the best will be acceptable.

'If you don't mind, the butter please.'

'Coming over, Adrian.'

'The marmalade there, Harry?'

'Wish the old lady would get some decent coffee in, right, Johnny?'

'Hear the news this morning, the bloody sewage workers' strike?'

'Nothing changes, does it, Henry?'

'Come on, lads, each to his appointed.'

'Yes, Mr Mawby.'

The men of the Service coming together with their individual areas of expertise in the operation, and all making the effort to pull Johnny into their nest.

Mawby and Carter, the last to leave the table.

'Distant, isn't he, Mr Mawby. Removed from us, like he's an untouchable, don't you think?'

'Self-dependent, and self-reliant, that's the way I see him, Henry, and that's what I'm looking for.'

'He's a cold sort of fish.'

'As he should be for what we want of him.'

'Do you know that he even brought his old army boots down here. Next to no luggage, but he insisted on the boots,

Smithson told me. You'd have thought he'd have turned them out months ago.'

'Let's hope he doesn't need them. Let's hope we're not into a cross-country scamper . . . Take him slowly, Henry, slowly and carefully.'

'Tell us about his health, Willi, his condition physically.'

Carter at the table with the big notepad, sometimes Mawby beside him and taking a lesser part. Willi sat in a straight chair in which it would be difficult for him to relax. Johnny sat behind the boy.

'He's an old man now, he's close to seventy. Up till his sixty-fifth birthday he used to go to a gymnasium that was in a sports club near our flat, but he strained himself and he has not gone back. We used to have a dog and he could go for walks with it, but it died several years ago. He said it was too much trouble to have another one. He has a medical check-up each twelve months that is done at Padolsk by the Army. He cannot walk far now. Always he used to like to walk, when Erica and I were younger he liked to go with us to the Hartz Mountains, to Wernigerode or Quedlinburg, and then walk in the hills and the woods. I think that he has a little rheumatism . . . Why do you ask these questions, Mr Carter?'

'That's not your worry, Willi. Just answer as best you can, like you're doing.'

In the afternoons in the sitting room, Johnny sat with Adrian Pierce. Military talk and the resurrection of familiar subjects of the old days before Belfast, before the trial, before the return to Cherry Road.

'You're going to be with a man who is expert in armour and its counter-weaponry. It's possible that the objective of the mission will not succeed, that you will not bring him over, but that you will manage to talk with him. It is possible that defection will be beyond him . . . And bloody daft it would be if the man we've sent has forgotten what the front end of a Main Battle Tank looks like. This is a sort of refresher course, Johnny, and by the time we pack you off I want tanks, armour plating widths, squash head, control guidance and all the rest of the paraphernalia running out of your ears.'

Always supper at seven, prompt on the clock, all of them sitting down, napkins spread, glasses filled with water or milk or Coca-Cola. Two tables pushed together. A cotton cloth that was clean each day. All watching the door to the kitchen through which Mrs Ferguson would come with the evening's offering. And after supper back to the sitting room for Johnny and with him Harry Smithson.

'We want you to know as much as is possible before you cross. You'll remember some of the basics from your "I" Corps days, forget that and listen to me. The DDR is a captive state. The regime of the Sozialistische Einheitspartei Deutschlands, that's SED in future, survives because of the permanent garrisoning on her territory of a minimum of 20 full strength Soviet divisions. Effectively the country is beholden to Soviet military command headquarters at Zossen-Wunsdorf outside Berlin. When you pull this one off, Johnny boy, that's where the squeal's going to come from, that's where the boot will be to kick every arse in sight to kingdom come. I said it's a captive state . . . Along a frontier of just under 900 miles with West Germany there is a cripplingly expensive set of border defences, with some 50,000 men deployed to keep their own brothers and sisters from doing a flit to the BDR. So start with an occupying force and the closed frontiers and you begin to get the sour taste in your mouth, you can call me a fascist if you want to and it'll give no offence, but that's my view of the place and I've been detailed to brief you. They enjoy living there so much that at the latest count more than two million nine hundred thousand citizens have skipped it, given their masters two fingers and run. That's the German Democratic Republic, Johnny. Perhaps I'm just an old right wing bastard, but I hate that place because it's sinister, it's tedious, it's drab.'

*

'Are you going to hurt my father?'

Carter's face slackened with surprise.

'No . . . nothing like that . . .'

'Why do you want to know so much about him, and about his holiday?' Willi cut across him, his voice strained.

'It's just routine,' Carter hurried. 'We're not going to harm your father, why should we?'

'You're lying to me, Mr Carter.'

'You've done very well so far, Willi, confine yourself to answering our questions.' The slip of Carter's control had been momentary. The cutting chill was once more in his voice. From where he sat Johnny saw it all, admired him for it.

'It's a lie,' the boy shouted.

The click of the door handle alerted Johnny and he turned to see George in the doorway. The boy too would have heard the door, realised its signal. Threatened from front and rear, Willi's protest was stifled.

'That's all right, George. No problems in here, are there, Willi?' A glacial smile from Carter. '. . . You were telling me, Willi, about your father's programme in Magdeburg. Let's start again with who he will be seeing there.'

The boy hesitated, he would have heard the door close. He turned full round to face Johnny. Johnny looked away, didn't meet him.

'There are many people that he will meet,' Willi said softly. 'He has many friends there. There is a pastor at the Wallonerkirche, he is a friend from many years, my father always attends the evangelist church, and the man who keeps the bookshop beside the Kloster Unser Lieben Frauen, he also is a friend. There is another pastor from the Dom, the cathedral . . . he will go to see him . . .'

In the bar of a Gasthaus on the outskirts of Wiesbaden, Adam Percy met with a friend from far back. The service's station officer resident in Bonn had driven the 100 kilometres of autobahn to see a man he had known from the days of the occupation and the first recruitment of German nationals to work in British funded intelligence gathering. Across the table from him, separated by two beers, was an employee of the West German Federal Intelligence Service, the Bundesnachrichtendienst, and well used to the private business that bypassed the official contacts between colleagues of SIS and BND.

Percy, elderly and overweight and unwilling to submit to the dieting prescribed by doctors during his London leave, quizzed quickly through the file that had been passed to him.

'You understand, Mr Percy, it was not easy for me to gain access for this. The section is not one that involves me.'

'I do understand, Karl, and it is a great favour that you do for me . . .' A costly favour.

'If you went direct to the section responsible . . . then there would be more for you.'

'Not the mysterious and marvellous way of London. No contact authorised, nothing on top of the table. Adamant about it.'

'You know about these people, Mr Percy? We regard them as dirt, as something evil, you know that.'

'Not for me to reason why. London commands, I provide. I'm a very humble person. Did you have to sign for the file?'

'Of course . . . you will be careful, Mr Percy, when you deal with this man . . .'

Percy closed the slim file that carried the name and photograph and identity card number of Hermann Lentzer, pushed it across the table past a small pool of spilt beer. 'Most careful, Karl.'

'They can burn you, these people.'

'It's not a character reference I want, it's a recommendation of effectiveness. I fancy I have that.'

An envelope followed the file across the table and into the German's attaché case. The two men drained their beers.

'You'll have seen a tank being brewed, Johnny, I'm sure you've seen it on the range. It's pretty revolting. They don't get out when they're hit by modern anti-tank shells. They get melted down, they get stuck to the inside walls, they blend in with the steel of the turret. There's no tank built that's invulnerable to the new armour-piercing and squash-head missiles. All we can do is try and minimise the areas of danger, that and teach the evasion procedures. The tank is the queen of the battlefield, when she's running rampant she's wonderful, incisive in the breakout. When she's outmanoeuvred, when the technology is against her, then she's just a death-box. They're developing their counter force while we're working on our hitting arm. It's always that way in military evolution, parallel lines. But now we have a chance to muscle up at their expense. That chance doesn't come often, Johnny . . .'

Pierce was drawing. Broad lines on the paper, the blunt nose and the guidance fins of a missile.

A man who identified himself as John Dawson walked into a travel agent's offices on a narrow, battered street close to Dublin's River Liffey.

It had been Carter's idea that Johnny's travel arrangements should be launched from the Irish Republic. Better that the visa and accommodation application should come from Dublin than London. Better, because that would provide the background to fog the computers and screening that the authorities of the DDR might bring to bear on Western visitors to their country.

Mr Dawson understood that the firm specialised in arranging holidays in eastern Europe and said that it was his wish to visit the German Democratic Republic. He wanted to see the city of Magdeburg, he'd read about it and it seemed a fine and historic place, and a good starting point for journeys to the Hartz mountains. He required a single room in the city and the dates that he could get away from work were between the 11th and the 18th of June. The young man behind the counter had looked up at the wall calendar, grimaced at the time left for him to make the arrangements, and promised that the telex requesting the booking would be sent that day to the East German Berolina Agency in London.

How would Mr Dawson wish to travel? He would go by train. From which West German city? He would go by train from Hannover. Did Mr Dawson wish the agency to book flights from Dublin to West Germany? No. Mr Dawson had business to fit in while visiting Britain. He would make his own arrangements to get to Hannover, but he would appreciate the rail tickets being purchased in Dublin. Would a £30 deposit be satisfactory? Perfectly satisfactory.

More details. Date of Birth. Place of Birth. Occupation. Passport Number . . . The information was given by a Secretary of the British Embassy in Dublin working to an exact brief. He offered the number of a passport that still lay in the basements of Century House awaiting the attention of the expert who would apply the various immigration officials' stamps for authenticity.

John Dawson was a teacher.

'I'm sure there will be no difficulty,' the young man said. 'When they pull their fingers out they can move quite quickly.'

'I hope so. It will be my first time there, a sort of holiday with a difference.'

'They passed their second constitution in 1968 guaranteeing the freedom of the individual, but it's not a document regulating the power of the state and its organs as it would be in the West. It doesn't curb the authority of government, it legalises that authority. The ideology of the system is with its citizens at all times because they've learned over there that the infrastructure is all-important. Everything is in pyramid formation, everything leads back to the Central Committee of SED. The base of the pyramid is very wide. There's the Freie Deutsche Gewerkschaftsbund which is the trades union organisation with more than 7 million members. There's the Freie Deutsche Jugend, the youth organisation, with $1\frac{3}{4}$ million kids on the books. There's the Pioneer Ernst Thalmann for the nippers between 5 and 14, 2 million of them. The Party, the SED, has 2 million members or just over. You can't get on in this society without belonging or having belonged, you can't just opt out and say you're not interested and then expect to pick up a foreman's job, or get a place at a decent college. And the system perpetuates its own security. It watches over people, smothers them so that they don't know where they can turn for commiseration. There are 500,000 Party cells at the baseplate of the Party. Eyes and ears, the espionage network if you put it that way. It's a honeycomb of ideological reliability. It makes for a suspicious, prying community where people believe in the right to inform on their neighbour or the stranger in their street. You have to be careful, Johnny, careful all the time. You have to watch yourself, because you'll be watched. You'll be mapped and surveyed by people who are more than curious about you. The moral is that you go slowly, Johnny, step by step. You don't talk to people there, you don't expect to find a friend . . . they can get 5 years inside for criticising the state to a foreigner . . . you go on your own, you stay on your own. Realise that and you can win, accept the isolation and you'll be fine.'

The telephone call for Mawby brought Mrs Ferguson scampering across the lawns to find him as he strolled under the back trees. The reply was back from Bonn. He was expected on the first flight of the next day. A man for him to meet. It was another step forward and an important step because it solidified the commitment of the Service to the operation. He was flying to Germany, and they were no longer at the stage of outline planning.

As he climbed the stairs to collect his clothes Charles Mawby was surprised that a flush of nervousness warmed his face.

'Tell us about Erica, Willi.'

'She is twenty-nine years old. She is loved very dearly by my father. In the last few years he has relied much on her for support, that is why she now works with him at Padolsk. She acts there as his secretary, and also as his protector. She answers his telephone and makes his appointments, in that

76

way she tries to see that he is not overstrained.'

'Would she be in the Party, Willi?'

'You want always to give the label . . . She is a person who has grown up in a state where the political system is communism. How then can she be anything but communist? How could she be a capitalist if she has never known capitalism? She knows only one colour, and that colour is red.'

'Is she committed to the Party, Willi?' Carter, wondering at Willi's evasion, recording the last question and the new line of Willi's answer in his notebook.

'Just labels . . .' Defiance bloomed in his cheeks. 'What do you know of life in Moscow, have you ever been there? Do you think the young people of the Soviet Union and the DDR spend their evenings talking of the grain harvest and the quotas in the building industry of workers' flats, and the composition of the Politburo, do you think that? Do you think they talk of the glories of steel production and the output of lignite? You know nothing of life there.'

'Don't be cheeky, Willi.'

'They are idiot questions.'

'I choose the questions . . . She was in the Pioneers?'

'Everyone is in the Pioneers. Every schoolchild has marched in Moscow on May Day. Everyone strives to better themselves.'

Carter looked across the table, carefully and slowly, weighing his words, creating pressure on the boy, loading it on his young shoulders. 'Tell me, Willi, if Erica knew that you were not drowned, but that you had defected, would she then love you or would she hate you? Would you be a hero to her or a traitor . . .?'

'You bastard.'

'Would she love you . . .'

'You have no right to ask.'

'I have every right. You have no rights. You have nothing, Willi Guttmann. Without me, without my help you have nothing. Answer me, would she love you?'

Johnny saw the boy crumple low in his chair, saw his body hunch and slide.

'She would hate me, she would despise me.'

'Why?'

'She would not have done what I did, not for the same reason.'

'Could she not have been in love with a boy, as you were with Lizzie?'

The boy spat out his bitterness. 'She loves no one. She is incapable of loving anyone but my father. She does not have the warmth or the heart to love a stranger, another man . . . Where is Lizzie?'

'Forget Lizzie.'

The boy was high again in his chair and his hands gripped the sides of the seat, knuckles clear and pale. The muscles gathered at the back of his neck. 'I want Lizzie to be here. I want Lizzie to be with me. You promised.'

'I said that you have to forget Lizzie Forsyth.'

The boy cried out, a wounded animal, deep wounded, the wood saw on the buried nail. 'How do I forget her when she is carrying my child . . .'

'She is carrying nobody's child. Not yours, not anybody else's. She's not pregnant and she's not coming to England. She's not coming because she doesn't want to.'

He was very quiet, silent but for the whimper, still but for the shaking that heralded the first tears. George was in the doorway and moving over the carpet with the disciplined stealth of the hospital orderly who must handle a troublesome patient. When George led Willi out of the room he had a strong hand at the boy's elbow. The door closed.

'Why did you do that?' Johnny asked.

'I don't really know,' said Carter.

'You scratched him hard.'

'I'm not proud of myself, Johnny,' Carter said. 'Just fractured a bit, I suppose. And what does it matter? The problem is bigger than the boy's sensibilities.'

'What problem?'

'Do us a favour, Johnny. I'm asking these questions to get crucial information for you, not for the pleasure of hearing my own bloody voice. The problem of persuasion, your problem. With the old man we stand a chance. We've evaluated that and we believe in the possibility of winning him. But how to cope with the sister, that's the new problem and Willi is the way round it.'

Chapter Seven

=

Charles Mawby, with the advantage of a diplomatic passport, was quickly off the plane and through Immigration. He walked at a busy pace through the Customs area and out onto the concourse and his eyes roved for the man meeting him. Adam Percy, SIS resident in the German capital, stood back from the waving greeters and welcome carriers who awaited other passengers from the London flight. Mawby saw him, strode forward, there was a brief and perfunctory handshake and they were on their way to the car park.

They looked what they were. The man on the ground who was the junior and at the airport to meet his chief from head office. The twinge of deference, had it been a good journey? The fact that the plane had not been delayed, the weather should hold up. With Percy driving they moved off for the autobahn heading south.

'What seems to be the form, Adam?'

'I held off calling you, Mr Mawby, until I'd lined a man for you to talk with.'

'Thank you for that.'

'We're going now to a village just the far side of Bonn, to see a man who deals in the matters we're concerned with.' The mole bulged on the left face of Percy's nose, his lips were flaccid and creased and bloodless. In the Service his name was synonymous with dogged and persistent endeavour. 'I'd heard some years ago of this group. Bringing people out of the East for cash, it's their speciality. They deliver – I checked the man out with Bundesnachrichtendienst.'

'Who do we deal with now at BND?'

'This was back door, an after hours request, as you wanted. The usual source.'

'Who are we seeing?'

'He's not the sort you'd have for cocktails, not a pleasing example of the human species, but that's not the job sheet, is it? His motivation would be categorised as political. A junior SS officer at the end of the war, but too junior to warrant retribution from the legal system. All the ideology was stored up and left to fester. He's a communist hater, and this is his way of goading them. He runs a small group that manages with a fair regularity to bring out unhappy citizens from the DDR in exchange for fat returns from their relatives and friends living on this side. Most of his scene of action is along the Berlin to Helmstedt autobahn.'

Mawby dived him a quick glance. 'That's possible, is it?'

'It's possible. Possible but hazardous.' Percy kept his eyes on the road.

'Not straightforward, not for people like this?'

'Hazardous, Mr Mawby, and that cannot be overstressed. In theory the DDR is obliged under the terms of the post-war Four Power Agreement to provide unimpeded motor access between West Germany and West Berlin. In effect over the last 2 years they have substantially raised the numbers of cars stopped and searched at the Marienborn checkpoint. The two principal methods of evasion involve persons hidden in a vehicle, or those provided with false papers, forged documents and attempting to bluff their way through. They're not idiots on the border, they've a fair idea what they're looking for ... there are some 500 West Germans serving time. The drivers, the fixers, the link-men, they'll testify to the thoroughness of the scrutiny at the border. There's a considerable intelligence effort mounted by the Staatssicherheitadienst that's aimed specifically at infiltrating the groups, giving them a length of rope and then strangling them.'

Perhaps even in the warm interior of the speeding car, Charles Mawby felt a faint and winnowing chill. Why did the wretched man start with the difficulties? Mawby had spoken in London of the feasibility of the concept, he had not lingered on the ruts and pot-holes in the road.

'How tight is our group?'

'How long is an Irish mile, Mr Mawby? The bad ones don't last, and this one has survived, that's on his side. Security is always going to be the greatest strain though. If nobody knows of them then they don't attract the trade, and they're commercial, so they need an order list. In a vague way they have to go out and tout for business. They have to be known, and the BND knows about our merchant.'

'You've called me over to meet this man, so what tells you he has the necessary security factor to be suitable for us?'

His politics. He detests them over there, detests and loathes them. His whole life is kicking them, and around him are like-minded people. To you and me his pay-roll is made up of thugs and fascists . . . It wouldn't be simple to infiltrate that kind of group.'

'That makes sense.' Mawby sighed a bellows blast of relief. The start of the good news, but the moment was short.

'You have to understand, Mr Mawby, that if you launch with this man you can expect us to be alone with him. Even if we subsequently change stance and request it, we'll get no help from BND. The authorities aren't friendly with these people. From the Chancellor down they're condemned. They're seen as jeopardising the free flow along the auto-bahn, the Soviets are for ever threatening that if Bonn doesn't take a firmer hand, stamp them out, then new controls will be asserted on the autobahn. They're an embarrassment to government here, the groups stand in the way of the gradual thaw in East and West German relations, so they're just not wanted. It's not an area where we'd have active co-operation.'

Mawby turned to watch the flow of growing crops and grass shudder past him, felt the trembling roar of an overtaking articulated lorry and trailer.

'I suppose we couldn't do this ourselves?' Mawby betrayed his unhappiness.

'You could, but you take a risk.'

'Explain yourself.'

'If you have a car with a British driver and you have

German passengers with German documentation then you invite inspection. You couldn't give British paperwork to Germans and just hope they weren't singled for questioning, and if it were blown . . . Good grief, they'd be scuttling for cover in Outer Mongolia.'

'Quite so.'

'You have to be distant from it, Mr Mawby. Distant from the group and above everything distant from the driver, so the leads and traces back are stifled.'

Mawby looked across at Percy, but the eyes were fixed on the road. Of course he was right and he could afford to be, because it wasn't down to him, the responsibility wasn't going to find its way to Adam Percy's pudgy back.

'How long do we have, before you want the pick-up made?'

'Our man is unavailable after the fifteenth of June,' Mawby said.

'That's sharp.'

'It has to be done in that time.'

'Not much scope for rehearsal, not before the first night. You'll have to hope everybody learns their lines by the curtain lift.'

'It has to be done in that time.'

'So be it,' said Percy. 'Perhaps we should wish each other luck, Mr Mawby.'

They bumped over the cobbled streets of Bonn, were held by traffic lights, cramped by cars as they crawled towards the south side of the city. Mawby had nothing more to say, nothing before the meeting was joined.

'Will your father take any work with him to Magdeburg?'

'Only if there were something very pressing. Only if there was a problem at Padolsk would they contact him.'

'While he's in Magdeburg is he subject to surveillance?'

'A guard, a policeman watching him? . . . I don't think so. Never before. But like every outsider, every visitor, his documents must go to Strasse der Jugend . . .'

'What's that, Willi?'

'To the offices of the City police. For the stamp.'

'Would the Soviet military be in contact with him, or GRU?'

'The Red Army, yes. They will know that he is in Magdeburg. They invite him each year for a dinner, perhaps to the garrison camp of the armoured division at Bierderitz . . .'

'That's to the east of Magdeburg?'

'East across the river. The GRU, no . . . there is no reason for the intelligence people to watch him.'

'You are sure he is not under permanent surveillance?'

'I am certain he is not.'

'There is no policeman that is attached to him?'

'There are none.'

'We are now into the age of the tactical nuclear concept and that means the end for fixed defensive positions. With tactical nuclear armouries the Maginot thinking is gone for ever. But you can only justify nuclear reaction to conventional attack if you have lost great tracts of land and territory, and if you have major hostile concentrations to aim the missiles at. The decision to go nuclear will not be made by a field commander, not by a man in denims with four stars on his cap, it will be made by a politician with political considerations uppermost and the risk of setting off a domino run of nuclear escalation giving him nightmares. So the military men on our side have to think in terms of meeting a conventional attack with conventional defence. The order of the day will be small, highly mobile units, low density and self-contained. Our tanks would be operating in platoon formation, four or five together and they will be met by Soviet mechanised infantry with manual controlled missiles. The infantry will have all the cover they want, wrecked villages, forestry, good and hilly terrain. The missile men can have a field day, and their equipment's off the Padolsk design board. You're with me, Johnny?'

The village was tucked within the twin walls of the valley. The church and main street low in the bed beside a stream

84

and the houses scattered indiscriminately above. The leaves were coming to the trees, the grass on the small lawns sprouted, the first flowers were opening. A quiet, private place.

Percy drove up a winding track. He scanned the gateposts of the houses for the number that he wanted. It was a split-level home, modern and freshly-painted and large. As the car drew up, there was a trembling in Mawby's legs, irritating and uncontrolled. They were a far cry from clubland, from the Service, from his home ground. He would rather have been anywhere, anywhere other than climbing from a car, stepping onto a track on the outskirts of a village south of Bonn, anywhere other than walking in this foreign place with morose Adam Percy for company. It was the expectable butterflies, first time at the sharp end for a year or so.

They went up the short driveway.

'No names, eh?'

'He won't want them,' Percy said.

Up to the front door, polished and heavy. Mawby looked behind him over his shoulder, nothing moved, nobody to observe the men in dark suits in the village setting. Percy pressed the bell button.

He was a big man who greeted them, a man of gross power and physique. A short neck, ears hugging his shoulders. A bullet head crowned with a shaven stubble of white hair. Heavy, muscled arms that stretched tight his high folded shirt sleeves. He loomed over them.

Best foot forward, Charles Augustus. Career men don't retreat, career men push ahead. Couldn't have delegated this one, could he? Couldn't have parcelled it off on Carter. This one was for Mawby. And he must not stare at the scar where a revolver bullet probably had nicked the skin high across the right cheek bone, and he must not curl his lip at the waft of cologne. You need him, Charles Augustus. More than he needs you, you need him. Just as you need Johnny Donoghue who killed a girl and never uttered a syllable of remorse. Just as you need the snivelling Guttmann. Just as you need Carter and the prig Pierce, and Smithson. All of them needed by Charles Augustus Mawby . . . God Almighty, what furniture. They followed the man into a room dominated by a single picture, a massive canvas of the reclining nude, white skin, angular limbs, a bush of hair, a summit of breasts. Mawby looked away, pained. What you'd expect of the man from what Percy had told him. But he had come to do business and so he sat in a mauve and green chair and smiled with all the warmth that he could muster.

There was the offer of a drink that Mawby declined; there was the brisk establishment of Christian names. The man called himself Hermann. He would ask questions to ascertain the nature of the assignment, then they would discuss practicabilities, then they would talk of the price to be paid.

'Is there a date involved, Charles?'

Mawby flinched from the familiarity. 'The thirteenth or fourteenth of June.'

'How many are there to be transported?'

'One elderly man and his adult daughter.'

'Where in the DDR are they living?'

'They will be staying in Magdeburg. On the fifteenth they return to Moscow.'

'They are Russian then?'

'They are German.'

'Who will make contact with them for the arrangements?'

'That will be our responsibility.'

'They could be brought to a point where a car could meet them?'

'We would bring them to that point, yes.'

'For two persons it is difficult to conceal them in a car, they would require documentation. Who would provide the papers?'

'We would provide them with West German passports and general cover material.'

'Is the face of this man known to the DDR authorities, would his picture have been in the newspapers?'

'Never.'

86

'You are anxious to make it so simple, Charles, but I tell you that it is not easy.' Hermann wheezed with theatrical effect, rolling his eyes to the ceiling.

'To me it is very simple,' Mawby clipped in response.

'Not so. If it were easy then you would manage your own affairs. And you give little time for the arrangements. You have not thought of the linking of the vehicle papers with the documentation of the driver, his assistant and the passengers. Those are two reasons why it is not easy. Thirdly . . .'

'Why is there the need of a second man in the car?'

'You know little of the documentation required for this journey, Charles. Any West German who makes use of the Berlin to Helmstedt autobahn is considered as a transit passenger through the DDR territory. His passport is stamped on entry and exit. So the driver will have his passport stamped when he leaves West Berlin. At a suitable moment in the journey he will collect two passengers, but they do not have the stamp and that must be attached while the car is moving towards the DDR checkpoint at Marienborn. The driver cannot do that, he is at the wheel, another must be there to do it. Understand me, Charles, it is not the stamp that is the difficulty, it is the signature that goes with the stamp. The signature for the passengers who are picked up must match with that on the papers of the driver. So the driver must have an assistant and he is the man who will attach the signature, and he must work in the moving car between Berlin and Marienborn, that is their check point opposite Helmstedt. You follow me, Charles?'

'I quite understand . . .' Mawby doing his best to take the lecture in his stride, as no more than his due.

'Thirdly, the people that you want taken from the DDR will have an importance, or you as foreigners would not be interested by them. You are not involved with bringing to freedom your friend or your relation, you are bringing someone who is of political use to you. If the pigs there catch a driver then he will stay eight or ten years in the gaol, not happy years. But if there is the smell of political action, if he is working for a foreign power then they will make more of it, perhaps fifteen years. It is not a safe business, you know that, Charles?'

'I'm perfectly aware of that.' Mawby trying not to catch the eye of the nude.

'The price would be 25 thousand marks. Twenty-five thousand marks for each passenger that we bring through.'

Mawby stiffened, felt a sweat bead spring at his hairline. The calculations swarmed over him. Three marks eighty to the pound. Thirteen thousand, one hundred and fifty sterling. 'That's bloody steep, Hermann, for a drive down the autobahn . . .'

The man was hunched in his chair, peering in surprise at Mawby. Adam Percy kept aloof.

'I did not suppose that this money would come from your own pocket, Charles.'

Mawby pulled for his rank. 'We have a certain influence in this country.'

Hermann laughed. A light, fine cackle. A small and diminutive noise from such a carcase of a man. 'Don't play with me, Charles. You have told me that an East German who is resident in Moscow will be in Magdeburg till the 15th of June, a man who interests a foreign agency. How long would it take the Volkspolizei to identify the man you want carried? I think a few hours only. Don't make threats to me, Charles.'

Mawby rose from his chair. 'I'll have to refer the matter back.'

'But don't sit on it. And remember that it is not your money.'

'I will ring you in the evening with the answer.'

'If you accept then we should meet again tomorrow.' Hermann grinned, climbed from his chair and advanced on Mawby with a hand outstretched.

The farewells were brief. Mawby and Percy walked briskly out into the late afternoon air, the nude at Mawby's heel.

Smithson sat in his armchair with the street map on his

knees, Johnny opposite him, after dinner coffee in his hands.

'Magdeburg had come through the war pretty well till January 16th in 1945, when the American air force came on the scene. Sixteen thousand people died that day and the inner city was obliterated, and I mean that. They started again with a heap of rubble and ended up with rows of flats, functional little homes for the workers. There was pre-war industry there and that's been expanded, mostly engineering. It's a major rail centre for the south-west of the DDR. the honeypot that originally attracted the bombs. Now it's a provincial capital with all the trappings, big parks, a crop of theatres and concert halls along with new developments towards the north, Neue Neustadt, Nordwest and Olvenstedt. There's only one hotel that's offering rooms to foreigners, the International, where you'll be, which is highly convenient to us, the cat will be right on top of the mouse . . . Now we'll turn to the policing of the city. There will be a unit of SSD there. There is a headquarters of the Volkspolizei Bizirksbehorde, operating out of Halberstadter Strasse 2, they're the provincial police. The town police, Volkspolizei Kreisamt, are little more than souped-up traffic men. Because of the proximity of the border there's a strong detachment of Schutzpolizei, they're security police and slightly down the ladder from SSD, also at Halberstadter Strasse. They keep their eyes open, their ears open. They look hard and they listen hard.'

The Deputy-Under-Secretary had a suite of offices at Century House. An outer room for meetings. A smaller room for his desk and easy chair. An annexe where he had the use of a single bed if he had no wish to return to his Hampshire home or to spend the night at his club. They were light and comfortable quarters, but too recent for his taste and like many of his senior colleagues he still hankered for the old days of the Queen Anne's Gate building and its peeling glories. The evening had blanketed the London skyline below his windows, the lights eddied on the

Thames beneath. The House of Commons steeples and clock-face swam in their floodlighting. Columns of cars nudged forward on the miniaturised Embankment beneath him.

Mawby's telex still lay on the desk of his private office. A good man, Mawby, a tried and trusted man, a man with a future, who might one day inherit this upper office. The telex from Mawby requesting authorisation for the payment of 13,150 pounds sterling to a German national for the lift down the autobahn to Helmstedt. Eight months of the Deputy-Under-Secretary's salary, quite a handful for the wide embrace of 'miscellaneous'. But he had authorised it without question. If it was good enough for Mawby, it was . . .

The telephone warbled.

The green receiver with the scrambler distortion devices.

'Yes.'

'Fenton here.' Peter Fenton, Director of the Security Service. Rather a tiresome voice.

'What can I do for you, Peter?' The Deputy-Under-Secretary was guarded when in contact with his opposite number from Security. Different men, different standards.

'Nothing that's very important . . . I just wondered if you felt the change of dates put out by FCO this afternoon for the DDR trade visit affected the business you were putting together.'

'You're ahead of me, Peter. I've been in one meeting after another, I haven't managed to get at my tray.'

'The visit of Oskar Frommholtz, FCO informed us because we have an escort commitment. It seems Comrade Frommholtz has asked for a change of dates. He was due here for the last week in June, that's been brought forward because he's a COMECON commitment on the original date.'

The Deputy-Under-Secretary fished in his memory. 'We trying to turn the trade imbalance, they looking for a foreign protocol . . . Why should it affect anything we're doing?'

'The visit will coincide with the Guttmann dates. Frommholtz will be being wined and dined on Whitehall when the good scientist is nippin over the border.'

'It's a covert operation, nothing to link it with us.'

'Quite right . . . if it works, but it would be a pretty mess if your nursemaid were picked up . . . Are you still there?'

'Yes, Peter.'

'I think the PM should know. I think the PM should sanction it. That's my advice anyway . . .'

'I'll not give it up.'

'Nothing went into the minutes of JIC. If he's not told, and if the thing trips, they'd have our skins.'

'I'll not lose this to a politician with a weak stomach and a short future.'

'That's your decision then . . .'

'Thank you for calling,' the Deputy-Under-Secretary said. 'Good night, Peter.'

He replaced the receiver. Perhaps he would say something to Downing Street. Not at this time, but later, something that would not arouse curiosity. Of course there was risk, but without risk the Service died, dried on the branch. And when he produced Otto Guttmann that would rank as a rare moment of success. A success that he would not tolerate the faint-hearted to deny him. And Fenton had no right to talk of failure, damned old woman wringing his hands. The Deputy-Under-Secretary sat at his desk and read again the message from Mawby. He had authorised the payment, he had stood by his Assistant Secretary. Mawby was a good man, young and a little green, but sound for all that. Mawby believed in the plan, that should be enough for him, shouldn't it? Security was always parsimonious in initiative, that was the difference between them and the Service. Mean, weren't they, when a bit of dash was required? The Deputy-Under-Secretary smiled. It was going to be a damned good show. He would not be balked.

With the curtains across the French windows not drawn, the lights of the sitting room lit the outside patio. From his chair Carter watched Johnny in the towelling top they had found for him and the loose trousers, listened to the thudding beat of his boots. There was an old oak garden chair on the patio. Right foot onto the chair, left foot following. Right foot onto the concrete flags, left foot following. The steady rhythm of the boots. The pumping of Johnny's breath. The press-ups. The jogging on the lawn. Only when it was quite dark, when the night had closed on the house would Johnny come back inside, and there would be a towel round his neck, and he would tramp towards the kitchen for a pot of tea.

Awesome to Carter because he was a desk man, who had not in recent years called upon the strength in his legs, the wind in his lungs. The division between them. Carter would be at the Departures desk in the airport concourse, or on the railway platform. Johnny would be flying on, Johnny would be travelling. That was the division, and Carter could not read his book as the boots pounded from the patio to the garden chair.

No movement since the patrol jeep had passed. Nothing stirred. And the ink darkness was cut savagely by the lights that fell on the fence, clasped it in false daylight, played on the sharp mesh and the attached guns.

Relief at four. Two more boys to climb the metal rungs on the inside of the tower and come to the closed platform 40 feet above the fields. Two more boys to take the places of Ulf Becker and Heini Schalke.

Open ground in front, 300 metres of grass, scythed twice a summer by workmen who were brought close to the wire and covered by the guns of the Border Guard. Open ground all the way from the electrified fence and the trip wires on the embankment of the railway line that had once served the brick works of Weferlingen, all the way to the vehicle patrol strip and the ditch and the fence with the automatic guns. Open ground.

Ulf Becker would never run on that open ground, not with Heini Schalke high and unimpeded above him in the tower. Not with Heini Schalke pulling the hard stock of the MPiKM against his shoulder and squinting with his pig eyes down the foresight. Not here . . . an impossibility here.

Cold in the shadow of the tower. Cold in the night air. Gone was the heat and the touch of Jutte. Find me that place, she had said. Find me that place, she had shouted from the platform at Schöneweide. But there was no place on the ground west of Weferlingen. If he were to come on foot to the south of the village, use the Siedlung Hagholz woods for concealment and cross the road that leads to the lime works, and stay beyond the old brick buildings of the railway yards . . . Then there was the tower and the night-sight binoculars, then there were the lights, then there were the fences, then there were the spring guns, and still there was Heini Schalke and a hundred more in the company.

A chill eddied in the tower, carried on the wind, bitter and penetrating because the windows must be open so as not to delay them if they must shoot and because the binoculars were less effective through glass.

Jutte, it is not possible here.

Find me that place.

Away to his left he saw the lights of the approaching jeep. The border, lethal to those who intruded on its ground, was alive only with armed and watchful men.

There was a pleasing peace in the house. Close to mid-night. Smithson and Pierce away to their beds. Carter back into his book. The slow hours of the late evening. The best time of the day for Johnny, when the quiet took command.

'You know, Johnny, we haven't a name for this caper, and we're under a month.' Carter looked up. 'We have to have a name for you.'

'Not a bloody Greek god, don't give me one of them.'

'Of course, lad. I've found it here, just the number.'

Johnny was amused. Johnny wondered whether Carter's hands ever sweated, whether he shouted at his wife, threw his temper at his children, whether he panicked, whether he screamed. He had seen a rough side with the boy, but that was tactical, that showed neither strength nor weakness. Carter would be escorting Johnny to Hannover, working on the fine detail of the pick-up. He'd want to have faith in this man, Johnny would want to trust him, to the full. The one who ironed the creased details of organisation . . . and who was filching ideas from a guide to European birds.

'What are you going to call me?'

Carter looked over the top of his reading spectacles. 'The Latin is *cinclus cinclus*. There are many names, different in parts of the country – water blackbird, water crow, water pyet. These are the characteristics . . . "straight, fast flight. Can swim both on the surface and under water, enters water by either wading in or diving, habitually walks submerged on the stream bed." That's what we want of our lad, creeping along the floor of the river while the Volkspolizei sit on the banks in blissful ignorance. I reckon that's rather apt. They call it most often the Dipper. I'm going to put it to Mawby. You'll be the Dipper man, Johnny. I think it's rather good . . .'

Johnny had not replied. There were feet drumming down the staircase. The crash of doors being wrenched open. George's voice angry and raised and cursing.

Carter snapped his book shut, drove his glasses into his breast pocket, started up from his chair.

The door of the living room arched towards them. George was in silhouette, the hall lights blazing behind him. Half dressed, hair dishevelled, eyes wide with anger.

'He's gone . . . Guttmann. I can't find the bugger anywhere.'

It was Johnny who discovered the imprint of shoes in the soft earth of the flower bed beside the rainwater pipe beneath the boy's window.

Chapter Eight

=

A slow May dawn, arriving at its own deliberate pace, maddening for the men at the house. They had searched the grounds as best they could with torches, had stumbled over the flower beds and through the rhododendron bushes and between the trees. They had arced their lights in the outbuildings, seeking the cover that a fugitive might use. They had seen nothing, they had heard nothing. Smithson and Pierce in separate cars had gone to drive through the lanes that skirted Holmbury Hill and its woods, roaring away down the drive in the early hours, and neither back yet. George, distraught and malevolent, still paced the grounds of the house as if believing that with the daylight a great truth might yet be found inside the perimeter fence. The nestling had taken to its wings, and George who had been given responsibility for the close supervision of Willi Guttmann had been found wanting. Perhaps that was why he lingered outside, avoiding the reproach of those who waited inside. Later he would find the boy's route over the wire, but it would be of token importance.

Johnny and Carter stayed in the living room, alternately brooding in silence and then conjuring fresh obscenities for respite. The fire had slipped to dull embers, the coffee that Mrs Ferguson had brought them was ignored.

'He's no money, the little bastard.'

'So George says.'

'He's no papers, no passport.'

'That's certain.'

'Where'll he go, Johnny?'

'He won't have thought of that. Just getting into the distance game, getting shot of us, that's all he'll be wanting.'

'He won't find any transport round here . . . there's precious few buses in day time, none at night.'

'He can take a car . . .'

Carter broke his pacing, swung round on Johnny. 'Don't pile it, lad.'

'It's a fact,' Johnny said quietly. 'He's five hours' start on you.'

'After what we've done for him.' The pacing resumed. 'Bloody well nursemaided the creep.'

'We've done nothing for him,' Johnny spoke to himself, as if alone.

'We brought him over here, offered him a new life . . .'

'We've done nothing for him. We've crippled him, chopped his foot off at the ankle . . . he won't be thinking well . . . at best he's an outcast for the rest of his natural, at worst he's a traitor.'

'We owed him nothing.'

'There's no basis for his loyalty . . . but he won't have a car.'

'I'll hang him by his bloody thumbs when I get him back.' Carter spat his anger across the room.

'You need manpower out there.'

'There'll be bloody hell to pay.'

'You have to call for help,' said Johnny. 'Anyone who can get your feet on the ground, and soon.'

'Rather it was any other bugger than me . . .' Carter walked without enthusiasm towards the mahogany desk on which the telephone rested. 'Johnny, it's not my field, tell me, where's he going to be?'

'Out there.' Johnny waved towards the hazed distance beyond the window glass. 'Not far and scared half to death, blundering off the trees. He'll be in the woods crying his bloody heart out. He won't be calm and he won't be rational. He won't have an idea of what he should be doing, where he should be going. He's not that sort of kid.'

'Hope to God that you're right.' Carter began to dial. 'I can just see Mawby's bloody face . . .'

*

96

The Night Duty desk at Leconfield House in London's West End, home of the Security Service, received and duly logged the telephoned advice from Henry Carter.

The clerk called the home of the Director. There had been a lengthy pause on the line and then a rattle of instructions, as if Security as well was involved in SIS's loss of their precious property.

Scotland Yard's Special Branch police were alerted, the description of Willi Guttmann telexed to their night operations room, the request was made for intensive surveillance of airports and harbours. A team of detectives would be hustled together and sent to Holmbury. Special Branch would undertake liaison with Surrey Constabulary and their headquarters on the hill above Guildford, ten miles from the scene of the disappearance of the boy. Surrey Constabulary would inform their outlying stations of a Missing Persons call and would add the rider that the matter was covered by Official Secrets.

More calls for the clerk.

The naval officer who had retired from the service with the rank of Vice-Admiral and who had been given the job of directing the country's D notice procedures was next on the list. The clerk explained word by word what he had been told to communicate by his Director. It was requested that advice of a D notice be served on all newspapers and broadcasting outlets urging them neither to publish nor communicate any material relating to the defection, arrival in Britain, and subsequent flight of Willi Guttmann. The clerk knew the wording well – Paragraph 4 Section a, 'You are requested to publish nothing about . . . the secret activities of the British Intelligence, or Counter Intelligence Services, undertaken inside or outside the United Kingdom for the purpose of national security.'

That was the necessary precaution. Once the civilian police were brought in the matter would be leaky as a sieve. Chatter among the wives, chatter in the saloon bar with most favoured journalists. Bring the civilian police onto the scene and security was at terminal risk.

The clerk's work done his imagination could wander and he sensed as a sharp smell the atmosphere on Night Desk at Century House across the city. For a long time the grin remained on his face.

The submission of his catastrophe to the Security Service had provided Carter with the required adrenalin to wake the Deputy-Under-Secretary. Should have done it hours before, shouldn't he? Should have done it when the men were still out hunting through the grounds. Should have, but he hadn't. Carter hadn't spoken to the Deputy-Under-Secretary for three years, could be more. Johnny watching, silent and sympathising.

Mrs Ferguson slipped into the room. Still in her dressing gown, still in her slippers, still with the pink curlers embedded in her hair. More coffee, steaming and augmented with a plate of biscuits. Both men might have kissed her.

When she was gone Johnny poured.

'I'm grateful for your help, Peter.'

The Deputy-Under-Secretary sat on the side of the bed in his usual room at the Travellers' Club. There was the faint drone of a vacuum cleaner on a faraway landing, the clink in the corridor of the tea cups and saucers being brought to the early risers. The garish ceiling bulb hovered over his head, accentuating the pits of his eyes, the concave bowls of his cheeks. The telephone rested on the sheets beside him.

'Don't think about it, it's nothing. If we can't help each other what can we do?'

It was a sharp barb. Fenton had long been the advocate of inter-departmental liaison, was a founder member of the 'bigger is best' brigade, had written a paper two years back on the desirability of merging Intelligence and Security, and had faced for his pains waspish opposition from SIS and its parent Foreign and Commonwealth Office. He was wide awake, in control and confident, but then Security never enjoyed the dinner round that was the privilege of the

Service. Peter Fenton would warrant a fraction of the hospitality that was available to the Deputy-Under-Secretary.

'I'm advised that this matter cannot be mounted unless Guttmann is co-operative.'

'More to the point, if a breath of this drops out of the bucket then there'll be half a dozen heavies from GRU or KGB on father Guttmann's shoulder crowding his vacation, yes? That is in the unlikely event they let him travel to Magdeburg.'

'There was no option, I suppose, but to bring in the police?'

'Had to be done. You want the boy and you want him fast. For that you need a manhunt. We don't have the necessary numbers and neither do you.'

'I hate to say it about ourselves, but it has been a pretty poor effort by our people down there . . .'

The rare candour cut at the toughness of the Director. 'Take my advice, leave the inquests till we have the boy back. Keep the court martial till we know the scope of the damage . . .'

'There'll be damage, but it's good advice.' There was the whiff of desperation. 'I'm not going to lose this thing, Peter.'

'We'll keep in touch through the morning.'

The Deputy-Under-Secretary began to dress, and he rang for the porter and asked if a cup of tea could be brought to him.

At first he had run hard.

Panting for air. Crashing through the undergrowth. Cannoning from the trees that loomed around him in the darkness. Sprinting where there were no paths. Around him were only the devastating sounds of his own movements and the thunder in the high leaves of disturbed pigeons. Running, crashing, panting, sprinting. But the boy's shoulder hurt him now, hurt far down in the muscles and wounded him in the hidden nerves by his collar bone and rib cage. The shoulder that had cracked into the low stone wall as he had pitched forward in the shallow, camouflaged ditch. The pain came often, surged and subsided. The intensity billowed with the exhaustion in his legs and the ache in his chest as he gulped for breath. He had no map, had followed no plan. He could only run. He ran with the darkness of the woods and trees closing on his flight as he passed, cloaking his trail. He knew that sometimes he had turned back on his path, that often he had sacrificed distance for the needs of concealment and so as to skirt the scattered homes beyond the trees. He could not calculate how far he had gone in the hours since he had climbed onto the rusted, rainwater pipe. Many hours, enough to waste his strength and exacerbate the throb in his forehead.

The wetness of the morning's dew gathered at his shoes and at the ankles of his socks. Water flaked to his arms and legs from the previous evening's rain on the leaves.

So where was Willi Guttmann running? What was his goal? Only a vision for company. Willi running to his Lizzie. The pigs had lied to him, the pigs had told untruths, had separated him from his Lizzie. Going to Lizzie.

In his tiredness he did not think of aeroplanes and travel documents and money and fresh clothes. Lizzie was outside the house, Lizzie was across the fence. Lizzie was out there, out beyond the darkness, and he was no longer in their cage. He had achieved a kind of freedom.

And they were going to kill his father. That was as clear as the lies they had told about Lizzie. They were going to kill him in Magdeburg – from a car – with a silenced pistol, by a knife thrust. Why else did they ask where his father would go in Magdeburg, who he would meet, whether he would be guarded? They had taken him from Lizzie, now they sought to take the life of an old man.

The day came with a hint of rain and the taste of the low, hill-hugging clouds. There was a wind, too, that caught the moisture on his clothes, tugged at them. The stamina for running had deserted the boy. The strength remained only to walk, to plod forward. There was nothing in his room that he could have taken that would have helped him. The bastards had left him nothing. Not even a bar of chocolate, not even a packet of sweet biscuits. Bastards, and he spat the phlegm from the dried soreness of his throat. He was walking and the trees now were sharp to his eyes, and the hedges clear and the pain of his shoulder concentrated his mind.

Time for the boy to think, and with the thoughts that came to his tired mind there welled a horrible loneliness, a hopelessness that was the friend of desperation ... He should break from the thinking, because thinking would hurt, would always bring to mind Lizzie and his father. And thinking would also be of George and his quiet shoes, and Mr Carter and his smile and the questions, and the one called Johnny who sat and listened and said nothing and who would be the man that killed his father. He had the eyes of a man who could kill, the one called Johnny, eyes that were never still ... Against a thorn hedge the boy flopped down. The brush of the wind could not reach him. He sprawled on his side and closed his eyes. So tired. Legs and arms draped haphazard on the soft grass. He must find someone to tell of the danger to his father. He must find someone to speak with of Lizzie and of the lies that had been told him. He would find someone ... He pushed himself up, tried to rise from the ground, but his energy was sapped, his will weakened.

He would find someone, but later.

From the towns of Guildford and Dorking and Horsham police units were moved into the area of the hills around Holmbury.

A photograph had been issued, plus height and weight, and a note of the clothes that the boy was believed to be wearing. There had been more than a buzz of interest at the police station briefings as the Superintendents had rolled their eyes and given the half wink and let it be known that this was a matter falling into the realm of national security.

Two car loads of Special Branch had travelled from London with the paraphernalia of fingerprint and

101

photographic equipment believing they were visiting a scene of crime, and the argument had been loud and vicious when George, heavy in aggression, had refused them permission to enter the grounds of the house without the prior authorisation of Henry Carter.

A party had come from Leconfield House, stern-faced, brush-moustached, unmistakably military men in civilian order.

They had gone with Carter to the sitting room and talked for more than an hour in an attempt to explore the mind of Willi Guttmann and gauge his intentions.

Johnny went to bed. Not his problem, not for him to hold Henry Carter's hand.

When the bank close to the Music Academy on Koblenzerstrasse opened, Charles Mawby and Adam Percy were there and waiting by the front door. This was where the SIS 'out station' in Bonn kept their funds for operational use. Percy wrote a cheque for 25,000 marks, Mawby scribbled the receipt that would go through Percy's paperwork. They were the first to be served, receiving a stack of 100 mark notes. Mawby counted them, Percy slid the money into a plain buff envelope, and then they were out onto the street and striding to the car.

The advance payment would be made, and the morning would be spent in the discussion of detail, the establishment of a liaison link, the understanding of the plan. With luck Mawby would be on the late afternoon flight to Heathrow. Percy had picked him up early from the Steigenberger Hotel, had not called at his office on the way and so the coded telex from Century House addressed to Charles Mawby lay unread.

They drove in heavy traffic out onto the Bad Gotesburg road. The money burned in Mawby's inside pocket.

'It's not the way I'd have wanted it, Adam. I'd have preferred our own people doing the driving. We can't contemplate it.'

'You have to allow for failure, and if the worst comes to

the worst then you absolutely cannot afford any connection.'

'It's the reliability of this man . . .'

'We can guarantee nothing. But he's as good as you'll
find, that's what I'm told.'

'They wouldn't play with us?'

'BND? The masters would, but not the man I talk to.'

It was a hell of a way to work, reflected Mawby. To take a
matter so delicate and rich and pass it to this thick-fisted pig
for delivery. But those were the rules.

'I don't know how you stick it here, Adam.'

Adam Percy looked with a trace of surprise at his
passenger. 'I don't fret much, Mr Mawby. That way it's just
about tolerable.'

The woman normally took her dog for a walk in mid-
morning if it were not raining. Not far, not more than a mile
from the farm gateway in which she could park her car.
Enough to let the labrador run and stretch in the fields and
sniff around and cock his leg. There were no sheep here off
the Ewhurst to Forest Green road, only cattle and the dog
would not disturb them and could be allowed to run and
ferret for himself far ahead of his mistress. She had thought
twice about going out that morning, but eventually had
risked it, armed with raincoat and head scarf. She stayed at
the edge of the field and looked up at the tree line and
beyond it to the squashed-down peaks of Pitch Hill and
Holmbury Hill and Leith Hill. Even on a threatening day,
with the mist low and muzzling the beauty of the trees, it was
an exhilarating outing. She was well bedded in her thoughts
when the barking of the dog alerted her. Hackles up,
shoulders flexed, back legs tensed and ready to spring,
furious at a centre of attention that was hidden from her
view by the hedge. He wasn't going to set up a fox . . .

'Rufus, Rufus, heel . . .' She ran forward.

He never came back to the call if it were a fox.

The boy lay on the ground. His knees were drawn up to
cover his stomach, his hands across his face for protection.

She stared down at him, then reached for the dog's collar and heaved the animal back and hooked the leash in the collar ring and took the strain as it rose on its back legs and pawed at the air.

The boy was soaked, his clothes drenched through, his hair streaked and tangled. Face white, eyes cowering. She would have run for her car if the dog had not been with her, but the animal gave her courage.

'What are you doing here?' Her voice shrill.

The boy did not reply, did not look at her, and his eyes were held by the slobbering, teeth-filled mouth of the dog.

'Don't you know you're trespassing? This is Mr Daniel's land . . .'

Now the boy gazed up at her. In her life she had never seen such terror. There was not the look of a gypsy, an itinerant, about him. Too well dressed for that, and by his face he was not someone used to sleeping in the rough.

'This is private property. You have to have permission . . .'

'Will you help me? Please help me, please.'

She recoiled, and the croak of the voice renewed the demand of the dog to be at the boy, and he wormed away.

'You'll try no tricks . . . or the dog will have you.'

'Please help me, madam. You have to help me.'

'Stand up, and don't you dare to try anything.'

A silly thing to say and she saw her idiocy from the moment that the boy, stiffly, awkwardly, began to rise to his feet. A helpless creature. His eyes pleaded, his shoulders hung limp. He stood in front of her.

'I was running from them,' he said.

'From whom?'

'They are going to kill my father. When he takes his holiday they are going to murder him . . . Please, help me.'

'I'm sure they're not.' Her reserve was tumbling, her curiosity winning.

'I have been a prisoner for two weeks now . . . they are going to murder him.'

The dog's barking had subsided and he sat now at his mistress's feet and his tongue lolled at his mouth.

'Where have you been a prisoner?'

The boy waved towards the dark mass of the woods, gestured behind him. 'There is a house there . . .'

The woman and the boy and the dog alone in the field, rain spitting on their faces.

'The one with the high fence round it – at the end of Maltby Lane?' She knew the place. Everybody in the villages close to Holmbury St Mary knew of the house. A fence of that height could not be erected around 6 acres of grounds without talk, talk that multiplied when it became known that 'government' was paying. She had seen the closed gates, and in winter had noticed the far flicker of brickwork between the bared trees. 'You'd better come home and have something warm and then I'll ring Mr Potterton, and he'll help you.'

She turned on her heel and started to walk back towards the farm gate. Her boots squelched on the grass and mud. The dog was close to her, and a couple of paces behind Willi Guttmann followed.

Carter slammed down the telephone and took the stairs three at a time. He ran down the corridor to Johnny's room.

Thank God. Thanks be to anyone who's listening. Down on his knees he'd be that evening at the old bedside, grovelling his gratitude. A sharp knock at Johnny's door and Carter's fist was on the handle and turning it.

'Come on, Johnny boy. Time to go and fetch the truant back.'

Johnny was thrusting the bedclothes away, swinging from the bed, groping for his trousers.

'You've got him?'

'Right first time.'

'Christmas and birthday rolled into one for George?' Socks on, shirt over his head, shoes at his feet.

'George looks tolerably pleased at the prospect of renewing his friendship with young Willi.'

Johnny was hurrying after Carter towards the door. 'He won't have had time to do any damage, will he?'

They went down the stairs in a scamper and clatter of feet. 'I haven't heard much,' Carter said. 'The little that did come through seemed to say that he'd been in the woods all night.'

'Then we're still on course.'

Carter sensed the satisfaction blooming from Johnny. Never panicked, had he? This was a cool one, steady and rational as he'd been every day since he'd come to Holmbury. This was the man for Magdeburg.

George was already in the driving seat, the engine ticking gently.

The directions they followed were not complete, but they had no difficulty in finding their destination. A slim country lane, with the high banks broken by the drives to the homes of those who could afford to live in the country, four bed-rooms and half an acre, and to commute daily to London. There were three police cars in the road, blue roof lights rotating, and a milling mass of activity that blocked the entrance.

George braked, cut off the engine, snapped open his door and was first out. 'Switch those bloody lights out, it's not a frigging circus.'

Two men from Security stood beside a uniformed Inspector. 'I've the place surrounded,' the Inspector said evenly, turning the cheek. 'Your boy is in there with the lady who found him and the local constable, chap called Potterton.'

'No photographs ... keep your eyes off his bloody face when we bring him out, and no talking to him.' George marched towards the closed gates.

'We'll hang around just to see you don't lose him again.' There was a smile at the mouth of one of the Security men. He spoke in a firm whisper and his words carried and he weathered the furious glare as George passed him.

George led to the front door, Carter and Johnny close with him. The doorbell chimed in a brief treacle melody. There were the sounds of a key being turned, a bolt with-drawn. The door opened. George surged forward to find his way barred by a uniformed policeman.

'Yes?'

'We've come for the boy,' snapped George.

'Everything's all right, officer,' Carter chivvied from the porch. 'We've come to take the lad back. We're most grateful for your help.'

'You should know, sir, that Mr Guttmann has made some serious allegations against . . .'

The droning country accent of the constable was sliced to silence by George. 'Forget them . . . where is he now?'

'Allegations which I shall have to report to my superior.' The constable would not be bulldozed, held his ground.

'Put that report in and you'll be digging potatoes for the rest of your natural. I'll make bloody certain of that.' George's voice was ice quiet.

'Don't do anything till you've heard from your senior officer, that would be the right course of action, I think.' Carter peered over George's shoulder, deftly poured his oil, and the constable stood aside.

Through an open doorway off the hall they saw Willi Guttmann, bare legs and naked chest under a loosely wrapped dressing gown, shrunk in a high-backed chair, gripping a mug of tea between his two hands. George was away, the hound after the stag. Into the neat and freshly papered and gloss-painted living room, muddied feet trailing on the fitted carpet. Johnny saw a woman sitting on a sofa close to the boy. Trim hair, tweed skirt, blouse and cardigan. Good imitation pearls at her neck, a dog that growled without menace at her feet. Her eyes shone in helpless, proud annoyance at the ravishing of her home and hospitality.

'Come on, Willi, get yourself dressed and we'll be on our way. I'm sure we've caused this lady enough trouble,' George said.

Willi stood up, put the mug carefully down on the chair arm.

'I've only just put his clothes in the washing machine,' the woman bridled.

'Then get them out, madam, if you would be so kind.'

She looked once at George, then at the impassive faces of Carter and Johnny, her nerve failed and she scurried for her kitchen.

Eyeball to eyeball, George and the boy. All the threat, all the intimidation absorbed in the devastated, pallid features of Willi Guttmann. George slipped off his raincoat and handed it without comment to the boy who undraped the dressing gown, stood for a moment in his underpants, and then drew the coat, many sizes too large, around him.

'Stay by my side, lad. All the way, and don't you bloody leave it.'

They walked from the room, Carter with them. Johnny heard their shoes grinding the gravel of the driveway.

The woman came back from the kitchen and handed to Johnny a supermarket shopping bag that contained the sodden bundle of Willi's clothes.

'What's this all about?' Chin out, aggressive now that the minder had gone.

Johnny grinned. 'It's called "national security", with all that that involves, all the rigmarole.'

'He said you were trying to kill someone.'

'If I were you I'd dig a hole and drop everything the kid said into it, and then fill the hole in and stamp the earth down. That's my advice.'

'You people, your sort, you make me sick.'

'That's your privilege.'

Johnny headed for the door, closed it gently behind him, and walked to the car.

Chapter Nine

=

As a couple that sits at breakfast the morning after an evening of vicious argument and tries to build bridges, so the community of the house at Holmbury led themselves back to the path of the social decencies. The talk was a little more strident, the laughter a little more frequent, the cheerfulness more overt. The flight of Willi must be erased. And Mawby was back again to inject discipline into the team, to stamp out recrimination, to lift and to encourage. Mawby understood leadership because that was his training from the time that he could stagger beyond the range of his nanny's arms. Mawby could take responsibility and carry the group towards efficiency and effectiveness.

But it was pretence and all in the house knew it.

Johnny recognised the fraud, and saw also the worry lines that settled on Mawby's face in the evenings, the glow of growing anxiety that was the bedfellow of the ticking off of the days on the calendar in the interrogation room. Sharp pen strokes towards the change of the month and the coming of June and the highlighted, bracketed dates.

Carter recognised it. He felt a keenness in his questions to the boy as if time was suddenly slipping. All the questions must count, all the answers must be clear and candid. They would not be repeated.

Smithson and Pierce recognised it. Johnny, the pupil, more attentive and straining to accept what they told him, and their own minds turned to the issue of how great an encyclopaedia they could cement into their man's memory in the intervening days.

Willi recognised it. The sessions in the morning were longer, sometimes spilling into the afternoons, and nobody shouted, nobody swore at him. This was the source of their information and at last he was treated with a grudging deference. Perhaps he had won a trifle of respect from these men. Perhaps their attention was closer to what he said. There were many things that Willi saw . . . The glimmer light that burned all night in his bedroom. The chrome bar, screwed into the woodwork, that sealed his bedroom window.. The camp bed in the corridor outside his door where George now slept, or lay on his back most likely, with his eyes opened and watchful.

A new and different mood for each participant at the house. And overriding and dominating was the calendar and the fugitive days of May.

Spring drifting to summer.

Squirrels on the lawn, leaping and chasing and thrusting out their brush tails. Rabbits coming with a boldness to the lawns from the shrubs. The small birds of the woods searching in the soft flower beds for grubs. And all unseen by the men in the house.

Meals in the dining room, briefings in the sitting room, questions in the interrogation room. Earlier in the morning, later in the evening. Longer days, more crowded hours.

Willi no longer in the centre and under the wide spotlight. Johnny there, Johnny superseding him. No time for walking and for casual conversation.

'Tell me, Willi,' says Carter. 'Your father's affections, who would they be stronger towards, you or your sister?'

'You won't have much of an opportunity to talk to him, Johnny,' says Pierce. 'But if you do, and before you get him in the car and lose him down the autobahn drive, then the critical areas are the warhead and the time factor between ignition and the completion of the target locking. It's conceivable that the Marienborn check will bust him. You see, Johnny, we'd hate to have gone to all this trouble and have nothing to show for it. You'll try and get something there, won't you?'

*

'You're a teacher,' says Smithson. 'But we can't pretend that you're on a study trip, we can't line you up a list of appointments at education institutions, not in the days we have available. So you have to be on holiday, a single man looking for somewhere out of the ordinary. That's why you're in Magdeburg. There won't be British there, highly unlikely, only other east bloc people. You just play the tourist with the maps and the pocket camera. Do the churches – the Dom and the Kloster Unser Frauen. Do the parks beside the river, do the Kulturhistorische Museum. For God's sake don't photograph bridges, railway sidings, anything military.'

The barrage of information increased. Sufficient to send Johnny to his bed each night reeling from its variety and complexity. Flesh growing on the old photograph of Otto Guttmann's face, blood coming to his cheeks, colour to his chin, life to his eyes. Finding familiarity and understanding with an old man.

Photographs of Magdeburg. Postcards in sepia, faded by sunlight. Twin towers of the Dom, cascades of fountains, the flats on Karl Marx Strasse. Brittle and modern and hollow monuments. They didn't help much, not so as Johnny would notice, but just gave a suspicion of comfort. Photographs and maps. The Stadtplan of Magdeburg that Smithson had used, scale of 1 to 20,000 and issued by VEB Tourist Verlag, lay creased on his bedside table.

Remember the police uniforms, Johnny.

Remember the MCLOS firing system.

Remember the distance from the city centre to the autobahn intersection.

Remember the capabilities of squash head and high explosive.

Remember the military train, Berlin to Helmstedt, via Magdeburg, remember the train times because that was sweet and clever, and that was Johnny's idea.

Carter and Smithson and Pierce, all of them feeding him, pouring the rich grain down his captive throat as if he were a turkey fattening for a feast. Each evening in his bed the minutiae seeped and swam in his mind and jockeyed for priority till he slept. This was the way back, this was the track to acceptance. The end of the shame of the Crown Court of Belfast and the field in South Armagh, was to be found on the streets of Magdeburg. The banishment of the disgrace of a teenage girl's funeral and the whipping sarcasm of the Lord Chief Justice, would be made on the Berlin to Helmstedt autobahn. A shit heap of a place to go for rehabilitation, Johnny would say quietly to himself. A shit heap, but he wanted back.

And his mother would be happy. She'd be pleased, if it worked out . . .

The Prime Minister moved easily amongst his guests.

A tall, angular, gaunt man who maintained an uncanny fitness on the privacy of a cycling machine and who believed that good health was the elixir for the self-confidence without which political leadership sagged and was spent. Around 60 visitors stood with glasses in their hands pecking at oddments of food in the first floor reception room of his official residence. A babble of talk and gossip. He liked these occasions at Downing Street, enjoyed making the home that he occupied while in office something more than a factory of daily government. Some diplomats here, some military, some cronies of the long years in the party.

'Nice that you were able to come, Barney, how goes it?'

'The villains of the media are behaving themselves.' The retired Vice-Admiral was an old friend, long trusted. 'Particularly last week, I was actually quite proud of them, all rallied round the flag like good lads.'

The Prime Minister nodded to his left to acknowledge a departing guest, thrust his fist to his right for a handshake of farewell. Distracted and content. Good to have some noise in the place, good to blow the cobwebs out of this archaic tomb. 'What was that last week?'

The Vice-Admiral laughed. 'The defector who tried the

double defection. Quite a flap really.'

'I didn't hear of it.' The Prime Minister ignored his duties as host, let the sea of people flow on either side of him, permitted his wife across the room to receive the smiled gratitudes and compliments.

'The East German boy, or Russian, there was some confusion there . . . we slapped a D notice down and Fleet Street and the broadcasters all fell into line. Very pleasing, not a bitch from one of them.'

'You have the advantage over me. What East German boy? What defector?'

'I'm surprised, sir. They seemed to think it important, they heaved me out of bed at some Godawful hour over it . . .'

The Prime Minister took his friend by the elbow and propelled him to an emptied corner of the room. He said slowly, specifically, 'They never tell me anything. They apply a "need to know" tourniquet to me. They believe they're autonomous, those people. Every time I chase them all I get is something about not wishing to disturb me with nonessentials . . . So what was this one about?'

The Vice-Admiral looked anxiously around him, seeking escape, no one caught his eye and the Prime Minister's hand still gripped his elbow. 'It's not easy for me to say, exactly. The bones seemed to be that an East German boy who had defected ran away from his debrief. Peter Fenton's crowd reached me because the police had to be called in to try and find the boy. They'd discovered him by the end of the day but there were police shoulder to shoulder for a few hours in south Surrey, it was the sort of thing that would have given the populars a bit of fun.'

'Why the devil can't I be told anything?'

'Perhaps it came through and you missed it, perhaps the secretaries didn't think it worth your time,' the Vice-Admiral was fishing and lamely.

'They have direct access to me. Whose pigeon would this be?'

'It was Security that called me . . . but it was on behalf of

SIS, the boy was theirs.'

'I'll teach 'em a damned lesson. I'll not be kept in ignorance . . .'

The Prime Minister's wife was at his side. He shouldn't be hiding himself away. The bitterness snapped from the Prime Minister's face and the public smile flowed.

'Of course, my dear, of course. Thank you, Barney, thank you for your guidance.'

The snow had crept from the grass a bare fortnight earlier leaving the ground bleak and without lustre. Far away the forests ringed the great expanse of the test firing range outside the town of Padolsk. No sunshine could pierce the ceiling of cloud that crushed down on them and in the long distance the target tank was wreathed in mist and indistinct to the watchers on the raised, plank dais. The generals always came from the Defence Ministry for a first time test firing.

Otto Guttmann in his suit and overcoat tried to separate himself from the military but the size of the viewing platform made this an empty gesture. This was when he was nervous, when even an old man who had witnessed and taken part in these occasions many times would feel apprehensive. Uniforms around him, heavy trench coats of sand khaki, polished boots of dark brown, wide brimmed caps that sat high on Slav featured faces, and the tongue that he had co-existed alongside without fully mastering. He was jostled for a place on the front row of the platform. He could deal with these men in his office or when they came to the laboratory, could stall and baffle them with the science of his trade. Now the reckoning. It was the first time that the mechanism had been put to the test of field trials.

The binoculars were out. A hush and an excitement and a score of eyes latched on to the group of soldiers in field combat dress who assembled the equipment from the solid wooden crate in which it had travelled from the workshops. Guttmann shuffled in impatience, but the soldiers were right to be methodical and painstaking. The weapon was new to

114

them, and he himself had instructed that procedures should be followed to the letter.

It was intended that combat should be simulated. The generals were anxious to see the weapon in active service conditions.

Far to the right a machine gun spattered through a belt of blank rounds. Out in the middle distance between the soldiers and the derelict tank there were crisp detonations and the swirl of smoke rising from the ground. Guttmann saw the glint of buried ecstasy on the faces of the older officers who watched, those who remembered, those who treasured their youth and the great battles of Stalingrad and Smolensk and Kursk. The thought was momentary, the distaste fast and quickly swallowed.

The soldiers had completed the assembly drill.

It was not to be a simple firing. First they must cross 200 metres of open ground through the crescendo of make-believe battle. They must weave and duck and crawl and take cover, above all else they must expose the equipment to the rough usage and tribulation of combat. Guttmann winced as the soldier who carried the warhead threw himself into a prepared trench and even at that distance he seemed to hear the thudding impact of the metal casing on the granite, long frozen ground.

Through the smoke, faint amongst the firing, came the orders.

The line on the T34, flame blackened, the useless hull and turret, the impotent damaged gun, a battered veteran of the fight against the Panzers, hit many times, holed like a colander and of use now only as a punch bag for the sport of the generals. None of them looked at Guttmann, all ignored him, all peered through magnified vision at the tank, the target. Men who wait for the death of a cock, or a bull or a pig that is wounded and that is trailed by the dogs. He wanted to turn away, wanted to create a chasm between himself and the men pressing around him. The grinning faces of expectation were all about him. The soldiers had stopped near to the top of a short reverse slope to the tank.

The launcher barrel would be peeping lethally over the rim, aiming, lining.

The single bellowed command. 'Fire.'

The flash of light.

Blinding, brilliant on a dulled afternoon. A moment of festive illumination that caught the crouching figures behind the launcher.

The warhead was away, shooting like a tracer a dozen feet into the air. Locking at that height for a fraction of time, the kestrel that needs for the last time to isolate the tuft of grass where the field mouse shelters, then is homing and scrambling for its prey.

Two kilometres it must travel. Striking low over the ground, beckoned to right and left, restored to target with the impulses transmitted by the aimer. A trail of light, and a rushing roar beating across the open range. On course, on target.

Otto Guttmann blinked in pleasure, felt the dry smile creeping across his cheeks and then wiped it as surely as if he had ripped his hand across his mouth.

The warhead veered far to the right, swung away in a sweet, looping arc till it was hastening at right angles from the tank. Two hundred and seventy-five feet per second ground speed. Three hundred kilometres per hour. Skimming the grey grass, hunting out the tree line. Out of control, beyond recall, mechanical discipline discarded. Breathtakingly fast. The concerted gasp of horror and astonishment from the platform was stifled by the distant report of the explosion amongst the trees. A blast of sharp flame that was short and edited and then a wallowing silence as the smoke gathered, was caught in the wind and taken from the trees.

There was a shuffle of feet and the heads were turned on Otto Guttmann and the eyes beneath the cap peaks struck and stung him. He must speak first. Always the inventor must explain, always he must offer a reason.

He stood his ground and faced them.

The smoke grew and drifted towards them, not hurrying,

116

not impatient, but dispersing gently from the impact point.

'You saw it, you saw it yourselves . . . the launch was perfect. The initial aim was perfect . . . It was only after that, afterwards that it went to the right. You have hurried me, I have told you that many times. The problem has been the protection of the circuitry of the aim mechanism. You saw with your own eyes how it was thrown to the ground. It is a delicate computer, not a sack of turnips. If the soldier had been careful then it would have been perfect.' He heard his own words as if spoken by another, recognised the guttural German resonance that always showed through when he spoke the Russian language. He saw the contempt on the officers' faces. He knew that he wheedled for their sympathy, sucked for their consolation, and could not help himself. 'I have to have more time to strengthen the circuits if they are to withstand abuse. It is not like Sagger, a rough machine with a cable to guide it. Electronic impulses are delicate . . .'

'When do we see it again?' The chill response of a Major General with a chest brightened by medal and decoration ribbons.

'Three weeks, perhaps more, perhaps less. It is complex . . .'

'It must withstand that treatment and more. It is to be a weapon handled by infantry not scientists.'

'I know.' Guttmann looked at his feet. He felt his inadequacy, that of the civilian who seeks to find explanations that will not satisfy the tunnelled minds of the military.

'Three weeks and we will be back . . .'

The wooden steps of the platform boomed under the weight of the descending boots. No backward glance, no understanding. Otto Guttmann was left alone to survey the range. They could come again in three weeks but he would not be there. In three weeks Otto Guttmann would have arrived in Magdeburg. Nothing deflected his annual holiday. At a brisk pace he set off to cross the open ground and talk to the firing team.

*

117

'PPS?'

Eight o'clock in the morning, the usual hour for the Prime Minister to buzz his Parliamentary Private Secretary, in the adjoining office.

'Good morning, Prime Minister.'

'I want an appointment made for the head of SIS to come here.'

'Urgent, sir?'

'Not so that we cancel anything, but I want 20 minutes of his time.'

'Twenty minutes with the DUS, I'll fix it. Will you want the PUS with him?'

'I'm not having the Permanent-Under-Secretary along like a damned lawyer telling him when to speak and when to shut his mouth.'

'There looks like a hole in the diary tomorrow morning.'

'That'll do,' said the Prime Minister grimly.

He was not the first Prime Minister of the United Kingdom voted into office since the war to believe that Intelligence considered him irrelevant to their operations. Not the first, perhaps, but he'd make certain that particular opinion went out of the window and down on to the pavement, and that the fall hurt.

Ulf Becker stamped out of the office of the commander of the Weferlingen company.

A lost sector map, a map dropped from a pocket on foot patrol, a map that could not be accounted for, a cause for punishment. Forty-eight hours confined to garrison buildings when not on patrol duties, one week's pay stopped.

A snigger in the dormitory sleeping quarters from Heini Schalke as Ulf Becker exploded into the room and began to fling off the best dress uniform that he had worn to mitigate the penalty.

Back in his denim fatigues, Ulf Becker fell on his bed, the dramatic gesture that was intended to show his contempt for the retribution raised against him. No talk from the other boys in the room. No hand of friendship reaching for him, no kindness or commiseration. This was the boy with the plague, with the yellow pennant hoisted. Shit on them, piss on them. Cowards with arse fluff on their cheeks . . . pathetic creeps, crawling to a system that punished for the loss of a map in the woods at the end of an 8 hour day of patrol . . . shit on them. And it would be on his record, and the penalty that had been awarded would hurry to his file. Would be there when the factory apprenticeships were considered and awarded.

And none of them who sneered, none of them who laughed behind averted faces, owned a girl such as the one in the possession of Ulf Becker. His boots smeared the dirt of the compound and vehicle park on to the blankets. Shit on them. His head rumpled the pillow on the bed. Piss on them.

And Jutte had spoken of the way to hurt them, the one way, the foolproof way. But it was not on the fence west of Weferlingen, not there . . . There were enough who tried, enough who believed the effort worthy. Why did they try, why did they challenge the fence, why did they risk their lives? What for them was worth death on the wire, in the foresight of an MPiKM, amongst the shallow buried mines?

The squeaking, oilless voice of Schalke was calling him. Time for the briefing, for the next duty in boredom on the frontier line. In his mind was the letter he would write, in his mind were the acid words of his company commander, in his mind was a future of hours spent with the eyes straining at fields and forests and only the sweat scent of Schalke's body for distraction.

Those who challenged the fence, from where did they bring the courage, from where did they unearth the dignity?

Much to consider for a young member of the Border Guard slouching along the corridors of his company head-quarters on his way to the armoury and the signing out of an automatic rifle.

'What are you going to do about it, Mr Potterton, that's what I'm asking you . . .'

119

Dennis Tweedle gazed across his living room at the police constable. Beside him on the sofa his wife, Annabel, picked fluff from her skirt, was ill at ease, demonstrated that the summoning of Frederick Potterton had not been her idea.

'. . . Your story and my wife's tally, no doubt on that. Mrs Tweedle does the right thing by this lad, brings him home for a cup of tea, thaws him out, starts to dry his clothes. Then we have this extraordinary story. Secret Service stuff, kidnapping, assassination behind the Iron Curtain. And what's the end of it? You're told to shut up and mind your business, my wife is insulted in her own home. So, what are you going to do about it?'

Avoid the direct answer, that was the governing philosophy of the constable. His examination for sergeant failed, his career on a promotion plateau, the village posting suited him well. A little burglary, a little swine fever, a little Highway Code instruction to the local junior school. This was quicksand for him. Dennis Tweedle with money in the City and a new Jaguar in the driveway was not a man to be trifled with, and neither was national security. Shifting ground all around him.

'The people that took the lad away, sir, they're genuine enough. They wouldn't have managed it past the Cranleigh inspector on the gate if they hadn't been. He came over especially, he's no fool.'

'Not the issue, Mr Potterton. The Inspector didn't hear what this boy had to say. Only Mrs Tweedle and yourself heard that.'

'I was told not to file a written report unless instructed to do so . . .'

'That's not good enough. If you won't take it further, Mr Potterton, then I will.'

'You have to be careful, sir, when the talk is national security. Bloody careful, sir, if you'll excuse me.'

'I'm asking for your advice, who should I complain to?'

The masterstroke from Potterton. 'Try your MP, sir. That's what he's there for . . .'

'That's a damn good idea, damn good, Mr Potterton.

120

Don't you think so, darling?'

'Absolutely, Dennis. A very good idea of Mr Potterton's.'

The constable was quickly to his feet. Time for withdrawal, time for pleading the call of work. Handshakes and thanks and he was off for his car. A chuckle to himself. The cat would be in the dovecote. A terrible old leech, the local Member of Parliament, never been known to let anything fall from his tacky hands once he'd taken it on as his business. If the Member made himself interested then that would show those buggers who'd been so happy to throw their weight about.

He reversed carefully in his car, not the moment to sully the paintwork of the gleaming Jaguar.

Chapter Ten

=

They left Mrs Ferguson standing on the step of the front porch waving to them, and George hit the car horn in a fanfare. A rare gesture that, for her to come to the door to see them off, as if a bond were building between this spidery woman and the men to whom she played a foster mother.

George driving, Carter beside him. Johnny and Willi Guttmann in the back seats.

Across the hills and down to Abinger, right at the main road and heading for Dorking between the avenues of ripening trees. Fast up the dual carriageway under the shadows of the grass shaven slopes of Box Hill. George drove the Rover with authority and there was a feeling of freedom that permeated them all, even Willi. Something of an event, a day's outing to London, something to anticipate with excitement. Each in his own way believed himself a prisoner of the house at Holmbury. For all of them the journey to the capital represented a truncated but welcome escape.

The boy looked around him with the full swing of his neck, the arc broken only when his eyes would have challenged Johnny's. This was the remaining area of his suspicions. With Carter he seemed to have an understanding of sorts, with George he had ploughed a bare field of co-existence, but with Johnny his trust was soured. Johnny and his role in the debriefings fuelled a degree of suspicion that the boy did not feel now for the others. Johnny who was deadly quiet and perpetually in alert motion, Johnny who seemed to be in increasing preparation for an unexplained action. Johnny alone was the block against Carter's protestations that no harm was intended towards his father.

When the countryside was gone from them after the Leatherhead by-pass Carter began to talk, directing himself to Willi, swivelling in his seat, relaxed and confident as if a new era had settled on them. Johnny sat close to the boy, tensed each time the car stopped at traffic lights or slowed behind a lorry, warily watching the boy's hands and the door catch.

'I can't tell you much, Willi,' Carter began, 'because that's not our way, that's not the style that we employ. But the incident of last week is forgotten by us and we've been impressed by your attitude since then. You have been most co-operative and we don't underestimate the value of the help that you have given us. We're going to continue to ask for that help, and your patience . . . in a few days' time, less than a month we're going to provide you with a bonus, a present in Christmas wrapping, that you wouldn't have thought possible. That's harder for you to believe than if we'd told you nothing at all . . .'

The boy listened in a glazed curiosity.

'. . . you have to be patient with us, as I said, you have to do everything that we ask of you. The worst part for you is finished, not for us, but for you. Help us and we'll help you, and the prize for both of us is very rich. All right, lad?'

The conflict seemed to rise in the boy's face. The implicit threat and the cold watch of Johnny beside him, confronted by the apparent kindness of Carter, the older man, with the words of honey.

'Yes, Mr Carter.'

'That's the spirit.'

'Yes, Mr Carter.'

'And now we're going to have a hell of a day out and a damn good meal, and we're going to forget about work and all those bloody questions and we're going to play the tourist game.' Carter held up a small camera to amplify his point.

And they all smiled, even Willi as if against his judgement, even George as his eyes hovered between the road and his mirror, even Johnny.

The Deputy-Under-Secretary walked from the Privy Council

Office in Whitehall, where his car dropped him, along the underground link tunnel to Number 10 Downing Street. A private man this, from a private world. None of the hundred or so tourists who gathered daily on the pavement across the road from the Prime Minister's home and office would have the opportunity presented them of inadvertently snapping with their cameras the features of the head of the Secret Intelligence Service.

Forewarned from a telephone conversation with the Retired Vice-Admiral, forearmed by an early morning situation report from Charles Mawby of the files that now carried the codename DIPPER, he believed he possessed protection in the coming encounter.

The Prime Minister's Special Branch bodyguard in the hallway on the ground floor rose sharply to his feet.

'Good morning, Mr Havergale.'

The Deputy-Under-Secretary saw the pleasure light in the veteran policeman's face. Good to find friends, to find them where he could.

'Good morning, sir, not a bad morning is it?'

'Not bad at all, and I think it's going to brighten a bit more.'

'Could be, sir.'

The usher beside the Deputy-Under-Secretary clicked his heels. 'The Prime Minister's waiting for you, sir.'

'Mustn't keep him waiting, must we, Mr Havergale? Must not delay the Prime Minister's business . . .'

'Right, sir. Nice to see you again, sir.'

The Deputy-Under-Secretary smiled coolly to himself. Briskly, confidently he followed the usher who led him up the wide staircase to the first floor, they paced the length of a corridor, their footsteps hushed by the carpet pile, aware of the murmur behind closed doors of electric typewriters, hearing the trill of a radio from upstairs that played light music . . . The Prime Minister's wife would be in the attic flat, not really a suitable woman, and she was said to tell anyone who would listen that she detested living over the

124

shop . . . The usher knocked lightly on a door.

'Enter.'

They always had their desks at the window and their backs to the doorway, these people. They always had papers that concerned them when a visitor was shown into the presence, leaving their guest standing in awkwardness and at disadvantage.

The papers were purposefully pushed away.

'Good morning, take a chair please.' The Prime Minister removed his spectacles, smiled without affection, turned in his chair. The Deputy-Under-Secretary sat himself down, wondered if there would be pleasantries and preliminaries. There were none. 'We haven't seen enough of each other since I came into office. I believe that one of my predecessors instituted a fortnightly meeting between Downing Street and the Service. I'm inclined towards resurrecting that habit.'

'I'm sure you read the minutes of the monthly meeting chaired by the Permanent-Under-Secretary, the meetings of JIC.'

'I read that.'

'And it's not satisfactory?'

'If I believed that what appears in a page and a half of transcript was the sum total of what was discussed, then I'd be tempted to wind the whole apparatus up, close it down. It's a thin sketch at best. You'll not disagree with that?'

'It contains the traditional elements.'

'Then the tradition isn't good enough.'

The Deputy-Under-Secretary was impassive, his eyes taken by a soup stain on the Prime Minister's tie. 'The tradition has not been found wanting in the past.'

'If that's true then I want to be in a position to make that judgement. I don't want to be merely told there are roses in the garden behind the high wall, I want to go into that garden and see them for myself.'

'If the JIC minutes are inadequate then I'm sure the Permanent-Under-Secretary will rectify that situation.'

'I'm not concerned with a carbon sheet of paper. I want a wider picture.'

'I doubt if you could spare the time for that, Prime Minister,' the Deputy-Under-Secretary remarked evenly.

'It boils down to the primacy of policy over the instruments of policy. Policy is in the hands of government. SIS is merely one of the instruments at its disposal.'

'I think I read that book as well, Prime Minister. A clever turn of phrase I thought at the time.'

The Prime Minister clenched his fist, caught at his temper. 'The issuing of a D notice is not a small matter. We try to keep secrecy within tightly defined limits, and I'm the one who may have to justify the imposition of such measures. I don't expect to hear of sanctions against the media days after the event.'

'The Service has not called for a new D notice in recent weeks.' There was a sweetness in the Deputy-Under-Secretary's voice.

'This East German boy, the defector, there was a D notice put on that, after he ran away . . .'

'And requested by Security, Prime Minister, not the Service. You should ask Fenton and he'll corroborate.' The Deputy-Under Secretary gazed calmly back across the room at his adversary.

'I don't have the time to waste in examining inter-departmental responsibilities . . . SIS held a defector, that defector escaped from their care. SIS called in Security and the police to recover him. A D notice was applied. Right or wrong?'

A grudging acceptance. 'Pretty much right, Prime Minister.'

'Why wasn't I told when the defector first came to us? Why wasn't I told of his escape . . .'

'Fairly small beer. A young fellow, a junior interpreter in the Soviet delegation to the Geneva disarmament conference. He doesn't rate very highly. If you want the detail, I can give it you, Prime Minister. Willi Guttmann aged 24, without access to secret and sensitive material inside the

Soviet delegation, meets an English secretary attached to the World Health Organisation. Their rendezvous is a bar called the Pickwick in central Geneva. She becomes pregnant, won't consider an abortion and persuades Guttmann to make his life with her. For that reason he defects ... Is this the material you feel cheated of, Prime Minister? ... The girl's family is quite well placed, I believe. Name of Forsyth. Chambers in the Inner Temple, her father ... Not a vastly edifying affair ...'

'Don't sidetrack me with irrelevance,' snapped the Prime Minister. 'A D notice was activated. A D notice implies a matter of national security, an issue that if revealed to public gaze would harm the interests of this country. In your own words the boy is small beer, how then does he warrant such a response?'

The Deputy-Under-Secretary was not a man to be stampeded. 'Two reasons, Prime Minister. Guttmann's method of defection has led the Soviet authorities to believe that he drowned in a boating accident, they are not aware that he is in this country and helping us, were they to have that knowledge we believe his life would be endangered and his family in Moscow would be open to reprisal. I don't think we would want that. Secondly, the boy has provided information on the new projected Soviet anti-tank missile system ...'

'And that you call small beer?'

'Information that is interesting to us because of our own preparations for the mass production of the Main Battle Tank of the late nineteen eighties. There are several thousand jobs dependent on that programme. Many of them, I believe, to be found in the constituency of the Secretary of State for the Social Services ...'

'And shouldn't I have been told of this? With a visit approaching by a senior minister of the German Democratic Republic, shouldn't I have known that someone with connections in that country is currently aiding our intelligence effort?'

Tell the Prime Minister and you tell how many? Which

127

aides see a memorandum, which personal secretaries? How many learn the contents of a file over cocktails and during weekends in the country? And not the occasion to speak of DIPPER, not the place, not the time.

'I will give instructions that in future you will be kept more fully in the picture. I trust you won't find our affairs tedious.' The Deputy-Under-Secretary was experienced in the tactical warfare of the civil service. It was unwise to join with a politician in head-on combat. You deflected attack, you retired in good order, you lived for another day.

The Prime Minister was sweetened. 'Don't think that I'm not sympathetic to the work of the Service. I think I know the procedures, but I want more than I'm getting in the way of information.'

'You must do as you think fit, Prime Minister. The Service will be gratified at the interest shown in its efforts. That interest, I trust, will be reflected in Treasury grants?'

That scored, the Deputy-Under-Secretary observed, forced the predictable sidestep. 'I think it goes without saying that it would be extremely disadvantageous to us were the East Germans to know of the presence here of this defector. They sell to the United Kingdom almost twice the value of goods that they buy from us . . .'

'You can rest assured that there is no action contemplated by the Service that would jeopardise the improvement of our trade balance with the DDR.'

The Deputy-Under-Secretary smiled from an open face at the Prime Minister. He thought of the Dipper bird, remembered what Mawby had told him. A dark and camouflaged little creature, hard to see in the gloom of a river bank, and it walked covertly on the stream bed. He remembered what Mawby had said of a contract man who would go to Magdeburg. Not the place and not the time.

He rose from his chair. 'I'll set in hand a small working party to see how we can keep you more fully informed without swamping your desk.'

*

They had eaten well at an Italian restaurant close to Victoria station, taken pasta and veal and drunk a litre and a half of white wine. Carter had paid, playing the father figure, extracting a wad of five pound notes from his wallet, explaining that he'd raided petty cash at Holmbury. On the government, he'd said, and no offence to Mrs Ferguson but this was the best meal they'd had in weeks. Much of the wine had found its way to Willi's glass, as intended.

In a little group they walked past Buckingham Palace and the red tunicked sentries, along the wide Mall where Americans and Japanese jostled for camera angles, they paused in Trafalgar Square and George bought a bag of nuts for Willi to scatter for the pigeons. They came down Whitehall and showed the boy the narrow entrance to Downing Street and passed on towards the House of Commons. Willi lapped up the history and George, who was always near to him, was a sure guide, humorous and interesting. Near to him, but never beside, always the few feet away so that Carter's Instamatic camera as it clicked incessantly would not include George in the pictures of the boy admiring and wondering at the sounds and sights of a great city. Carter used two cassettes of film.

They moved in a regulated, planned formation. Carter leading. George alongside Willi. Johnny in the rear and sliding for the background each time the camera came to Carter's eye. No reason that he should have worried, the photographic section would have painted him out.

Johnny wondered what the boy thought. Wondered how sharply the experience of escape and return to the house had cut. Wondered why the boy had not mentioned the girl again from Geneva. Wondered how he would respond to Carter's appeal for friendship and help. Didn't know any of the answers, didn't fathom the mind of the boy, alien to Johnny. But then Willi Guttmann was a prisoner and his feelings would be masked and closed, flies tightly zipped, protecting himself. Not the only prisoner, Johnny, was he? Not the only one who's trying to be a good kid because that's the way towards remission. Johnny and Willi, two of a kind. Both used, second-hand persons. And after the work was finished, what then for Johnny and Willi? Forget Willi, what then for Johnny? He didn't give a shit for the boy who walked in front of him. So what then for Johnny when the work was finished? . . . No way of finding the certain answer until he came back from Magdeburg with Otto Guttmann in his pocket . . .

They had an ice cream each, dripping from cornets, and George cleaned Willi's mouth with his handkerchief, and Willi said it was good ice cream, and Carter said that it bloody well ought to be at 8 old shillings a portion.

They started back for the car. All tired, all footsore.

One morning a week the Member of Parliament for Guildford held open house at his constituency offices.

Ten till twelve on a Wednesday and that was sufficient for him to be able to boast each time that he sought the electorate's support that his door was always wide to those in difficulty. They came in a hesitant dribble to ask whether something could be done about the drain that smelled by the bus stop, whether there could be an additional pedestrian crossing for the school children, whether there could be greater police presence to combat young people's vandalism, whether the transport service could be improved. A telephoned message from the Member of Parliament would motivate the local Council to action. But not many of the class and affluence of Dennis Tweedle availed themselves of the opportunity to meet him at the public 'surgery'. The likes of Dennis Tweedle were private patients, met for lunch in London or for a drink at a club in St James's. But Tweedle had said that he must see his Member of Parliament that day, could not wait for a more socially convenient occasion, and so had waited out in the corridor with the rest, subject to a hard wooden bench and the exhortations of the party slogans on the walls.

When the Member had entered the Mother of Parliaments he had believed that after a shortish apprenticeship he would be invited to the Despatch Box to argue with the authority of ministerial responsibility behind him. But the party had fallen on barren years, long rejected. A team of hard fisted, abrasive tongued men and women now soared in the new order. Time had slipped by the Member for Guildford. The back benches of the House of Commons were his fate. He found a solace now in aspish criticism of his youthful but more senior party colleagues, and prided himself that this was useful to democracy.

The snake sting of his tongue had acquired him a certain notoriety that to be maintained must find frequent replenishment from cause and case history. He was a very suitable candidate for Dennis Tweedle's complaint. 'He repeated it again and again, the boy, the allegation that his father was to be murdered in the German Democratic Republic by members of the British Secret Intelligence Service. They showed intolerable rudeness, these people, just barged into the house, not a word of thanks for what my wife had done, stripped the clothes she'd given him right off the lad and took him out half naked when what he needed was warmth and kindliness.'

He had endured two more of his constituents, fought to concentrate on their worries, and hurried them away. Left to himself he telephoned the headquarters of Surrey County Police and requested an appointment with the Chief Constable.

He reflected afterwards that many would have warned him that this was not a fit matter for his concern. Any number of his colleagues at the Palace of Westminster would have offered that advice.

But such an attitude would have marked the betrayal of the true role of the backbencher. That was the opinion of Sir Charles Spottiswoode, Member for Guildford.

In the sitting room Carter broached the whisky bottle, handed a generous glass to Johnny. The two men alone.

Willi and George away upstairs. Smithson and Pierce not back from a day with their families.

'I think we deserve it, but the day was fine, the pictures will be just right.'

'They'll stir the old man up,' Johnny said thoughtfully.

'Mawby rang while you were in the bath. He's coming down tomorrow, early. He's having dinner with the DUS tonight.'

'That's nice for him . . .' Johnny looked up, away from his drink and saw the uncertainty in Carter. '. . . Do we have a problem?'

'Mawby says the DUS is a fraction nervous. The Prime Minister called him in, gave him the acid about not having heard of Willi, the D notice did that for us. He was going on about the need for more consultation between the Service and Downing Street . . .'

'Will he get that?'

'Shouldn't think so,' said Carter cheerfully. 'The DUS regards politicians as passing ships. But there was a bit more than that. The PM was jittery about the defector damaging trade negotiations between us and the DDR. Mawby says that all this bloody government thinks about is export statistics.'

'What does the PM say about DIPPER?'

'I fancy the DUS told him the truth, and nothing but the truth, but I get the impression that the bit about the whole truth might have been mislaid. The PM wouldn't have said anything about DIPPER for the very simple reason that he's rather in the dark about it.'

'What does that mean?' Johnny swigged at his glass.

'It means that it's a bloody good plan, and one that's getting better, and it's not going to be screwed for a turbine engine order.'

'It's a hell of a way to carry on.'

'That's what I was thinking, but it's the usual way.'

Johnny pondered, head resting in his hands, cheeks enveloped. He sat very still, thoughtful, wrapped in himself. Carter stared out of the window into the cloaking darkness.

'I'll want a gun,' Johnny said.

'What do you say, Johnny?' Carter murmured, his attention distanced.

'I said that I'll want a gun.'

Carter swivelled towards him. 'That's not on, Johnny, you know that.'

'Not to carry through the frontier, but to pick up there. I want one.'

'It's not cops and robbers, you know.'

'When we go for the autobahn, I'll want to carry a gun.'

'It'll never be agreed to, you know that. If anything happened . . .'

'Exactly right, if anything happened . . . if one idiot stands in the way. If one Schutzpolizei holds his hand up . . . What do you do? You won't be there to tell me. Not you, not Mawby.'

Because that was the crucible, and Carter wasn't travelling. He'd be at Helmstedt and waiting. Kicking his heels at Checkpoint Alpha and thinking of the restaurant they'd take over when Johnny came through. Carter was the blunt end man. And Carter couldn't read this young man, young enough to be his son, young enough to have had the small front room of his home, young enough to have earned in Northern Ireland the mauve and green ribbon of active service, young enough to have killed there . . . How do you love a young man, offer yourself as parental substitute, when he's slaughtered a child, shown no public remorse? And Carter didn't know him, could not search a path into the mind of the man they would send to Magdeburg. And he would only be waiting for him, waiting with a restaurant reservation.

'I'll see what I can do.'

'We wouldn't want a little thing to stymie us.'

Carter showed a beleaguered, tired sympathy. 'I'll argue the case for a gun with Mawby. Don't worry at it.'

He carried the bottle to Johnny. Something terrible in those watchful, clear lit eyes, something that frightened him, that made him want to turn his back on the man who had shot a teenage girl and wept no tears.

'You're a cold bugger, Johnny.'

'I'm a contract man,' Johnny said, and his eyes blinked and the brightness had fled.

Ulf Becker jumped easily down from the lorry's tailboard. He didn't look back to see how Heini Schalke coped with the drop. He held his pack lightly with one hand, trailed his rifle in the other. Dirty, hot, bathed in his sweat he stopped in front of Company Orders, the board on which duty rosters were posted. Becker sniggered, pointed out the carbon typed sheet to those who followed him.

Battalion at Seggerde directed company at Weferlingen to provide two sections in the morning in support of company at Walbeck. An epidemic of measles was responsible. Much laughter, much ribaldry. And welcome ... Becker's name on the list of those to be sent the eight kilometres south from Weferlingen to Walbeck.

Anything for variety, anything to change the outlook of the sugar beet fields across the wire, and the farm houses, and the road junctions, and the viewing platforms where the British troops and the Bundesgrenzschutz and the Zoll Customs men came to peer across at them ... and there was no hope of breaching the fence at Weferlingen, no justi-fication there for writing a letter to a girl in Berlin.

Chapter Eleven

=

Carter opened the door silently, and walked on his toes towards the bed. Johnny sleeping and lit by the early morning sunshine. Carter intruding, as if creeping into the room of his daughter when she had been small. And this one had a child's face too. Relaxed and easy breathing, a calm set mouth, the legs drawn up and silhouetted under the bed-clothes. The defenceless, vulnerable posture of sleep. Carter carried a china mug of tea to the bedside table and grimaced at the street map of Magdeburg that had been left crudely folded beside the lamp. Bloody awful bedside reading. Switch yourself off from the day's work with a street map of a ghastly city of chimneys and furnaces in the German bloody Democratic Republic. Poor bastard. Everything so neat in the room. As if Johnny infiltrated himself between the furnishings and fittings, disturbed nothing, moved nothing. Clothes all in the wardrobe, or folded on the chair. Shoes together and slippers beside, as if for kit inspection. Means more than that, doesn't it? If his possessions aren't strewn on the floor, if he doesn't leave his mark in the nest, then he's a stranger here. He doesn't believe that he belongs. The return of the thought, the thought that came many times to Carter . . . They did not know this man.

'Johnny, Johnny.'

He started in the bed, tightness on the face, the peace gone and fled. A sharpness of movement, the fast clearing of the mind. Carter had thrown a pebble into still waters. The private face was gone, Carter would not recapture it.

'Johnny, I brought some tea for you.'

Johnny propped on one elbow. Johnny gazing at him and seeking a reason. Johnny who slept so tidily that the parting of his hair was still intact.

135

'I brought some tea.'

Brought some tea because that was a personal gesture, that was a bridge between pointman and planner, that was the way Carter hoped to span the chasm. Carter could not have said why he needed the relationship, nor where could be found its importance to DIPPER. He knew only that without it there would be an emptiness, that the mission would have no heart. And if there were catastrophe then Johnny would need the knowledge that he belonged and was a part of something greater that supported and upheld him. That was why Carter had gone down to Mrs Ferguson's kitchen and boiled the kettle and made the tea.

'Playing the housemaid?'

'I never sleep at weekends, I never just lie in. When I'm at home, when we haven't a show on, then I'd be out in the garden or walking the dog . . . I thought you'd like a mug of tea.'

'Thanks.'

'I always like one myself, early on.'

'You were right to wake me. I'm trying to marry the post-card snaps to the map. They're both ersatz, substitutes.' Johnny yawned, threw back his head, scratched at his chest. 'I was at it late last night, must have been at it a couple of hours after we went up.'

'You'll be all right, Johnny. We all think so, we're all very pleased with the way it's gone so far.'

'Thanks.'

'It's a special day today, Johnny, did you know that?' He was playing the parent figure, couldn't help himself.

'What day is it today?'

'It's the first of the month.'

'What happens on the first of the month?'

'It's the first of June, come on . . . it's the day Otto Gutt-mann goes to Magdeburg.'

'You brought me a cup of tea to remind me? Just for that?'

Carter flinched. 'Not like that, no. I just thought it was a bit of a landmark for us all. I'm sorry, I should have let you sleep . . .'

'Not to worry.' Johnny heaved himself out of bed, shook his head to achieve the effect of a bucket of cold water poured on his face.

'I spoke to Mawby again last night, after you'd gone up. He's off again to Germany, not coming here today. About the weapon, I worked on him a bit . . . he's not happy but he's agreed . . . he took a bit of persuading . . .' There was a pride in Carter's voice at his achievement against the habits of the Service. 'There'll be a drop-off point organised for you in Magdeburg . . . You know we're going outside normal practice on this one, it's irregular.'

'What are you giving me?'

'Probably the APS, the Stechkin. Nine millimetre, twenty round magazine. They'll get one with a tubular shoulder stock which'll bump the range up to a couple of hundred metres.'

'That would be right.'

'I suggested to Mawby that if you were to be armed we had better make it effective. In for a penny, and that nonsense. We can also make available up to 4 fragmentation grenades, we reckoned the RGD 5s. That makes the pay load all east bloc . . . might confuse them a bit.'

'Good for you.' Johnny had begun to dress, peeling off his striped pyjamas.

'It wasn't easy to get Mawby to agree.'

'I'm sure it wasn't.'

Carter fidgeted on his feet, wondered whether he should withdraw. If he did so then he would have aborted the whole journey up the stairs with the mug that still cooled on the bedside table, untouched.

'Not that the weaponry affects the main problem, the persuasion of old man Guttmann . . .'

Johnny's eyes lit up. 'Of course it bloody doesn't. Why do you think I go off each night and sit in this bloody hole? Why do you think I'm always first away in the evenings? . . . Because all the crap downstairs doesn't help me with the main issue. I'm not a bloody idiot you know.'

Carter stumbled for the door. Felt a pain, a desperate

137

sadness and his mind was filled with the anger of Johnny's face, the anger that was the overcoat of fear.

As he went out of the room Johnny called to him.

'Thanks, thanks for bringing the tea. Give me five minutes and I'll be with you for breakfast.'

A small voice, a small brave voice.

Erica Guttmann tilted her window seat back, waved away the stewardess with the meal on the tray, and was content to sink and flow with the even motion of the aircraft. Non stop to Berlin-Schönefeld. High above the cloud layer, distanced from the turbulence. Her eyes were closed, her hands limp on the seat arms, a magazine lay unopened on her lap.

So tired from all that had gone before.

Otto Guttmann sat, as always, upright and serious, considering a technical journal, hissing between his teeth either in exasperation at what he read, or at the pleasure of new discovery. She wore the new skirt and blouse that she had bought for the holiday, she had made the effort to lift her morale. Her father was dressed in his perennial dark suit, scornful of concessions towards a vacation.

He had wearied her in these last weeks. First the task of confronting the lethargy that had seeped over him after the news of Willi. And when at last there was light and his cold grief had thawed imperceptibly there had been the sledge hammer set back of the firing range at Padolsk. The experience had left him flaccid and without enthusiasm for the breakaway from his laboratory and drawing board. Erica had to sort the clothes that he would take with him, Erica had to pack his suitcase, Erica had to write the letters to the friends in Magdeburg and give their arrival and departure dates. In his depression the old man had renewed his work on the guidance circuitry of the weapon, calling for greater effort from his technical team. Driving himself, pushing forward, moving beyond the perimeters of possibility for the health of an old man. Let the bastards do it themselves, she had told herself. He had earned his retirement, was owed a rest haven far from the badgering complaints of the generals from Defence . . . But it would not be granted. Their thanks would be confined to the few scientists and military officers who were detailed to walk behind his casket and stand in patronising quiet while the speeches were made over a worn down corpse.

Once she had pushed her hand against his and squeezed the hard, boned fingers and he had leaned towards her and his roughened lips had kissed behind her ear. The smartness of her new costume would have appealed to him. The perfume that an officer stationed at Padolsk had brought back from Romania and which she had dabbed against her skin would give him pleasure. Her long and carefully brushed fair hair would draw his pride.

From the cockpit came the pilot's information that they had entered the air space of the German Democratic Republic at Schwedt to the north of Berlin. They had received landing permission. The weather on the ground was clear and fine.

The drone of the aircraft engines switched in tone as the Tupolev sagged through its descent. She roused herself, straightened in her seat and looked at her father. Still trapped in his reading, still remorseless in his study. Pale cheeks. The small puff of cotton wool at his neck where he had slashed the skin while shaving in the hurry of the early morning at the flat. His hair, greying and unruly after the barest efforts of the comb before they had locked the front door of their home.

Absently she reached across his waist and buckled his seat belt.

'A few more minutes, then we land.'

His eyes, huge and blurred through the lenses of his spectacles, turned to her and he nodded. She thought, perhaps, it would have been better if she had held his head against her shoulder and let him weep with the fluency of an old man.

Better if he could have wept, better if he could have shared.

139

How could Willi have allowed himself to die? How could he have been so stupid?

A courier from the Service brought to the house at Holmbury the buff envelope that contained the rail tickets and the voucher for the hotel. The Dublin travel agency had enclosed a photostat of the relevant pages of the West German train timetable.

A second class seat had been booked for John Dawson on the Inter City from Frankfurt to Hannover. There he must change. At two in the morning he would connect with the train that crossed the frontier. Obeisfeld in East Germany would be reached at 28 minutes past 3, Magdeburg at 25 minutes past 5.

'I'll be in a great state to take on the comrades,' remarked Johnny.

'It's better that you go at night and through a little used crossing, they won't be very bright,' said Carter soothing. 'You'll be able to sleep the rest of the day.'

'And not much after that.'

Time rushing past them. Time crushing and burdening the men on the DIPPER team.

They marched towards the company headquarters' operations room. Not inside, of course, not within sight of the most confidential wall maps of the Walbeck sector. Outside on the beaten down mud, lined up and at ease until the company commander was ready to come from his den and beard them. A blackboard was brought and a large scale map hung to it and a marker cane was produced. The two sections came to attention when the company commander emerged. Beside him Ulf Becker sensed the effort of Heini Schalke to get the contours of his fat arse and fat belly into dashing line.

Not a bad fellow, the company commander seemed at first sight. He wore the insignia of a major on his shoulder straps. An older man, one of the originals from the days far back when the National Volks Armee was formed and the

Border Guard was raised as an integral part of the military forces of the state. Didn't seem flamboyant, nor pompous. Didn't walk with the strut of a martinet. Ulf Becker knew his officers, knew what to scout for. He'd be a Party man, he'd hold the SED membership card in his tunic pocket, wouldn't be an officer without that, not a major anyway . . .

The Politoffizier stood behind. Becker watched him. The head of an owl, the body of a stoat. They were the pigs, the ones who set soldier against soldier, the ones who primed one man to offer the studied indiscretion to the other in the watchtower or the earth bunker and waited to see if the confidence were reported. They were the pigs. It was their work to ensure that no soldier trusted his colleague, their work to ensure that on the border no soldier owned a friend. Too close to the fence for that, too close to the green grass beyond the wire.

It was a new thought for Ulf Becker, a new species of complaint for him. It had not been so before he had ridden on the S-Bahn train in Berlin with Jutte.

The major called them forward, told them to gather round him, to be near to the map.

'My name is Pfeffel, you are all most welcome to the Walbeck company. You will be with us for some days and we will endeavour to make your stay with us as happy as we can manage. The Walbeck sector of the anti-fascist defences of the DDR is not entirely similar to the area that you are accustomed to patrolling at Weferlingen. Our company frontage lies on either side of the Walbeck Strasse that before our liberation from Nazism by the Red Army linked this coalmining village with that of Emmerstedt now in the BDR.' The major stabbed with his cane at the map, identifying the village and the mauve line of the frontier. 'Walbeck is different to Weferlingen because here the terrain is less friendly to us. To prevent crossings of our frontier by saboteurs from the BDR we have had to clear considerable areas of forestry. The whole frontage of our sector is covered by forest and as yet the programme for the building of towers is not completed. We have to maintain the highest

141

level of patrolling. Where the ground is difficult for us we have found that only increased vigilance and watchfulness can compensate.'

The major had completed his speech, smiled at the young men and retreated to his command post. An NCO followed with a briefing of the duties they would face, and the rosters they would work.

Ulf Becker listened closely, absorbed the details of the sharp curves in the frontier line, the pockets of dead ground where special care must be taken, the positioning of the bunkers, the frequency of the routine of observing the fence from the Trabant jeeps.

If he had watched the boy the Politoffizier would have been impressed by this young soldier's apparent keenness to begin his work with the Walbeck company.

Ulf Becker had 8 more days to serve in the National Volks Armee on the border. He would then spend 3 more days preparing for his demobilisation at Battalion at Seggerde. After that, Berlin and the status of civilian . . . Berlin, where Jutte waited for a letter.

From the armoury he drew the standard MPiKM of the border, and two magazine clips of ammunition. He was assigned to a junior NCO and awarded the night watch in the 40 feet high, square based concrete tower dominating the overgrown and tree strewn Walbeck Strasse. There was much cover on either side of the fence there, he was told, high alertness was demanded.

It was a short meeting at Bonn/Cologne airport.

Adam Percy had driven up from the German capital to be told that their business could be completed inside the airport. He wondered why Mawby had bothered to come, why their conversation should not be conducted by telephone or telex. Looking for reassurance and comfort, wanting his hand held and stroked with the news that all was according to plan and schedule. Ridiculous, Mawby flying over to be told that the German aspect was advancing. But not for Adam Percy to query the motives of his masters, not for 'out station Bonn' to question and deride.

Percy was able to confirm that Hermann Lentzer had allocated a driver to bring the car from Berlin to Helmstedt. He had also been informed that a forger had been found who would ride in the car to doctor the transit papers. A BMW 520 would be used for the run, stolen within the next 3 days in West Berlin, resprayed and with changed number plates and fraudulent documents. Better that way than using a hired car which was often subject to closer scrutiny at the border, Percy had remarked.

"They want to know, Mr Mawby, if we'll be giving them advance knowledge of the pick-up point?'

'No.'

'Tell them when they start the run.'

'When they start the run. It's a financial transaction, an unpleasant and dirty one.'

Percy did not betray his feelings. 'I'll pass that on.'

'Stay close to them, won't you . . .'

'They're as good as any. How good that is remains a matter of judgement.'

'It's the weakest link we have.'

'When you play around over there all the links are weak.'

They were sitting in the self-service cafeteria. Two coffees, two sticky cakes. Sitting with their heads close in a caricature of conspiracy.

'What's our man like, Mr Mawby?'

'We have no doubts that he'll cope. He has to . . . It will be the biggest show the Service mounts this year, that's what Dus says.'

Percy circled his spoon in the murk of his coffee. 'They're always the ones that go sour.'

'You're a damned pessimist.'

'That's been said before, Mr Mawby. You'll forgive me for saying so but I've also been called a realist. I'm an out of London man. All the plans that I make have to be put directly into operation. You get a bit jaundiced about the infallibility of programmes that descend from Century House.'

'Concern yourself with the autobahn run,' Mawby said acidly.

'I will, don't you worry, Mr Mawby.' Percy gazed back at him over his cup and his cake. Perhaps he should tell Charles Mawby that a sparrow from Wiesbaden had telephoned to report that he had let slip to his superior a British interest in Hermann Lentzer. Perhaps he should report to Charles Mawby that his secretary had twice fielded calls from a senior official of BND with the answer that Adam Percy was out of his office. Perhaps he should say to Charles Mawby that he had pleaded a cold to avoid attendance of a routine liaison meeting at which he would have sat opposite that same senior official.

Just a bloody nuisance, wasn't it? A bloody nuisance but peripheral to their business. And Mawby was paranoid about Lentzer and the autobahn run, Mawby would be heaving into the ceiling if the indiscretion were known to him. Better left unsaid. And it would all be smoothed over, the ruffled German feathers, when Mawby's show was curtained down.

Percy walked with Mawby to the departure gates, shook his hand and summoned a bleak smile and confided that he was sure that all would be well.

When he was back in his car, before starting the engine, Percy wrote in his memory pad a gutting of the instructions that he had been given about the transhipment of firearms and explosives that would be sent from London to Bonn by diplomatic bag, and which he must then arrange for delivery to East Berlin. Not a complicated task for him, the moving of a package to the British Embassy in the DDR's capital, but a wretched chore. All of those years that he had been in West Germany, a working lifetime of commitment, and still there were wet eared young men out from London like Charles Mawby who regarded him as little more than a messenger.

He imagined Mawby back in London, and the quip in Century House, 'Awkward old cuss, that Percy in Bonn, right for retirement time', but he'd seen them off in the past, the youthful and ambitious Assistant Secretaries, he'd survive Charles Mawby.

When Adam Percy was angry his ulcer hurt, and he bit his lower lip as he started the car.

Together the Member for Guildford and the Chief Constable of the county walked around the policeman's garden. Both men had heavy diaries of appointments and a Sunday afternoon provided the opportunity for them to blend their free time.

His wife did all the work, really, the Chief Constable had remarked. She was the one with the fingers to bring on the flowers and shrubs. He confined himself to keeping the grass cut, and he'd be doing that later, and that was a heavy enough hint that Sir Charles Spottiswoode should explain the reason for his visit.

'In confidence, right, that's understood . . .?'

'I'm always cautious of confidence. I'm a policeman, not a priest in confessional.' With his pen knife the Chief Constable sliced away the sucker stem from a rose bush.

'I've come to a friend for corroboration, and advice.'

'Try me. We've known each other enough years, we don't have to lay down ground rules.'

They paced the prim paths with the clear cut borders, they admired the blossom of the pear and apple trees, they bent to examine the rhododendron buds, they looked in the greenhouse at the coming tomatoes. And Sir Charles Spottiswoode talked of what Dennis Tweedle had told him at first hand, and what he had heard once removed of the experiences of Annabel Tweedle and Constable Potterton.

The Chief Constable led his guest to the centre of the handkerchief lawn. 'If it wasn't you I was talking to, if it was just your ordinary fellow from the public, then I'd say forget it. But a Member of Parliament doesn't have to forget anything. The incident at the Tweedle house took place, that I know. A young man being brought to the house in a state of distress, the local constable summoned and matching the boy with a missing person we'd been told to raise heaven and hell to find, that's all copper bottom. That end of the

145

county was crawling with spooks and to put it most kindly they were cavalier with my people. I can neither confirm nor deny what was said to Potterton in the Tweedle house, I've made it my business not to find out. I heard separately from Special Branch that the matter was connected with a property at Holmbury. We all know about that place and we leave it to itself . . . if it caught fire I doubt they'd let the Brigade in. I imagine that everything you say is true, and I don't want to know.'

'I only asked for corroboration.'

'You've had that . . . and in confidence.'

'In confidence.' The Member smiled and his hand touched the Chief Constable's arm, gripped at his shirt sleeve. 'We don't have private armies in this country. We don't tolerate people being dragged out of private homes by faceless men who aren't accountable . . .'

'You're not going to shout this lot off the rooftops?'

'It will go to the Prime Minister. All the smell, all the nastiness I'll tip on his desk. He won't love me for it, but a backbencher who does his job isn't there to be loved by Cabinet. They had no right, no authority to treat this boy in that way . . . and it'll not happen again.'

'You didn't come and see me, did you?'

'As you said, we've known each other enough years. It's a wonderful garden, it does your wife great credit.'

There were no porters to carry their two suitcases at the Hauptbahnhof at Magdeburg.

Erica lifted them down onto the platform and started the long slogging trek down the steps to the tunnel that ran underneath the tracks and that emerged in the hallway of the station. There was a warm and clammy heat, as if rain might lurk in the sun haze. She shouldered her way through the crowds that milled between the ticket windows and the information kiosk and the sweet and cigarette shop. Her father trailed behind, carrying her handbag and magazine and his briefcase. In front of them stretched the wide square of ornamental lawns and laid out flower beds and beyond that the grey façade of the International Hotel. The bags were at her feet on the pavement outside the station, and she flexed her hands and braced her muscles. A Soviet army corporal, far from home, loading freight onto a military lorry looked with a longing at the tall, slender girl and was slashed with the contempt of her glance. She wished Renate had been there to meet them, but Renate had written to say that she would be in Sangerhausen in the south because her aunt was ill, and she was sorry and would be back in Magdeburg as soon as it was possible. And her father's friends were not at the station because Otto Guttmann had dithered in posting his letters and the service between Moscow and the DDR was awful and she had not been prepared to nag him into earlier action. What an idiotic, unhappy way to arrive in a far away city, and God alone knew why they had to take rooms in that hotel, why just once they could not accept the invitation of friends. No one there to help her, and too short a distance for a taxi. Erica hurried forward, bent by the weight of the suitcases, and Otto Guttmann was panting as he tried to stay at her heels.

A pretty girl, an old man, and the start of a summer holiday.

Chapter Twelve

=

The days at Holmbury had slipped, tumbled, fallen away.

It was as Johnny would have wished and Carter was sensitive to the needs of his man. The final days for Johnny and the moments when he might brood in solitude were denied him. Pace and camaraderie were the order of the moment.

For Carter the atmosphere stretched back his memories to the days when he had been young and a new recruit of the Service and attached to Special Operations Executive in the last years of the war, when he had worked with men to be parachuted into occupied Europe. Thirty-five years later, 35 years of continental peace and nothing changed. The same tensions, the same belly flutters and loud laughter, the same fear of failure and the willing hopes of success. That was how Carter had learned to cosset and protect an agent, that was how he had acquired the knowledge of when to pamper and when to bully. They were all frightened, the young men who would suffer the abrupt snapping of the umbilical link, they all wanted their hand gripped by Henry Carter. This lad would not be pitched out of a swaying, slow running Mosquito bomber on a clouded night. He would take the train at 2 in the morning from Hannover . . . Didn't matter a damn, didn't alter the basics of the mission. Whether by parachute, whether by second class rail ticket, Johnny was going into enemy territory. There wouldn't be many who would recognise that destination. They wouldn't know, and fewer would care, that a young man was flirting with his life because he had been chosen to journey on their behalf. You're a maudlin old bugger, Henry Carter would say to himself.

It was going to be a hell of a show, one of the best.

Well, it had to be, didn't it?

They had all worked so bloody hard for this one, all of them.

Early in that week Carter drove Johnny to Aldershot. They went in the late afternoon, skirted the garrison town and presented themselves at the Guard House of the Parachute Regiment depot. Carter had parked in front of the lowered barricade across the camp entrance and slipped into the building to present his letter of introduction and to have his credentials inspected. A lance corporal in para smock and with the distinctive maroon beret jauntily worn had come with him to sit in the back of the car and act as guide to the range.

Carter and Johnny walked from the car towards the warrant officer who waited for them. They were led to a brick built hut, the formal army rectangle and on a chair was a smock and a pair of denim trousers, and on the floor was the weaponry. Johnny changed quickly. A long time since he had worn khaki and camouflage. Something stabbed at him, something from the far past, and the sweat ran a little on his forehead. Carter noticed and battered Johnny on the shoulder, won a slow and distant smile.

The warrant officer held a dark, paint chipped handgun, the outline frame of a metal shoulder stock, and in his other hand there dangled a cloth bag tied fast at the neck. Carter and Johnny followed him out onto the open ground and towards the firing zone. A red flag whipped high on a shaved larch post. Not a smart and neat and tidy place. Divoted ground, the wheel ruts of turning Land-Rovers, few trees, rough and worn grass. To the front there loomed a sloping wall of sand, fenced with long cut logs, and rising proudly before the wall was the blackened cardboard cutout in the shape of a human torso.

They stopped 50 yards from the target.

'Were you ever on a range before, sir?'

'Yes,' said Johnny, little more than a whisper.

'Military or civilian?'

'Military.'

'General or individual firing?'

'Both.'

'You are familiar with the procedures?'

'I know the procedures.'

The warrant officer lifted the gun for display and speedily screwed on the shoulder stock, then reached down to the bag and pulled clear three loaded stick magazines. He talked with a calm competence, a man familiar with his trade. 'They asked us to provide a Stechkin, had to get one out of the museum and re-arm it. We had one from the NLF in Sheik Othman back in the Aden days when One Para snaffled it. I've fired it myself and it works, won't blow your head off. The Soviet military don't use it now but it's available to the security police throughout the Warsaw Pact. Automatic, fires as long as the ammo lasts while the trigger's depressed. It's a blow back mechanism with the option of selective firing . . .'

'I've read about it.' Johnny wanted to feel a weapon in his hand again.

'There are some RGD 5s as well, we'll come to them later. Do you want wool for your ears?'

'No,' said Johnny.

Carter drew back, separated himself from the pair as they closed and Johnny bent to watch the loading of the pistol. Half a lifetime since Carter had handled a gun. Something vulgar about them, something crude that was abrasive to the modes of the Service.

Over 15 minutes Johnny emptied the three magazines into the target. Standing aimed shots, crouched on one knee and with both fists clamped on the weapon for steadied marksmanship, diving and rolling and firing in a whirl of movement, running on the spot for 15 seconds and then at the shout of the warrant officer the pivot to blast at the torso. All the drills, all the routine. Single and automatic. Planned and spontaneous.

And then the grenades and Carter was waved by the warrant officer into the observation tower with its shrapnel pocked walls and it didn't interest him to watch through the viewing slit as Johnny threw and dived to the ground.

When it was quiet Carter came down the steps and saw the

warrant officer examining the firing target and from that distance he could read the cheerfulness on Johnny's face. The man who had eclipsed some personal barrier, won back some trifle of respect, and Johnny was talking, animated and fast ... But it was against all the rules to take a gun. The team would have to live with that because Johnny was the one who was travelling, Johnny was going to Magdeburg.

Johnny loped away and headed for the hut. Carter and the warrant officer walked after him.

'What's he like?' Carter asked with diffidence.

'If it's one to one then he'd survive, perhaps with a bit to spare. I'm taking it that this isn't just a refresher, I'm reckoning that the next time would be for broke. Well, he'd be all right. It would be an unlucky bastard that faced him.'

'Thank you.'

'But don't forget that I said one to one.' The warrant officer's stare beaded into Carter's face. 'Not one to three, not one to four. The best men don't win then.'

'It won't come to that.' The doubt swam at Carter's mouth.

The warrant officer made no reply. Carter was anxious to be gone, to get clear of this place and back to the house at Holmbury. He waited at the door of the hut for Johnny to come out dressed again in his civilian clothes, and then they were in the car and away towards the main road. Carter drove fast, hammering the accelerator more than was usual for him.

Johnny turned in his seat towards Carter. 'I want to go a couple of days early, spend a couple of days in West Germany on my own.'

'Why?'

'I want to talk German again, just for a couple of days.'

'We can get people down to Holmbury for that.'

'That's how I want it. I think it's important. Just a couple of days, just for listening. I wouldn't ask if I didn't think it was necessary.'

'It's a bit bloody late to be mucking things — why didn't

151

you speak earlier?'

'Before, I didn't think it necessary, now I do.'

'It's ridiculous, you swanning about over there just for language – bloody daft.'

'It's my neck in Magdeburg, Mr Carter, not yours.'

'I'll talk to Mawby.' Bloody contract man, thought Carter, not the same as if it had been a staffer.

They were back at the house in time for dinner. Johnny was in good form that evening, even chatty, even making jokes. And he asked for a whisky before he went to bed.

'. . . What happened when you were called to the Tweedle household, Potterton, and the things that you subsequently heard do not fall, in my judgment, under the heading of police business,' the Chief Constable intoned. 'I've not asked you for a written report because in these matters it's better that paperwork doesn't exist. When you deal with security and intelligence people the only safe course is to believe that they know best, otherwise you're in a can of worms. I am formally instructing you not to discuss this episode with any person without my express permission. If a slanging match is going to start I won't have my force as the punchbag in the middle. Is that clear?'

'Perfectly, sir. I'll be away back to the village then, sir.'

The Chief Constable watched his man leave. Perhaps he had overplayed the heavy hand, but it would be for the best.

The Chief Constable had available to him lines of communication through to the Director of the Security Services. The channels existed, protocol would not be breached if he were to utilise them. It was possible for him to warn Peter Fenton of the information gathered by Sir Charles Spottiswoode. Possible, but not desirable. What applied to his subordinates was also relevant to himself.

The Trabant jeep bumped and whined along the concrete patrol strip. Three kilometres west of Walbeck, where the frontier split the Roteriede woods. The jeeps were always noisy, victims of the petrol that was mixed for the sake of economy.

To the left of the driver was the 'Sperrgraben', the deep vehicle ditch.

Beyond that the 'Kontrollstreifen', the ploughed strip that was harrowed and virgin and waiting to betray footmarks and human disturbance.

The driver's eyes ranged from the road to the smoothed earth and on towards the 'Metallgitterzaun', the metal mesh fence, dark from weather, lightened only by the cement poles and the close set 'Automatische Schubanlagen'. All of this section was covered by the automatic guns.

The driver would be the same age as Ulf Becker, but a smaller, slighter boy. Short in conversation, high in a patronising parade of his sense of duty. Boring little pig, Becker thought.

But Ulf Becker also followed the orders of their NCO and studied closely the cover and terrain that slipped past them. Becker looked right. Past the occasional signs that warned of mine fields. Past the watchtowers and earth bunkers. Past the communications poles where a portable telephone could be plugged in if there were radio failure. Past the scrub bushes that grew on the ground that had been cleared. Past the high tree line of pines that lay a full 100 metres back from the patrol road. The border here followed inevitably on the rolling contours and gentle hills of the woods. The engine would strain to the minor summits before the coast down into the next valley. Not like Weferlingen, not flat and easily observed. Dead ground, covered ground, hidden and secure. A good place this, two kilometres on from the watch-tower on the Walbeck Strasse where he had spent a night on duty. But the earth bunkers were manned at dusk and the men there carried the infra-red binoculars . . . they could be skirted. The jeep patrols were frequent after darkness . . . their lights and their engines removed the possibility of surprise. But there were the Grenzaufklarer, the specialist troops whose duty patterns were not posted, whose patrol programmes were not divulged . . . that was a chance.

Becker's hands gripped the stock and barrel of the MPiKM that rested against his legs.

The whole matter was a chance.

In the pocket of his blouse was Jutte's photograph, encased in cellophane protection. He would have liked to have looked at it, drawn it out, and gazed at the grey shades of her face in the picture. Not in front of this bloody pig.

The whole matter was a chance.

But the greatest barriers were away in the seclusion of the woods. Not here in the final metres but back and beyond the Hinterland fence, back and beyond in the Restricted Zone. Not one obstacle there, but a dozen.

Did Ulf Becker have the guts for the challenge?

Not until he had seen the Hinterland fence . . . but that was evasion of the principle.

He must see the Hinterland fence. What if that, too, offered the possibility? . . . Then he must see the Restricted Zone.

And if that, too, offered the possibility? Then . . . they would shoot them here. Shoot them if they were found near the wire. The high velocity bullets in the magazine of the MPiKM, capable of killing at a range of a kilometre. What would they do at 25 metres to the body of Jutte? A sweet, clean and perfect shape. How would she seem to him when the clip of shells had dropped her.

They would butcher the two of them, the guns on the wire, the guns of the patrols. Arc lights flashing, illumination flares falling, attack dogs barking. Jutte, bloody in death and thrown into a jeep such as this one. Ulf Becker, bones fractured, bowels ripped by gunfire, slung beside her. No mercy inside the Hinterland fence, no pity within the Restricted Zone. He could not make the commitment until he had seen more. And he remembered her, on the platform at Schöneweide, heard her voice that was ringing and sharp, saw her eyes that were bright and bold in the dimness of the station lights.

Ulf Becker spat down onto the roadway.

There were many who had entertained the possibility, and

where were they now? Shuttered in the flats and factories of the Deutsche Demokratische Republik, bound to women and babies, trapped in stinking apathy. The opportunity would only come once, it would go with the sureness of night, it would never be repeated. If he did not find the place at Walbeck then he must stand amongst the ranks of those who had harboured a dream and who had failed to discover the determination for the final assault at the fence.

Even to contemplate it was idiocy . . . Then Ulf Becker was a creature of the herd.

Better alive and a machine tool worker, than dead . . . Then he had deceived the girl.

The driver brought the jeep to a halt. Becker waved to the earth bunker and was rewarded with a white hand acknowledging his gesture and protruding through the firing slit. The driver swung on his wheel and drove back the way that they had come.

The slow routine of holiday was settling on Otto Guttmann. The pace of Padolsk was abandoned, the endeavour of the laboratory sidestepped.

In those first three days he had been to the Palast-Theater to see an old Italian film. He had cruised at snail pace in the Weisse Flotte boat on the Elbe-Havel Kanal to Genthin – all day and for 7 marks. He had browsed in the bookshops of Karl Marx Strasse and beside the Kloster Unser Lieben Frauen, handling with something like reverence the range of books in his native tongue. He had sat with a magazine and a small beer, at the open air café looking across the Alter Markt towards the old and renovated Rathaus. He had watched the young people of Magdeburg, laundered and fresh in their uniform of sports shirts and floral frocks. He had dreamed, and closed his mind to the slide rules and drawing boards and the firing range.

The sunshine blessed, warm and clear air bathed him.

Now he went, slowly and in his own time, to visit his valued friend at the Dom, the cathedral. A friend of his own generation and one long revered because he was a pastor of the Evangelical order, living in a dilapidated cottage sandwiched between the high cathedral walls and the sloping banks of the Elbe, a man who had not compromised.

Not easy he thought as he walked beneath the great twin towers of the cathedral, to carry on the work of a pastor under the rule of socialism. Not simple to watch the church that one treasured stripped of its influence and authority, left merely as an institution of worship to the elderly, denied its former role of administration over the kindergartens and the youth clubs and the hospitals. The erosion of the church's position had been managed with a subtlety. No jackboots and no padlocks. The sprawling new housing estates rose without a church in their midst, young Christians found it even harder to gain the coveted places in secondary and higher education, political precepts ruled. His friend, the pastor, had struggled on through succeeding years, prepared for boldness when bravery would win the day, prepared for acquiescence when subservience dictated the greater advantage. A man who over many years had earned Otto Guttmann's admiration and love.

Men in the latter days of their lives. Men who could gossip and chuckle with a private and closed humour. The pastor would shrug with pain when the scientist told him of his work at Padolsk and put his short and muscled arm up to Guttmann's shoulder and squeeze the sparse flesh. Old men, who in their talk could offer comfort the one to the other.

Their meeting was heavy with affection and cheeks were kissed in a spontaneous happiness and they gazed into each other's faces. The advances of age were ignored and they complimented themselves on their health and put aside their misfortunes. The pastor held tight at Otto Guttmann's hand when the death of Willi was talked of.

Later there would be a salad lunch. Guttmann explained that Erica was with her friend. He had no more commitments for the day and much to speak about.

The two men walked on the medieval flagstones of the cathedral cloister, far from the factories of the city, far from

156

the industry and its chimneys. They sucked at the air that was rich with the scent of the freshly cut grass of the inner lawn.

They sat close together on the settee. Erica Guttmann and Renate, the friends since childhood.

It was a man's flat, no doubts that her friend was the lodger. The choice of the wall pictures told her that, women with naked backs coyly turned and water colour renderings of apples and lemons in china bowls. The furniture was gaunt and inappropriate to the small room. Cardboard cased files draped the shelves, no books, no ornaments. A living room, a bedroom, a bathroom, and a kitchen, the home of a single man.

'Can't he do better than this, the senior man of the Schutzpolizei?' Erica giggled with the conspiracy of her question.

'There's the fat cow, his wife. She has the old home and he can't boot her out. At his level he's supposed to be the living legend of domestic rectitude. It's bad enough for him having it known that he's taken me in, if he heaves her then the whole town will be clucking.' Rich laughter from the two girls.

'I nearly collapsed when I had your letter, you and a policeman. You'll tell me, won't you, what he's like?'

'Like a bull,' Renate said quickly, evasively. 'He'll have a hert attack the rate he goes at it.'

A sorry little silence flitted on them. Out of place for Renate to have said that. Erica had no boy, had never written of one in her monthly letters, seemed to shun them. Over many years she had talked to Renate of lovers and always her interest carried the eddy of insincerity.

'Am I going to meet him?'

'He said he'd come home for lunch. Not my cooking that he wants, it's to see you. He says I talk interminably about you.' Renate paused, a brittle smile at her mouth. 'I hope you like him, and there weren't many to choose from, you know.'

'Rubbish.'

'I'm not a little chicken any more.'

'Rubbish.'

There was a key in the door, the sound of feet scraping a mat. The Schutzpolizeipresident for the city of Magdeburg, Dr Gunther Spitzer, came into his living room. The homecoming of the Director of the Security Police.

Erica was drawn from her chair. The girl who over the telephone could turn down the request of a Soviet Army full colonel for time in her father's office found herself standing and wiping a sliver of perspiration from the palm of her hand against the seam of her dress. A mountain of a man, advancing across the small room, a cloud crossing the face of the moon. Renate, casual on the settee, unconcerned and flicking her fingers in greeting. Erica shuffling and unable to look away from the ribbon scar that trailed from the centre of his forehead to the straggled bush of his right eyebrow. Unable to see beyond the heavy jowl cheeks where the stubble won through the pale skin. How could Renate have chosen this one?

'Darling, this is Erica . . .'

'I am very pleased to meet you, Fräulein Guttmann.'

His hand was pushed forward. Clothed in a glove of thin black leather. God, it's a bloody claw. A thought ravished her. How did he touch her, her friend Renate, with this . . .? Did he wear it in her bed? Did the claw run against her skin?

'I am very pleased to meet you, Dr Spitzer.'

The hand was withdrawn, seemed to fall to the side of his jacket. 'You live in Moscow, I understand. I have never been there. Only outside Moscow, once I was 40 kilometres from the Red Square. That was where I left my hand. It was 38 years ago. Since then I have not wished to try again to reach that place.' He smiled. 'Your father is enjoying his stay in Magdeburg, I hope.'

'Very much, thank you.'

'Has it been a busy morning, darling?' Renate intervened, as if to offer rescue to her friend.

'Quite busy. I have been talking to the driver of a car that was stopped at Marienborn. The car had been broken down for 2 hours on the autobahn before it reached the check-point. The car was searched and in the boot was found a man and a woman and a baby. The baby . . .'

'I didn't mean a case history, darling. I'm sure it's of no interest to Erica.'

'The baby had been tranquillised so that it would not cry and alert the frontier guards at Marienborn. When the boot was opened it was found that the baby was dead, probably suffocated in the heat caused by the delay of the engine trouble . . .'

'God . . . God . . .' Erica felt her stomach heave, felt the bile pitch to her throat.

'You didn't have to tell us that,' Renate blazed.

'The driver of the car is a West German, also a heroin addict, also he was paid 3,000 west marks. He will be fortunate if his sentence is less than 8 years. I have been quite busy this morning talking to this driver, finding who sends these criminals into our country . . . My sweet, I have a table at the Broiler Gaststatte. We should go now.'

Renate went into the kitchen to turn off the gas taps, abandon the meal that she had prepared.

As they walked down the stairs to the street entrance of the building, Erica felt a growing sadness, a deepening loss. She had lost a friend. They would never talk again, not as they had before.

'Did you get my note?' Sir Charles Spottiswoode caught at the PPS's arm. He had followed him from the Chamber to the door of the Members' Tea Room.

'About what?' The PPS rocked back. This one the same as most of the old fools, halitosis and no one with the courage to tell him to suck peppermints.

'I requested a meeting with the PM.'

'He's under fair pressure at the moment. I haven't fixed anything.' The PPS tugged at his arm, hoping to break the hold and was unsuccessful.

'I want to see the PM and soon.'

'Can't someone else help you?'

'It's the PM I want to see.'

'What's it about?' It was not suitable for the PPS to be involved in public argument. A corridor of the House of Commons was a very public place.

'Not your business.'

'I'm hardly going to waste his time on that basis. He's got four days in Scotland, then the economic debate . . .'

'The more you delay the harder your soft arse will be kicked when I've seen him.' Spottiswoode's voice rose, drawing a honeypot of attention, and his grip on the PPS's coat tightened.

'You'll get to him, I promise. I'll fix it while we're in Scotland.'

'Monsieur Foirot, is that you . . . can you hear me? It is Sharygin.'

'You have a very bad line.'

'Sharygin . . . from the Soviet Residence . . . you can hear me?'

'You are very faint . . .'

'I am calling from Moscow . . .'

'I can just hear you, Monsieur Sharygin, how can I help you?'

'The boy who drowned, you remember . . . the accident with the boat on the lake . . . Guttmann . . . has the body been found?'

'No.'

'I did not hear you, Monsieur Foirot . . .'

'The body of Guttmann has not been found, we have not found it . . . if it had been recovered the Residence would have been informed.'

'Of course, of course . . . but it is abnormal this length of time . . .'

'Yes.'

'You agree that it is abnormal . . . that you have not found the body is strange.'

160

'I am a policeman, I am not an expert of the lake, but I know it is abnormal.'

'You cannot explain why the body has not surfaced.'

'I cannot explain it.'

'I see . . . thank you, Monsieur Foirot.'

'For nothing, Monsieur Sharygin.'

Johnny stood on the patio, gazed out into the darkness beyond the crescent of light from the french windows. He shook his arms gently beside him, trembled the muscles in his legs, wound down from the heights of his exercise session. The last time that he would strive for greater strength in his thighs and at the stomach wall and for his lungs. The last evening at the house. The last of everything.

'I brought you a cup of tea . . .'

Johnny stiffened, turned, saw Mrs Ferguson, still in her apron.

'That's very sweet of you, thanks.'

'Mr Mawby's just come . . .'

'I heard the car, I'd better be getting inside.'

'You're away early in the morning Mr Carter says.'

'That's right, on my travels, something like that anyway.'

'Keep safe, Johnny.'

His hand shook and the cup rattled in the saucer and the tea spoon chimed against the china. He heard her feet pattering back towards the rear door that served the kitchen. For a few moments he watched the cloud gunning across the face of a small moon, picked out star patterns, then abruptly swung to the french windows, opened them and stepped into the living room.

Mawby stood in the centre of the carpet, Carter was sitting reading, Smithson and Pierce played backgammon near the fire. That's the team, Johnny, that's the Dipper's back-up. As good as you could expect, as bad as you were likely to find. Pretty average, and why should it be anything else? Johnny took a chair near the window.

'Fit and ready, Johnny?' Mawby said heartily.

'As fit as I ought to be.'

161

'I wanted to see you before you went off, that's why I came down. Henry put your case about going these two days early, said you wanted to rub-up your language in West Germany for 48 hours . . .'

'That's right.'

'You kept it for the last, sprung the idea late.'

'I said to Mr Carter that I thought it important.'

'I'm not making a thing of it, Johnny. I'm not forbidding it . . .' Mawby paused and Johnny saw his tiredness, the strain at his eyes and the nerves that chipped at the façade of calm. 'You're in Magdeburg, and we're not, I understand your attitude. There's something that I've said before, but which I want to emphasise again . . . if it goes nasty, if it starts to slide, then you quit. You don't risk capture. It's critical that you remember that. If it's falling apart, out you come, regardless of any other consideration. Is that clear?'

'That's very clear, Mr Mawby.'

'Good hunting. We'll have a bit of a party when we meet up again.'

There was a half smile at Johnny's face. 'I'll look forward to that.'

'I expect you want to get yourself a shower, and put your things together . . .'

There was an awkwardness settling in the room, all grown men and none knowing the script of the occasion.

'I'd like to do that.'

Mawby stared at Johnny and the gleaming public confidence of a few seconds before had been stripped. A naked and uncovered face.

'It's a good plan, isn't it, Johnny . . . it ought to work . . .'

'Doesn't matter if it's a good plan or not. It's the one that we have. Good night, Mr Mawby.'

'Good night, Johnny,' Mawby said. 'And good luck . . .'

Johnny closed the door quietly behind him, slowly climbed the stairs. Time to pack the few belongings that he had brought from Cherry Road.

Chapter Thirteen

=

The routine of the house at Holmbury had swiftly changed course.

Johnny gone, Mawby back for a night and then away, Smithson and Pierce heading for London.

A house of echoes and memories as it had been many times before. And the moment for the boy to be told.

Two mornings after the exodus Carter took Willi outside. A fine, cheerful morning and Carter pushed a wheelbarrow with a fork in it and handed a hoe to the boy and suggested that if the weather held up they could put in a day's weeding and tidy the old place. They needed some fresh air, had been cooped up long enough, had earned the right to unwind before the launching. The wheelbarrow dented the grass as it was taken to the middle of the lawn in front of the house and Carter gazed around him at the acreage of flower beds with their vermin weeds. Where to start . . . begin with the roses. It had been an impromptu idea over breakfast, and so he was dressed in his familiar two piece suit. He tucked the ends of his trousers into his socks. They would have to clean their shoes meticulously afterwards or Mrs Ferguson would scalp them, but nobody had ever thought to provide wellington boots at the house, nobody had ever thought of gardening as a useful therapy for defectors. George would be watching them from the patio, sitting on the oakwood bench and pretending the newspaper he had collected from the front gate held his attention. George would be watching the boy.

They started at the rose bed. Willi hoeing at the grass tufts, loosening them and throwing them into the barrow. Carter discarding his jacket onto the branch of a small birch and turning the cleaned earth. They worked close to each other, a few feet apart.

'You remember when we went to London, what I said then, about helping us?' Carter puffed and his hands rested comfortably on the fork's handle.

The boy chopped at the grass. 'I remember, Mr Carter.'

'I said then that if you helped us, we would help you.'

'You said something like that, Mr Carter.' Willi did not look up, no emotion on his face. A neutered thing they had made of him since his return to the house.

'We are very pleased with the way that you have helped us, Willi, and in particular with the way that you co-operated after Johnny came down here. You've earned the truth from us. And with the truth you'll be able to help us all the better in the last stage of what we plan.'

Willi gouged at the earth beneath the grass roots.

'What is the truth, Mr Carter?'

Carter hadn't reached Johnny and he hadn't reached the boy. He remembered how he had once heard his neighbours talking over the garden fence and unaware that he was within earshot. 'He's a dull old cove', the husband had said; 'a proper queer blighter', the wife had replied. Not a man who excited trust, was he? God knows, and he tried. And the suit and the briefcase and the tale of government business and the long periods away, they weren't Henry Carter's fault. But that was the verdict of his neighbours. Dull and queer . . . If he couldn't find Johnny's soul then he must find the boy's.

Carter said, 'It's our hope, Willi, that within a week you will be reunited with your father . . .'

The boy's head flicked round. A voltage charge through him. Eyes wide, mouth sagging, hoe held limp.

'. . . within a week we will have your father in the West. You will be together again. Your father, yourself, and we presume your sister also. That's what we have all been working towards. That's what everything that has been happening here has been aimed at. We are bringing your father out.'

Carter smiled with affection, saw a tear dribble on the cheek of the boy, saw the hands clench in astonishment.

164

God, it was unfair what he had done to the kid. Unfair, and he looked into the opened face and saw the disbelief faltering with the child-joy.

'The DDR are releasing my father to emigrate?'

'No.'

'It is not possible then . . . how is it possible?'

'I said that we are bringing your father out.'

'You will try to bring him through the frontier?' the boy challenged and the happiness was sinking.

'We will bring him out on the autobahn.'

'What does my father say of this?'

'At this moment he is unaware of the plan.'

'My father has not been told, he does not know?'

'No.'

'And the authorities in the DDR have not given permission for him to leave?'

'No.'

Willi threw the hoe down onto the ground, slapped his hands together to shake off the earth. He spoke very quietly.

'You take a great risk.'

'We have worked very hard at the plan, Willi.'

'The risk that you take is not with yourselves, it is with my father and my sister. You endanger them.'

Carter gazed into the small and now frightened face of the boy. 'We think that we have minimised the risk to them. Everything has been thought of, most carefully.'

'Johnny is the man who is going to see my father in Magdeburg?'

'Johnny will talk to him.'

'What will he say to him? How will he persuade him to make the journey?'

Carter sighed and his composure was diminished. It was not the path the conversation should have followed. There should not have been the gun rattle of questions, only gratitude and wonderment was wanted from the boy.

'I don't know the details, Willi,' Carter said. Evasive and

165

with his confidence derailed. 'That's Johnny's side and Mawby's. But without you, Willi, the chance slackens. I'm very serious . . .'

'Without me the attempt will fail, or without me my father will not be persuaded to make the journey. Which, Mr Carter?'

Little bugger, clever question. Carter could have slapped him. He held himself, dragged at the reins of self-restraint. 'If you ever want to see your father again you do exactly what we tell you during the next week. Everything, to the word, to the letter, without question. Understand this, Willi, we'll try to bring him out anyway, we'll make that attempt. If you obstruct us then we may fail, if you help us then we have a better chance. It's very simple, Willi.'

'Why do you want my father? He is an old man. Why do you ask him to do this?' Like a cat with a field mouse, the boy would not release the meat from his mouth. 'You threaten him, why? You endanger him, why?'

'You're his son, I should have thought you'd be grateful for what we're doing.'

'I'm not a fool, Mr Carter,' the boy's voice was rising. Behind him George had eased up from the bench, folded a newspaper and placed a stone over it to save the pages from the wind, and was coming across the lawn. 'I'm not an idiot. You do not do this for charity, you do not do it for me. Perhaps even for him you do not do it. Why can you not leave him to live in peace for his last years?'

'Then you'll never see him again.'

'You make a bait of me, you make me as a tethered goat. I am the bribe that you offer him . . .'

'You said that he loved you.'

'I said that he loved me. I answered your question, I did not know why you asked . . .'

Carter gripped at Willi's arm, trying to turn him, trying to succour him. Earnest and encouraging. 'We've been thorough, Willi, as thorough as possible. There's no danger to your father. He's going to be safe, and he's going to be with you.'

The boy shrugged the hand away, was at his full height and the colour glowed in his cheeks.

'Who gives you this right to tempt and taunt an old man with the love of his son? What authority do you have to chance the wrecking of my father's life?'

'Without your help we may fail . . .'

'You're evil, all of you. You and Johnny and . . . the man who comes and you all crawl to.'

'With your help we may succeed.'

The tears ran fast now on the face of the boy. 'You play a game with the love of an old man.'

'It won't be like that, lad.' Carter hated tears, was always terrified when his wife wept and he was useless and clumsy and unable to comfort. He tried to put his arm on Willi's shoulder and was pushed away. 'It won't be like that, I promise you, Willi.'

Deftly Carter waved George back. He bent down and lifted the handle of the hoe and passed it again to the boy. Then with his fork he started to dig at the earth that he had trampled flat and beside him he heard the scraping of the hoe and the thud of clotted weeds hitting the walls of the wheelbarrow.

It was a gloomy pilgrimage for the Prime Minister.

The West of Scotland was traditional misery for the politician in office. More of a disaster than a development area. The crowds that had come to see him heckled, the press that had questioned him carped at his answers, the managements that he had met dropped their heads and spoke of bleak forecasts for the future. And damn near a whole week to be spent there. He had walked through shipyards, through shopping centres, through engineering works and with each day he had believed less and less in the buoyant words of his speechwriters.

There were three cars and two police motorcycle outriders in the convoy that drove at speed for the new housing development at Cumbernauld. His speech in reply to the Mayor's welcome rested typed in his jacket pocket. The red boxes of government papers were in the car behind him that carried the Downing Street team of civil servants. He could sit back in his seat, spaced from his PPS by the arm rest and talk without constraint, confident that at least here he was saved from badgering dispute.

'It's the shame of being away for so many days, the diary is. clogged solid when we're back in London,' the Prime Minister murmured. 'Is the weekend clear?'

'Not so as you'd notice, sir. We're hoping to get you off to Chequers after lunch on Friday . . .'

'Thank God for that. It's the closest thing to heaven in this job, going down there, the only thing about it that Dorothy likes.'

'It won't be all fun time. You've a constituency garden party speech on Saturday afternoon, and you've the East German Trade Minister as your dinner guest in the evening.'

'Riveting entertainment that will be.'

'Sunday's clear . . .'

'Small mercy after Saturday night.'

The PPS scrutinised the large desk diary that he regarded as perhaps his most important possession of work. 'Small mercy as you say, and it's heavy too before you can run to the country, sir. There's Cabinet, Overseas Policy and Defence, Questions in the House, and the Censure debate, that's Thursday . . . And one more cross I haven't fitted in yet. The Member for Guildford, Spottiswoode, he wants to see you.'

'What about?' the Prime Minister drawled, he was close to sleep.

'Wouldn't tell a lowly minion. But I'm to have my backside kicked if it's not attended to, that's a promise.'

'He's a poisonous old bastard, like every other passed over politician. A buffoon who has to be tolerated because he gets a damned great cheer at Party Conference each autumn. Fit him in at the House on Thursday evening, I'll see him in my room while the debate's on.'

*

'Good of you to have come in, Charles, you must be up to your neck.'

'A touch frantic, sir. The lad goes over tomorrow night . . .'

'I remember the feeling. A long time back, but I don't suppose things have changed much.' Late evening, and Charles Mawby had been called to the Deputy-Under-Secretary's office high in Century House, and had been sat down with a glass of amontillado sherry. 'Always a little fraught in the last few hours.'

'We've worked pretty hard at it, it's been a good team effort, and I'm very happy with the freelancer . . .'

'From what you tell me you chose well, doesn't sound the sort of chappie who'll let you down.'

'He's level headed enough, I've a deal of confidence in him.'

Mawby talked of the specifics of DIPPER and this was an armchair session, a conversation without pen and paper. There were few questions to interrupt him. It was perhaps the highest enjoyment known to the Deputy-Under-Secretary, to bask in the commitment of his subordinates, to hear of their skills and preparation. He heard again of Johnny and the progress of the last days at Holmbury. He listened to the résumé of the plan for the autobahn pick-up. He was told of the documentation that had been printed to bring Otto Guttmann and his daughter through the Marienborn check. He nodded in approval as the need for the forger in the car was explained. His face tickled in amusement at Mawby's scathing word portrait of Hermann Lentzer.

'It's first class, Charles.'

'We're all of us pretty happy with it.'

'And you've every right to be. You seem to have been up all the cul-de-sacs, given them the once over, and fenced them off. We don't deserve to have this go wrong on us.'

Mawby hesitated. Easy here in the safety and cosiness of the Deputy-Under-Secretary's office, simple to be confident and assured. And he hadn't stressed the vagaries of 'local conditions'. He had not highlighted the shadow areas of uncertainty.

'It can't be watertight, sir. There has to be an area of the imponderable . . .'

'Of course, Charles . . . I understand, I've done it myself. I stood once at Helmstedt waiting for a car to come through. Hideous experience, in '49 or '50, damned cold and middle of winter. Three days I was there, and the car never came. Seemed important at the time.'

'I think we're fine with this one.'

'I'm sure you are, and when you've a few more under your belt you'll wonder why you ever worried.'

'The concept is straightforward. That's been the planning strategy from the start. No frills and no histrionics. I'm relying a lot on that.'

'I don't think you do yourself justice, Charles. You'll ring me when you have the old man over . . .'

'You'll know immediately.'

The pleasant smile slipped from the Deputy-Under-Secretary's face, exchanged for a keenness that beckoned attention from Mawby. 'There can't be a slip, not with this one. Downing Street have a senior East German minister in tow when you're tripping down the autobahn. I don't want any embarrassments, no messes on the floor. You're with me . . .?'

'At Downing Street, do we have approval or ignorance?' Mawby asked, the junior man intruding into the uplands of policy, the nervous question.

'Just ring me when you're all wrapped up, Charles. I'll be waiting for the call.'

From his room in the Prime Minister's Glasgow hotel, the PPS telephoned the House of Commons office of Sir Charles Spottiswoode.

'Good evening, Sir Charles, I've spoken to the Prime Minister about your request for a meeting. He's a very heavy schedule when he gets back to London, but he'll see you on

Thursday in his room at the House. He wants to hear the start of the debate, and then he'll have to make the revisions for his own speech, so I've written you in for 6.30 . . . It's been nothing, Sir Charles, the PM is always anxious to be available to the back benches . . . It's kind of you to say that . . . Good night . . .'

Pompous old beggar. Sweetness and light when he'd won his petty victory. He dived for the shower, and his dress suit was laid out on the bed and he was late for dinner and the Prime Minister hated tardiness.

It was close to midnight when the transport dropped Ulf Becker at Company in Weferlingen.

His last duty of service with the unit on the frontier and they had seemed none too happy to let him go from Walbeck. The epidemic of measles was spreading and the two sections were staying on in their reinforcement role. At least he was spared Heini Schalke's company on the road back, just himself and a morose Feldwebel who drove the Trabant jeep in silence. It had to be a senior NCO to justify the paperwork required to set aside the strictures of the ten o'clock curfew inside the Restricted Zone. There had been a few goodbyes at Walbeck, some of the seconded Weferlingen boys had wished him well and spoken without enthusiasm of a reunion; Schalke hadn't joined them, had stayed with his book.

They had taken their last pint of blood from soldier Ulf Becker, had him out all day from dawn with sandwiches for lunch and soup from a flask in the early evening. Not that he cared. Not that hunger and tiredness would worry the boy, and the damp from the rain that had caught them without their capes. Ulf Becker had tramped and driven for more than ten hours behind the Hinterland fence, he had patrolled both sides of the Schwanefeld to Eschenrode road, with his eyes wide and his hopes soaring. A good briefing they had given him . . . trip wires on this track, acoustic alarms on that path, dogs running on fixed wires on this sector, the road block round that curve and hidden by that bank . . . a good, sweet, kind and conscientious officer had been with them and had been at pains to make certain that the new boys from Weferlingen knew the scene at Walbeck in the most minute detail.

The Feldwebel set him down at the gates of the barracks, didn't acknowledge his thanks and sped away into the night. He'd have a woman or a beer waiting for him, otherwise there would have been no lift. Becker went in search of an officer to report his return and then roved through the kitchens that were darkened and cold; nothing to eat. He went into the communal room. There was another boy there, a lonely one that he barely knew beyond that he was short of friends and likely to pester anyone within his range for company and gossip. Becker slumped into a chair. Too excited for bed, too exhilarated for sleep. His mind was alive with the memories of woodland tracks, alert with the width of the cleared ground straddling the Hinterland fence, brimming with the fall and rise of the land, the density of the woodland.

'Hello.'

'Hello,' said Becker. He must have smiled, his face must have thrown some warmth.

'I'm on leave tomorrow.'

'Wonderful.'

'I'm going home, the first time that I've been home since I've been here.'

'Good.'

'Back to Berlin, that's where my home is.'

'That's good.'

'Don't misunderstand me . . . it's not that I'm not enjoying the work here. I mean, it's a privilege to be posted to the Border Guard . . . it's an elite force, it's an honour to be entrusted with such work . . . I don't complain about it, we're in the force to work, but I think that I've earned my leave.'

That's right lad, trust nobody, not in this pit of snakes.

172

Perhaps you hate it, perhaps you cry yourself to sleep each night, perhaps the homesickness chokes you. But don't tell. Trust no bastard . . . Make out it's a holiday camp.

'You are going to Berlin tomorrow?'

'My home is in Berlin. My father is a building worker. He is an old Berliner, from the Tiergarten district. I will have a fine welcome when I get home, they will all want to know of the work that I am doing . . .'

'How long are you going for?'

'I have three days there. There will be a party at home. It is only a 72 hour pass and then I am back here. I am looking forward to being here for the summer.'

'Would you take a letter for me?' There was a hoarseness in Becker's voice.

The boy recognised the change, was cautioned by it. 'A letter?'

Becker raced his explanation. 'It's Monday, right? I'm going to Berlin on Friday. I have a girl in Berlin. I want her to know that I am coming back for the weekend. You know how it is, you know, don't you?'

'You want me to deliver a letter tomorrow to your girl?'

'She lives on Karl-Marx Allee. Near to the cinema and the Moskva Restaurant. If you are taking the train from Schöneweide you must go through Alexander Platz, it's 5 minutes' walk from there.'

'I suppose that I could . . .'

'I'd really be most grateful.' As if Ulf Becker's gratitude mattered. Gone in the morning for Seggerde and demobilisation. On the way out of Weferlingen and uniform. The gratitude would never be recompensed, and the idiot hadn't the brain to see it.

'I will do that for you.'

'Give me 5 minutes to write something.'

He loped down the corridor to the Operations Room, was given two sheets of scrap paper and an envelope, came back to the communal room and settled at a table.

'Just give me a few minutes, right?'

'Fine,' the boy said. He would tell his father that he had many friends in the company.

Ulf Becker wrote fast in his spider crawl.

Darling Jutte,

I have found someone who will deliver this. I am coming to Berlin on Friday night or early on Saturday morning.

You must make some excuse to be away on Saturday night, perhaps an FDJ camp. You must bring waterproof clothing and something warm. Buy two rail tickets – returns – for Suplingen which is a camping place west of Haldensleben.

We should meet on Saturday morning at 10.30 in front of the Stadt Berlin, Alexander Platz.

I have found that place.

I love you, Ulf.

Weferlingen Monday June 9th.'

He folded the two sheets of paper, put them into the envelope, licked that and stuck it tight, and wrote on it the address to which it should be delivered.

'I'm really very grateful to you.'

'It's nothing.'

Of course it was nothing . . . because if this bastard were at Walbeck next week and Ulf Becker and his girl were in the rifle sights then he would shoot. He would shoot, and there would be no crying over it, not from him and not from any of them in the company.

Would he have written that letter in the morning? After he had slept, when the light had come again, when he'd queued for breakfast, when he had made his bed, when the barracks throbbed in activity, would he have written it then? But it was written and it was in the boy's blouse pocket, and Jutte would have it when she came home in the afternoon of the next day.

'Good night,' said Ulf and walked from the room to his bed.

Over the years it had become the habit for Carter to buy a gift for presentation to Mrs Ferguson on the last morning of the occupancy of the house. Sometimes some flowers, sometimes a piece of imitation jewellery, sometimes a box of dark chocolates.

That would be his final duty before leaving for Heathrow and his flight to Hannover, and George and Willi would go from neighbouring Northolt by regular Air Force transport to West Berlin. He had checked the house to ensure that the traces of DIPPER had been stripped, and the maps were down from the walls, the photographs removed, the bags packed, the mood sombre. They would leave a barren, sterile house.

In the kitchen Carter gave Mrs Ferguson a packet of embroidered handkerchiefs, and she thanked him reservedly as if mistrusting her ability to hide her feelings.

'But we'll be back soon, we're not offering you much peace, Mrs Ferguson. You'll barely have time to get the duster round and change the beds. Back in six days, you'll have the house full on Sunday night. George and I, Mr Smithson and Mr Pierce, and there'll be another gentleman and a girl coming . . . perhaps you could manage something nice for the girl's room, make a bit of a home for her.'

'I'll see to it, Mr Carter.'

'It's a bit quiet, I suppose, when we've all gone.'

'Quiet enough, but I'll have enough work to keep myself busy . . . will Johnny be using his room on Saturday night?'

'There's no call for him to be back. Bit of a freelance, Mrs Ferguson, he won't be involved after the current bit of nonsense.'

'The girl who you're bringing, she can have his room,' Mrs Ferguson said briskly.

When they were all in the car and the luggage stowed in the boot she waved to them, and stood a long time on the steps after they had gone before returning to the kitchen.

Adam Percy came into the office, hooked his coat to the back of the door, and was followed inside by his secretary and her memory pad.

'There was another call from that fellow in BND, the one who's been trying to reach you, he said he should see you . . . that it was imperative.' She was a tall woman, attractive in late middle age, wearing well the widowhood inflicted by the death of her husband on a dirty, snow scattered Korean hill. She had worked for Adam Percy for 14 years.

'Call him back in the morning, tell him I'm on a week's leave to England and fix an appointment for the week after.'

She would lie well for Adam Percy. She was accustomed to that task.

Standing on the viewing gallery on the roof at Hannover Airport, Johnny watched the passengers emerge from the forward door of the Trident. Henry Carter was one of the first down the steps.

Chapter Fourteen

=

A taxi took them to the railway station in Hannover. At the 'Left Luggage' they lodged Carter's case. That was where he had left his own bag, Johnny said.

They had hardly spoken in the taxi, nothing of substance, not until they had walked out of the station with the evening falling and found the café Augusten and taken a table far from the bar and the loudspeaker that played undemanding piano music. Many hours to be absorbed before Johnny's train. Carter ordered a Scotch with soda water, Johnny a beer, and the drinks were brought to them by a tall girl with flowing dark hair, and a tight shirt and a wraparound skirt. It would all have to be accounted for, that was the way of the Service, every last beer and sandwich and newspaper would have to be down on the printed form. They wouldn't ask Johnny for receipts, not from Magdeburg.

A pleasant enough little bar. Later it would fill up but this was early and the alcove with the large round table was their own and offered them freedom of talk.

'How's it been, Johnny?'

'Fine, just fine, what I wanted . . . I talked some German. That was what I wanted . . . that was important to me.'

'Where did you stay?'

'In Frankfurt . . . well, it was only two nights. I found a place . . . I was hardly there. I just walked about . . . I went where there were people. That's the important thing, to hear voices, to hear inflections.'

'It was really important, was it, Johnny?'

'Of course it was, or I wouldn't have gone . . .' Johnny stamped on the question. 'I said what I wanted to do and I've done it.'

'I just wanted to know,' Carter said evenly. 'It wasn't the

way that we would normally have done things.'

'It was the way I wanted it.'

'We were very fair with you, Johnny, nobody tried to block it.'

'I go over tonight a fair amount happier for those two days. Is that good enough?'

'Good enough, Johnny.' Carter looked across at him, tried for the meeting of eyes and wondered why his man lied, and knew that the time before the train was no occasion for interrogation. Unhappy, and he must let it slide. 'We've felt all along on this that what's right for you is right for the operation. That's governed everything.'

Johnny smiled, the cheeks cracked, the teeth shone.

The light was too pale for Carter to judge and assess the sincerity.

'You've done everything that I could have asked for. I've no complaints, Mr Carter.'

But then Johnny had never really had any complaints, Carter thought. Only the gun and the two days in Germany, otherwise he had never objected, had never argued for a different course of action, a different tack of approach. As if he never quite believed that the work and preparation at Holmbury would ultimately be translated to actuality, to a train journey towards Magdeburg. He'd find out soon enough, wouldn't he? Carter slipped a glance at his watch. He'd find out in the small hours on a station platform where the uniforms were strange and the manners cold. At Obeisfelde as this night was running its course for John Dawson, alias Johnny Donoghue, short contract operative of the Secret Intelligence Service. It was difficult for Carter to know how expertly they had prepared Johnny. Gone through the book, hadn't they? All the military science, all the political science, all the psychological science. All of that to burst out of the poor bastard's brain. So that it was dripping out of him, so everything was second nature, old and familiar. That was standard procedure, that was easy. But harder to come across to the man and breathe the reassurance into his lungs.

178

More than a month they'd had Johnny; and Carter, sitting in a café near the central station of Hannover, did not know whether a rope bound the two of them together. He should have known that, shouldn't he, should have been certain of that? Did it matter? . . . Perhaps not . . . Of course it didn't matter. Not going on a joy trip to see the London sights. Going on a survival run, wasn't he?

Nasty that Johnny had lied to him, out of character. Carter saw the girl hovering near their table.

'Another Scotch, another beer, and then we'd like to eat something, please,' Carter called cheerfully. There shouldn't be weighted silences, and leaden hesitations in the byplay of conversation. Must have been like this in the trenches, Passchendaele and Ypres and the Somme, when the Staff Officer came down from Brigade to explain the plan and knew that after the coffee was pressed on him and drunk that he would be going back to the cosy billet and they'd be heading forward into the mud and the wire and the machine guns.

Carter fumbled onwards.

'You didn't write any letters when you were at the house, Johnny. You know we didn't even do a blood chit form . . .' What are you at, Carter? There has to be a blood chit form, there has to be a next of kin procedure. Should have been wrapped up on the last night at Holmbury, over drinks and with suitable ribaldry, should have been done then, not when the next stop is Platform Eleven on Hannover Station. Should have been, but it hadn't. 'You didn't get in touch with anyone?'

Johnny looked quizzically across the table. 'You wouldn't have expected me to send out a rash of postcards.'

'Let's put it formally. If there's any . . . trouble, an accident, something like that . . . well, who we do we notify?'

Johnny let him sweat. The girl came with the drinks. Carter paid and she reached in the leather purse she wore behind her apron for the change. She left the menu on the table.

'We have to have a name, Johnny.'

'Charlotte Donoghue, number 14 Cherry Road,

Lancaster,' Johnny rapped. 'You'd better write it down.'

A notebook was produced and a Biro pen. Carter wrote the name and address carefully. 'Anyone else?'

'No-one else.'

'It won't happen, of course, but it's part of the paperwork. I'd get my balls chewed if I hadn't looked after it.'

A tremble at Johnny's eyelids, a quick half smile. 'If it happened you'd go easy with her . . . Promise me that.'

'I promise you that, Johnny.'

'She's an old woman, and alone. She doesn't know about this sort of thing.'

'I'd make it my business to do it myself. Does that help?'

'That's fine, thanks.'

Johnny's hand snaked across the table, gripped at Carter's, squeezed it. The gesture of affection and gratitude. Carter blinked. Christ he was too old and the thread too worn and the steel too rusted, too old to be sending young men across frontiers.

'She hasn't understood anything for years,' said Johnny quietly. 'It's a fair old time since she had anything to cheer about . . . She was very proud in the Sandhurst days, each time I went home in the kit she always seemed to be about to head for the shops because she wanted me to go with her down the street and hold her bag and have everyone see how well her kid had done . . . The trial crucified her.'

'I can understand.'

'You can, perhaps, but try and tell a pensioner widow how it is. Little Johnny's across the Irish Sea fighting terrorists. Little Johnny's away and trying to save the lives and property of decent people from the forces of evil. Little Johnny's on hush work but it's very important. Little Johnny may be in line for a medal, a bravery gong . . . That was all right for her, that was simple enough, and then it changed, didn't it? . . . Little Johnny's charged with murder, he's under arrest in army custody, he's before the Lord Chief Justice, he's accused of handing down "untrustworthy evidence", he's slated for bungling. He's a bloody failure . . . That's a hard meal for an old woman to swallow. It's shame that hurts the old people.'

'I understand, Johnny,' Carter whispered.

'I was engaged, you'll know that from the file. You'll have read that. The bitch treated me as if I had the scabs. Just a bloody letter. Didn't come to Belfast, had her father answer the telephone when I called from the airport to say it was "Not Guilty" . . .'

'Just the one girl, was there?'

'Just the one,' the savagery bit in Johnny's words. 'I bloody near smashed my mother . . . It's not the English way, is it? A man close to bloody middle age and living with his mother and talking about her. Get type-cast, don't you? Into the realms of the pansies . . . She was crippled, really cut about. I owed her something. You know that? We're both bloody owed something . . .'

'We'd better have something to eat,' Carter said.

He would remember Johnny for the rest of his life, remember the hand that had held his in the vice grip, remember the tremble of the hard man.

They had soup, and a schnitzel each with fried potatoes and sauerkraut and a litre of sweet wine from a carafe and watched the bar filling and the fluent noise of people who had no care, no sense of crisis. Pretty girls and young comfortable men and a random affluence and no attention paid to the two outsiders who sat at the far table and slowly cleared their plates. A cup of thick dark coffee, and then Carter went to the bar and the girl wrote quickly on the receipt slip and added for him, and Carter thanked her, and they edged their way through the throng and the silky warmth, and went out into the night.

The noise of the café Augusten dogged them as they walked away along the narrow pavement. They alone with work to be accomplished, they alone set aside from the noisy happiness of a bar in the centre of Hannover. There was nothing more to be said that was relevant, they went in silence.

181

First to the 'Left Luggage' and the collection of the bags. They stood then in the middle of the walkway that runs underneath the platform and track and solemnly checked Johnny's wallet and inside pockets. The identity of Johnny Donoghue was erased. No envelopes, no bills, no driving licence, no credit cards. John Dawson supreme. Around them the station shops were closed down, darkened and locked. The tourists' place, the flower stall, the sex cinema, the newspaper and book stand. Hours still to wait, but not in this place of the whores and the pimps and the police in pairs.

Johnny in fawn slacks, and his anorak zipped over his sports shirt and trainers on his feet and the boots bulky in his bag – as it should be for a tourist. They walked up the staircase to Platform Eleven. Like a bloody morgue, Carter thought. Midnight on any station in Europe, home for creeps and queers and misfits, like a bloody desert because only the parasites have business on a station when the clock shows past midnight. Carter shuddered, held his arms across his chest. A few of the platform benches were occupied, there was the tramp of the feet of the military police patrol of the Bundeswehr, the trilling clatter of a kicked soft drink can, but overall a great quiet in shadowed light. Carter took the mood of Johnny, noticed the tightness of the skin on his cheeks and the way that he fidgeted with his hands. He kept his peace.

The Warsaw express came and went, east to west. Johnny hardly seemed to notice it, didn't turn his shoulders to watch the disembarking passengers and the surveillance of the Bundesgrenzschutz on those who had crossed through and now smiled with an ebullience as if the grey life was however temporarily behind them. Into the early, soft hours of Wednesday morning. Just a few days, Johnny, you'll be fine . . . Fussing like an old woman, Henry Carter, and Johnny was on the bench beside him and his eyes were closed now and his breathing regular and his face gentle. Not a gentle creature, though, was he? Pulled the bloody trigger on the Armalite, hadn't he? Dropped the kid, killed the girl,

182

slaughtered her. And his mother would have been proud to have known him, proud with her chest swollen at the dosage. Her Johnny in a hedgerow with a high velocity rifle at his shoulder and a round in the breach and his finger curled on a cold trigger. Well, somebody has to bloody well do it, someone has to scrape the dog shit off the pavements, someone has to make life clean and sweet smelling for the wife of Henry Carter, and the daughter of Henry Carter . . .

The loudspeaker announcements came fierce and sharp.

Just before two o'clock and Carter could have done with the pullover folded in his bag.

The impending arrival of the express from Cologne. Service D441. For Wolfsburg, Obeisfelde, Magdeburg and Zwickau. Carter shook Johnny's arm lightly, saw him start into wakefulness and brush a hand across his eyes as if to clear a veil.

The big engine edged towards them. The coaches with the livery paint of the railway system of the Federal Republic. The scraping of brakes and steam hissing from between carriages.

'All right, Johnny?'

A wry grin for an answer. Johnny stood up, seemed to shake himself and with his bag in his hand walked across the platform to the carriage door. Carter opened it for him.

'Take care of yourself . . .' Carter said, a little stammer in his voice.

Johnny climbed the steps, and there was a frail grin of amusement and then he was gone along the corridor and looking for a compartment to himself. Carter searched along the line of windows, and found where he had settled. He hurried to stand underneath Johnny. Like a father and son, exchanging farewells, as if their next meeting would be long postponed. Carter strained to see into the shadow of Johnny's face.

'I'm an old fool, I know that . . . but be careful.'

'You worry too much,' a softness from Johnny.

'Probably . . . Take care, Johnny. And don't forget the whole team is with you.'

Johnny laughed. 'Don't walk under a bus,' he said.

The guard's whistle shredded Carter's thoughts. The train began to move, slowly at first, then catching its speed, drawing away, opening the gap.

Johnny waved, once and briefly. The window was drawn shut.

Carter stood and watched the going of the train till the red tail lights were lost to his view. An old fool, that was what he called himself. Pathetic, and he was about right, wasn't he?

He went back to his bag that he had left beside the bench and set off for the staircase and the change of platform that he would need to catch the first train of the morning to Helmstedt.

An hour to wait, an hour alone with his thoughts of Johnny.

Charles Mawby presumed it to be an old custom of military hospitality and rejoiced in the provision of a cut glass decanter, liberally filled with whisky, on the dressing table of his bedroom. His day clothes folded and put on a chair, wearing his pyjamas and dressing gown, he poured himself an ample tumbler. He would brush his teeth later.

It had been a fine evening, with good company and good conversation. The Brigade Commander of the British garrison stationed in West Berlin was the cousin of Joyce Mawby. It was not unnatural that he should forsake the hotel that the Service had allocated for his party and find accommodation for his team inside the protected compound that fringed the pre-war Olympic Stadium. Mawby would stay in the Brigadier's quarters. Smithson and Pierce had been farmed out to more junior officers' homes. George and Willi Guttmann were found a room with twin camp beds above the Brigade communications centre which offered security for the boy, peace of mind for his guard, and the presence of an armed Military Police Sergeant on the outside door.

He had talked more than was usual for him, drunk more

184

than he was accustomed to, found himself free and at ease. Mawby was introduced to the dinner party guests as being from Foreign and Commonwealth Office, and his presence had raised no eyebrows. It was a chance to escape from the anxieties that would dog him over the following four days until he received the telephone call from Carter in the early hours of Sunday morning. Only once had the spell of re-assurance and conviviality been broken. At the dinner table had been a colonel of the Intelligence Corps, serving his third year in Berlin.

Mawby asked with a casualness whether many escaped in these days from the German Democratic Republic across the city's dividing wall.

'Damn few,' the colonel had replied cheerfully. 'Not for lack of trying, not for lack of effort, but it's down to a trickle. That's not peculiar to Berlin, there are hardly any making it across the whole of the East/West border. They've spent a fortune sealing it and now they're getting their money's worth. Even after the DDR 30 years anniversary the gaols are still stuffed with kids who've had a go and failed. It's a pretty risky business, and don't let anyone tell you otherwise. I don't reckon I'd care to try it.'

The talk had switched to the new government in London, the capabilities of the Prime Minister and his Cabinet, the likelihood of further defence spending cuts. The passing of the port around the table had served to dismiss the one moment that threatened Mawby's confidence.

By the time that he was ready to switch off his light Mawby was a little drunk. And why not, he reflected.

Rubbing the towel across her shoulders, Erica Guttmann emerged from the bathroom. A close, hot night and she hoped that the shower would enable her to sleep.

It had been an endless, dragging, dreadful day. A walk in the late morning to the Zoologischer Garten, a lunchtime snack there, a doze in the sunshine and then back to the hotel to change into a clean dress while her father took a new shirt and then another concert to be endured . . . He never went to hear music in Moscow and the city brimmed with ballet and symphony orchestras and chamber music quartets. Never went, and instead saved his trapped enthusiasm for the Magdeburg fortnight. Beethoven at the Bezirksmusikschule on Hegel Strasse. Back to the hotel for late dinner before the dining room closed. She had seen her father to bed, sat and talked with him in his room and enjoyed the evidence that his strength and purpose were ebbing back in the days away from Padolsk.

She moved with a quick grace across the room, tall and light footed, slender and fast, the towel draped at her waist. No traffic moving on Otto von Guericke Strasse. There wouldn't be, they didn't have cars in this dreary, factory ridden camp. Even Moscow was better than here, even Moscow and God knew there were only trifles there. But these were her twin homes, these were the towns where she would grow old. Complaint would not help her, nor dissatisfaction, nor dreams of the different world carried gently into her room by the hotel radio tuned to jazz music from Hamburg.

And her life was drifting, notching up anniversaries, and the petal prettiness of her youth would soon fade. Then she would be a matron caring for an old man, and when he was gone she would be an orphan with a faded face and nothing to call her own. Home was not Moscow because the barriers of life ensured that there she did not belong. Home was not Magdeburg because that was a city of concert halls and theatre seats and parks with chairs that were suitable for an old man who could not walk far without resting.

If she left the window open then the early trams would wake her. If she slept with it closed then she would drown in the sweat pool. That was the decision with which she wrestled without resolution while waiting for the relief of sleep.

Past Wolfsburg and first light coming diffused and uncertain, nibbling at the colossus of the power station, at the huge emptiness of the car parks underneath the towering and illuminated advertisement for Volkswagen. The train clattered forward, rolling with its speed, surging between fields and woodlands.

Johnny sat alone in a bare carriage. Who travels on the night train from Cologne to Zwickau? Not many, Johnny, not what a railroad would call a profit making exercise. It was cold in the carriage and Johnny wrapped his arms round him and zipped his anorak and stamped his feet. Not tired any more, not a vestige of sleep catching at him. Closing in around him, wasn't it? The carriage and the night pressing in on him . . . Wolfsburg station had been the last chance to turn back, when the BGS man came into the compartment and Johnny had shown his passport and seen the puzzlement on the frontier policeman's face. Only a fool wants to go over there, the eyes seemed to say. Too bloody right, brother. Only a fool and Johnny.

On a long swinging arc now, bending to the left the train shuddered and the first sight of the lands that fringed the track drifted to him. The lights were clear and bright in a ribbon line in front of the train. Like the lights for the autobahn. That's it, Johnny, that's what it's all been about . . . Those lights, the lights as far as you can see, the strip across the full width of the window. Keep looking, Johnny, and then you'll see the watchtowers, great big bloody monstrosities, and then you'll see the wire. The wire and the watchtowers and then you're nearly there. That's the overture, Johnny, and it gets better after that. Quite a bloody show it will be. Not one to disappoint Johnny Donoghue.

The train heaved and struggled on the steel frame of the bridge.

The bridge at Obeisfelde, the bridge over the Aller.

The train bucked and swayed and was slowing. Take it in, Johnny, all there for you to see. Two lines of wire, three and a half metres high and floodlit and past . . . gone behind. Can't see the frontier wire any more . . . can't see it because you're inside now, Johnny. Inside their bloody cage.

But there never was an opt-out, was there? Not since the morning in Cherry Road when the men came, not since then.

187

The first train through that Wednesday and it roused the dogs, brought them barking out of their kennels, yapping and pulling at the running wires alongside the track. Big brutes, fierce and hostile, hungry and aggressive. Another tower, looming close to the carriage and Johnny caught the vision of the pale face that peered through the opened glass on the high platform. Wire alongside the track. Wire as far as he could see and lights hovering over the line and obliterating the pale power of the bulbs in the carriage, hurrying the day forward, punishing the darkness. The train was slowing, the wheels grinding.

Nervous, Johnny? Be a bloody idiot not to be.

The train stopped. Johnny sat in his seat. Moments of desperate, complete silence, then the banging of the doors opening.

Where it starts. Good luck, you bugger. On a prayer and a wing. Poor old Carter, touching a coronary, he'd be.

The compartment door was wrenched back. Four men. Dull green and grey uniforms. Two with holstered pistols, two with sub-machine guns. Johnny drew his passport from the inside pocket of his jacket, offered it without request along with the travel folder from Dublin.

The passport was scanned by one man, the folder was opened. Three other men staring at him. Johnny low in his seat. Difficult to be comfortable, impossible to be easy, not with guns and men in uniform close and pressing. The message from Dublin had said that he would simply present the hotel voucher and the visa formalities would be handled then and there on the train. Some hope, Johnny boy. There was an indifferent gesture of the head, the indication that he must leave the train. He pointed up to the rack and his bag and it was lifted down for him. The compartment doorway was cleared for Johnny to pass. His thigh brushed against the metalled barrel of a snub-nosed gun as he stepped into the corridor.

'To Kontrol.' The guttural, cracked order.

Far from the café Augusten and the pretty men in their

tight trousers and open shirts and hanging necklaces. Far from the pub on the corner of Cherry Road. Far from the bustling attention of Mrs Ferguson displaying her breakfasts. Into the bloody cess-pool, Johnny, far from everything you've known.

There was a chill in the air as he walked the deserted platform. A crisp morning and a clear sky. He passed the guards who watched the train, passed the guns and the dogs on their leashes. Don't look, Johnny, don't rubberneck. Eyes front, straight and steady stride. Into a long, low building. The first photograph of Comrade Honecker cheaply framed, high on the wall. You'll get to know him, Johnny, because he'll be staring at you from everywhere that's public, with the greying hair that was freshly combed and the steel glasses and the thin lips and the uneven teeth. You'll get to know the First Secretary of the Party. He remembered the story that Smithson had told, the banning of the revue in Leipzig the previous year that had shown Comrade Honecker rehearsing in front of the mirror for spontaneous meetings with his supporters. Brave bastards they'd have been, the actor and the theatre manager, and Smithson said both had lost their jobs, both had been scrubbed from public life. Good morning, Comrade Honecker, you don't know me now, but you will, you'll hear of Johnny, you'll hear of him and it's going to bollock your Sunday morning, it's going to wreck the taste of your coffee.

Johnny walked to the counter, again offered the passport, and stood and waited as it was taken. His face was checked with a quick glance against the photograph, there was a wintry smile and the stamp was produced with the flick of fingers for money. Fifteen West German marks. The stamp thumped down filling a page. A one week tourist visa. A postage stamp was licked and stuck. Another stamp across it. The entry point into the DDR was noted. Another stamp. The wave that he should move on. God, doesn't anyone speak in this bloody place? On to Customs.

'Tourist?'

189

'Yes,' Johnny said, and tried to demonstrate the enthusiasm of a holidaymaker. 'Yes, I'm here for tourism.'

'Coffee?'

'No. I don't have any coffee.' Should have brought a bottle of Scotch, though, because he was ready for one now, ready to pull the top off the bottle.

He was waved on past last year's slogans on the wall. Thirty years of DDR achievement, 30 years of progress and advancement. That was last year, that was sweetness . . . Past the photographs that were faded and that showed the interior of a power station, and a line of combine harvesters in a sunlit field. Gripping stuff, Johnny, rich in inspiration . . . He went to the Staatsbank. A tired looking girl at the desk behind the glass and one customer to serve. None in front of him, none behind. All the other passengers locked on the train, only foreigners allowed off to clear their documentation. They'd all be pensioners, those from the other carriages, the old ones that they allowed out because they were useless, unoccupied in the factories, non-contributors to society. Only the old ones were accorded permission to travel outside the borders of the DDR to visit relatives in the West. Coming home, weren't they? Coming home to the guns and the uniforms and the dogs. He changed 200 West marks at one for one.

Johnny took a seat in the station café, looked again at another Honecker, waited for the train search to be completed. He shivered and sat very still wishing he had something to read, and officers from the Border Guard marched in their boots behind him and took two tables and ordered tea. It was the right way to come in, Johnny, in the middle of the night. It had been a cursory and sloppy check. But that's for starters, Johnny.

The door onto the platform opened. Another man, another gun, another wave for him to follow. He picked up his bag and walked to the train.

One hour and 7 minutes later Johnny was in Magdeburg.

The sun was rising and it would be hot later and the station was busy with people. He walked out onto the pave-

190

ment and was confronted with the view of the International Hotel. Bloody inviting it looked, but then anywhere would have been inviting if it boasted a bed booked in the name of John Dawson.

What the hell are you doing here, Johnny? Don't know. Might be able to tell you on Sunday morning. Not till then.

their trailers, along the avenues of flats that were short of paint and creeping towards dereliction. First on Sandtor Strasse, then on Rogatzer Strasse, through the district of Alte Neustadt. Not much benefit derived from the 30 years of struggle. You're thinking like bloody Smithson, Johnny, spilling all his propaganda, all his prejudice.

Perhaps . . . Nothing much to excite him in the shops. Tins and sausage in the butchers. Cabbages and beans and potatoes in the greengrocers. Clothes that were angular and drear in the narrow fronted window of the ladies' dress shop. Perhaps old Smithson was right, perhaps he was on course. Twice he slipped around a street corner and waited for the signs of a following tail, and he found none, and no interest seemed to be shown in him by the two boys in the blue shirts of the FDJ who hurried past him, nor by the green and white police car that cruised smugly on the street. No tail that he knew of, no one following and observing. And what was criminal about a tourist strolling on Rogatzer Strasse?

The railway line was in front. Easy to see because it was built high on an embankment. He looked at his watch. Smithson had said that it would take him 20 minutes to reach this point. Just about right. An exact man, Smithson, for all the cynicism, one who knew the value of information that was tested and proved. On time. Johnny climbed the metal footbridge over the line and busied himself with his map. A bad place to wait, a bloody awful place.

The train eased along the track. Nothing particular about the engine that was huge, oozing power, and that carried the initials of the Deutsche Bahn, the railway of West Germany. The main line from West Berlin to Helmstedt. He had not come to the bridge to see the engine, it was the carriages that he would observe. Ordinary and nondescript until his eyes caught the brilliance of the red and white and blue. The bloody old Union Jack, the flag attached to the carriage walls. The British military train on its daily run. A restaurant car and men with grey hair and trimmed moustaches tucking into their toast and scrambled eggs. The windows of the kitchen section were wide open to expel the grill fumes and the Army Catering Corps chef was taking time off from his frying pan and looking out. He would have seen the lone figure on the bridge above. There was a corporal in camouflage dress who had positioned himself by a window in a carriage farther back. The train moved slowly, negotiating the junction of points. Time enough for Johnny to view the sight and scenes. He wanted to shout, wanted to wave and communicate. The old Union Jack slipping through Magdeburg each day, a journey of impertinence, the maximum of effrontery. The historic legacy of the transit right of the Allied powers to West Berlin. And it was gone from him. He hadn't seen the East German troops who rode escort in the forward and rear carriages; complacent and on their arses they'd be, smoking and reading the day's *Neues Deutschland*. Right on time the train had come, mark that down as a bonus, Johnny.

A long walk now. And this was not tourist country and Johnny must forge on as if there was a purpose in his direction, as if he had the reason and the right to tramp past the factory entrances and the power stations on the Aug-Bebal-Damm. Guards of the National Volks Armee, with MPiKMs and magazines attached, watched the side roads leading to the city's heavy industry complex. Not a place to linger. Few houses here, just machinery and decay and old brickwork and heaving chimney smoke. On your way, Johnny. But better to walk, because then your eyes are brought into play. You see nothing from a train, nothing from a trolley bus, nor from a tram. You have to walk because that way you remember what you have seen. It was Wednesday morning and there was much that he must remember before Saturday evening and there would be no opportunity to retrace his steps. See it now, remember it now. Wide, flat, colourless country, pimpled with squat factory sheds and high rise chimneys.

Like a dividing ribbon the autobahn lay ahead.

Down the autobahn the car would come for the rendezvous and the pick-up of Otto Guttmann. Jumping the fences early, Johnny, light years till then. Not true, three and a half days. Not even worth thinking about . . . God, they'd kept that in short supply, they'd hoarded and they'd played the miser with Johnny's available time. But that was the plan, to press forward and sweep the target up in a rush, above all and above everything deny him the opportunity for reflection and consideration. Sounded good at Holmbury, but stretched and creaking beside the Magdeburg intersection of the autobahn.

The autobahn bridge of grey, weathered cement straddled the road. There was a steady surge of traffic above him. Mercedes and Opels and Audis and VWs and the throbbing articulated lorries plying the isthmus strip between West Germany and West Berlin, drivers with documents and permit for transit through the DDR. Johnny looked quickly over his shoulder. And that was wrong, out of character for his cover. Suppress it, Johnny, shut it down. He walked under the bridge and saw the sharply curving slipway to the autobahn down which a car coming from Berlin would travel and beside it the bushes that were leafy and would offer concealment. There were no houses on the far side of the city to the autobahn, no factories, only a gravel works more than 300 metres farther beyond the bridge. An unseen place, a covert place, and here the car would come and take its load and spin its wheels and be away again within seconds back onto the racing circuit of the autobahn. A deviation of less than half a minute . . . That's the plan, Johnny. That's what Charles Mawby and his dark suit and his club tie have been sweating on. Not Johnny's problem, not his concern how fast a car swivels and how quickly the driver guns an engine back onto the autobahn. Johnny's concern was the bringing of an old man and his daughter to this seedy patch of undergrowth where the cover was draped with old newspapers and the ground littered with beer bottles and household rubbish. Christ, that was enough, wasn't it?

Johnny walked on. Putting the briefings of Smithson into pictures.

He went through the gateway of the Barleber See camping site. Past the administration building, past the rows of planted tents, past the yellow sand of the lakeside beach, past the children that played with buckets and spades, past the men and women that walked listless in their swimming clothes. Jesus, and what sort of a holiday was this? A fortnight beside a flyblown lake 3 miles down the road from the power station or the chemical works or the railway engine repair yard. He reached a wide patio where the tables were shaded by multi-coloured umbrellas. Take more than that, Johnny, to swing the Barleber See camp site into life.

A bar here. The prospect of a large beer, the chance to ease his boots loose. And it would be the train back after the beer.

Smithson had done his homework. The pick-up place was good, right for concealment. The camping place was good, right for whiling away the hours till he was ready to head for the autobahn slip road. Have to give Smithson a pat when he saw him. Johnny rummaged in his pocket for coins, paid for the lukewarm beer and ambled to the comfort of a chair.

It had been a good morning.

Well, good as far as it went . . . and how far was that? Everything was gloss before the contact was forged. One step at a time, Johnny. He would see Guttmann tonight at the hotel. Not to talk to, of course, but to look at and evaluate.

One step at a time.

The desk in front of Valeri Sharygin was cleared, all the work finished that must be completed before his departure to New York. From his office in the headquarters building he carried the single sheet of typed paper down the stairs to Transmission section and the bank of telex machines and operators. He still smarted from the apathy of the KGB colonel to whom he had explained that day the unanswered queries in the case of Willi Guttmann and a yacht out on a foul afternoon on the Lake of Geneva. Down many flights of stairs, along many corridors, and with each step and stride Sharygin's annoyance increased; he might have been with his children, at his home with his wife, he had no need to expose himself to a superior officer's sarcasm and poorly disguised scepticism. But the body of young Guttmann had still not been found, and without the corpse an area of ill-defined suspicion was entitled to remain. The matter remained in Valeri Sharygin's mind, irritating and marginally obsessive.

With faltering enthusiasm he had asked his colonel whether KGB in Germany could ascertain with certainty from surveillance of Doctor Otto Guttmann whether he, at least, believed in the death by drowning of his son. He had been told peremptorily that manpower in Berlin did not run to such poorly substantiated luxuries.

He had suggested that GRU might complete the investigation, and been slapped down for the suggestion that military intelligence should take on the spade work of KGB.

He had followed the one course left open to him.

The Schutzpolizei in Magdeburg would follow without question a directive from Moscow. They alone were lowly enough in the ladder of east bloc security to accept instruction from a major in KGB. And he did not ask much of them, only the confirmation that would dash his diminishing caution in this matter.

The message that he brought to Transmission section was addressed to Doctor Gunther Spitzer, Schutzpolizeipresident of the city in which Otto Guttmann and his daughter now took their holiday.

The noise of the argument billowed from the shop onto the street pavement.

Erica Guttmann was window gazing and easily distracted. She cocked her head and sought the source of the shouting. The radio and television shop was in front of her. She was in no hurry, had nowhere to go, and the baying carried the prospect of amusement. Through the opened doorway she saw the crowd gathered at the shop counter – gesturing hands confronting the assistant at the record counter. The shop would only just have opened from the lunchtime closing and the young people would have lined up patiently outside for the new delivery of records and found when they were admitted that there were none for them. A mirthless grin dappled her face. Pathetic . . . Not teenagers, these ones, but boys and girls in their twenties with their tempers roused because they could not buy music with the money they had saved. Then the crowd was surging. Up to a hundred and sprinting from the shop, stampeding across the Julius-Bremer Strasse towards the Centrum. She crossed after them, caught by the silly excitement of the rush. Into the Centrum, avoiding the counters of clothes and cosmetics and china, off into the depths of the shop. The newcomers joined the already formed twin queues that shuffled towards a wooden trestle table where piles of long playing records were stacked. She saw the pleasure of those who examined with a kind of love the sleeve of the record they took away.

No choice for them, only the one label, and one copy for each customer. Something discarded by the West and dumped, and picked on here with a humiliating excitement. She idled closer to the trestle table. The name of the artist was Nana Mouskouri. Erica pulled a face, she had never heard of this woman, of this singer. But then Erica Guttmann was no longer a child, she had no feelings for the moods of the queue beside her. She would never have stood in line to buy a record. She would never have screamed if it were denied her, she would never have sulked if she had gone home without the prized possession.

There was no accommodation for such trivia in the life of Erica Guttmann.

The contented mood in which she had dawdled in front of the shop windows was destroyed.

Time to turn for the hotel because she had with docility accepted her father's wish that they should go to the Dom before dinner, another concert, another recital. And then they would meet Renate and her friend in the hotel restaurant. Renate with her man, Renate satisfied by a security policeman with a claw. She had been surprised, perhaps annoyed when it had been suggested that this Spitzer wanted to meet her father.

She had no long playing record and she had no lover. She had an old man that she must care for, and company for dinner that was unattractive.

Erica's foot stamped the pavement as she marched back to the hotel. And it was hot and the stains from her exertion were visible at the armpits of her blouse.

Adam Percy had taken the Berlin flight. From Tegel airport he telephoned Mawby and arranged a meeting in a café on the Kurfusten-Damm.

Over afternoon tea in the sunshine he reported that he had spoken that morning to Hermann Lentzer, that he was assured that no difficulties had arisen and that Lentzer himself would be driving to Berlin from West Germany and arriving in the late morning of Saturday.

'Cutting it a bit fine, isn't he?'

'That's the way he wants it,' said Percy, 'so that's the way it has to be, I suppose. He does the trip pretty frequently.'

'The car, the driver, the second man to handle the passports . . .?'

'I'm afraid he wasn't very specific.' Percy sipped gingerly at the warm cup. 'All he did was to tell me that everything was in hand. That's his style.'

'He's an uncommunicative swine.'

'Has to be if he's to survive in that business, and he's a survivor.'

Percy would stay now in West Berlin.

The dispositions were complete. The team was in place. A chance to catch their breath before the whirlpool broke over them at the end of the week.

'Everything all right at this end?' Percy asked.

'Couldn't be better.'

'And the Magdeburg end?'

'Carter saw our lad onto the train, said he was in fine shape.'

'Good,' said Percy, and there was a heavy flatness in his voice.

He believes in nothing, this one, thought Mawby. Almost a degree of insolence, Mawby reckoned and he'd have something to say when he was back at Century House next week.

With her key Jutte Harnburg let herself into the flat. A long day in the engineering faculty behind her, a long night in her room ahead. Examinations at the end of the month. Even for second year students at the Humboldt there were examinations that had to be passed. And necessary for her to make a good show because her father was the Director of a Kombinat and much was expected.

'Jutte?' The voice spread from the living room. 'Is that you, Jutte?'

'Yes, Mother. It is me.'

'A young man was here. He came with a letter for you.'

'Who was he?' she said indifferently, hooked her plastic coat on the stand in the hall.

'A young man from the Border Guard. He said he was a friend of that boy Becker that you see.'

'He brought a letter?' Jutte dropped the bag of books onto the floor, ran into the living room.

'I put it on your bed. You did not tell me that you were still seeing the boy.' Frau Harnburg sat in front of the television with a tray and teapot and a plate of cucumber sandwiches. Between mouthfuls, she spoke. 'Your father would not be pleased to hear that you still see Becker. Your father says the boy is nothing, that he has no career. His family is nothing, not even prominent in the Party in the quarter where they live . . .'

'He pesters me a bit, there is nothing more than that. He was at a camp a few weeks back, I cannot help who else is there.' The trembling gripped her, trickled through her legs, kissed the coolness of her arms. She turned away, hid her face from her mother.

201

'Your father will be pleased to know that.'

'There is nothing for him to know.'

'Have you much work tonight?' Her mother asked the question in sorrow. She was from a former generation where girls did not concern themselves with engineering. A pretty girl she had wanted for her only child, someone whom she could pet and beautify and take credit from, not a daughter that slaved at a drawing board and wore stained overalls in the Humboldt's workshops.

'Enough to last me three evenings, and there'll be more tomorrow.' Jutte grimaced.

A fat bitch with a fat arse and a fat pompous husband to sleep beside. God, how they'd scream and howl, the pair of them, if they knew that Ulf who is nothing and has no career had spilled himself on their precious sheets. They'd rip them and burn them, and the noise would lift the roof, and the shrieks would bring the neighbours running.

'When is Father coming home?'

'Soon . . . he rang me at lunchtime, he has to go to the Council of State to meet with the Trade Secretariat. The Secretary is going to London tomorrow. Your father is one of a select few who are required to advise him on certain contracts that may be offered. Your father is well thought of by the Secretary . . . perhaps on another occasion he may even accompany a delegation.' The woman bled with pride.

'I'll go to my room, it's better I start the work before supper.'

It was the one virtue of the burden of study that she brought home that the books freed Jutte from the punishment of attending the living room seminars of the evening when her mother theatrically fed her father the cues for him to relate the anecdotes of his contacts with the high and mighty of the Central Committee and the Politburo.

She had a small room in the flat, barely large enough for the bed and her table and chair and the chest for her clothes and the hanging wardrobe for her dresses and coats. A sleeping and working place only, a room where she came as a stranger and a visitor. Not home, not her own, because her mother would root through the drawers for evidence of her life outside the flat. Not even her own pictures on the wall, those instead that her mother had wished on her. The framed photograph of Jutte in the dress of the FDJ at camp in the centre of a group of happy and toothy girls, and beside it the picture of her amongst a thousand others marching on a May Day on Unter den Linden in front of the Memorial to the Victims of Fascism and Militarism.

Jutte held the envelope and ran her fingers on the sealed flap. It had not been opened and refastened. She ripped the envelope apart and read the words written in Ulf's writing.

Had she really meant it? On the platform at Schöneweide, had it been just to tease him because he was frightened that he would lose his train, and the discipline of the military overwhelmed him? But her uncle in Hamburg had told her of a home that waited for her, and a job and a future. Her uncle in Hamburg had said that it was necessary for one in the group to have an intimacy with the border sector that would be crossed. Her uncle in Hamburg had said it could be achieved, and that was before she had met Ulf. That was not the reason that she had lain on the bed beneath the boy, and splayed her legs and caught him with her arms . . . That was not the reason. There were many boys she could have gone with. Why Ulf? Why the frontier guard? Why was her boy, the one she had chosen, the one who would know the sector at Walbeck?

She had told Ulf what she wanted of him, and he had done it. She had told him where she wanted to be taken, and he would guide her. She had taunted his courage, now she must prove her own.

'Jutte,' the voice whined behind her closed door.

'Yes, Mother,' she said brightly.

'What does the boy say in his letter?'

'Only that he will soon be coming back to Berlin in a few weeks' time and he asks if he can see me.'

203

'It is kinder if you write and are frank with him, tell him there is no chance of you meeting again.'

'I will write to him next week, soon enough then. And Mother . . .'

'Yes, Jutte?'

'I really have to work tonight. I have some difficult things to do. I have to be quiet.'

There were apologies and the scraping retreat of the slippered feet. Shit, that would make her miserable. Back to her tea bags and cream cakes and not knowing what was in the letter. That would wound the cow. Jutte opened a book on her desk, took her writing pad from her bag . . . What would they do to them, her parents, when Ulf had taken her across? How great would be the shame, how far would be the tumbling fall of disgrace? Perhaps her father would lose his job, certainly the prospects of promotion to the permanent staff of the Secretariat. Influence gone, friends gone, because who would want to be the confidant of a man whose child had won such disgrace? Jutte would drag them down, down so that they suffocated in their humiliation.

The book lay unread.

She wondered how they would make the journey from this place called Suplingen, how they would cross. It could not be difficult or Ulf would not have written to her. There could not be great danger. She sat very still in the evening light of her room and tried to read and failed until the room dripped darkness and she heard the voices that heralded her father's return and the syrup of her mother's welcome.

It could not be difficult or Ulf would not have written to her.

He was at the Stettiner Hof, a small and vintage hotel . . . His wife would have liked to have stayed here on holiday, Carter thought . . . Low ceilings, dark woodwork, stairs that creaked in age. Not a bad room, simple and functional with a bathroom across the landing. But he'd mixed his seasons, muddled his habits and the evening had come and he was wide awake, and not hungry either because he'd eaten a big meal at 3 served by the proprietor's wife in the empty dining room.

The afternoon had been wasted with a stroll out onto the medieval Holzberg that sloped, cobbled, down the hill, surrounded by the timber and plaster houses that were made for postcards and holiday photographs, nothing to impress Henry Carter.

With evening there was at last some purpose to Henry Carter's day. He took a taxi from the Stettiner Hof to the NAAFI Roadhaus. That was what he had been told that he must ask for, not that he was searching for a cup of tea or a hamburger or a plate of chips.

Two kilometres short of Checkpoint Alpha the Roadhaus offered the British armed forces a last staging post before the drive along the autobahn through East Germany to their garrisons in West Berlin, access guaranteed by the four power post-war agreement. There was a Military Police unit stationed here, secure communications by radio and telephone and telex, and repair and towing facilities for service personnel luckless enough to blow a gasket or overheat an engine on the autobahn.

The Union Jack fluttered in the last minutes before coming down from the flag pole. At the Guard House Carter explained that facilities had been arranged for him. He was expected and that brightened him, he had resigned himself to an hour kicking his heels while they checked him out. Ushered straight to the major's office, and he was left by himself to telephone Mawby in West Berlin. There wasn't much for him to say, only that he'd arrived, was installed, was groping his way around and would put in a detailed reconnaissance in the morning. And Mawby sounded confident, and said the Berlin team were in shape and raring to go. Bloody Mawby, never a doubt up his sleeve. Well, just the once, just the once at Holmbury on the eve of the launch. Must have been his menopause then, right out of character.

When Carter came out of the room the major was waiting. An apology, the excuse that supper would be on the table at home, but if Mr Carter cared for a drink there was the NAAFI bar. Carter watched the major leave in his car, he'd never met a military man yet who was happy in the company of civilian intelligence.

The bar was little more than a hatch surrounded by the decoration of the wall shields emblazoned with the insignia and mottoes of the army and air force units that had stopped over the years at the Roadhaus before the drive to Berlin. It was a wide, airy room, some tables for eating, some easy chairs. The requisite portraits of the Queen and her Consort and the carefully stacked piles of back numbers of *Country Life* and *Woman's Own* and *Punch*. Carter was back in the realm of the familiar.

There were two men at the bar, elderly and black uniformed, white shirts and black ties, and two white crowned caps on the stool beside them.

'Good evening, the name's Carter.'

'How do you do, Charlie Davies.'

'Pleased to meet you, Mr Carter, I'm Wally Smith.'

They'd be good for some beers thought Carter, good for some company. His estimation was correct, his hopes were justified. For several minutes they chewed over whether it would rain in the next 24 hours, whether at last the summer had come. They swapped winter anecdotes, how much snow there had been in southern England as against north-east Germany. They discussed the merits of the Stettiner Hof as a hotel, whether he could have done better. Gentle and pleasant conversation at the end of a piggish day.

'You'll forgive me, Mr Davies, but the uniform stumps me. I haven't come across it before,' Carter said.

'BFS . . . British Frontier Service . . . you're not alone, no one's heard of us. After the war we were up to 300 strong, but they've cut us so hard there's damn all lead left in the pencil. I'm called a Frontier Service Officer Grade Two, and there's three more that have Grade Three rank, that's all that's left along with a half dozen that do customs work for the forces on the Dutch border.' Charlie Davies spoke with a cheerful gloominess.

'What do you do?'

'On paper it says that we're supposed to keep Chief Service Liaison Officer at Hannover informed of the day to day situation on the IGB . . . that's Inner German Border. We do that and we accompany all army and RAF patrols within five kilometres of the frontier,' Wally Smith chipped in. 'In effect we have to know every damned inch of it from the Baltic down to Schmiedekopf, and that's 411 miles. It's our responsibility to see that no idiot goes where he shouldn't and starts a bloody incident going.'

'It's a fair old stretch of ground,' Carter said with sympathy.

'We manage . . .' confidence from Davies.

'Kind of . . .' doubt from Smith.

'What line are you, Mr Carter?' Davies sipped easily at his beer.

'Foreign and Commonwealth Office.'

'Do you know a Mr Percy, we sometimes see him here?' Davies drained his glass.

'Adam Percy, from Bonn, you could say we're colleagues.'

It had been done easily, the establishment of credentials, the presentation of Carter's pedigree. The talk moved on to civil service pay, the prospect of pensions being linked to inflation indexes. All were men of a common age and experience in their careers. Davies and Smith had bought a round, Carter had reciprocated.

'You'll be around for a few days, Mr Carter?'

'A few days, yes.'

'We're here most evenings, if you're at a bit of a loose end, if you're on your own and you'd like a bit of a natter.'

'That's very kind of you. I'll be using the communications tomorrow evening, round the same time . . .'

'Probably see you then . . . You'll forgive us, it's been a long day. There was a flap on south of here this morning. A silly bugger like me should know better than to get up and take a look . . .'

'What sort of flap?'

'Two kids had a go at the wire. One made it, God knows

207

how, bypassed the trip wires for the SM 70s ... the automatic guns on the fence ... the other kid didn't have the luck. They're shitty bastards over there, don't let anyone tell you otherwise, they had the kid who was hit hung on the wire for an hour ... his bloody leg was off. Looked about sixteen ... I didn't see the one who came over, the BGS had whipped him away.'

'Doesn't sound very friendly,' Carter said quietly.

'If they'd stuck a transfusion in for him they might have saved the kid. They don't hurry themselves, not when some poor fucker ... you'll excuse the French, Mr Carter ... not when he's hanging on the wire. Not very friendly, as you say, that's why I've been taking a few jars tonight. Like I said, we'll see you again.'

Carter walked back from the Roadhaus to the hotel. He walked briskly in the darkness, and he thought of Johnny. 30 miles down the road, behind the Inner German Border, Johnny upon whom they all depended.

He sat in the wide, high entrance hall of the hotel, deep in a black leather armchair and faced the 3 doors of the lifts.

More than 45 minutes he had been there, waiting calm and detached, rested by an afternoon sleep and a bath. He would stay there and watch, half the night if necessary. The old photograph trampled its picture in his mind.

Johnny would know him when he came.

There was a chorus of accents and languages in the chairs around him. The coaches and officials of a basketball team from Bratislava who were waiting for their bus to take them to a reception. The excited chatter of three Libyan students who talked noisily and nervously because the surroundings were strange to them. A soprano singer and her accompanist from Vienna. A trades union delegation from Cracow. A group of Red Army officers in their walking out best uniforms who celebrated with vodka the promotion of a colleague. The sounds eddied at his ears and Johnny was oblivious to them.

Erica Guttmann came first.

Tall, slim, fair haired and tanned skin. Wearing a dress for the evening. Distracted as she stepped from the lift, concerning herself with holding the doors open so that they should not close on the old man who followed her. No hesitation for Johnny. The fast, quick clarity of recognition, as if he'd seen him yesterday.

An old man, a little bowed and stooping, but with a firm stride. The suit hung on him as if age had wasted his stomach and dropped his shoulders and the shaping of the jacket and trousers was now obsolete. A domed, wrinkled forehead and wisps of white hair, metal rimmed spectacles. As Willi had said he would be, as the boy had described.

Erica had slipped her hand through the angle of her father's arm. She swept the hall with her eyes and found no satisfaction and whispered in her father's ear. He nodded agreement and the two of them went carefully and in step to the side of the reception desk and stood, examining and quizzical, in front of the framed and printed sheet that carried the timetable of Magdeburg railway station.

He was fast out of his chair and across the hallway.

Johnny hovered behind them, listened and watched as the old man adjusted his spectacles to peer at the close print, and Erica's fingers darted at the relevant information.

'The one at 11 is too late. It has to be this one, just before 9 . . . it goes at 8.52 . . . I will book the call tonight for us to be woken in the morning . . .'

She led him away, spared no look for Johnny, left him the freedom of the timetable. He leaned forward to see the place where her fingers had played. The 8.52 via Oschersleben and Halberstadt to Wernigerode. Willi had talked of Wernigerode. Willi had talked of the annual pilgrimage to the town in the Hartz mountains. It suited Johnny well, was very adequate for the plan that had been conceived at Holmbury.

Johnny moved back into the centre of the hall. It took him some moments to find again the Guttmanns, father and daughter. Their backs were to him and they were talking to another girl and with a stout giant of a man. Johnny saw

209

the glove and the scar. The girls talked fast and with the animation of friends. The men stood stiff and apart and seemed to spar with their words, in the guise of strangers. The girls in front, the foursome headed towards the glass doors of the restaurant. Time to find a table for one, Johnny, not too near the band. Time to try the food, lad.

Johnny smiled up at Comrade Honecker and followed into the restaurant. Otto Guttmann had seemed older than he had expected. At the finish line of his career and that would be polite. And he was going to have a bastard time from tomorrow. Going to be wracked so that it hurt, deep pain, deep agony, because that was the plan that Mawby had endorsed. That was the way it had to be, wasn't it? Otto Guttmann was to be bent and crushed and broken. You're a nasty bastard, Johnny. Right . . . and that's why you're here, that's why you were contracted to drive an old man half out of his mind with grief and dreams.

The restaurant seemed full and Johnny stood in the doorway and searched for an empty chair and tried to catch the eye of the head waiter.

Chapter Sixteen

—

Johnny stood outside the station entrance and looked across the square towards the International Hotel. He was early and his return ticket to Wernigerode was already in his pocket. Otto Guttmann would be late, because he was on holiday and he would be coming in a hurry and probably in an ill temper, and the girl would be fretting. And they would be confused and Johnny would be calm. That was the way it must be, for every hour and every minute that stretched before him in Magdeburg. Johnny, with the reins tight in his fists.

Now 8.30 and the workers were scurrying for their offices and shops, for their desks and their cash counters and their construction sites. The slogan in front of him, 12 feet off the ground and 30 feet long, read 'DDR 30 – Werk des Volkes fur das Wahl des Volkes!' Impossible to know how many believed in the collective exhortations for greater striving and effort, impossible for Johnny to gauge how many of those brushing and bustling past him believed in the doctrine of 'the work of the people for the welfare of the people'. Don't they have any selfish buggers here? Just a myth, or is there really a Utopia that confronts capitalism? . . . They wore pressed and laundered clothes and dulled tired faces.

The presence of the Red Army at the station emphasised for Johnny the width of the bridge that he had crossed at Obeisfelde. Send them into apoplexy, wouldn't it? Johnny Donoghue, former holder of the Queen's Commission, former officer of the British Army Intelligence Corps, currently under contract to the Secret Intelligence Service, standing on the pavement outside the Hauptbahnhof of Magdeburg and running his mental check over their units and dispositions. Have a heart attack, wouldn't he, the

Soviet military security commandant for the city? He saw the long serving men with their wide caps far back on their heads and badges of rank on their shoulders and their baggy trousers and floppy blouses. He saw the new recruits, some with the Asian tan and the narrow eyes of the far eastern territories and whose uniforms were poor fitting and whose boots were polished.

The Russians seemed to Johnny to dominate the station with their manpower and their transport. But this was what he had been told he would see, because this was a command area and Pierce had dinned that into his memory. Johnny saw the civilians thread and weave between the foreign troops, watched them ignore each other. Quit the rubber-necking, Johnny, that's the way you're noticed, that's the way the questions get asked. He walked away, turned his back on the military movement.

It was as he had thought it would be.

Otto Guttmann trailing his daughter. They came past him, Erica leading by two strides and heading straight for the ticket counter and leaving her father to rummage in his pocket for coins for a newspaper. She would feel the burden of him, wouldn't she? Too fine a girl in her looks and bearing, as she stood in line in haughty impatience for the tickets, to be anchored to an old man. He wondered how they paced their evenings, what common ground they found for conversation. He swatted the mood away and set off in a leisured pursuit down the passageway to the platforms.

Across the track a troop train was loading. Children and wives, prams and parcels being stowed up the high steps and into the carriages. Men of the Soviet Military Police and the local Schutzpolizei overseeing. Johnny the interloper. The families of a Signals Regiment returning to the Ukraine.

The loudspeakers blared the warning of the arrival of the train for Wernigerode.

Erica had her arm at her father's elbow. Johnny stood close and saw their heads merge as the girl whispered in her parent's ear. She laughed and he smiled, their crisis of departure was overcome. The train pulled into the platform and Johnny watched them climb on board and then walked to the next carriage.

He felt in his pocket for the envelope that contained the photographs, was reassured by the reminder of their presence and settled in a seat.

Sir Charles Spottiswoode drove fast along the A3 to London. The Volvo had brought him many column inches of comment and publicity in the national media after his well-documented claim that the British motor industry produced vehicles of such poor workmanship that he, a patriot, had been forced to take delivery of a foreign produced motor. The Member for Guildford rejoiced in the brickbats that had been hurled at him, revelled in the abuse heaped at his doorstep.

But those who saw him as little more than an amusing by-product of public life had misread their man. The aggression and bitterness that haunted him were cultured in privacy. When he bit, he bit deep. He was not ignored.

The Prime Minister was seeing him that evening. In his mind he rehearsed the story that he would tell of the removal from a private house of a terrified young man at the hands of the louts of the Intelligence Service. He would demand the answer to his question of who sanctioned such behaviour, and by what legal right. The reputations of men previously unaccountable to Parliament would suffer, they would cringe away from the affair. That he guaranteed.

The team of Schutzpolizei had not concerned themselves with Johnny. He'd felt the nerves wriggle and fidget in his body as they came into the carriage. Two men and two women. Navy blue trousers and navy blue skirts. Sexless powder blue blouses. Snug little pistols holstered at the waist; East German manufacture and a copy of the Soviet Makarov that in its turn was the copy of the West German Walther PP. Johnny tensed, slid his hand to the passport that he had collected from Reception before leaving the hotel and that carried the stamp of the Volkspolizei opposite his visa page. All trains going into the border areas were checked and under surveillance. Wernigerode was less than a dozen miles from the frontier, just routine. They had moved slowly, scraping their eyes over the passengers in the carriage. By the time that they were level with him Johnny had seen the pattern that they followed. The teenagers, the young ones, the kids with anoraks and rucksacks, they received attention. Those who were going into the hills and forests towards the frontier, who were walking and camping in the Hartz, they were asked for their papers and tickets. The kids who had never known another life, who were ignorant of another colour, they were the risk. They were the runners.

Johnny stared out of the window. He repeated the catechism to himself. Not to take an interest, not to follow the gruff questioning and the hesitant answers. He must detach himself, follow the lead of people around him who closed their ears and eyes and minds. He wanted to smile and suppressed it. Out in the field, flat and stretching to a distant horizon was a corral of wire and floodlights and imprisoned inside was a single engine crop spraying aircraft. One last year, one this year . . . the way to the West at tree top height . . . the hope that the frontier guards weren't too accurate with the MPiKMs and the machine guns in the towers. Take a bit of nerve to lift a plane and fly out, a matter of courage and a fair load of luck. Up you, Comrade Honecker, because there were people here with nerve and courage and luck, and that's why a little aircraft has to have wire of 10 feet in height stretched round it. The man on the seat opposite Johnny would also have seen the plane, and his eyes were blanked and expressionless. Johnny pondered on what he thought of the sight, and had no possibility of knowing.

The Hartz gleamed green and lofty above the agricultural plain. He mused away the last minutes of the journey and was at the carriage door when the train stopped at Wernigerode station.

Otto and Erica Guttmann were not difficult to follow. Their pace and their steps were predictable.

Up the hill and towards the old, close knit town.

Into the Markt Platz where the hotels were and the tables and chairs were set and the stalls for the sale of vegetables. They had a coffee and Johnny surveyed them from a distance.

Along the gentle climb of the Burg Strasse, where the houses were timbered and painted, where the church was ageing and weeded, where the tourists were Party members and union officials and factory workers and holidaying with their families at the FDGB hostels.

By the bridge and over the shallow river. Johnny kept a gap of 30 to 40 yards between himself and the couple.

Across the road was a low roofed, century old stone chapel. There was a stall in front where an elderly woman guarded bundles of cut flowers, cheerful when set against the darkness of her clothes. Willi had talked of the cemetery, of the pilgrimage to the grave that would be made by Otto Guttmann and his daughter.

Johnny quickened his stride, closed the distance and reached in his inner pocket for the envelope.

Erica had paid for a spray of roses that were red and bold and erect, her father carried them and they nodded their thanks and passed into the cemetery. They threaded their way between the family plots. The old man struggled to maintain his straight, firm walk and his shoulder was tilted to his daughter as if he leaned more heavily for support. The grave they found was narrow, and there were tufts of grass sprouting between the gravel chips. With a quick gesture of annoyance Erica Guttmann bent down and snatched with her fingers at the grass stems and threw them to the pathway, then rose to stand in silence beside her father. A full minute Otto Guttmann waited, until the tears ran on his cheeks, and the tremble of emotion played at his lips, then he ducked and placed the flowers against the headstone and retrieved himself and stood again in stillness.

You're a pig, Johnny, you're the man in the night at the window of the Nurses' Home. A foul, nasty creature ... Turn the screw, Johnny, turn it so that it hurts and brings agony. You're a pig, Johnny, and you don't give a shit.

Erica walked away from her father, leaving him to his inner contemplation, to the memories of the woman who had been his wife and given him his children, the memories of the woman who had died in the car that he had driven. Memories of holidays with a son and a daughter and picnics in these woods. Memories of shared happiness. Erica was away from him and her back was turned and she browsed among other stones, other inscriptions, other flowers.

Johnny sidled forward, whittled the yards down, came to Otto Guttmann's shoulder.

'Doctor Guttmann ...'

The old man's head cocked, jerked up at the stranger's voice. A spell broken, a mood disintegrated.

Johnny slid the envelope into the opened palm of Otto Guttmann's hand and as the fingers clenched and the eyes spun he was gone. Gone fast, gone because the work was finished.

Johnny didn't look back, did not expose his face, hurried in a fast walk to the cemetery gate. You've taken a chisel and hammered it into him, chosen the place where he'd be most vulnerable and beaten the sharp edge into him. You've destroyed him, Johnny.

On his daughter's arm Otto Guttmann climbed the path of stamped earth through the trees above the cemetery towards the Feudalmuseum.

This was the show piece of the town, the towering and restored castle that perched on a rock crag pinnacle above the houses. Several groups of walkers passed them because his steps were hesitant and the toes of his shoes bruised the stones in the path. Erica would notice nothing, would relate his stumbling progress to the graveside visit, equate his condition with the emotion generated by the cemetery.

He had looked once at the photographs in the envelope. Once also he had glanced at the words written on a single sheet of paper.

'If you ever wish to see your son, Willi, again, tell no-one of what you have been shown.'

In his mind there was a pandemonium of confusion. Five photographs of his son, cheerful and with a smile and clothes that he had not owned when he had left Moscow for Geneva. Willi on the streets of London because Otto Guttmann knew the symbols behind his son's back . . . the red double decker buses, the policeman with his conical blue helmet, the monuments that were international and famous.

The photographs said to him that Willi was in London. But Willi was drowned in the Lake of Geneva.

His body had never been found.

That was explained. The man from the Foreign Ministry who had telephoned had said that it was possible in those waters for a corpse to stay submerged for many weeks. Possible, but unusual.

Which image should he take, which image should he accept? Willi with his face swollen and his stomach distended, caught in the weed, held in the slurry of the lake mud. Willi, drowned and dead and the file closed. Was that his son? . . . That, or the boy who posed with the grin and the wide smile of the photographs.

If it were a cruel trick then who would have the viciousness of mind to concoct it? The taunting of an old man with the resurrection of his son from the winding sheet.

They had come under the arch of the castle gatehouse, they had paused to find the coins for the admission charge, they had stepped into the strong light of the battlements adorned with cannon. He had no recollection of the man who had come in stealth behind him, could remember nothing of his face or features. He could recall only a slouched and disappearing back and the feel of the thin paper of the envelope in his fingers. If the palm of his hand had not been able to find the clear edges of the photographs in his pocket he would have known he had dreamed, imagined, that the mind of an old man could be harsh and vindictive.

He made an excuse to his daughter. He must find a lavatory. He would only be a few minutes. He left her to gaze down from the high walls across the panorama of the houses set in trees in the slope of the valley, and beyond to the rising woodlands and the Brocken mountain.

Behind a bolted door, cramped and closeted, he took the photographs from his pocket. The pictures admitted no possibility of doubt, nor of deception. Even in the meagre light he could see there was nothing fraudulent, no super-imposition, no trick . . . Willi in the centre of London . . . He felt his knees weaken and reached for the whitewashed walls for support. The tears flowed and he wept without inhibition. Willi, his son. Willi, walking and alive and breathing the good air. He found his handkerchief, wiped his eyes and snivelled into its folds.

Why had the man come with such subterfuge? Why had he not stayed to offer explanation? Why did he torture him with such cruelty? When Otto Guttmann joined his daughter on the battlements she quizzed him sharply as to whether he felt faint, and he said that he was well.

This year, as every year, they set off to tour the state-rooms of the Feudalmuseum.

Too early for lunch, too early for the train back to Magde-burg, Johnny meandered along a wood path away from the cemetery. To his right, half hidden from him by trees was the road winding to the horizon of the hills. That would be the road to the Brocken, the summit at 1140 metres above sea level, the highest peak in the Hartz. Pierce had spoken of the Brocken, of the antennae of the Soviet technicians, of the principal Warsaw Pact listening post in the DDR. Triple towers rising into the skyline that could monitor NATO radio transmissions across West Germany. Less than 10 miles away and the most sensitive installation in the country and close to the frontier. And down the road he'd be drifting into the

Schutzzone that Smithson had warned of. He retraced his steps, turned his back on the far hill and its pylons.

The sign of the forking of the paths directed him to the Wildpark Christianental.

There were deer and pigs here that gazed sorrowfully from inside their wire lined compounds. A fox in a cement floored cage stared back at him and having no escape curled itself again into a fur ball. A wild cat scurried for its artificial cave. They were not the creatures that caught at Johnny's eye. It was the birds of the mountain that drew him. The buzzard and the sparrow hawk, the harrier and the peregrine, the merlin and the kestrel. Each with his stumpy wooden perch, each with his own chain for denying flight. What the bloody place is all about, a great sodding empire of clipped wings and restricted movement.

And Johnny would cut Otto Guttmann free. He would have loved to take a wire cutter to the birds, loved to watch them climb and soar again in the upper currents of the wind.

Suppose Otto Guttmann won't come, rejects it, won't entertain the drive down the autobahn ... what then, Johnny? Cut the wires on those birds and they'll rise. Guttmann is the same, or he's a bloody lunatic.

It had taken Johnny half an hour to walk through the Wildpark. In front of him was the main road into Wernigerode.

Nothing more for him to do in this town. The dart had been thrust into the mind of Otto Guttmann. Its poison should be given time to run.

He would catch the early afternoon train to Magdeburg.

A pleasant sunshine in West Berlin. Crowds out on the Kaiser-Damm and the Bismarck Strasse. The people of this frenetic, isolated city around which 11 Divisions of the Red Army were stationed bobbed in and out of the department stores, crowded the pavements, jostled for seats in the cafés.

With the Brigadier's wife as his guide, Charles Mawby was shopping. He had bought a cut glass vase for Joyce, now looked for something for the children. And he was frittering time, eating at the hours that stood before the launching of DIPPER's run. He was poor company for the Brigadier's wife, little that was amusing in his conversation, and the shopping expedition did nothing but aggravate the cutting edge of his impatience. The obsession that he could not share trampled on him. He carried full responsibility yet he would not be in Magdeburg when Johnny Donoghue met Otto Guttmann. He would not be on the autobahn for the pick-up. He would not be at Marienborn when the documents and passports were produced. He had taken responsibility but when the Dipper bird soared he could not influence its flight.

In three days the mission would be done with, finished. Either way, success or failure, it would be completed. In his working life he thought that he had never felt such choking awareness of the stakes for which he played.

On a scheduled Interflug flight the Trade Minister of the German Democratic Republic and his advisory team arrived at Heathrow.

The group was taken by car from the apron to the Queen's Building suite where was waiting for them a welcoming party formed of a junior minister, two senior civil servants from the Department of Trade and Industry and the East German ambassador to London. There was much smiling as the interpreters grappled with the introductions, many firmly clasped handshakes, an impression of lasting friendship. The Trade Minister was an important figure in the regime and the Party, a member of the Politburo, one of the 'old guard', a colleague of the founders of the 'other' Germany, a friend of Ulbricht and Stoph and Grotewohl and Pieck. A hardline man whose political career had been at its peak when Stalin sat in the Kremlin, an advocate of the march of the Red Army into Czechoslovakia.

The pleasure shown by Dr Oskar Frommholtz at his reception was a patchy mask, as if the guard over his face sometimes slipped to allow suspicion to flourish, the glimmer of caution to cloud his warm words. There were short speeches, polite applause and then the Trade Minister was led to a News Conference.

It was not an auspicious start to the visit.

When a senior functionary of another country, whether from the socialist or capitalist camp, came to the German Democratic Republic a room full of journalists was guaranteed. All the trappings of serious scribblers hanging on the words of the visitor, and arc lights and microphones and turning cameras.

To hear Dr Frommholtz there had gathered only the Press Association, the airport news agency of Brenards, the BBC world service, and the representative of the communist *Morning Star*. Interest had been muted, the questions sparse until the proceedings were brought to a sharp close. The request by the PA reporter for information on the release date of a young East German writer named by Amnesty International as a Prisoner of Conscience and charged with espionage ended the conference. The chairs had been snappily vacated, while the visitors sulked and the hosts twitched in embarrassment.

Facing the first Censure motion that the Opposition had tabled since he had assumed office, the Prime Minister had reacted with annoyance to the charges of incompetence and maladministration thrown across the Despatch Box of the House of Commons. In the morning he had been tetchy with his colleagues in Cabinet and Overseas Planning and Defence. In the afternoon he had given no quarter when fielding his twice weekly Questions. Uneasily his supporters on the benches behind him had cheered as he steam-rollered his opponents on the far side of the Chamber.

He had sat on in the front row of government when the Censure debate had commenced aware that he could expect only a difficult and acrimonious passage when his own time came to wind up the government case before the 10 o'clock voting division. He had heard out the opening exchanges, then with a walk of theatrical indifference left the Chamber.

Now in his private office the Prime Minister was weighing

the paragraph cards of his speech when his PPS introduced the Member for Guildford, Sir Charles Spottiswoode.

'Nice to see you again, Charles.'

'Good of you to see me, Prime Minister.'

'You'll take a drink?'

'A small gin, thank you.'

The PPS poured the drinks at the walnut cabinet, and excused himself. He had no doubt that with the third party gone the pleasantries would be short lived. Within 15 minutes he would have concocted a reason to return and break up the session.

The two men watched the door close.

'What can I do for you, Charles?'

'You can clear up a rather unpleasant and unacceptable bit of government action in my constituency.' Spottiswoode watched with a fleeting smile the flicker of discomfiture on the Prime Minister's face.

'Go on . . . let's have the complaint, and the reason why it was necessary to bring it to me.'

Spottiswoode dramatised a moment of silence, pondered his tie, brushed his nose with a handkerchief. 'In the hills between Guildford and Dorking, at Holmbury, is a country house that many years ago was taken over by the Secret Intelligence Service, or one of their agencies, a hush-hush place. A bit over a fortnight back, I have the exact date in my briefcase, if you want it . . .'

'That can wait, go on.'

'. . . a bit over a fortnight back, a young man with a German name but some sort of Soviet connection escaped from that place and was discovered half frightened to death – and I emphasise that, scared out of his wits – in a field between Ewhurst and the village of Forest Green. One of my constituents found him. Nothing appeared in the papers, of course, because government slapped on a D notice. You presumably were aware of that, Prime Minister?'

'I was aware of the use of a D notice which applied to the presence in this country of a Soviet defector. That notice is still in force, Sir Charles . . .' The admonition was sharply put.

Spottiswoode stiffened. 'You call him a defector, Prime Minister, which to me implies someone who has chosen and quite voluntarily to come to our country. This young man was in a state of abject terror when found, which I suggest is hardly the characteristic of a willing participant in whatever matter the Intelligence people were hatching . . . I will continue. He was taken to the home of my constituent, soaked and chilled, and while he was there he specifically requested protection from the people holding him at Holmbury. He made a most serious allegation there in the presence of the householder and the local constable who had been summoned by telephone. He claimed that he was being forced to provide information which was to be used to facilitate the murder of his elderly father. I understand that his father is a citizen of the Soviet Union, but of East German extraction and that he takes his holiday in the country of his birth each summer, where the killing will take place. This young man alleged that the plan was far advanced, that the actual assassin was present at Holmbury.'

'It sounds a complete tale of fabrication.' A flush was in the Prime Minister's cheeks, the testiness in his words.

'I haven't finished. I'm sure you'll want to hear me out . . .' Spottiswoode said. 'As a result of the information being passed through police channels that the boy had been taken to the house of my constituent, these freebooters from Holmbury were told of his presence. They arrived, abused the police there, were vilely rude to a most pleasant lady, and dragged this young man from the premises half naked. There was no question of returning him into the hands of his former captors of his own free will.'

Anger was settling on the Prime Minister's face. He should have been sitting quietly, brooding with his speech, left to himself and his closest cronies. 'I'll look into it, you can be sure of that.'

'It's my hope that you will look into it, and most thor-

223

oughly at that.' Spottiswoode was not to be easily moved from his bone and the marrow fat. 'Personally, I think it's a damned scandal if government agencies can cloak themselves in secrecy to cover what is at best disgusting behaviour, at worst a heinous and criminal act . . .'

'I have said, Sir Charles, I will look into the matter.'

'This is not a land of private armies, nor is this a police state. We should not tolerate Security and Intelligence carrying on like bandits . . . I have assumed throughout this interview, Prime Minister, that the actions of these people at Holmbury in this case do not have government approval . . .'

'You won't expect me to pass comment on that.'

The Prime Minister shifted in his chair, his fingers twisted on the fountain pen in his hand. Irritation and embarrassment. Could he admit that the Service often acted without informing the head of government? Well enough known that was a fact, whispered about in the corridors of Westminster that the Service was a law to itself. But not for him to say in his own office to a querulous backbencher that he did not control the day to day activities of SIS. Admit that and he was not fitted for the high office he held.

But this was the grey area of the unmentionable – National Security – the area discussed by politicians with the same enthusiasm that a table of cigarette smokers will bring to the topic of terminal cancer. One of his predecessors, Harold Macmillan, had told the House that 'it is dangerous and bad for our national interest to discuss these matters'. Another occupant of Downing Street, Sir Harold Wilson, had written that a Prime Minister questioned in this field should phrase his answers to be 'uniformly uninformative'.

'I trust that those responsible in this case will be brought to heel and sharply. It would be unfortunate if people in this country, hard working and law abiding people, were to believe that there are agencies here that operate above democratic life . . . beyond your control, Prime Minister.'

There was a knock and the PPS came into the room. He coughed for attention.

'I think there are one or two points that have come up in debate that you might wish to rebut, Prime Minister . . .'

The Prime Minister gazed steely eyed across at the back-bencher. 'Thank you for your time. As far as is possible I will inform you of what I discover. I'm most grateful to you.'

'Thank you, Prime Minister. I hope I've been of help.'

They shook hands. With Sir Charles Spottiswoode gone the Prime Minister smacked a clenched fist onto the cards for his speech, scattered them across the table. The PPS, without comment, swept up his glass, took it to the cabinet, filled it heftily. No oil for the troubled waters, gin would have to do the job.

On a Thursday evening in Bonn it was usual for a representative of the Bundesnachrichtendienst (BND) to meet with a senior official of the Bundesamt fur Verfassungeschutz (BfV). It was the regular conversation on matters of mutual interest between the Federal Intelligence Service and the Federal Internal Security Office. Consultation between the two agencies had been demanded by successive Chancellors after the retirement of General Reinhard Gehlen, who had founded BND after the war and run the organisation with autonomous secrecy. It had been determined that never again would an arm of the secret service be permitted such free ranging power, and if BfV maintained a gentle spy role over the more senior brother there would be no complaint by the political administration.

There was always much for them to discuss. The damaging and publicised drain of defecting government secretaries to the East, the knowledge that within the Ministries existed the deep sleeper agents positioned by East Berlin, the efforts of DDR operatives to prise their way into the lives of lonely, menopausal female clerks. There were grounds for constant vigilance, the stability of the nation was threatened. It was little more than 5 years since the worm had crawled to the very heart of the apple, since Willi Brandt had resigned after the discovery that an East German spy had nibbled his way to the Chancellor's private office.

The early talk in the office of the BND representative had concerned the vast scale of Positive Vetting procedures authorised by government. The files were now locked back in their holding cabinets. Neither man was in a hurry to be on his way though their main business was completed. For each this had been the last appointment of the day and all that faced them was the traffic on Koblenzer Strasse, the tedium of the homeward journey. One produced a packet of cigarettes, the other his pipe. Time to ease back in their chairs, time to replace their pens in the inner pockets. The liaison worked well. They were old friends, men who had worked as young officers in Fremde Heere Ost, the section of staff officers in the former Wehrmacht that had concerned itself with Eastern front intelligence. They could confide in each other.

'Did you know that the British . . . SIS . . . had been round us, their man here, they sought a recommendation. They wanted a name of one of the organisations for bringing people from the East.' The BND officer dragged at his cigarette.

'They haven't been to us.'

'It was not a request through the usual channels, there is a procedure for the exchange of information, they did not use that.'

'And before they had been asked for what purpose they needed such information?'

'The intention must be clear . . . they wish to bring someone from the DDR.'

'They live in a delusion of their former times.' The BfV man coughed through the pipe smoke. 'Thirty-five years after the war, and you find those of them that believe they are still the occupying power.'

'Nothing about this was handled properly. I telephoned their man for guidance on their intentions, he was not available and he did not call back. He cancelled the usual liaison meeting for last week, so again we did not talk. Now they have said that we will meet next week . . .'

'Which will be when their business is completed . . . they think they can walk over us.'

'It poses a difficulty, certainly, if we adhere to the policy of the Chancellery at this moment. Escape across the frontier is totally discouraged when aided by commercial organisations. If the request for the information they sought had been properly presented I doubt that it would have been granted. You have the risk of our involvement in a potential incident.'

'Whose name were the British given?' There was a glaze of hostility in the BfV man's face.

'Lentzer . . . Hermann Lentzer . . .'

'A Nazi, I know of him.'

'The British should not have gone about their business in this way, not in the country of an ally, a close ally. And afterwards when they have gone back to London, when they have dismantled their circus it is we who are left with the recrimination and sniping from East Berlin. And bad at this time, with the meeting of the Chancellor and Honecker coming . . .' The BND officer shrugged, enough time had been used. The Koblenzer Strasse traffic would be thinning.

'What are you going to do about it?'

'The Chancellor will not thank me for drawing him into the matter . . . The British would accuse us of gross interference in their plans, whatever they may be . . . I am going to do nothing.' The BND officer was on his feet, briefcase in hand.

'They never change, the British . . . they have never learned to accept their new place.'

As they parted a few minutes later in the car park a persistent drizzle sprayed them and the lights gleamed and shone and cast far shadows on the streets. His temper aroused by what he had been told, his forehead ploughed with irritation, the BfV man rattled his horn as he nudged into the traffic flow.

A black and miserable evening and a slow trek home.

*

Outside the door of his private office the Prime Minister accepted the congratulations of his supporters. Many crowded round him and his ears rang with the acclamation of their praise.

'A triumph, Prime Minister . . .'

'Absolutely marvellous stuff, sir, just what the party needed . . .'

'Quite destroyed them, kicked them where it hurts, damn good . . .'

The Prime Minister's face was set, furious and aggressive. His eyes ranged the corridor for the arrival of his PPS from the Chamber. The decision was taken on the course of action he would follow. Was it supposed to be one man government? Was he supposed to oversee every bloody department of Whitehall? Those buggers from the Service playing their games, living prehistoric dreams. He had been softened up and knocked down by an arrogant fool and that treatment from Spottiswoode outweighed the sycophancy gathered around him.

The PPS came smiling to the Prime Minister's side.

'Fine show . . .'

'What do I have tomorrow?'

'TUC economic committee at 10. Egyptian ambassador at 12 and he's lunching. Away for Chequers at 3.' The PPS marshalled the timetable effortlessly.

'Get hold of the Cabinet Secretary,' the Prime Minister said quietly. 'He's to bring the SIS man to Downing Street at 9 tomorrow . . . That's an instruction.'

The PPS slipped away from the gathering throng around the star of the night. He was baffled. Why on an evening such as this should the Prime Minister speak with such anger?

Chapter Seventeen

——

Friday morning. Johnny rose at six and dressed at once. The noise of the first trams and buses of the day boomed along the street below his window. Friday, and the coming of the critical hours.

He sat at the table and took a sheet of hotel notepaper. Otto Guttmann would have followed instructions, would not have reported the contact. That was Johnny's feeling and he had backed it by sitting in the foyer the previous evening and watching. He would have seen the policemen coming to the lift . . . there had been none . . . Better to use the hotel paper, to blazon the proximity, because anything that disturbed the old man suited Johnny's purpose. He wrote the clear directions that Guttmann should follow and on the reverse side drew a map of the route to the railway bridge by way of Sandtor Strasse and Rogatzer Strasse. Simple, bold lines for the map. He slipped the paper into an envelope and sealed it.

Johnny took the lift downstairs, walked out into the street and towards the square behind the Centrum. It was where he had seen the telephone kiosks. He rang the number of the International, spoke in natural German, and asked for the number of the room of Dr Otto Guttmann. He was a friend, he said, later he would be sending a book to the hotel and he wanted to ensure that the package was correctly addressed. The girl on the switchboard would be busy at this time of the morning with the waking calls. Over the line he heard the yawn, then the turning of paper as she searched for the information.

'Doctor Guttmann, or Miss Erica Guttmann?'
'Doctor Guttmann.'
'Room 626.'

'Thank you.'

Johnny replaced the receiver and strolled away. It had rained in the night, but the day promised well and the banking clouds were falling behind the Elbe and the sun flickered after them. He went back to the hotel and to any who watched him in the hallway he would have seemed a man who had slept badly and taken an early walk to freshen himself. Unremarkable behaviour. Johnny had been a good pupil to Smithson.

He nodded the day's greeting to Comrade Honecker . . . he took the lift to the sixth floor.

There was a maid in the corridor with her trolley and bucket and brooms and stacked clean sheets. Johnny waited, admired a grim water colour of hills and lake shores until she had found a vacated room where she could work. He walked the length of the corridor looking for 626, and paused outside Otto Guttmann's door.

He looked once over his shoulder, heard the sounds of muffled radios in the rooms, the soft voice of the maid as she sang. The corridor was empty. He bent and pushed the envelope under the door. He knocked. There was a distant, indistinct grunt of acknowledgement.

'A letter for you, Dr Guttmann,' Johnny called softly.

'What . . . ?'

'A letter for you under the door.'

'Who is it . . . what time is it . . . ?'

Johnny heard no more. Away down the corridor, light-footed to the lift. The old man would not be quick to find his light switch, stumble to the door, turn the key. If he bothered to search for the carrier of the letter then he would find only a corridor frightening in its emptiness.

Johnny dropped into an armchair across the hallway from the restaurant. He made himself comfortable and waited for the breakfast service to begin.

'What should we do?'

Erica was by the window, a willow figure in a long cotton nightdress. The letter was in her hand, the photographs were spread on the low table beside the easy chair. Erica was pale and her lips bit tight.

'I have to go to the bridge, as I am told.'

Otto Guttmann stood in the centre of his daughter's room. His dressing gown hung from his thin shoulders, his hair wisped and straggling, his eyes confused.

'What if it is a trick . . . ?'

'It *is* Willi in the photograph.'

'It's horrible, evil . . . the people who have done this . . .'

'They know that I will follow, to find Willi.'

'Who would tell us that he is alive, who would tell us in this way?'

She gazed into her father's face and her hair that was not combed fell across her cheeks. Erica who was his leaning staff at Padolsk, on whom he depended. Erica as fearful as a child in a darkened house.

A smile broke the smoothness of the skin at his mouth. 'The pictures are taken in London . . . in the centre of a NATO capital. If they are not a fraud then Willi has gone to the military opponent of the Soviet Union.'

Her fingers crumpled the single sheet of paper, dropped it to the carpet. 'Then Willi is a traitor . . .'

'That is how he would be seen by many.'

'What will they want of you?'

'I don't know,' the old man said simply.

'They will want your mind.'

'I don't know.'

'What are you going to do?'

'I must go to the bridge.' Spoken with tenderness, spoken by a man who has seen the precipices of grief and does not believe he can be hurt any further.

'You can go to Renate's friend, to the Schutzpolizei . . .'

'Then I have disobeyed the instruction.'

'It is your duty to go to the police . . . to the Spitzer . . .'

'Then I do not see Willi.'

'If it is not reported, then we have joined the conspiracy, you see that?'

'I am too old to be afraid.'

231

'Willi is with our enemy . . .'

'In the photograph Willi is happy, as if he has found friends . . .'

She came quickly to him. The slender arms circled his neck, the softness of her mouth nuzzled against his bristled chin.

'I will come with you to the bridge.'

They stood together a long time, drawing on each other's courage, and the photographs lay on the table, and Willi's smile was with them. They could hear his voice and see his face in laughter. Willi's presence was overwhelming. Their cheeks were damp when at last they broke apart to begin to prepare to face the day.

The Second Secretary, Commercial, slipped out of the British Embassy on Unter den Linden, and hurried towards the bridges over the Spree river. His briefcase weighed heavily in his hand. Twice he stopped and turned in one movement . . . surveillance of embassy personnel by the Staatssicherheitsdienst followed no regular pattern and he rated his chances of going without observation as best in the early morning. Before eight and the tourists not yet on the streets.

He was the junior of the two SIS men attached to the embassy staff and working under the wing of diplomatic immunity. This was not the work that he enjoyed, playing the old delivery routines. He was an analyst, an interpreter of information.

The contact would be an older man, an East German national long employed by the British and with an account at a bank in Zurich. Not that he could use the money. But the day would come, the forged passport, the train through the Friedrichstrasse checkpoint. But the contact was not encouraged to think of that time, urged only to soldier on.

For five minutes the Second Secretary sat on a bench in a square across the river and under the Television Tower, then opened his briefcase and took out the package. It was wrapped as for a present. After another minute he left it on the seat, under a newspaper. When he walked back towards the bridge he did not try to watch the collection. Once over the river he stopped at the café beside the History Museum and ordered himself a coffee and a pork sandwich.

It was a vulgar scandal when a foreign intelligence service mounted an operation from Federal territory with neither the courtesy of liaison nor the consideration of the repercussions. Vulgar and arrogant.

Since the assault on the Lufthansa jet at Mogadishu, since the British had loaned two 'storm experts' and their equipment, since hostages had been freed and terrorists killed, the British had taken too much for granted. The congratulations and thanks offered by the Chancellor to their Prime Minister had left them with an illusion as to their rights.

Any connivance, official or otherwise, in the use of a commercial organisation to breach the frontier was potentially disastrous. Transit on the corridor autobahn between the Federal Republic and West Berlin was based on a fragile enough agreement, the Soviets had talked only eighteen months before of renouncing the arrangement if the Bonn government did not take action to curb the escape groups. The British were blundering onto thinly frozen water, and without authority.

Once in his office the man from BfV switched on his electric kettle, and selected two tea bags from the packet in the lower drawer of his desk. He phoned his clerk to provide him with the file on Hermann Lentzer, he ordered an immediate surveillance put on the man, he started the process of discovering the time schedule of the operation for which the British had employed him.

That done the temper that had lingered with him from the previous evening was improved. He would not have admitted that pique or spite fuelled the remorseless attention he now turned on Lentzer. He regarded himself as a good servant, committed simply to the welfare of his country.

233

On the table behind his desk the kettle spluttered and the lid bounced over an eruption of steam.

The Prime Minister sat shoulders back, erect and straight.

On the sofa, with his legs crossed and with the unhappiness of a man drawn into a dispute for which he has no stomach, was the Secretary to the Cabinet.

'Take a chair, please.' The Prime Minister was aloof.

'Thank you, Prime Minister,' the Deputy-Under-Secretary said firmly. That was what he had learned over the years. The maxim of no surrender. Stare them out and don't whimper. Stand your ground. He looked at the Cabinet Secretary and smiled and received for his pains only a turned head. He would find no ally there; not in this room, not at this moment. Worthwhile to know.

'We had a discussion a few day ago over the areas of consultation that I required between your Service and Downing Street . . .' Measured words from the Prime Minister.

'I remember, sir. I've asked my people to get something onto paper, there'll be a minute through in the next few days.'

'. . . Our discussion then followed my complaint that a D notice had been requested without ministerial approval following the disappearance of an East German defector who was in the hands of your people.'

'That's about correct, sir.'

'At that meeting you provided me with a sketchy brief . . .'

'I explained the young man's relevance. I told you of an area in which he might be of some help to us.'

The Prime Minister ignored the interruption, swept on. 'You led me to understand that this defector was being questioned because he had some slight knowledge of a Soviet anti-tank missile system.'

'I said that, yes.'

'In leaving me with that impression you were at worst lying to me, at best being less than frank . . .'

'You must be mistaken, sir.' The golden rule of the civil

234

service and practised now by the Deputy-Under-Secretary. Never lose your temper, not with a politician.

'I believe that I am not mistaken. I am informed that at the time we last met the Service was already well started on a project involving the father of this defector. I am informed that a team had been gathered together for a clandestine operation in the German Democratic Republic. I am additionally informed that the objective of this team was the assassination of the father of this defector . . .'

The Deputy-Under-Secretary gaped. 'That's just not true.'

The Prime Minister gestured him to silence. 'I will not tolerate autonomous action of this type. I will not permit killer squads to be sent abroad.'

'I said it's not true.'

'I demand that this operation, whatever its state of advancement, shall immediately be cancelled. I don't mean postponed, I mean cancelled. Is that clear?'

The Deputy-Under-Secretary closed his eyes, allowed the quiet of the room to swim in his mind. The time for persuasion. No option but conciliation. 'Prime Minister, there is no plan to kill this young man's father. His murder has never been considered. The plan that the Service has initiated is not histrionic. It is a straightforward and, we believe, valuable exercise . . .'

'I've made my decision.'

'Our target is no more or less than to bring about the voluntary defection of a top authority from the east bloc in the science of Manual Control Line of Sight missiles. He is holidaying in the East German town of Magdeburg. It's close to the frontier and we are offering him the opportunity of following his son into exile.'

'I repeat . . . I want this plan called off, finished with.'

'The defection of this man would be of enormous advantage, not only to this country but to the military technology of all the NATO nations. It is extremely rare that a man of this calibre comes within our reach. The opportunity should not be missed . . .'

'You haven't been listening to me. I demand cancellation . . .'

'We are close, this very morning, Prime Minister, to achieving our objective. We hope for his arrival in West Germany within the next 48 hours. The prize of this defection, sir, is incalculable, I must stress that. All of my senior officers agree on the value of this man.'

'The issue is not the importance of the information this scientist can give you. The issue is whether the personnel of the Secret Intelligence Service institute policy in the United Kingdom, or whether that function remains in the hands of the democratically elected leaders. Because that point does not seem to have been understood I intend that a lesson shall be learned. The operation is cancelled.'

Damned, damned, damned fool. The Deputy-Under-Secretary squirmed. Pompous, priggish, damned fool. And from where had the leak come? The house at Holmbury? The hours when the boy was loose, when Mawby was in Germany, when an incompetent wretch called Carter was in charge?

For the first time the Secretary to the Cabinet intervened. A softly spoken man. A hesitant, cultured voice. 'Perhaps, Prime Minister, we should hear the nature of the plan to bring out Doctor Guttmann. Perhaps before we make a final decision on this mission we should hear an assessment of the risks of detection for the operation, as seen by the Service.' His influence was vast in the offices of Downing Street. Few decisions of national importance were taken in the face of his disapproval. 'And perhaps DUS can outline the worth to us of this man?'

The Deputy-Under-Secretary was aware of the shimmer of interest from the Prime Minister. He probed steadily forward with his argument. 'I've one of my best men running this show from Germany. Naturally I've studied his plan, most closely. I have no hesitation in telling you that it will succeed.'

'The Service has behaved with extraordinary arrogance . . .'

'We deliver, Prime Minister,' said the Deputy-Under-Secretary evenly. 'In the early hours of Sunday morning we intend to deliver Otto Guttmann.'

'The plan has been conceived in flagrant violation of the conditions I laid down at our previous meeting.'

'In the 1980s this country will be building a thousand Main Battle Tanks of new design. We have a small army and for it to be effective we must provide excellent equipment. If Guttmann comes to Britain those tanks will benefit in performance and protection. I urge you, Prime Minister, to reconsider.'

'You can't be certain of success. You can't be certain the whole thing won't blow in our faces. I'll not have myself put in the position of Eden in the '50s, having to tell the House he wasn't told that Intelligence were putting a diver under a Russian cruiser docked in Portsmouth harbour . . . of Macmillan who wasn't told that his Minister of War was sharing a call girl with the Russian naval attaché . . . of Alec Home who wasn't told that Security were offering immunity to that fellow Blunt . . . I'll not have myself made a fool of.'

'I can assure you, sir, you'll not be made a fool of. By the weekend I would anticipate that it will be within your power to share with our NATO and American allies what we confidently expect will be the most sensitive information available to the Western Alliance for many years. I'm sorry if that seems a bit of a speech, but that's how we rate Otto Guttmann.'

The wheel had swung, the pendulum had swayed. The Prime Minister wiped the moisture from the palms of his hands. 'You believe that risk has been eliminated from this affair?'

The Deputy-Under-Secretary felt the flush of victory. 'I do, sir.'

They talked for a few more minutes. The Deputy-Under-Secretary explained the details of the run along the Berlin to Helmstedt autobahn, he spoke of the armoured deficit between the tank forces available to NATO and those of the Warsaw Pact. He titillated with an abbreviated biography of

an unnamed agent who had travelled to Magdeburg. Ultimately he offered an apology for what he conceded to be a
want of frankness on his behalf.

The Deputy-Under-Secretary and the Secretary to the
Cabinet left the Prime Minister's room together.

In the corridor the Secretary to the Cabinet whispered, 'I
hope to God you're right, that risk has been eliminated . . .
because if it hasn't then there's nothing on this earth that can
save you. You'll be carrion for the crows.'

On an ageing typewriter Dr Gunther Spitzer drafted his
reply to the communication from KGB headquarters in
Moscow.

A quite puzzling matter for him because no explanation
had been offered as to why KGB's own operatives were not
involved, nor any of the other Soviet organisations that
might have been expected to handle the enquiry. And as he
typed, and crossed out what he had set down, and typed
again, he remained confused as to what in fact was required of
him. He could report that he had met Dr Otto Guttmann,
had dined with him, that the drowning of his only son had
been spoken of. He could report that the scientist was still
deeply affected by the death, to the extent that he, Spitzer,
had not felt decently able to press further. Without doubt
the grief was genuinely felt, not counterfeit.

Of slight consolation to the Schutzpolizeipresident was the
knowledge that his prompt response to Moscow would be
noticed, his efficiency would be recorded. Moscow had
much influence.

He wrestled again with the text and called through the
open door of his office for more coffee.

George as the minder, Pierce as the watcher, accompanied
Willi Guttmann on the British army train out of West Berlin.
They'd dressed the boy in the standard tweed jacket of a
British officer in mufti, given him a tie and a check shirt. Just
right he seemed to them, like any young lieutenant from the
Berlin garrison.

The daily routine of more than 30 years was enacted at the East German frontier. The carriage doors were locked after the guards had clambered aboard. A small, sealed cell the train had become as it wound through the East German countryside. Before taking bacon and egg in the restaurant car, Pierce had reserved a compartment, bluntly evicting a Dental Corps major. He had seen that the window opened. He had repeated again to Willi where he should stand.

Willi had said little as he toyed with his food. Pierce wondered how he felt, how he would react to seeing his father again . . . if indeed the old man came to the bridge . . . he couldn't put himself in the boy's mind and after a moment's reflection saw no particular reason why he should.

It was aggravating that he would have to stand behind the boy when they rolled through Magdeburg. He wouldn't get a decent look at the scenery, and the scenery meant Johnny. Not that he'd be standing at the old man's shoulder, but it would have been special to have seen him. The man they had moulded at Holmbury, it would have given Pierce a particular pleasure to manage a glimpse, however brief, of Johnny's face.

Past Genthin and half an hour out from Magdeburg Pierce made the move for them to return to their compartment. His own excitement consumed him. They were very close now, close enough almost to finger the success of the DIPPER mission.

Johnny distanced himself by a full hundred yards from the bridge. It was bad to have to wait in one place for long, conspicuous, and he willed that the train would be on time.

They had done everything that he had demanded of them in his note and they were standing now, the old man and the girl, in the centre of the bridge and their eyes never wavered from the track that stretched away towards the Biederitzer Busch. Frail and unsafe they seemed to Johnny, close together for comfort, Otto Guttmann holding tightly to his daughter's arm.

The train came, crawling over the tangled web of converging rail, slow and noisy and swaying. Their eyes scanned the length of it, searching into the windows of the forward carriages.

'The third carriage, Father . . .' Erica cried. The hoarseness grabbed at her throat. 'The third one, the second window . . .'

'Willi . . . Willi . . .' The faint call of the old man, his voice cudgelled and overwhelmed by the pounding wheels.

They were so near to him. A few feet only. The letter had said that they should not wave, and Otto Guttmann's hand clutched at the material of Erica's raincoat, and her own fingers were across his, stifling their movement.

For only a few seconds the hallucination lasted, a trifle of time, and the train had cleared the bridge.

They were left with the images, the sharpness of the memory. Willi at the window. Willi shaved and clean and with his hair combed. Willi with the strained face and the eyes that seemed to call mutely to them. Willi pleading that they should follow, and no path shown to them, no signpost given. There had been two men behind Willi, standing back in the compartment, their faces in shadow.

They came down the steps of the bridge.

The ribbons of tears ran on Otto Guttmann's face. 'The moment is tainted . . . we should be happy, Willi is alive, more than I ever prayed for . . . but there is an evil. You saw the flag of the British on the train . . . it is not for kindness that they have shown him to us . . .'

'Why did they do it?' Erica, saucer eyed, her voice strident.

In front of them a man turned his gaze away. A well-built man, youngish and powerful. The man had been watching them, watching as they negotiated the steps of the bridge. He had stood out, strangely different, the clothes and the gait guaranteeing that they noticed him. Otto Guttmann stared, entranced, captured by the diminishing silhouette of the man who walked away on Rogatzer Strasse, threading his steps between the broken paving stones.

Otto Guttmann flinched. He had seen the contact man, he

had seen the man they had sent.

'They are all around us, like rats near an animal that is about to die,' he said quietly.

'What do you mean?' Mid-morning. Daylight swamping the city that Erica had known since childhood. Traffic on the roads, people in the streets, the business of the community under way on every side of her, and she was frightened.

'When they are ready they will come close and say what they want of us.'

'Who are they?'

Otto Guttmann shook his head sadly. 'It does not matter . . . we must go back to the hotel.'

'I should go to Spitzer, Renate's friend,' Erica said.

'Do that and you kill me.'

In front of them the man did not deign to turn and watch them again. In a little time he was gone from their view. In a business like this, Guttmann knew, nothing would materialise by chance. Everything was calculated, everything was weighed and tested before being allowed to go forward. It would have been intended that he should see his torturer, the courier who thumbscrewed an old man's mind. They would leave him now, leave him to brood and curse. Only when he was broken would they come.

Holding fiercely to Erica's hand, Otto Guttmann started back for the centre of Magdeburg.

Through the afternoon Johnny slept in his room. He was not tired but he knew no other way to chip through the hours till it was time for dinner. He had undressed, slipped under sheets, closed his eyes and tidied his mind. Two more days and he would have Carter fussing round him, Mawby pressing his hand. Two more days and he could make the telephone call to Cherry Road and he would be standing high on his pride. Two more days and the killing of Maeve O'Connor would be purged. There would be a hell of a party in Helmstedt, he thought of that before the release of a shallow, mottled sleep.

*

241

A thousand yards from the International Hotel a middle-aged man dropped a parcel into a deep litter bin behind the back doors of the Kulturhistorische Museum on the narrow Heydeck Strasse. He hid the package with a shallow covering of refuse.

Friday afternoon was the right time for a litter bin 'drop'. The last clearing of the week by the city's cleansing department would have been made in the morning. The bin would be untouched until Monday. The man retraced his steps to the Hauptbahnhof. He would have less than 20 minutes to wait before the departure of the express to Berlin.

She was sorry, very sorry, said the housekeeper, but the pastor had gone for the day to his niece in Cottbus. She told the caller that he would not be back till very late in the evening because it was a long journey to make in one day. Was the matter urgent? Could it wait till the morning? The pastor would be at the Dom all the next morning, she knew that for certain. She took a pencil and wrote down a message on the notepad beside the telephone. The pastor would find it there when he returned.

'Doctor Otto Guttmann telephoned. It is most important that he should see you. He will come to the Dom tomorrow before lunch.'

A pall of smoke floated over the shell of the T 34 tank. There was much laughter, cheerful banter, as the generals came down from the viewing stand to their transport. Both of the prototype missiles that had been made available for the test firing had run with unerring aim towards their battered target. There was a round of drinks for them when they reached their staff cars.

'The opportunities for evasion to a tank commander are negligible.'

'When is the German back?'

'Guttmann returns in two days.'

'Where is he now?'

'Still in Magdeburg.'

'He should be told of the success of the firing. He deserves congratulation.'

'We have witnessed the birth of a famous weapon . . .'

The message from Padolsk went via Defence Ministry in Moscow to Soviet military headquarters in East Germany at Zossen-Wunsdorf, was then relayed to Divisional head-quarters for the Magdeburg region. An army motorcyclist brought the communication to the International Hotel, and took it by hand to the sixth floor because he must bring back a signature of receipt.

The motorcyclist was admitted to the hotel room by a girl, tall and blonde and who at a different time might have been considered striking and pretty. She was pale, and her eyes bulged in the aftermath of weeping. The room was dark from the gathering night, the lights had not been switched on, the curtains had not been drawn, open sandwiches from 'Room Service' had not been eaten. An old man sat by the window, seemingly unaware of the intrusion until the girl brought the docket to him and he wrote his name quickly, then reverted to his empty stare across the skyline of the city.

After the motorcyclist had withdrawn, his boots beating away down the corridor, Erica Guttmann ripped open the envelope.

'It is from the commandant at Padolsk. The test firing was successful,' she said without emotion. 'They say it was com-pletely satisfactory . . . they offer their warmest congratula-tions . . . they call it a triumph of military technological development . . .'

She passed the sheet of paper to her father. As if with reluctance he held out his hand to receive it, then peered at the typed words in the half light. Abruptly he opened his hand and let the paper flake to the floor.

By the finish of the working day the reports ordered by the BfV official were arriving at his desk. An efficient and effective organisation. The safe return of the homing pigeons.

The neighbours of Hermann Lentzer had been spoken with, discreetly.

His telephone had been tapped at the local exchange, with official authorisation.

His personal file had been taken from the archive collections at Wiesbaden and teletyped to Bonn.

Gazing through the shallow lenses of the spectacles that he wore for close work, puffing occasionally at his pipe, the man from BfV read through the material that had been collated for him.

Lentzer in a training battalion of the Waffen-SS and finding his combat baptism in the 33 day battle to obliterate the Warsaw Ghetto, the battle that was fought until every Jew inside the perimeter was either dead or in transport for the extermination camps. Lentzer, who had stood guard at the fences of Auschwitz in the latter months of the war before slipping into peace-time obscurity. Now, Lentzer the trafficker.

They came again, these people. Their filth was never destroyed. Where was he now? . . . The young man who had fired his rifle into the tottering, tragic remnants of the Ghetto, who would have marched the emaciated prisoners to the bulldozed pits of Auschwitz . . . What was his punishment? A secure future and immunity from prosecution. A big house in a pleasant village outside Bonn, a big car to drive, a big account in black at the bank. Where was the repayment of the debt for the disgrace of his country? They were scum, these people, scum at the rim of the cess-pit.

He read on.

Hermann Lentzer was going to Berlin. That afternoon he had made a telephone call, he had announced his arrival time. He had spoken to an Englishman and neither had used their name. He often went to Berlin, the neighbours said, because sometimes they saw beside his rubbish bins the plastic bags that carried the names of the stores on Kurfusten-Damm and Bismarck Strasse. And when he travelled, Lentzer went by car, the neighbours said. He

244

would use false papers, the BfV man reflected, but the car would not change, the number plate would not be altered . . . How could the British associate with such dirt? Was this the courtesy of an ally?

The lights threw into relief the gloom beyond his window. Late in the evening and the building was quiet and empty save for a scattering of night clerks . . . All the frontiers of the world could be crossed. Through the minefields and wire and high walls there were hidden corridors of communication. The BfV in Bonn could make contact with the SSD in East Berlin. The route was tortuous but could be managed.

He wrote on his notepad the details of the model of Mercedes car driven by Hermann Lentzer, its colour and number plate. He pondered then for a few moments. The bastard deserved no sympathy, no mercy. The British had made their own bed, they could lie on it, and they had not consulted on a matter that if it failed or succeeded would bring only nuisance to the Federal Republic.

Without emotion he weighed the correctness and the consequences of the action he had proposed to himself. The British had stepped outside the agreed guidelines; he had no responsibility that he owed them. And if he jeopardised the British plan? They had had the opportunity for consultation with the Federal authorities, they had not availed themselves of it. They had avoided the queries raised by BND.

He remembered the displacement camp in which he had stayed for two years after the war. Temporary barrack buildings near to Celle, swill to eat, thin clothes to wear through winter, and the guards of the British Army of Occupation behind the fence with their jeers and cat-calls and the arrogance of the victor. Two years as a number and he had committed no offence, only served with what he had believed to be an officer's honour in the crumbling Wehrmacht. That was how they had treated him, and now they hired an animal, a criminal like Lentzer to do their work for them.

But that was not the reason that he would make the telephone call. The defence of the interests of his country would

245

govern his action, and this was a time when the policy of the Chancellery demanded an improvement of relations with the 'other Germany'.

He dialled the home number of a young art teacher living in the city of Stuttgart.

After his dinner in the restaurant of the International Hotel, Johnny set out for Heydeck Strasse. Alone on the streets, with only the echo of his footsteps for company, his own shadows swinging to meet him.

One last push in the morning, Johnny, then the bloody thing's finished.

Chapter Eighteen

═══

Standing on a chair, Johnny stowed the package on the wardrobe shelf above his hanging jacket and spare pair of trousers. Saturday morning.

The package was lighter than when he had brought it into his room because the Stechkin automatic pistol now rested on his hip, held there by the pressure of his belt, pressed against his skin. He had armed the pistol, slotted it with a magazine. There were extra blankets on the shelf and the maid had already tidied his room while he had taken coffee in the hall and guarded the package between his legs. It would be safe on the shelf, safe till the grenades and the other magazines and the shoulder stock were needed.

When he left the room he locked the door behind him, pocketed the key. Down the corridor to the lifts. Johnny let himself out at the sixth floor.

How do you feel, Johnny? Bloody grim, like nothing ever before. Worse than standing before the Lord Chief Justice when he'd finished the summing up, put down his pencil, sucked at the stuffy air of the courtroom, pronounced his verdict. Worse than then. Worse than that time when he'd turned into Cherry Road and known that all the neighbours knew, and known his mother would be in the kitchen and all he would see of her welcome would be a cup of tea.

Just a job, Johnny, just do your best. Go tell Mawby that, go tell Mr bloody Mawby in his pinstripe suit.

Room 626.

They're all behind you . . . Mawby, Carter, Smithson and Pierce, even old George, they're all behind you. Right behind, back over the bloody border.

Room 626.

Corridor's clear. Get on with it, lad, don't hang about.

His legs were tight and his muscles fluttering, and there was a pain in his stomach and the forward gun sight bit at his buttocks. In you go, Johnny.

He knocked at the door, knocked twice and sharply.

The girl was in front of him. The dullness of the corridor and the light of the room behind her contrived to shadow and grey her face. He saw the blotched smears at her cheeks, the trembling of her fingers at the door jamb.

Johnny spoke in German. Curt and boorish because he must dominate from the start. He had come to issue instructions, not to plead, that was the Holmbury doctrine. 'I'd like to see your father, Miss Guttmann.'

He was expected. There seemed no surprise, only a deep tiredness that he read from her eyes, and almost the trace of relief that a nightmare might be nearing its end. She gestured that he should come into the room, then as an afterthought she moved aside to permit him to pass her.

An obsessive fear of flying led to Hermann Lentzer using his car for the long journey from the outskirts of Bonn to West Berlin. After Cologne he would join the E 73 autobahn that would take him beyond Dortmund. He would transfer then to the E 8 and from there it was straight for 280 miles via Hannover and Braunschweig and Helmstedt to Berlin. The Mercedes would swallow the distance.

His documents rested in a leather handbag on the imitation fur cover of the seat beside him. His radio was tuned to the station designed for long distance travellers, light music interrupted only by news of road works and traffic accidents that might cause delay. When he returned the following day he would be hugely richer and more importantly he would have kicked the pigs of the DDR, bruised their testicles, chalked up one more scream of pain and anger.

If the frontier crossings were not slow he would be in West Berlin by early afternoon.

Otto Guttmann was sitting in a low chair near to the window. Johnny towered over him.

'Doctor Guttmann, we have some matters to talk of.'

'We have been waiting for you . . .'

'Have you followed the instructions, have you spoken to anybody of the photographs and the train?'

'Only to Erica, only to my daughter.'

Otto Guttmann wore the visage of the priest, of one who has been persecuted and who has felt the slings and arrows. He was not lying, Johnny knew that. The quiet, steady, deliberate voice could not have mustered an untruth.

'Willi is alive and well, Doctor Guttmann. This evening he will be waiting fifty kilometres from here . . .'

'Waiting for what?' The old man's head swayed as he watched through the window the careering flight of a pigeon.

'He will be waiting for you, Doctor Guttmann. From midnight he will be waiting at Helmstedt, waiting for you both to come through the border.'

'It is a sick, cruel game that you play . . .'

'Not my game, Dr Guttmann. It's the facts that are sick and cruel. You've been in mourning for a boy who's fit and strong and breathing, that's sick, and that's a fact. Your son defected, that's cruel, and that's a fact. We didn't make him, we didn't know him till he came over. If that hurts, I'm not to blame. But there's another fact . . . tonight Willi will be waiting and you can join him.'

There was a grim smile on Guttmann's face.

Did you leave him too long, Johnny? Too long, so that the introspection has strengthened and not broken him. Not clasping your bloody hand in gratitude, is he? Far from it. There was a calmness about the old man. A serenity, a sense that he was above and beyond anything that Johnny could do to him.

'It is not possible for us to go to the West,' he said simply.

'It *is* possible. It is arranged, and it will happen.'

'I am an old man. Once I had a wife and she is lost to me. Once I had a son and he too was taken. I no longer believe in promises. I trust only in Erica's love. That is enough for me.'

Harder, Johnny, go harder. Obliterate the disbelief. You have to, Johnny, you have to be bloody vile. 'Doctor Guttmann, listen carefully to me. Your son had no accident on the Lake of Geneva. His actions were intended only to deceive, they were eminently successful. Of his own volition Willi came to London. Once there he renounced the countries of his birth and of his adoption. He has put himself at our disposal . . .'

'You are British?' The whisper, the incredulity from behind.

Damn the girl, damn her for the spoiling of the mood, damn her for bringing her father's gaze darting to the source of interruption. 'Be quiet, Miss Guttmann. He put himself at our disposal. He co-operated fully with us. He is well and happy now, you can see that from the photographs. He has told us of you, Doctor Guttmann, he talked a great deal of you . . . he is ashamed of the hurt that he has caused you. Six weeks ago we began to plan a way that would bring you in safety to your son's side. By this time tomorrow you will be reunited with Willi. If you follow me that will happen – I guarantee that, Doctor Guttmann – if you do not take this chance the opportunity will never be repeated. You have one chance, one chance only that you may take advantage of. A car will come down the autobahn tonight from West Berlin. It will carry the necessary documents. The car will pick you up and drive you to Helmstedt. The offer stands for this night . . . for this night only . . . there will never be another car . . .'

Johnny saw the old man's eyes drift away from him.

Otto Guttmann no longer listened. 'You know that I am elderly, you think, too, that I am a fool?'

Johnny was halted and the words, careful and rehearsed, deserted him. There was a limpness in his reply, forced by the bluntness of the question. 'I know that you are no fool, you have a reputation for brilliance in your field of study.'

'You believe that at this time my grief for Willi is keenest. You believe that when I come to Magdeburg next year I will be less susceptible to your blackmail.'

'You owe these people nothing, Doctor Guttmann.'

'And what do I owe to your people?'

Johnny hesitated. He glanced back over his shoulder at Erica, wondered whether she was a source of support. She stared back at him, bland and impassive. 'We offer you freedom, Doctor Guttmann.'

The old man stared at Johnny. 'You are the representative of freedom? You who spy on me, you who hides himself without a name. What is freedom to you?'

'You should know better than to ask, Doctor Guttmann,' Johnny snapped back. 'You have lived in Hitler's Germany. You have worked in Stalin's and Khrushchev's and Brezhnev's Russia. You should know what is freedom.'

'If I follow you what is the price that I must pay?'

'You will make your own choice on the repayment of the debt. That is the freedom that we offer you.'

'You know my work?'

'Willi told us.'

'You know that the team I direct has been working on the prototype missile to succeed Sagger?'

'Your son told us.'

'You know the prototype has been completed and tested?'

'We assumed the project was in the final stage.'

'Yesterday that prototype was fired at Padolsk, and I have received a message of congratulation from General of Ordnance Grivchenko. You cannot know that?'

'Of course not.'

'You are young and no doubt brave to have come here, you are clever and resourceful or you would not have been chosen. I ask you those questions so that you may appreciate that I am sceptical of angels who speak with the motives of mercy and freedom. You want me only as a traitor, as a turncoat.'

The silence hung in the room. The memories of the briefings at Holmbury turned in Johnny's mind. Stand your ground, they'd said. Don't debate and don't argue. Let the blood ties gnaw at him.

'You must decide where your affections lie. It may be

251

many years in your life since you have had the opportunity to choose your own future. You have that chance now. The choice lies in whom you betray. It may be Defence Ministry in Moscow, it may be your son who will be at Helmstedt tonight.'

Not bad, Johnny. Smithson would have enjoyed that. Otto Guttmann had turned back to the window and the grey cloud basket.

'What is your name?'

Johnny swung round to face Erica Guttmann, pirouetted on his toes. 'It's Johnny.'

'You ask much of us, Johnny,' she said. 'We have a security here, of a sort . . . You ask us to go blindfold after you.'

'Yes.'

'It is a crude bait that you offer.'

'Yes.'

'This car, it will really come?' She was urging the confirmation from him.

'I promise that the car will come.'

'What is the danger to him?'

'We are careful people, Miss Guttmann. There is no danger.'

'He loved Willi,' she spoke as if her father were no longer in the room. 'I think he loved him more than he loved my mother . . . there is no risk to him?'

It was Erica who they had said at Holmbury he would have to claw his way past to get to the side of the old man, and Johnny saw only sweetness and worry and the tumbling in her mind on the decision that would be hers to make.

'There is no risk . . .'

'I will talk to him.'

'Yes.'

'You will come again, later.'

'Yes.'

'When will you come?'

'You have all the hours of daylight to talk. All the day. By evening you must be clear on your intentions. There is no argument after that. If you accept then you follow me without question.' A half smile, a little chuckle came to Johnny. 'You should come, Miss Guttmann, ride the wind beyond the fence. Willi is waiting there and a great horizon . . . don't turn your back on it, don't choose this bloody drab heap.'

'Come again in the afternoon.'

'You should not talk of this . . . if you were to go to the police, if anything were to happen to me then it would go badly for Willi, that's obvious, isn't it?'

She looked at him without anger, without surprise, showed only a smear of disappointment. 'Are the threat and the bribe the only words of your language?'

Johnny walked past her and closed the door quietly behind him.

Sitting by the window in the breakfast room at the Stettiner Hof Henry Carter planned his day. There were only a few courses open to him. He thought that he'd buy a shirt down in the old quarter, on the Neumarker Strasse. He thought he'd wander up to the NAAFI Roadhaus and have a lunch of something and chips and a bottle of beer. He thought he'd have a siesta before the evening vigil at Checkpoint Alpha. At least by the evening he'd have company. Pierce and George and Willi had gone through to Hannover on the military train, they'd spent the night in the close security of the British army camp at Paderborn. Pierce had telephoned to report that Willi's behaviour on the train had been faultless. They would all come back to Helmstedt for the end of the run. A treat for Willi, and he'd earned it. Carter thought that it might be time for him to talk with the boy about the girl Lizzie in Geneva, put the record straight, and it would be the right occasion because the boy would have his head stuffed with the reunion with his father and sister.

It was a subdued, close morning in Helmstedt. Carter hoped the sun would have broken through before he started the trail up to the Roadhaus.

*

They ran towards each other across the wide, white pavings of Alexander Platz, sprinting, racing to be together.

Ulf and Jutte beneath the mountain of the 'Stadt Berlin' Inter Hotel. Hands around each other's necks, fingers deep into each other's hair, lips pressed against each other's cheeks. With the world to watch, with the stores calling the Saturday shoppers, with the square crowded with tourists and visitors, she hugged against him, squirmed herself close to him. No words, no talk, only holding, only kissing. It was a warm morning and he felt the roughness of her heavy sweater and the waterproof anorak hung from her elbow. If she had worn the clothes that he had asked for then she would have the rail tickets tight in the pocket at the waist of her trousers.

Instinctively he led, his arm around her shoulder, towards the S-Bahn station on Alexander Platz.

Jutte had told her father and mother that she was camping for the weekend. She had made her farewells short and cheerful and temporary, pecked at the cheek of her father, squeezed the hand of her mother . . . she had not thought whether she would see or hear of them again.

Ulf had survived the annoyance of his father that within hours of his demobilisation he should need to take a weekend with the FDJ out of Berlin. His mother had sat in the kitchen while the father and boy had conducted their whispered argument in the hallway.

He wondered how soon they would hear of his escape. Within a day perhaps, not more than two, after the crossing. The little room where they spent their evenings in front of the television and the electric fire would be crowded with the men of the Schutzpolizei. Submission from his father, terror from his mother, and they never in trouble before. And when his father professed his surprise, astonishment at the action of his son, would the policemen believe him? And if they did not believe him . . .? Emotion trapped in Ulf's throat, tears caught in his eyes. He did not want to harm them, not his father or mother. They had done nothing to deserve the retribution of the Party.

Jutte's forehead nuzzled against his chin. 'You have found the place?'

'There is a place where it can be done.'

'Where we can cross?'

'Where it's possible, yes.'

'I will not be frightened, not with you.'

For more than 3 hours Otto Guttmann had sat in the small sitting room in the cottage of the pastor beside the Dom. He had come alone, and Erica had gone to walk in the Pionier-park and had said that she would support his decision, she would follow his choice. The burden was on his back, laid at his door, and one friend to turn to.

Otto Guttmann told the pastor of his work at Padolsk. He went over in detail the events as he had known them surrounding the drowning of his son. He had relived the visit to Wernigerode and the passing of the photographs which he showed to his friend. He talked in a voice stumbling with pain of the sight of Willi from the footbridge over the railway. He recalled the words of the Englishman who had come to his hotel room.

What should he do? he asked. Where lay his loyalty?

The pastor had not interrupted. Only after the housekeeper had carried in on a tray a plate of cold meats and a pot of tea was the monologue exhausted.

He was a small spare man, the pastor. The gestures of his hands as he spoke were quick, decisive. His voice was lulling, persuasive. He had known humiliation and rejection, he had worked all his adult life in the community of Magdeburg. He showed no surprise that his friend had visited him, only an acceptance of the enormity of the option. The words he used were thoughtfully chosen.

'You are a scientist, Otto, a manufacturer of terrible weapons of warfare. I am a pacifist, I have been so ever since the bombers came to our city and 16,000 persons were slaughtered in the holocaust and the firestorm. If you stand before me as a scientist and ask me where your duties lie, then I cannot help you, I offer no advice.'

The cup in Otto Guttmann's hand trembled, tea slopped to his trouser leg.

'. . . But you are, too, a Christian, you are a believer, and there we are joined. As a Christian your blood runs as freely as mine, as if we were brothers. We know what it is to worship alone, we have the comradeship that comes from the mocking of an atheist society, we have suffered the nobility of hardship for our beliefs. In this country it is an act of courage to attend public worship. You remember when the pastor from Zeitz, you remember the name of Brusewitz, you remember when he immolated himself on the steps of his church, poured petrol over himself and took a match, to draw attention to the harassment of young Christians in our society, you remember him? They called him an idiot and said that he was deranged. And after his death, we who were his fellow Christians, we debated amongst ourselves as to whether we had compromised too far with the Party. To me, Brusewitz is as near a saint as we will find in our time in this place. He made the supreme sacrifice in the flames, the sacrifice of Christ. His example was one of heroic faith, and his death demands that we of the church must stay and fight for his ideals, we cannot abandon our people. I speak as a cleric. I could not go, my fight is here.'

The pastor poured more tea, took another slice of meat to his plate and cut it with neat and precise movements.

'You do not have those chains on you, Otto. Neither you, nor your daughter. You are free to go. There is no shame in withdrawing from persecution, no disgrace. Your time runs quickly, you have deserved a latter peace. You should go to the comfort of your family. You have the right to find your happiness. There is no duty that obliges you to remain.'

They went together from the pastor's room and into the high, vaulted cathedral, past the tombs topped by stone carved knights, past the shrapnel pocked figure of Christ, past the place where the leaking roof threw water down on the flagstones. They went to the front line of chairs arrayed in front of the altar. For several minutes they prayed in silence.

Outside in the sunshine they shook hands.

The pastor smiled. 'I will think of you, my friend, I will think of you often.'

His engine idling, his radio playing, a packet of sweets close to his hand, Hermann Lentzer sat in his car at the head of the queue at the Marienborn checkpoint. A kilometre behind him and barely visible up the hill were the fluttering flags of the United States of America and France and Great Britain. He was close to a square-based, tall watchtower, he was hemmed in by the wire that enclosed the checkpoint. He was impatient because it was some minutes since they had taken his passport, and those of other drivers in the queue who had been behind him had already been returned. They had been free to drive away on the autobahn.

He drummed his fingers irritably on the steering wheel and tried to show his annoyance by staring out the young face of the Border Guard who stood in front of the bonnet of his car. Usually it was quick, usually only a formality to gain clearance for the autobahn corridor. Behind him a driver hooted as if to protest that Lentzer by his own choice was blocking the road . . . stupid bugger.

The fright came slowly, nagged at him gradually, gathered in his stomach. There should not have been this delay. He had never waited so long before at Marienborn. The driver who had hooted passed him and Lentzer scowled at the man's enquiring glance.

Alone in his car, the business of the border around him, a warm lunchtime, the sun high, and the sweat gathering in his armpits, running underneath his vest. There had never been a delay like this at Marienborn. Two hundred metres back towards Helmstedt were the steel barriers that when dropped lay at windscreen height, they could lower them in 6 seconds . . . no going back, and the Border Guard in front with the sub-machine gun slung from his shoulder and his eyes never leaving the Mercedes.

He wiped his forehead, and fiddled with his radio, and took another sweet. Not until they were all around the car and a pistol held hard against his ear was he aware of the Border Guards. They pulled open the door and dragged him from his seat. His hands were first flung across the car roof while they frisked him for a weapon, then pulled behind his back for the handcuffs. Never upright nor still enough to protest, he was frogmarched into the administration block.

A Border Guard, unable quite to conceal his fascination in the finish and fittings of the Mercedes drove Hermann Lentzer's car behind the building and parked it amongst the unit's lorries and jeeps.

An inexact science, wasn't it? No bloody text book to tell Johnny the technique necessary for the persuasion of a man to abandon the life of 35 years and turn his face towards strangers. Willi was the bludgeon in his argument, but Guttmann had shown a resilience that he had not expected. The girl was different, strange that, as though Willi had talked of a casual friend and not of his sister. The girl would bend her father, perhaps.

Now Johnny could wait no longer for his answer.

Again it was Erica Guttmann who opened the door to him. Again the old man was sitting in the chair beside the window. Erica moved to stand beside her father.

'We will come with you,' Erica said quietly.

A great smile split his face. God, he could have shouted, lifted the bloody ceiling off the room.

'Thank you.'

'It is not because of anything you have said. It is for a reason that you would not understand.'

'It doesn't matter.'

'It is not just because of Willi that we are going with you.'

'It's not important why.'

'We put our trust in you. If anything were to harm my father after the promise that you have made, then it would lie with your conscience for the rest of your life.'

He was taking them to the bloody autobahn, packing

258

them into a car with only forged papers to protect them, and all the skill and all the vigilance of Marienborn waiting for them, and the shield they looked for was Johnny Donoghue's conscience. The bombast in him peeled. God, who'd chance as much as their freedom on Johnny Donoghue's word?

'Nothing will harm you.'

'What do we have to do?'

Johnny clenched his fist so that the fingernails cut at the palms of his hands. Trust was devastating, trust could crucify. A brave old man, a brave and pretty girl, and both watching him in naïveté, hanging on his words.

'You should have dinner tonight in the hotel. After that you must walk across to the Hautbahnhof and you must take the train on the local line to Barleber See . . . there is one just after eight, another 20 minutes later, you can take either. At Barleber See you must walk along the path towards the camping site. Before you reach the tents you will find a cafeteria and a place where people sit in the evening. You wait there and I will come to you.'

'There are many things that we should know.'

'None of them necessary,' Johnny said drily. 'Do you sew, Miss Guttmann?'

A hollow, shy laugh. 'A little.'

'In the drawer of the room desk you will find the hotel's needles and cotton. All the labels on your clothes show them as made here or in Moscow, they must be removed and replaced.' Johnny handed her a small plastic bag filled with the identification of manufacturers in West Berlin and Frankfurt.

'Will we be searched?' The nervousness narrowed her lips.

'It's a precaution,' said Johnny.

The telephone rang from the hallway, called through the door of the darkened bedroom. An insistent, howling whine. It stripped the provocation and the tease from the face of the woman. It drew an obscenity from the man who drove his gloved fist into the softness of the mattress to lever himself

259

better from her body. He rolled beside her, his face clouded in the shades of frustration. The telephone was a prior claim on him and he shrugged away her reaching arms, and strode naked and white-skinned to the door.

No sheet to cover her, Renate screamed at the broad back, 'Tell the bastards to go to hell . . . you said they would not call you on a Saturday . . .'

She watched him through the open door. The anger withered, the giggles rose. Her lover in profile at the telephone, thin and spindly legs, only the glove to clothe him. She shook with quiet laughter.

'Spitzer . . . I will come immediately . . . nobody is to talk to him . . . the SSD should be informed that I have taken personal charge of him . . . that is all.'

The telephone was slapped down. He made for the heap of clothes around the bedside chair, pulled on his underpants and vest.

'Aren't you going to finish . . .?'

No response. Preoccupation with the shirt buttons, with the trouser zip, with finding a missing sock.

'What's so important . . .?'

He laced his shoes, retrieved his knotted tie, slid his jacket from the back of the chair.

'When are you coming back . . .?'

'I will not be coming back tonight.'

'On a Saturday . . .?'

'A man has come to see me and I have waited 7 years for the meeting.'

She saw the excitement bright in his small blue eyes, and not for her. She knew the language. Some poor swine shitting himself in an underground cell at Number 2, Halberstadter Strasse. Sitting in a corner and shitting himself. And Spitzer would enjoy it, more than being with her on the big bed. And better at it too, better at terrifying a snivelling cretin in the cells than satisfying Renate.

As the front door slammed she buried her head in the pillow and pounded it with her fists.

*

Under the canopy of the petrol station on the edge of the Grunewald Park beside the Berlin approach road to the E6 autobahn, Charles Mawby and Adam Percy shaded themselves and waited.

They had arrived early for their rendezvous with Hermann Lentzer, but that was Mawby's way, he said. Never be late if you don't have to be, always give yourself time, easier on the nerves that way. They looked up the road, watched for the car that would come with Lentzer and the two men who would make the drive to Helmstedt.

'I've enjoyed Berlin, Adam, rather an exhilarating place I felt. More going on than I'd expected. You hear of it as a sort of ghost city, all the young people leaving. I thought it was rather lively.'

'I suppose I come too often to notice,' Percy said dourly.

'I'd like to bring the wife, I reckon she'd be fascinated . . . bit bloody expensive, have to keep her on a rein. Do you ever bring your wife, Adam?'

'My wife died three years ago, Mr Mawby.'

'God, I'm sorry . . . I'd forgotten.'

'I wouldn't have expected that to be remembered back at Century . . . I'll get some coffee from the machine. White and sugar?'

And they'd drunk the coffee and found a rubbish tin for the beakers, and Mawby had started to flick his fingers, and he'd looked at his watch, and paced out into the evening sunlight, and come back to Percy.

'A damn good holiday we're having. Joyce and I when this is over. Reckon I'll have earned it. Taking the kids with us, of course. A package trip, but that's the only way you can afford to go these days, down to Greece. Where are you going, Adam?'

'I usually go up to a place near Hull, my sister's family. They put me up for a fortnight, they're very kind.'

'I've heard it's very nice there, Yorkshire, isn't it?'

'Seems to rain the fortnight I'm there.'

'Does it? . . . I hope this bloody man isn't going to cut it fine.'

'He was very exact with his timings, but from what he said, he's a bit adrift.'

'You stressed the importance of the schedule?'

'Of course, Mr Mawby . . . I'll get another coffee.'

And the concern grew and the worry was bred and the anxiety draped their faces. The pump attendant gazed with undisguised curiosity at the steadily increasing discomfiture of the two Englishmen who had come in their office suits to stand in his forecourt.

'He couldn't have misunderstood anything, Adam?'

'He had it all pat, Mr Mawby.'

'He's late, you know that?'

Percy looked down at his wrist. 'He's five minutes short of an hour late.'

'It's the centre of the whole damned thing, the car . . .'

'I know that, Mr Mawby. He's a greedy bugger, he'll be here.'

'Well, he'll get cut down to size when he comes.' Mawby's voice rose and he slapped against his legs the briefcase that contained the two passports of the Federal Republic.

'Would you like something more to drink?'

'Of course I bloody wouldn't . . .' Mawby strode away and stared again down the road, searching for a crimson BMW. Angry now, taut and stressed, stamping his feet as he walked. A little of panic, a little of temper.

Two hours after the time that Hermann Lentzer should have come, Percy went to a coin box telephone beside the cash desk. He was gone a short time. When he returned his face was pale, sheet white, and he faltered in his stride towards where Mawby was waiting.

'There was a contact number that Lentzer gave me. A woman answered . . . she yelled at me, hysterical . . . some whore that he shacks up with when he's in Berlin. She said it was on the DDR radio that Hermann Lentzer was held this afternoon at Marienborn. Those bastards have got him . . .'

'Will he talk?' Mawby blurted.

'How the hell should I know?'

Petrol spilled from an overfilled tank. The attendant who held the nozzle did not notice. In fascination he watched the two Englishmen, toe to toe and yelling.

It was raining heavily but then it always did on the second Saturday in June, the day of the village fête. The chestnuts that separated the graveyard from the vicarage gardens dripped steadily on to the roof of the marquee. Only the sale of used clothes and cakes and the White Elephant stand were sheltered; the other stalls were all outside and braving the elements.

But the fête must go on. Without its fund raising the primary school would have no books, the church organ no maintenance, the steeple would have to wait for repair. In wellington boots, waterproof trousers and his shooting anorak the Deputy-Under-Secretary understudied his wife on the Garden Produce and Plants table. He always left a number where he could be reached and that was why the surly daughter of the vicar came splashing across the quagmire lawn to find him.

There was despair on the Deputy-Under-Secretary's face when he came back and the water ran on his neck and stained his collar. 'I won't be able to go to Hodges's tonight. I'm sorry, dear.'

'Not the bloody office?' she commiserated.

'I shall have to go to Chequers.'

'What does he want?'

'I've requested the meeting. There's a bit of a mess . . .'

'They're a boring crowd at the Hodges', you always say we'll never go again . . .' she said irrelevantly.

'Darling, tonight I'd have given my eye teeth for a boring evening,' the Deputy-Under-Secretary said. He turned to accept a customer for the last of the potted fuchsias.

At the Campingplatz 'Alte Schmiede' in the woods outside Suplingen tents could be hired for the weekend, and sleeping bags. Just the one they used. Ulf and Jutte wriggling with laughter into the warm constriction of the bag, no clothes, no impediments. The tent was pitched slightly less than 12 miles from the Inner German Border and due east of Weferlingen. Before they had negotiated the constraints of the sleeping bag Jutte had several times asked Ulf how and where they would make their attempt. He would tell her in the morning, he had said . . . for now she was safe in his arms.

The cell door in the basement corridor crashed shut. As the officer in uniform beside him thrust the bolt across, Gunther Spitzer wiped a blood smear from the leather of his glove with his handkerchief.

'He will know now who he is with . . . in a little while when he has had time to frighten himself we shall start again.'

Chequers was no easy place to find at night. Far from any main road, outside the village of Great Kimble, a pin-head in the Chiltern Hills, 30 miles west of London. It had taken the Deputy-Under-Secretary more than three hours to negotiate the winding roads with only his taciturn personal guard for company.

An ugly building it was too. Ridiculous that this should be the best that the nation could provide for the Prime Minister's country retreat.

The official cars were parked in an orderly line in the courtyard at the back. The dull cigarette flares betrayed the chauffeurs who waited for the dinner to be finished, the guests to depart. The Deputy-Under-Secretary was shown to the Long Gallery and requested to wait.

Would he like a drink, a cigar, the day's newspapers?

He wanted nothing, only the ear of the Prime Minister.

The dinner party was continuing, the Prime Minister was hosting the Trade Delegation of the German Democratic Republic, and would come as soon as was convenient now that the Deputy-Under-Secretary had arrived. He smiled ruefully at the young man who had escorted him into the house. He was content to wait until it was suitable for the Prime Minister to leave his table. The great irony, the coincidence that could make him vomit ... East Germans munching the food and swilling HMG's wine on the floor below and offering their dining room toasts of comradeship and friendship and co-operation ... and Mawby berserk beside a telephone in Berlin, and an agent loose in Magdeburg, and a mission triggered, and damn little but catastrophe in prospect.

The Prime Minister swept through the door. A brandy glass for an orb, a cigar for a sceptre. A little flushed, a little loud, a little overwhelming. Saturday night, the night off, the night without crisis, and the Deputy-Under-Secretary recognised the inroads of the decanter and the bottle.

'What can I do for you, my friend?'

The Deputy-Under-Secretary sketched the news that had been relayed to him by Century House.

'What am I supposed to bloody well do?'

'I thought you should know the situation, sir, and I've been very frank.'

'I had a damned promise from you, Deputy-Under-Secretary. I remember your words, you told me risk had been eliminated ... that's what you told me ... it was a bloody lie ...' And his eyes rolled and his brow furrowed, and he sought to concentrate his resentment.

'Everything you were told yesterday, sir, we believed at that time to be true.'

'I told you myself, I told you to cancel it. I gave that instruction.'

'And after deliberation with Cabinet Secretary you changed your mind, sir.'

'You're a crafty bugger, Deputy-Under-Secretary, you've trapped me ... You tricked me, you've landed me. I'm not afraid of taking responsibility for my decisions, but I damn well expect the briefings to be straight. I've the right to demand that.' The Prime Minister's anger was sudden.

'We have to face the fact, sir, that there can be repercussions. They will be questioning this man with whom we have dealt. We have to be prepared to deny their allegations. We may have to ride a bit of a storm.'

'The run can't be managed?'

'At this notice we don't have the paperwork capability. More important, if this man provides them with information then the pick-up zone is compromised.'

'You have to wind it all up . . .?'

'Yes.'

'And your man there, what happens to him?'

'He has to get clear . . . we have to hope that's possible. We'll not know till the morning the extent of the damage.'

'There's no way to salvage something . . . you can't pull anything back from it?'

'I'm afraid not, sir.'

'It's a damned shame. You know I'm really rather sorry. I think I'd started to root a bit for this freelance fellow of yours. Things are going to be horrid for him, I suppose.'

'That's fair comment.'

The Prime Minister shrugged, tried to focus his eyes on the Deputy-Under-Secretary. '. . . Are you sure you won't have a drink yourself?'

'Thank you, sir, no. I'm going back to London. I ought to be on the road . . . I am desperately sorry, Prime Minister.'

'It's a damned shame.'

The fool doesn't understand, the Deputy-Under-Secretary thought. Getting high, loosening his collar with the German Democratic Republic, sliding his feet under the table. But he would understand in the morning, and God help the Service then.

He left the Prime Minister to his cigar and his glass, an empty room and the unlit grate, left him ruminating behind closed eyes.

Time to run for London. Time to be in Communications, to be watching the telexes and reading the telephone transcripts.

The Deputy-Under-Secretary brooded in the back of his

car while the bodyguard drove towards Century House.

What in Heaven's name had Mawby thought he was at? Six weeks he'd had to plan DIPPER, all the resources and finance he'd asked for. And it ended like this, in crawling apologies to his Prime Minister who was tipsy in the company of the opponents of the day. What a damned mess . . . Where did the blame lie, at whose door? He had pushed Mawby hard, pushed him because that was the way to gain the best from an ambitious Assistant Secretary. Pushed him too far . . .? He remembered the caution that Mawby had shown in his office on the last night, at the final briefing. The fiasco would lie on the desk of the Deputy-Under-Secretary.

The Prime Minister had called it a damned shame. Not for Mawby, he would be shuffled, slotted into Agriculture and Fisheries or Social Services. A damned shame for the Deputy-Under-Secretary, and he'd called it the best show of the year.

'Family well . . .?'

'Very well, sir, thank you. The little girl's just starting school.'

'I don't suppose you see much of them.'

'Not too much, sir, no.'

Not the problem of the Deputy-Under-Secretary. He would see all he wanted of his wife and sons and his grand-children, all he wanted of his home in the country. He wondered whether the bodyguard would be allocated to his successor.

Under the lights that hung from poles that were intended to provide the Barleber See Cafeteria with the happy image of a holiday playground, Johnny saw Otto Guttmann and his daughter. Their clothes identified them to him. The only man in a suit, the only girl with a city raincoat over her shoulders. In the shadows, hidden by the perimeter darkness of the patio, Johnny circled them. Better to be safe, better to know if they had buckled in their resolution and gone to the Schutzpolizei. He was very thorough; the lavatories, the back

267

of the bar where the bottle crates were stacked and where a man could hide, the trees around the café. He watched the faces of the campers who had come to talk and drink. He saw no surveillance, no watchers.

He strolled to their table and they managed an unobtrusive welcome. Then Johnny went and queued at the bar and came back with two small beers and an orange juice for the Doctor.

Chapter Nineteen

=

As the last of the campers were leaving the cafeteria for their tents and the shutters of the bar came down, Johnny rose from the table, tapped at his watch, motioned to Otto Guttmann and his daughter that it was time. The path was dim lit and they walked close to each other and twice the old man bumped into Johnny's back.

I don't know why they're coming, thought Johnny.

The contact had been too slight, too transitory for him to make the judgement. Damned if he knew why they were coming. Too old, too settled to be purchased by the trinket attractions of the West. Too cynical to be bought by the elusive breezes of freedom across the fence. Too weary to be lifted only by the promise of a lost son at Checkpoint Alpha. Perhaps he would one day comprehend, if at a future moment he met and talked with Otto Guttmann. He had expected more fight from the girl, more hostility.

All questions, Johnny, and questions are wasted breath.

They kept to the centre of the gravel path that widened when it left the trees. It was flanked now by low slung holiday tents and there were the lights of portable gas lamps, and the glow of cookers, and radios played the interminable orchestra music of the East's airwaves. A couple were in dispute, another kissed in the privacy of shadow. A child urinated noisily behind a flapping canvas screen. There was the dull, constant drone of the traffic on the autobahn. Johnny leading, Otto Guttmann and Erica following. Where are you taking them, Johnny, to what salvation, into which Shangri-la land? Another question . . .

No questions, no answers, not until the rear lights blazed away onto the autobahn, not until the train pulled out of Obeisfelde and straddled the Aller Bridge.

They turned out of the gateway of the Barleber See site, and went along the road that Johnny had walked on the first morning. Seemed a century ago. In front of them the autobahn bridge towered and the racing lights of the cars were suspended, carried on puppet strings above them. A hundred yards from the bridge Johnny stopped and he took Otto Guttmann's hand and whispered to him that Erica and he should stay, that he would be gone for only a minute. Johnny hurried forward. The fast, trained reconnaissance. He was clear in his mind what he was looking for. On the open road that passed under the autobahn a waiting police car could not be hidden.

Johnny came back to them. He reached out in the darkness and his fingers touched the hem of Erica's coat, and she started as if in shock and her hand clutched his wrist. Poor bitch, frightened half to death.

Gently he pulled his arm clear of her and they started to walk again towards the approach road. Only the autobahn lights to guide him. He would want to see Erica again, Johnny thought, when it was over.

They came to the approach road that snaked up to the traffic lanes. Johnny held one of Otto Guttmann's hands, Erica the other. As if at a signal they scurried forward, bent low. Their feet stampeded on the tarmac and then they were buried in the undergrowth. The branches whipped at their faces, low roots caught at their feet, the grass sank and heaved under their shoes. Johnny knelt and they followed him down. Near to the autobahn and the cars and lorries hammered towards Helmstedt above them. The sweet and sticky smell of green leaves and green grass was around them. The damp of the evening clung to their clothes. Johnny moved and wriggled in the bushes before he found the view that he wanted, the road down from the autobahn on which the car would come. He looked at his watch. Fifteen minutes, perhaps a little more or less. He felt Erica against him and the softness of close-clinging summer clothes, and he heard the breathing of her father as if the short run to their hiding place had winded him.

'Well done,' Johnny whispered. 'Strange carry-on, isn't it? But this is the way it happens. For all the cleverness we end up with grass stains on our knees. Silly.'

'How long to wait?'

'Fifteen minutes, Doctor Guttmann. Around midnight, The pick-up has to be open-ended, you can't be exact as to how long it will take the driver from Berlin. They should have practised it, but we still have to wait for them.'

'What will happen?' Erica's voice pitched high and nervous.

Johnny playing the expert. Making believe that most weeks of his working year he slogged his way into the German Democratic Republic and lifted the best of the Warsaw Pact scientists ... 'The car will come off the autobahn at this turn off. When he's turning he will flash his lights once, at the top of the incline. About where we are you'll have seen the "Give Way" sign, he stops level with that. The driver will get out and look at his tyres, one by one, the passenger will open the door behind him, the near side. You have to move fast, Erica first, Dr Guttmann, you follow. The car spins and it's back to the autobahn. I wave and find a beer.'

'You don't come with us?' Erica shrill and close.

'I have my own way out.' The smile wiped from Johnny's face.

'Who will be in the car?'

'Germans, who work for us. They have the paperwork for you to have been travelling with them from West Berlin. You are from Frankfurt ... you have been to see an aunt in Berlin, what you like. It's very straightforward.'

'Why don't you come with us?'

'He does not come with us,' Otto Guttmann said quietly, 'because if it is not straightforward he does not wish the involvement of being in our company ...'

'That's nonsense ... four is enough in the car, and a foreigner would only complicate.'

Johnny edged a little way from them. Not the time for a debate on the plan, he should separate himself. His gaze was on the gap between the bushes and the upper curve of the approach road. Waiting for the car, for the transport. He checked his watch. He was very tense and his legs were cold and numb. Staring into the darkness for flashing headlights. He was half aware of the low pitched conversation behind him, what they would do the next morning. Warm baths and newspapers, and talking to Willi and whether there might be a church service they could attend, and with Erica gone what would happen to the cat at the laboratory at Padolsk. How Erica would need new clothes and Otto Guttmann would need money.

Bloody innocents, Johnny thought, like a couple of kids from the provinces going to London for the weekend.

Again he looked at the luminous face of his watch. Come on you bastards you're not going to be bloody late, are you? Not tonight. Please God, not late tonight.

It was easy for them in the approaching car to see Carter.

The floodlights on the tall stanchions at either side of the road highlighted him as he stood in front of the two storey building, and beneath the sign. 'Allied Check Point'. The rooms were bright behind him and a Military Policeman sometimes came to the window and wondered at the presence of the bald and elderly Englishman who waited patiently while the traffic ran steadily past him from west to east. Some strange beggars came at night to Alpha, he would have thought.

They parked the car behind the Bundesgrenzschutz passport control and walked the last few yards to Carter. Pierce was spruced in a three piece cement grey suit, a closed rose bud at his buttonhole. Willi trailing but with an eagerness in his face and a bounce in his step. George was a pace behind the boy and dressed as if for winter, a roll neck sweater under the leather coat.

'The road was foul, that's why we're late. Have you spoken to Mawby?' Pierce asked Carter.

Willi stood a little away from them. Clean in his new

clothes, fresh with the air on his face, hair waving and falling.

'I tried to call him earlier. He wasn't on the HQ number . . . but that was some time ago . . . I've been stuck here waiting for you, I didn't want to go off to chase a phone in case they came through early.'

'I'd give a fair bit to know if they took off from Berlin on time.'

Willi motionless, Willi peering into the growing lights that edged forward from the far cluster of the Marienborn checkpoint across the shallow valley, across the line of the watchtowers and the wire and the whitewashed strip on the road that wheels had worn to a smudge.

'They could be here any time now,' Carter said.

'Did you leave a number where you could be reached?'

'Berlin Military know I'm at Alpha. Mawby will be beside the phone later, when I report the arrival.'

Willi with his hands clasped, his trousers pressed, shoes cleaned. Willi watching the cars approaching across no-man's land.

Pierce turned his wrist, looked down at his watch. 'Shouldn't they have been here by now?'

'They might have been, but they're not late yet.'

The door of the building flew open, spilling out light, bathing the faces of the men who waited, tensed faces, harassed tired faces. The Military Police corporal hesitated.

'Excuse me, gentlemen . . . is one of you a Mr Carter?'

'Yes, it's me.'

'You're wanted on the phone, sir. A Mr Smithson, in Berlin.'

Carter shrugged, went into the doorway, disappeared from Pierce's sight.

Willi saw him go . . . Willi with the stress at his mouth, the flicking wet tongue. Willi with the picture of his father bulging in his mind. Not knowing which car to watch for, restless, pacing.

'Where the hell have you been?' shouted Smithson, distant and furious, and in Berlin.

'I'm at Alpha . . .'

'I know you're at bloody Alpha now. Why didn't you call in?'

'I did and nobody knew where to find Mawby.'

The Military Police in the office turned their heads away from Carter as his face flushed and his forehead knitted in anger. In front of the electric fire their alsatian dog stirred, cocked its ears towards the raised voices.

'What a fucking shambles . . . not that it matters now, it's off . . .'

'What's off?'

'What do you bloody think? The run's off . . . Do you want it in one syllable words? It's off, there's no fucking car coming. They've knocked off the pick-up merchant coming through the border . . .'

'How?'

'About the least relevant question you could ask on an open line, Carter. Just take it from me, no car has left Berlin, no car is gong to leave. It's finished, the whole thing.'

'What am I supposed to do, what does Mawby say?'

'Find yourself a fat frau and a bottle of whisky, that's my advice . . . Mawby's past answering questions like that.'

Carter put the telephone down. He thanked the Military Police corporal for coming to look for him.

Carter stepped back into the night wind, into the drone of the traffic, into the shadow of the high lights.

Willi was watching him. Willi would know. A bloody idiot could see the message, read it from the way he lurched across the concrete, from the way he winced his eyes, from his sunken shoulders, from the way he stumbled to Pierce's side. Willi staring, Willi absorbing.

'The car's not left . . .'

'Cutting it fine, aren't they?' Pierce had not looked at him, still peered up the road.

'. . . and it's not coming. Not now, not ever.'

'What?' Pierce had spun to face Carter. George scrambled towards them.

Willi alone, Willi abandoned, Willi within earshot.

274

'It's finished ... DIPPER's called off. The pick-up maestro was arrested at the border checkpoint, he must have been driving into Berlin ...'

'You're levelling, Henry?' Pierce in disbelief and his mouth sagging open.

'Smithson said so, and he called it a fucking shambles.'

'God ... so what's going to happen to them, out there ... when the chappie starts chattering ...' Pierce cut himself short.

Willi was going. The stride into a trot. The trot into a run. The run into a sprint. Willi going past the shimmering white of the flag poles, along the central crash barrier. Willi going for the faded line that crossed the road.

Carter and Pierce rooted to the ground.

George struggling for speed, but heavy and flat footed. The white line looming, a car going east and slowing to avoid the boy who ran down the long hill, hugging the centre of the road. George losing ground. The voice drifted back to Carter, weak and carried on the breeze, the panic softened by distance.

'Come back, you little bugger. Willi, come back ...'

Willi over the white line, Willi the victor of the race. The searchlight on the tower platform locked on him, circled and held him, followed him on down the road. Brightness all around and Willi ran with the beam that slowly traversed and accompanied his progress.

From where Carter and Pierce stood the cocking of the machine gun in the tower was sharp and unmistakable. The scraping of the metal spring, the crack as the mechanism locked the bullet in the breech. It would have been deafening to George, he could not be blamed for throwing the towel. The searchlight covering the boy, the machine gun covering George. Willi growing smaller, retreating into the bend of the wide road. George was rock steady, standing on the white dividing line.

Carter thought he was about to be sick.

He saw a jeep stop beside the running boy, it was stationary for a few moments and then reversed towards

275

his report to Moscow pealed in his mind.

Faintly at first, in the distance, Johnny heard the choral song of the sirens, hurrying from the south, from Magdeburg. The fox that is aware of the baying of hounds, and he reacted, rising to his knee, seeming to sniff around him for confirmation of danger.

A swelling of noise and closing. He groped in the darkness and took the arm of Otto Guttmann. He felt the dragging at his anorak as Erica clawed with her fingers to find him. The fear of the hunted was shared. No argument, no discussion. Father and daughter clung, one to each of Johnny's arms as they came from their hiding place and began to run back towards the camp of Barleber See. They swung off the road and onto the track and Otto Guttmann heaved and gasped for air, and Erica in her shoes tripped on the rough chipped stones, and Johnny looked back. The cluster of blue lamps was nearer, the wail of the sirens grew. The Stechkin banged against his hip, the grenades danced in his pocket. Johnny pulled them off the track, onto the grass and away behind the line of tents. He would set a cruel race and as he ran his mind was tugged to the alternatives open to him. Precious few, Johnny.

Where are you going, Johnny? Going west, west is the way to Cherry Road, west is the way back.

West is where the bloody minefields are, and the fences and the machine guns, right, Johnny? Right, darling, bullseye first time.

Are you going to ask the Doctor and his daughter if they fancy the glory ride with Johnny? Not now, later. Enough on the rubbish heap, without sifting for detail.

Perhaps they don't want to go, thought of that, Johnny? Thought of it and ducked it, they'll come . . . with the sirens blasting in their ears, they'll come.

They're going to slow you down, they'll be lead on your back, and the order for difficulties was quit and run, remember that, Johnny? But a promise was made, that's the end of it. A bloody promise was made.

The old man tried to keep with them, heavy going and he wheezed and coughed. Johnny on one elbow, Erica on the other. The three of them careering through the trees, and all the time the sirens in the wind.

A wasp's nest disturbed by the gardener, that was the headquarters of the Schutzpolizei on Halberstadter Strasse at past two in the morning. Lights erupting in the upper windows, desks manned, telephones busy. There was no reason for Gunther Spitzer to doubt the scale of the catastrophe that had befallen him.

From the International Hotel he was told that the bed of Otto Guttmann was undisturbed, so was that of Erica Guttmann, so was that of a British tourist travelling under the name of John Dawson. His men were at the hotel now, swarming through the rooms, hectoring the staff. Right under his eyes they had been, right under the nose of Gunther Spitzer who had entertained the Doctor and his daughter to dinner. And the report he had transmitted to KGB would take pride of place in the ammunition aimed at the Schutzpolizeipresident.

The telexes went variously to the Ministry of State Security in Berlin, to the offices of SSD, to the duty desk clerk for the Red Army's military intelligence section at Zossen-Wunsdorf, to the home of the First Secretary of the Party at the privileged village of Wandlitz seven miles from the Berlin city boundaries. Fury, recrimination, abuse, burst like a monsoon over the second floor office of Gunther Spitzer. And in the eye of the storm would be the arrival of the men from Berlin, and what he had done to retrieve the disaster would be analysed and criticised because a head must be found for the block.

In a high whining scream he demanded greater efforts of his subordinates.

From his bed in the guest wing at Chequers, the Trade Minister of the German Democratic Republic was roused by the telephone. On the line was his country's ambassador to

Britain. A matter had arisen of great sensitivity and delicacy involving relations between the two countries, a matter that could not be communicated on an open line. The Minister should know that the ambassador was about to leave the Residence for the Embassy where the text was expected soon of a message from the First Secretary to the Prime Minister of Great Britain. The ambassador anticipated that he would be at Chequers before dawn.

The conversation had been monitored by the Duty Officer in the Chequers' switchboard. It was debated whether the Prime Minister should be woken.

'Frankly, if he's to be in the firing line in the morning and you'd seen him just before he turned in, you'd leave him in bed,' advised a civil service aide. 'He was well maggoted, and beauty sleep's going to be like gold dust for him.'

The interpreter at Chequers for the visit of the East German delegation had translated the tape recording of the telephone conversation. The Prime Minister was permitted to sleep on.

In Berlin Brigade a scrambler call had been patched through for Mawby to talk from the offices of Military Intelligence to Century House and the Deputy-Under-Secretary. They talked curtly, unemotionally of the night's events. Both men at that moment lived in a house of glass, neither would hurl rocks. Later it would be different, later the bitter inquest would begin. Mawby had said that there was no further business for him in Berlin, he would be returning to London in the morning. After the call he walked back across the floodlit parade area.

The Brigadier was waiting up for him. There was a champagne bottle in a silver bucket on the sideboard, a linen napkin draped across the neck. The Brigadier looked at Mawby's face, at the shamed eyes, at the pale cheeks. From the cupboard in the sideboard he took a decanter of whisky, poured two fingers, no water, no ice, handed a tumbler to Mawby.

'Was it that bad, Charles?'

'Worse than bad, it was bloody awful.'

'A fiasco?'

Mawby drained the glass, spluttered. A wisp of mischief crossed him. 'I'll tell you how bad it was. Ten years ago if this had happened it would have been a resignation job.'

'And now . . .?' The Brigadier refilled the glass.

'I can't afford to bloody resign. I'll just be kicked sideways, I'll never have responsibility again. You asked if it was a fiasco . . . It is and it can get worse. It's all blown now, it's wide as the open sky, and we have a man in there. A train left 15 minutes ago from Magdeburg to Wolfsburg, if he's not on the train then he's locked inside. That's his only chance. They're reporting in Signals down on the border that the whole bloody place is awake, there's heavy traffic on their police net. He's our man, and if picked up then . . . then . . . it's just a bloody disaster.'

They went to their bedrooms. In the morning the champagne bottle would be returned to the kitchen refrigerator, and Mawby would retrieve two green backed passports of the Federal Republic of Germany from the corner of his room where he had hurled them.

Johnny's flight took him through the camp site and the woods around it, and to Barleber See station.

A primitive place for vacationers and few else. There were no lights nor life nor activity. Five hundred yards away was the autobahn and racing cars and twice Johnny saw that signature of the police, the inanimate and travelling blue lamp.

In front of him was the fragmented pattern of the street lights of Barleber, more than a mile away. When the moon came he could see the far, flat horizon spread beyond the village. No trees, no cover, and he remembered how he had seen it when he had come back on the train on the first day. There were open fields between the railway and the village.

'We have to go on,' Johnny whispered.

'He can't, you can see that,' Erica hissed in his ear.

'If he has to be carried, so be it. We have to go on.'

283

woods, only in the depths of the Landschaftschutzgebiet that stretched from the town of Haldensleben behind them to the outskirts of Walbeck village. They would cut through a nature zone, crossed by few roads, with few villages.

They went out of the Campingplatz hand in hand. Two products of the regime, two machine-tooled children of the Party. Her blonde hair was whipped back on her shoulders by the wind. Their stride was bold and long. Two young people on whom the Sozialistische Einheitspartei Deutschlands had lavished care

'How long will it take?' she asked, and the leafy light played at the tan of her cheeks.

'If we go hard we shall be close by tonight. We rest for a few hours and we watch. Tomorrow, early in the morning, we go over.'

So sure, so confident, he seemed to her. She kissed him quickly behind the ear, and did not see the quaver at his lips. In a few minutes they were hidden by tall trees, walking a carpet of fallen autumn leaves, alone together in the territory of wild pigs and fallow deer and foxes. Jutte dreamed of Hamburg and of the car of her uncle and of the house in which he lived. Ulf thought of the automatic guns and the wire and the watchtowers, and of Heini Schalke and an MPiKM high velocity rifle.

Carter stayed by the barrier at the station of Wolfsburg until all the passengers had left the train. Not many of them on the early train of the day out of Magdeburg. And never really a chance that Johnny would have been with them. Straightforward enough at Holmbury. Johnny to see the Guttmanns into the pick-up car, then back to Magdeburg for the station, and nobody had drawn a blueprint for the plan if the autobahn ran off schedule. A wasted journey for Carter and he'd known it before he started. Johnny wouldn't quit, not before it was hopeless, he would have stayed at the autobahn intersection. Stayed till the train was lost to him.

What would Johnny have done with the Doctor and Erica

Guttmann? Carter couldn't know, doubted that he knew his man well enough to make the judgement. The order was quit and run ... it would be a hell of a thing for his man to do, but that was the order.

He had heard from Pierce the report from the Signals monitoring unit, that police activity across the border had risen sharply from the small hours of the night. The codenames for prearranged road blocks had been called, reinforcement detachments had been summoned, search parties were co-ordinated. Johnny would have stood a chance on the first train of the day. Not after that. They'll tear the bloody carriages apart till they find him.

Back to Helmstedt, back to sweat it through. Mawby and Smithson were returning in a few hours to London, Percy would fly to Bonn. Pierce and George had been told to take the first aircraft to Heathrow. Carter was to be left to gather up any information that might seep through. Of course it would be Carter who was left behind, because Carter was too junior to field the blame that would be ambushing the senior men of DIPPER. Better off where he was. He would hear of Johnny soon, that was certain. He would hear of an Englishman arrested in Magdeburg.

God knows we conned you, Johnny. Conned you rotten.

He drove back from Wolfsburg on the secondary road to Helmstedt. Through small villages that were timbered and attractive. Through fields that were tended and flourishing. Along the line of the frontier. The border was perpetually with him, as a ribbon of wire and torn earth. Beyond it were distant and faded hills and protective woods that his eyes could not penetrate.

The border drew him, as a cliff edge will a man who suffers vertigo. He turned off left and drove into the sleeping, Sunday morning of Saalsdorf. The wire was in front of him, away across a field. He walked from the car and threaded his footsteps between the lines of young barley. Trying to share something, wasn't he? Trying to share something with Johnny, and the only way that he knew was to go to the fence and stare across at the closed country beyond.

'Five hundred yards from the border there's an electrified fence, that's the Hinterland.'

'You can take us through an electric fence?' A spark of awe from Erica.

'. . . Or under it, or over it. It runs damn near the whole length of the sector. We have to cross it if we are to get to the frontier.'

'What is at the frontier?'

'When we get there, when we're near it, that's the time to talk about the frontier.'

Erica persisted. 'Have we done well so far, Johnny?'

'We've done well, and it's all still in front of us. You've seen nothing yet, just a few lamps and sirens . . .'

They started to walk. Johnny took his bearings from the gathering sunlight. The same procedure as before. Erica on one side, Johnny on the other, husbanding the strength of Otto Guttmann.

'Why do you do this for us?' the old man asked.

'It's my job.'

'I say again, why?'

'It's the job I was given . . .' Johnny said. 'A contract I was given . . .'

'By people who were not worthy of you, who did not provide the car. Why not abandon us, make good your own escape?'

His voice was close to Johnny's ear, and his tone was gentle in age, persuasive in pitch. No witnesses, no tape recorders, nothing to recall and keep in perpetual memory what Johnny might say. No justification for a further lie.

'I have to do it, Doctor, it's a way back for me. It shakes off my past. You know in battle, in combat, some men go far up the road towards their enemy and get medals for courage, most of them go that far so as not to be called cowards . . .'

'We would never accuse you of cowardice,' Otto Guttmann said quietly.

'We shouldn't talk any more,' clipped Johnny. 'The sound carries a long way. We make enough noise already.'

They had started at a brisk pace. Johnny had no complaint.

In the Long Gallery at Chequers where the previous evening he had heard of the breakdown of the DIPPER plan, the Prime Minister played host to Oskar Frommholtz, Trade Minister and Politburo member of the German Democratic Republic. The two men were alone with the Downing Street interpreter.

The Prime Minister had showered, had then taken breakfast in his room, had telephoned the Deputy-Under-Secretary for the latest reports. He was told of the flight of Willi Guttmann. He knew that the Magdeburg police radio had broadcast descriptions of a British passport holder travelling under the name of John Dawson, and of Doctor Otto Guttmann and his daughter, Erica. He knew that checkpoint searches at Marienborn had reduced motor traffic on the Berlin road corridor to a trickle. He was given a brief outline of the East German manhunt to draw in the tatters of the mission.

So the meeting demanded of him now by the Trade Minister was the first of the crisis that would break about his shoulders. And crisis it was, he had no illusions. Much greater than the dismemberment of the adolescent relations between the United Kingdom and the German Democratic Republic. That could be coped with, managed. That was inconsequential to the wider crisis. The damnable incompetence of those people over in Germany would involve him in the recrimination of the Chancellor in Bonn. The Federal Republic was involved because DIPPER had launched from their territory, utilised their nationals, avoided the channels of co-operation. A wretched business the whole damned thing. There would be reverberations in Washington, they were always fast enough to raise questions of the efficiency of their British cousins when an intelligence mission was bungled. If the European newspapers sniffed at the scandal of a botched operation and printed, then the domestic protection of the D notice was invalidated, and the with this scientist, sling him on his shoulder and jump that fence of yours? I find it most distressing that your government should stoop to such smears and untruths . . .' The Prime Minister turned to the interpreter. 'The strongest words you've got, Rodgers, I don't want any prissiness.'

'Last night . . .' the Trade Minister snapped his reply to the interpreter. 'Last night a spy who came to the city of Magdeburg under the name of John Dawson intended to kidnap Doctor Otto Guttmann, a most eminent scientist, and to smuggle him illegally beyond our borders.'

'You should pass to the First Secretary my advice that he should be most careful of the weight he attaches to the gossip of this Guttmann boy . . .'

'We have incontrovertible evidence.'

'When you are my guest, Trade Minister, do me the goodness of hearing me out. It would be most unfortunate if the ramblings of a jilted youth were permitted to sour British and East German co-operation. I would not welcome anything that jeopardised the good relations between our countries, certainly not a concocted story like this. Where is this British agent, this saboteur?'

'In a few hours he will have been arrested.'

'So the evidence is quite unsubstantiated?'

'To us the evidence is satisfactory.'

'To me it sounds ridiculous. I would like you to stress to the First Secretary my total commitment to the bettering of understanding between your country and ours. From the hospitality shown to you here you will have seen for yourself the value we have put on your visit. Are you forgetting that because of a youth's hysteria, I hardly think so . . . You haven't touched your coffee . . .'

'Thank you . . . I must return to London.'

'You're due in the Midlands tomorrow, the Lucas and British Leyland factories.'

'If I have not been recalled to Berlin.'

'That would be a very great disappointment to the people who have tried to make you feel most welcome here.'

'I must consult with the First Secretary.'

'My advice is that he should not be precipitate in his actions. Assure him, please, that should he provide concrete evidence of the presence of a British agent in the German Democratic Republic, evidence incontrovertibly proved by his arrest, then a most far reaching enquiry will be instituted into the behaviour of our Services. The First Secretary has my word that I know nothing of this matter.'

'I have no doubts that such evidence will be produced.'

'My warmest regards to the First Secretary.'

'Thank you.'

After the withdrawal of the Trade Minister and the interpreter, the Prime Minister reached for the coffee.

He pondered to himself. He had come to the cul-de-sac after all and he was linked with the Service. All that he had feared and sought to avoid had happened, and he was hamstrung in the web that the Service wove. The same web that had caught Anthony Eden on the affair of Commander Crabbe. The same web that had dictated the bland denials from Harold Macmillan that Harold Adrian Russell Philby was a lifelong traitor. The head of government could not dissociate himself from his Intelligence establishment. He had bought himself a little time, and had not yet counted the cost of the purchase. The Trade Minister's scarcely civil departure had indicated that the message would be relayed to the First Secretary, it was possible the advice might be accepted.

Now he must await a miracle. The freelancer that he had been told of, a man called Johnny Donoghue, must bring an elderly scientist and his daughter through this impenetrable border. A border that was sealed tight, the Deputy-Under-Secretary had told him, a border that was festooned with automatic guns and minefields. That alone could save him from the humiliation of involvement in the DIPPER failure.

He drank his coffee. All a question of faith, he supposed. And in the matter of political miracles he regarded himself as an agnostic. Beyond possibility to believe the freelancer would offer salvation.

His wife came into the room, two Prayer Books and a Bible in her hand.

'We really must hurry, darling.'

'I suppose so,' said the Prime Minister. 'I'm not feeling terribly like church.'

Carter came out of the communications wing at the Roadhaus. All despondency and gloom in London, all waiting for the Berlin team to come trooping back for the inquest of the afternoon. He was told that the name of John Dawson had been heard on the Magdeburg police radio. He'd be sitting on his hands and hoping that the dust would have settled before he, too, received his travel orders.

He walked across the car park to the NAAFI bar. Yes, he was on duty. No, there was no harm in a couple of beers. Sunday lunchtime, wasn't it?

'Morning, Mr Carter,' a big cheerful welcome. 'Christ, you look as if it was a hard old night. Come for the hair of the dog, have you?'

Charlie Davies of the British Frontier Service leaned easily against the bar.

'Good morning, Mr Davies.'

'Found myself short of fags, so I popped in for some. Cheapest ones you can get here, cheaper than duty free at the airport, that's what I told the wife.'

'Yes, it was a bit of a rough night . . .'

Charlie Davies called for two beers.

'Going back soon, are you?'

'I don't know . . . I mean nobody's told me. They can run the shop well enough without the likes of me.' Carter smiled ruefully. 'If I was here six months they wouldn't notice back there.'

The warm grin slipped from Davies's face. 'There's a fair old flap over the other side,' he said dropping his voice. 'I was talking to a BGS fellow . . . they're tearing the cars apart at the checkpoint, there's a mile's tail-back at Marienborn. Good job it's Sunday, be right chaos if the lorries were on the road as well. It's said the security on the autobahn is really fierce . . .'

'I know,' said Carter. As a seeming afterthought, he added, 'Would you care to take a breath of fresh air with me, Mr Davies?'

The NAAFI manager had recently laid out a rough putting course beside the drive way. An RAF sergeant and his wife and small daughter were coaxing a ball down the green. Out of earshot of Carter's low and hesitant voice.

'You'll forgive me for what's going to sound a pretty daft question, Mr Davies . . .' Carter stared down at the thick tufted grass. 'But what's the chances of a chap making it out right now?'

'Depends who he is, what he knows.'

'Resourceful, thirtyish, fit physically . . . I don't know how much he knows.'

Davies looked at his companion with a strand of sympathy. 'Your lad over there, is he? Is that what's stirring them up?'

'Could be,' said Carter.

'He's about five foot ten . . .?'

Carter gazed into Davies's face.

'. . . dark brown hair, a blood spot on the right side of his nose.'

'Something like that.'

'Calls himself Johnny, doesn't bother with the last name. Accent a bit north country.'

'He was here?'

'A week ago,' said Charlie Davies carefully. 'He had two days here . . . came out with us in daylight and kept us talking half the night.'

Two missing days, Johnny wanted to brush up on his German. Clever, thoughtful Johnny. Come to the border to find the experts, the men who know. Slipped into place. Johnny buying his own insurance, Johnny taking his own precautions. Johnny disbelieving all the bromide that Mawby and Carter poured down his throat at Holmbury.

'It's Johnny that I'm waiting for,' said Carter. One turn round the course completed. The sergeant's daughter squealed with delight nearby.

'What was the question again, Mr Carter?'

'The chance of him making it . . .'

'On his own, is he?'

'I don't know.'

Davies considered. 'He spent the whole of his second morning in one sector, he seemed satisfied enough with what he saw. He's not a lad that talks much, is he?'

'If he was coming he would have started early this morning, but not in circumstances of his choosing, you know what I mean?'

'If he made it to the fence, when would he be over . . . that's what you're asking?'

'Yes.'

'We talked about that. I said to him that most of the people that get across have lain up for a full 24 hours in the immediate area, soaked up the patrol patterns, that sort of thing.'

'And so . . .'

'If he followed that he wouldn't come tonight. It would be Monday night that he was giving it a go.'

Carter sighed, breathed the air that now carried the faint moisture of hope. 'What was the sector that he looked at?'

'He seemed to like a piece of what we call the Roteriede forest, just about opposite the village of Walbeck on their side . . . I'll run you out there tomorrow morning.'

'Thank you.'

'We all thought him a hell of a nice bloke. He came back to my place and had a meal with the family, got everybody laughing. He knows all there is that's important about the last few yards, but what you see from our side isn't the half of it. You know that, don't you . . .?'

'What time shall I come in the morning?'

'Try about 10. I'll have cleared the post, we'll take a coffee and then run out there.'

'You never answered my question,' Carter said in mild reproach. 'His chances?'

300

'And you didn't answer mine, Mr Carter, whether he's on his own . . . I'll put it this way, if he hadn't been here this week then I'd say Sweet Fanny for his chances. He soaked everything we could give him on the border, and he'll need that and the rest. If he's passengers in tow, and they're not of the same quality . . . well, then it's obvious, isn't it?'

Carter nodded morosely.

'I'm out of turn, Mr Carter, but it's a bit queer to me, the whole business. You in Helmstedt, Johnny over there, and you not knowing your lad was here this week casing the place . . . I'll tell you what he said. Nobody had spent five minutes working out how he was going to run for home if whatever he was up to slipped . . . I knew he was going over, he said as much. He reckoned you'd left him bare arsed, that's why he came to see us.'

'As you said, Mr Davies, out of turn . . . I'll see you in the morning.'

Carter felt like an old man as he walked to the Stettiner Hof and the bed that he had missed last night. An irrelevance on the pavement as the procession marched by. He had no power of intervention, could do nothing to affect the fate of Johnny. Run fast, Dipper, run deep. He remembered the rifle that he had seen in the hands of the guard beside the river, the height of the wire and the automatic guns that had gleamed in the early morning light. And Charlie Davies said that wasn't the half of it.

Willi Guttmann had been taken from Gunther Spitzer's office.

He sat now in a bare walled ante-room with a man who watched him in silence, who wore thick lensed spectacles close to his face, and who had not removed his raincoat. Through the morning he had talked with many people, teams from SSD and Soviet Military Intelligence and KGB had come from the East German capital to interrogate him. His run from Checkpoint Alpha seemed not to impress them. When he asked about his father the questions were ignored. They were interested only in Holmbury, the men he had talked to there, and the limits on information of Padolsk that he had given to the British.

If they had not reunited him with his father, if they had not told of Otto Guttmann's arrest, then that could mean one thing only. His father and Erica and Johnny were running, running blind and hard for safety.

He ate his lunch from a steel tray, stringy meat and boiled cabbage. His father's survival from capture lay in the hands of Johnny. He remembered Johnny at Holmbury, quiet and reflective and sitting in a chair behind him as Carter questioned. Johnny who laughed rarely and distanced himself from the others. He remembered when he had looked down from his bedroom window high in the house, down on to the patio and watched the evening work-out, the strengthening of legs and shoulders and stomach. He heard again the pounding of the boots.

And he had betrayed Johnny, he had spoken of him to the men from Berlin, and Johnny alone could take his father and Erica beyond the reach of their punishment.

Willi pushed the tray with the half emptied plate away from him. The man who sat across the table said nothing and Willi dropped his head into his hands.

Gunther Spitzer had been sent home for the night because men of greater seniority had taken over the organisation of the hunt for the scientist, his daughter and the agent of British Intelligence. A stranger had sat in the chair behind his desk and given orders to his staff, newcomers had handled his telephone. They came and went through his door without acknowledgement.

When he reached his flat the tiredness and self-pity and frustration broke over Renate. She was the only target within reach.

She lay on their bed and her moaning, whimpering, trebled in his ears as he stayed hunched in the chair across the room from her. The blood from the cut below her right eye seeped to the pillow covers. The bruises spread in technicolour at her throat.

He had screamed at her with an anger she had never seen before.

'You must have known . . . You told me nothing . . . you were her friend. She would speak to you, you must have known . . . You made me pay for their dinner, you made me bow and scrape to him as if he were a great man, you must have known . . . Bitch, bitch, and you have destroyed me . . .'

And through the accusations he had punched and pummelled her. She had not fought back, just cowered and used her arms to protect herself from the agonies inflicted by the gloved hand.

'She didn't tell me anything . . . I promise . . . she said nothing, Gunther.' A small, low, choking voice.

During the day the trains to the West were searched with great thoroughness. All stopped at the Marienborn junction where the lines were enclosed by high wire. Border Guards with machine guns flanking the carriages, eight man teams climbing aboard with torches and rods for poking into the narrow recesses of the roof, with ladders and a painstaking commitment to the task. The delays grew, the trains ran late.

The tracker dogs brought from Magdeburg found the place of crushed and trampled grass beside the approach road to the autobahn, but lost the scent on the roadway and sat sadly at the handlers' knees. New orders came for widening the hunt.

It was seven hours between the time that the schoolmaster of Barleber reported the theft of his Trabant car to the Volkspolizei Kreisamt and the arrival of that information on the desks of the men who had come from Interior Ministry.

And the trail grew cold.

There were no grounds for panic amongst the men who directed the manhunt. No reason for anxiety. Let the Englishman and his followers run and blunder in the countryside. They must come to the border, they must flee in that direction. There they would be taken. Inevitable. They would be driven towards the frontier, the fence and the guards.

From the Battalion headquarters at Seggerde the instruction was broadcast to the companies at Lockstedt and Dohren and Weferlingen and Walbeck that special vigilance must be maintained. At Walbeck Heini Schalke listened to his Politoffizier's briefing. The bright new stripe on his tunic arm ensured his concentration.

The river was behind them, but the chill of the water he had waded through clung to Johnny's legs, and his shoulders ached from the weight of the piggy-back rides he had given to Otto Guttmann and Erica. Two journeys with his boots sliding on the mud bed, groping for firm stones. Up to his waist in cold, filthy water, and perhaps a small sewer emptied into the river. He stank when they were over, and there was no time to dry himself properly. He had tried to wipe himself down with a handkerchief that became a sodden mess, he had dropped his trousers to his ankles and wrung them, he had chafed his legs for warmth. The Doctor and Erica had watched him in exhausted silence.

And then they had gone on, headed west with the Aller forded.

By hugging the woods, avoiding the roads, skirting the warning signs that forbade entry without the precious permit paper, going on tip-toe past a pair of Border Guards who smoked and talked, Johnny led Otto Guttmann and Erica into the Restricted Zone.

Where once the trees had been felled, where there now grew dense and sprouting undergrowth, he called a stop. All of their nerves twisted by the long and escalating risk of discovery. Time for a halt, time for the bivouac. No blankets, no food, no drink. Nothing but the chance for rest. Under the canopy of the forest the evening came quickly, slanting the shadows, tricking the eyes.

They sagged down onto the ground. Erica tended her father, mopped the damp from his forehead, loosened his collar, eased off his shoes. The old man was white faced,

frighteningly so, his breathing was ragged and the failing
light played at the cavities of his eyes, the hollows of his
cheeks.

Food, Johnny, the poor beggar needs food. And only
Johnny could make the decision as to whether to forage for
Otto Guttmann. He should never have brought them with
him . . . but Johnny had made a promise, and a promise was
as binding as a contract . . .

The sound of the voices swept the thought from his mind.

Furtive voices. Those of a boy and a girl. There was the
crack of a broken branch, there was the snapping of a
broken frond. Johnny's finger went to his mouth, the urgent
plea for total quiet. Who else would come to this bloody,
forbidden place at this time? Johnny eased the Stechkin
from his trouser waist, checked that it was cocked, saw the lie
of the safety catch. Who else would come to the bloody
killing zone?

Johnny gestured to Erica that she should stay still. With
the sureness of a stalking cat he was gone from her sight.

Chapter Twenty-one

===

To Ulf and Jutte the forest was a dangerous and alien place. There was no safety here, no gratitude from them for the dark, cloaking cover of the trees and thickets. They huddled close to each other, his arm on her shoulder and her face rested on his cheek. They talked in low, guarded voices, in fragmented sentences that often were stifled as they listened to the night sounds around them.

'When we are across, Ulf, what happens to us, where do we go?'

'To the first farm, the first house . . .'

'How will they welcome us?'

'. . . they will give us something to eat, they will call the authorities.'

'The police will come to see us?'

'They will take us to a place called Giesen . . . north of Frankfurt . . . they will give us money there . . .'

'Is the money a reward for what we have done?'

'It is just to help us begin our lives.'

'I want to live in Hamburg, where my uncle is . . .'

'Then we will tell them, Jutte, we will give them his name.'

'My uncle has a big factory there, he is the owner of the factory, all of it belongs to him. My uncle is a rich man . . .'

'Perhaps he will help us when we are ready to leave Giesen.'

'My uncle will give me a room.'

'Perhaps he will not want to have the two of us living there . . .'

'He said he would be kind to me.'

'We have to think of the future, Jutte.'

Her head moved angrily away from his face. 'I'm not exchanging one prison for another. In Berlin you could have had a little flat and some cheap furniture. I am not going to Hamburg just to become a housewife . . . I am going there to live . . .'

'Yes, Jutte, we are going there to live together.'

'. . . of course, Ulf, of course.'

She leaned her head back to his shoulder and he felt the cool, paper-smooth skin, and he knew that he loved her, that he could not believe that he would ever love another girl. And the price that he must pay for her love was high, as high as the close mesh fence, as high as the crack of the automatic guns, as high as the cry of the Hinterland sirens.

'Did you hear something . . .?' Jutte was rigid, alert.

'Nothing.'

'Something moved . . . close to us . . .'

She pointed with her hand into the inky darkness, a wasted gesture. He sensed her fear, the panting of her breath.

'I heard nothing.'

'There was a movement . . .'

'Perhaps it was a pig, there are many here.' He remembered once, patrolling in the Spellersieck woods near where the Soviets had their observation bunker, how he had startled a pig. She had had all her young with her, seven or eight of them. He remembered the crash of their rushing flight, his own terror.

'Nobody would come here?'

'Not this close to the border. Not in curfew. There would only be the guards. You'd hear them,' Ulf said viciously. 'You'd hear their blundering feet.'

'Would the pig hurt us?'

'Nothing will hurt you, I would not allow it . . .'

They laughed sweetly, privately, together and his arm tightened on her shoulder. He wondered if the moon would come, whether the patrols had changed their night routine, whether there had been a variation since he had left the Walbeck garrison.

From the fold in the ground where he lay, Johnny could

sometimes see the boy and the girl. Momentarily the moon's brightness would light on the flash of the boy's teeth, a glimpse of the white collar of the girl's blouse. Otherwise two indistinct, merged shapes. Only their voices were clear. Johnny had come silently with the stealth of the expert. He had moved, once, at the bite of an insect at his stomach. A quick, stifled action.

Johnny lay still and listened.

'. . . Are you going to love me, before we go . . .?' The tease from the girl now that the fear of wild pigs was passed.

'Not now . . . not here.'

'Why not?'

'Because . . . because we have to run tonight.'

'Won't you have the strength?'

'Later . . .'

Johnny like an old man in a dirty raincoat who hides his hands and slinks close to teenagers at night.

First he had come, holding his breath and his nerves screaming, the Stechkin targeting on the voices, and as he had absorbed the talk of young people he could let the spring unwind. He put the safety catch on.

Same as you, Johnny . . . but fantastic. Fantastic that in the thousands of square miles of woodland along the frontier, under the same bloody trees, facing the same bloody sector, there should be another group . . . Fantastic . . . He had heard the girl goading the boy, the boy's gentle answers, and he had been relaxed by the tempo of their talk. He imagined the hands of the girl sliding under the shirt of the boy and he pushing her away, and her mouth nibbling at his ear and him twisting his face . . .

The enormity of what he knew sledge-hammered Johnny.

Going tonight, weren't they? Going over during these hours of darkness. Footsteps across the ploughed strip, and the follow-up of lights and searches and dogs. New patrols to follow, intensified activity as the Border Guards tried to claw away from their failure. If these two went over then every man in the Walbeck company would be out at night for a week. That was the procedure, that was what he had been told. They seal it tight once there's a breakout, never the same place twice.

If they go over then you're broken, Johnny.

If they go over, Johnny has to up sticks and head on down the fence to where it's quieter, to where the panic button's been left unpushed. Otto Guttmann could not withstand another cross-country hike. A forced march and a day without food, that's the final limit. What to do, Johnny? What to do with a tricky little obstacle in the way of Mawby's plan, and Henry Carter's hopes? What does the training tell you? You blast them out of the bloody way. But they're just kids, kids that Smithson would want to kiss for their courage, and they've the same right to slip the fence as you have, Johnny. That's morality, that's logic, that's for outside the Restricted Zone. You couldn't do it, Johnny. Not to a girl who wants a purse full of Deutsche marks and a walk down Jungfernstieg in Hamburg city centre. Not to a boy who has the idea that freedom is a flat that he's saved for and furniture he can afford. You couldn't do it, not follow them to the Hinterland fence. Not take a stick and throw it against the Hinterland fence, activate the alarms, home in the patrols, guide the guns. If they caught them on the Hinterland then the patrolling the next night would be at normal strength, right for Johnny and Otto Guttmann and Erica . . . you just couldn't do it.

No one to ask. No one to query the point with. Johnny makes the decisions. Johnny alone. Mawby would say to blast them out of the bloody way. Carter would say to find a way to head them off, negotiate and compromise.

What do you do, Johnny?

Once he had stood in judgement over the life of a girl and once is twice too many, and Maeve O'Connor in a village grave under Slieve Gullion mountain.

She had never seen the wire. If he told her the whole truth of it he would terrify her.

'When we go from here, Jutte, there is no turning back.

From the first step we go on.'

She nuzzled against him with her cheek and nose. 'I know.'

'If we are to go back, it is now.'

The kiss was soft on his lips.

'Jutte, listen . . . we have to be very quiet when we leave this place. We take a path that leads to a woodman's hut. At one place in the path there is a trip wire. I know where it is, and there is a track that the patrols use to go round it . . . We come to a woodman's hut and then there is the first cleared strip where there is the Hinterland fence. It is less than two metres high, but the top half is of strands of wire that have alarms and lights that are triggered if the wire is disturbed. Jutte, you have to remember this . . .' He took her face in his hands, he was so frightened himself, so frightened for her, tears welled into his eyes. 'At the point where I am taking you the Hinterland is close to the border, closer than elsewhere, 400 metres. With your help I can climb the fence without fouling the wires. You come then and when you climb the bells will ring. We have to go very fast then and we carry sticks. The last fence is three and a half metres high and is fitted with automatic guns. I will throw the sticks against their wires to fire them, then we climb again . . .'

'I understand.' Jutte with a faint, threadbare voice.

'When we climb you must have your hands inside the cuffs of your coat. The wire at the top is very sharp, you will remember that?'

'Yes.'

'Jutte, we have to run all the way from the Hinterland to the border fence. There will be noise, men shouting, perhaps they will shoot . . . you must never look back, you must follow. Wherever I lead, you must follow.'

'And you will be with me, close to me?'

Ulf kissed Jutte on the forehead, then pulled her down and snuggled her against his chest, cramped her body against his, felt the beat of her heart and the warmth of her blood.

'We have to go, Jutte . . .'

They rose to their feet and began to grope their way towards the path, between the bushes and the bracken. They did not see the fleeting shape that trailed them.

They were young and they had each other
    They had the capability.
    It was not a plan that Johnny would have entertained. They would career between the Hinterland fence and the border with the lights and alarms behind them . . . Johnny would go with circumspection, weigh each step and evaluate each problem. And Johnny had the carcase of Otto Guttmann to slow him, and there was no love . . . only a bloody job, only a filthy contract he had signed with Charles Mawby on a grey May morning. They had the capability, and if they were successful then Johnny and Otto Guttmann and Erica would not cross the following night.
    Better to fail, Johnny, better to fail and to know yourself . . .

    Only a stick thrown against the Hinterland fence, and the guards and the jeeps and their guns would be alerted. No witnesses to the treachery. And he'd live with it every waking hour of his life, every sleeping minute. It could be justified, too, just a silly girl who wanted a shopping spree in Hamburg, not rated high on the pecking order beside Otto Guttmann from Padolsk.
    You don't have the stomach for it, Johnny.
    The padding of their feet on the path drew him forward. What would they have said, the Guttmanns? The Doctor and Erica who he had brought to the border. Would they say the kids should go to the Hinterland? And not there to be asked, were they? Only Johnny to decide.

They had come to the woodman's hut.
    The fence was clear in front of them, flickers of light at the diamond mesh of the lower wire, and above that the strands that were electrified. The first barrier. An eerie, desperate quiet in the woods behind them and beyond. For a full minute they stood and listened to the deep silence that

311

rocked back at them from the tree walls. They were remote from each other, straining their senses, frightened and coiled.

'You are ready?'

Ulf felt against him the nodded agreement, the constant shiver.

'You remember everything that I said?'

'Yes,' she said, her mind empty.

'Never look back . . .'

'I love you, Ulf.'

Only the love of the girl would have taken him forward. For nothing less than the dream and the promise would he make the step towards the wire.

He squeezed her hand and broke away and went to the back of the woodman's hut where were stored the logs and branches for kindling fires. He had seen the wood piles as he had patrolled, and they were where he expected to find them. In the darkness his hands ran over the lengths of wood until he had found three branches, all that he needed for his purpose.

'Close to the border is the vehicle ditch, we lie there, protected, while I explode the guns.'

'Yes.'

Still she does not understand, after all that he had said. Lucky Jutte. Then he had taken her hand, and with a quick, sharp stride he tugged her towards the fence.

The Hinterland fence rose above the level of her eyes. The trees beyond were very close, and opposite her a path opened into the woods. Ulf tossed the branches high over the top wires. Jutte bent down with her fingers locked together and felt Ulf's boot scrape into the palms, his hand on her head steadying himself. She braced her muscles, gathered strength for the impetus of the push that she would give, waited for his command.

A moment of standing time.

'Now . . .' The hoarse whisper from Ulf.

She heaved her hands upwards, felt his body thrust past her into the air and knew that her strength had failed her, that his leap was false. She stood, petrified, as the wires sung with his impact. A shadow in front of her face, wriggling for support. In the same instant the siren avalanched into her mind, and Ulf's flailing boot smashed against her face.

A hundred metres from them, as if in unison with the alarm, the twin red and green lights flashed out the position of the disturbance.

'Help me ... help me.' Ulf screamed, suspended and frantic.

'What do I do ...?'

The noise swelled, rose from a growl to a crescendo.

'Push me ...'

She saw the threshing arms grasp at a cement post. She reached to her full height and thrust at his body with her fists, pushing him away into the blackness, over the fence.

Even as he fell Ulf could picture the scene at the command bunker. As he dropped and the grass rushed to take him he could see the small white bulb winking on the console. The bursting activity that the light would merit. The charge of the duty personnel towards the microphone that linked the bunker with the radio receivers of the foot patrols, and the watchtowers, and the earth bunkers.

He landed hard, awkwardly, and the pain was immediate, coursing through his ankle. They would be running for the jeeps.

'Give me your hand ...'

Jutte's cry was far from him, detached and unreal. He was so tired, so weak, he wanted only to rest on the cool grass beside the fence, he wanted only to lie and sleep there. In shock, in exhaustion, in agony. But the siren in the air would not let him sleep, the siren and the pain in his leg, the pain and the cry from Jutte.

'Help me. Stop fucking snivelling, help me ...'

'Go back ...' screamed Ulf.

'We can't ...'

'We have to.'

'Help me.' She spat the words at him through the close mesh.

313

She leaped at the wire. The fence rocked, sagged under her weight. She climbed, lost her footing, fell back, climbed again. There was a new sound to compete with the siren, a new intruder. Jutte was not aware of it, knew nothing but the effort of heaving herself astride the top of the wire. Ulf heard it, heard and recognised the running roar of the jeep. He staggered to his feet, lurched as the river of pain burst in his shin and thigh, retrieved himself, stood uncertainly and waited to break her fall.

She dropped from the wire and her weight and swinging arms caught his chest and his face and both together they were pitched to the ground.

Jutte springing to her feet, Ulf sprawled on his back. She saw his face, saw the snapped shut eyes that tried to squeeze out the pain. She saw so clearly, down to the glistening sweat beads at his neck. Ulf was floodlit in her gaze, and she was puzzled and could not realise the source of light.

Even when the jeep had braked she still could not understand the coming of the light. She wrenched at Ulf's arm to drag him upright.

'Come on, pig, run.'

Hatred for the fallen Ulf Becker boiled in her. Scorn grappled at her mouth. She was the daughter of the Director of a Kombinat, he was the son of an engine driver . . . she had given him her trust and he had failed her. Her uncle had said that one of the group must know the border if there was to be success, and this was the one that she had chosen, this was the one she had found and given herself to, this one . . . this shitty pig.

'Get up . . . get up.'

A single shot.

One round fired from a rifle with a killing range of a 1,000 metres. The guard with the rifle at his shoulder and the bright stripe on his arm stood less than 30 metres from Jutte Harnburg. The bullet nicked one of the strands of electrified wire and so was tumbling when it struck her upper back.

She fell, flung and smashed over Ulf Becker. Her blood

314

flew at his face. Her mouth was wide in anger, her eyes frozen in contempt.

By the Jeep the sergeant said, 'Why did you shoot?'
'I thought she was going to run,' replied Heini Schalke.

In the tree line Johnny turned away, retraced his steps along the path. The Stechkin had been in his hand when the jeep had braked. Stupid, really. Futile and unnecessary, because there had never been the chance of intervention. Never on, never an option.

He could not have saved them. He walked on a dry path with the same precision as he had in coming, heading for the place where he had left the old man and Erica. It would have been a wasted sacrifice. They had wanted an animal, ice cold and devoid of feeling, when they came to Cherry Road, they had made the right choice . . . He would never lose the image of the girl's fury ridden face.

The price had been paid, access to the border had been bought. He would go the next evening with Otto Guttmann and Erica.

Away behind him was the noise of the jeep engine. They would be taking their trophies back to the command bunker, the girl who was shot, the boy who would be their prisoner.

His head small and frail in Erica's lap, Otto Guttmann slept.

The shot had not wakened him, nor the siren that murmured in the trees around them, nor the flinching of his daughter at the stealth of the approach sounds. Her arms guarded his face as defiantly she waited.

'Erica . . . it's Johnny . . .' The whisper from the darkness, and then the shadow loomed close, silent and fast, until he crouched beside her.

'The shooting . . . the noise . . . I thought it was you. What happened?'

'A boy and a girl tried to cross . . .' The gruff response, unwilling answer. 'The guards fired on them.'

'You saw it?'

'I saw it.'

'Did they succeed, did they go?'

'The girl was killed, the boy was captured.'

'You saw it all happen?'

'It was pathetic, they were children, they behaved like children.'

'But brave . . .?'

'Brave, yes . . . in everything else they were pitiful. I listened to them when they were talking, before they went forward . . . then I thought they had a chance, I thought that until they came to the Hinterland, the first wire . . . it finished there. There was never a chance for them.'

'And for us . . .?'

Determination deepened his voice. 'We go tomorrow, we go tomorrow night. For us it is different.'

'How is it different for us?'

'Because I am not a child,' Johnny said savagely.

He eased himself down onto the ground and stretched out beside her, felt his hand brush against her arm, wanted to hold her, wanted to cling to her, wanted her to gather him as she had her father.

'What would have been their idea of freedom, Johnny? What was their dream?'

'He wanted to rent a flat and buy furniture. She wanted a pretty frock from the shops in Hamburg.'

'Did they talk of their freedom, what it meant to them?'

'It's an empty word; it means nothing.'

'Nothing to you, Johnny, everything to them. If someone comes to this place, dares to come here, then a flame must burn . . . The absence of freedom is outside your experience.'

'I have to sleep, Erica.'

'Can you sleep when you have seen a girl killed?'

Johnny's eyes were closed. Exhaustion crawled through his body, mushroomed in his mind. 'When we are across, then we can talk of freedom . . .'

'Too late then . . . you must know what is freedom before you lead us to the wire.'

'It's not important.'

'You think people will risk their lives for something that is not important?'

'It's just a job. Erica that's the total of it, that's all.' Johnny propped himself up on his elbow. 'I've been paid to do it, I've taken the money. I've an old mother and she needs cheap sausages from the corner shop, and electricity and coal, and a new coat for the winter, and I buy them. I'll pay for them because I came to Magdeburg. You understand? I don't fool with clever words like freedom . . . The girl tonight, all she wanted was some pretty clothes, a new High Street to walk down. That was an idiot reason to get killed.'

'You're cruel, Johnny . . .'

'The boy with her, he loved her. They talked of love and it was wasted breath. There's no love now because she's wrapped in a bloody blanket and dead, and he's in chains in the cells.'

'Did she love him at the end?'

Johnny peered into her face. 'Erica, for Christ's sake leave it . . . it doesn't matter about love, another bloody irrelevance, all that matters is a plan to cross the wire. Love isn't the bloody leg up . . .'

'Are we going to cross the wire, Johnny?'

'I don't know . . .'

He sagged back onto the ground and his head was resting on the matted grass and the bent bracken. He unloaded the grenades from his anorak, squirmed down in search of comfort. His hand rose and grasped at the night air and Erica took it and pressed his fingers close to her and gave them warmth.

'When Willi went from Geneva, was it to find his freedom?'

'You have to ask him.'

'Something more than those two you found tonight, what Willi was looking for. Tell me it was something more, Johnny.'

'He must tell you himself . . . I'm sorry, Erica.'

Chapter Twenty-two

=

It was the pressure of her hand over his mouth that woke him. The first sensation he knew was of the weight of her fingers on his lips. Even as his eyes functioned and his mind turned he had grasped at her wrist. He could not move her, not until he was awakened and aware, not until he saw the fingers of her other hand splayed in the warning for quiet. She pointed to the undergrowth in the direction of the path.

Johnny heard the voices. Low, casual, in conversation. The voices of young men. Erica was hunched above him and beside her a few feet from Johnny was her father, alerted, wrapped in the girl's coat. Dreadful, the old man looked to Johnny, his age accentuated by the lack of the razor, by the unbuttoned collar, by the hair that had not been tended. And Erica showed the haggard reward of a night without sleep. Stupid creature to have given her coat away and to have sat through the night in a skirt and a blouse and a light cardigan . . . bloody daft. The whole night standing guard over them, husbanding her strength to play sentry while the men slept. Shame caught at Johnny, he'd slept and he'd rested, and he had not thought of the girl.

The Border Guards would be working through the area. They'd be at the Hinterland fence and trying to track back along the route of the couple. There was no reason for them to search with great thoroughness. One dead, one captured, and no trail beyond the Hinterland. And if they had dogs then the dew would have formed over the scent of Johnny's tracks and he had been scrupulous in his care for movement in the undergrowth.

The voices passed, not aroused, not interested. Erica's hand withdrew from Johnny's mouth. The Stechkin dug at the small of his back and he pulled it from his belt and laid it on the ground beside him.

'They'll be up and down the track for most of the morning, then it'll tail off . . .'

'My father is very hungry.'

Hungry and ill, Johnny thought, and at the limit of his resources; a passenger to be coddled.

'We can't move from here, not for hours . . . none of us.'

'Look at him . . .'

The old man met his gaze with a rare, fluttering smile, but that was bravery. Otto Guttmann sought and failed to conceal his helplessness. Johnny's resolution sagged.

'Perhaps later I can go and look for some food . . . but it is a great risk.'

'We haven't the clothes to sleep like this, in the open . . .'

'I know.'

'But you will try?'

'If it is safe to do so I will try.'

'And tonight we go?'

'When it is dark.'

'What do we do for today?'

Johnny grinned, dredging a measure of cheerfulness. He would not allow them to play clock-watchers. Keep the morale alive, because Johnny must lead as they must follow, keep their limbs and minds active.

'I've a job for each of you . . .'

He saw their interest quicken. Johnny reached for the coil of rope that had been taken from the Trabant, passed it to Erica.

'. . . near to the wire is rough ground, about five metres across, then working backwards is the vehicle ditch.' With the flat of his hand he smoothed the earth beside him. With his finger he mapped the lines. 'I have to have at least two lengths of rope that will reach from the fence to the ditch. I want you to unravel the rope and make the lengths that I need from the strands.'

'And for me?' asked Otto Guttmann.

'Figures for you, Doctor . . .'

'Explain.'

319

'The Hinterland fence is one metre eighty-five high. At the top of it metal stanchions project at a forty-five degree angle and carry wires that we cannot disturb. I propose to put a small tree trunk over the wire and bind it to a cement holding post with the cables from the car engine. We will have two more poles and tie them together at the top so that they rest from our side of the fence against the post and clear the tension wires. It will be like a ladder, the struts will be simple to tie in position. From you I must know how long the poles will have to be if they are to avoid the wires.'

'That is very easy.'

'That's the plan . . . and bloody good luck to it.'

Like taking children to the seaside, finding something for them to do, designing a sandcastle and giving them a bucket and spade. Erica soon with a tangle of rope streamers on her knees. Otto Guttmann with a brightness on his face and a pen in his hand and an envelope on his lap. A diagram and a column of figures spreading over the paper.

'The projection of the stanchion, how long is it?'

'Fifteen centimetres . . .'

'You are an exact man.'

Johnny gazed at Otto Guttmann. 'A boy and a girl came to the wire last night. They failed at the first hurdle because they had no plan. One is dead, one is captured because they had no plan, they were not exact. They believed that will alone was enough.'

'And it is not?'

'It is suicide.'

Otto Guttmann pocketed his pen. 'On our side of the fence the poles should be three metres and thirty-eight to the knot, so three metres and fifty is adequate overall. The pole on the far side that is tied to the post should be two metres and fifty-six . . . that is what you wanted to know?'

'Right.'

'You did not manufacture this plan after the autobahn . . . before, you thought of this?'

'Yes.'

'Because you never believed in the car?'

'I believe in nothing that I am not myself responsible for.'

'And when you talked to us, when you gave us the guarantees of safety, and you pleaded that there was no danger, did you then imagine that at the last we would go this way?'

'No . . . it was only myself.'

'And we are a hazard for your safe crossing of the border?'

Johnny saw the old man's composure, examined the lined and unshaven face, and the eyes that were alive and piercing. 'Without you it would be easier for me . . .'

'Why do you take us?'

'It was what they sent me for,' said Johnny quietly. 'It was the reason for coming . . . whatever happened to the car from Berlin that didn't alter the reason.'

Otto Guttmann persisted. 'Were we wise to trust you, to put faith in you?'

'I don't know . . .'

'I went to see a man in Magdeburg, my oldest friend, a pastor at the Dom . . . I am proud of my faith. We talked of a man called Brusewitz who burned himself to death to bear witness to the conditions of worship in the country of my birth. Brusewitz faced fire, what we have been asked to do is trifling in comparison with the sacrifice of that man.'

'To cross the fence is your protest?'

'It is the only protest that will affect them. When you have taken me across then that is what I will speak of . . . you know there are many ways in which they scourge our church. When they needed room for factories it was the churches in Leipzig and Potsdam that were destroyed to provide the ground. When they wished to widen the road into Rostock it was a church that was demolished. When 15,000 of our brother Catholics wanted to go for their annual pilgrimage and worship at the cathedral of Erfurt they were told the ceremonies were forbidden, on that day the square outside the cathedral was required for the performance of the Soviet State Circus . . . My gesture is a small one, but it will be noted.'

'It will be noted,' Johnny grinned. He took himself as a fly to the ceiling of the office of the Politburo on Berlin's Marx-Engels Platz, to the corridors of Defence Ministry in Moscow, to the laboratories at Padolsk. They'll go bloody mad, Doctor.

'Where will Willi be?'

'Near the border but perhaps today he has gone back to London.'

'It will be wonderful to see Willi. I will be an old man and cry and make a fool of myself.'

Johnny glanced across at Erica. She was looking at her father. Radiant, gentle, and proud. The love blossomed from her.

Later he would take the spade and hack down some birches for the cross-struts of his ladder and dig up some young larches for his main poles, later he would leave this private communion between father and daughter. Later because the guards who examined the Hinterland fence must be given their time.

In two small clusters the Border Guards who were off duty stood in the parking area at the rear of the barracks of the Walbeck garrison and watched as Ulf Becker was led from the building to a Moskwitch car by two plain clothes men of the Schutzpolizei. His wrists handcuffed behind his back, he limped heavily and was supported by his escort. He searched among the faces for a covert greeting.

Heini Schalke was there. Straight-backed, belly protruding, unable to disguise his triumph. Schalke who had aimed the MPiKM and who would get a cash reward and extra leave, and who had won the chance of another stripe on his arm, of another favourable entry in his file at Battalion.

The boy who had carried the letter from Weferlingen to Berlin was there. Nervous and hanging back because he did not know the extent of his implication, only that the boy who had befriended him and asked the favour was in the custody of those who would extract a confession on all matters that interested them. It was the first day of his secondment to Walbeck. He did not meet Ulf's eyes, looked away.

Willi Guttmann heard the key turn in the door.

A mug of coffee was brought to him.

'Has my father been found, and my sister . . .?'

They had not been found. He would be told when they had been found.

The door was locked again. Behind the thin window curtains he could see the trellis of bars.

They had been most careful with Willi Guttmann. They had removed his shoe laces, his trouser belt and his tie, and had locked him in an upper room at Halberstadter Strasse.

He was past weeping, had cried himself to sleep the previous evening after the first detailed interrogation by the man from Berlin. There were no more tears as he lay on his back and stared at the ceiling light behind the protective wire.

Carter was shown into Charlie Davies's office.

Handshakes and Nescafé. Wally Smith was there and another man that Carter had not met before.

He wouldn't mind waiting, would he? A few things to be settled, then they'd be off.

Carter looked at the walls and their huge mosaic of black and white photographs. Photographs of the fences, of the National Volks Armee at work, of the Border Guards, of patrol boats on the distant side of the Elbe river, of the SM 70 automatic gun, of the PMK 40 and PMP 71 mines, of watchtowers and earth bunkers, of jeeps and transport lorries, of the RPK drum magazine machine gun . . . photographs that covered three of the four walls. On the fourth wall, from ceiling to floor, was a map, 1 inch to the mile, with its covering and Chinagraph symbols, showing the border.

When they were alone Charlie Davies lit a cigarette and came and sat beside Carter.

'Taken an eyeful of the pictures, have you? Well, you

323

should, because that's what's out there. Two million sterling a mile we reckon it's costing them, and that's big money for those bankrupt buggers . . .'

'It sort of clears the mind,' said Carter faintly.

'But they keep coming, God knows why, and about a dozen a year make it that we know of, a dozen a year along 411 miles, they're the ones we hear about. I don't know about the American sector, shouldn't be different. A dozen a year, and we're told there's 2,500 in the gaols that didn't make the run . . . and there's the ones that buy it . . .'

'The ones the bastards shoot . . .'

'Or the minefields, or the SM 70s . . . one last night, not on the fence itself but on the Hinterland. The alarms went off and there was a shot reported. I had to think of Johnny, didn't I? The BGS monitoring set the record straight. A girl was killed and a boy captured . . .'

'Johnny . . .?' mouthed Carter.

'They were both East German nationals. We reckon it's on the Hinterland that most of them fail though it's difficult to be exact. Last night there was a fair bit of radio chatter, that's because they're all keyed up for your lad and his customers.'

'They shot the girl dead?'

'They don't piss about.' Davies stabbed out his cigarette. 'Time we were off. There are some military doing a border recce north of Helmstedt, one of the other lads was taking them but I've put them under my wing. The East Germans are used to seeing me with troops, so if we go out in a big jolly party it's less conspicuous.'

'However you like it.'

They didn't talk in the car because Charlie Davies's German civilian driver was at the wheel. They drove north and met the troops in the village of Brome. Two Land-Rovers, a party of junior officers and senior NCOs. A pleasant group interested in what they had seen on the Elbe the previous day, and anticipating what they would find on the second half of their formal patrol. Men from a cavalry regiment, wearing their camouflage scarves jauntily, carrying their unloaded weapons easily and happy enough that for a few hours they had escaped the demands of their Chieftain tanks. The stops were frequent, as Charlie Davies with the skill of an expert guide handled their tour.

They gathered at a border marker to look through the close mesh wire and watch a work party of Pioneers erecting a new watchtower.

'The last one blew down,' said Davies. 'With them in it and all. Fair old night it was, hell of a wind and rain too. Down south in the Hartz there was a stretch of mines 2 kilometres long, which means 6,000 mines laid, and 2,000 of them went up when the rain cleared the earth off their pressure plates. Like bloody Guy Fawkes night . . .'

Through binoculars they stared across the sloping grasslands to the hill with its tree line and the Soviet Army observation bunker and listening post, and admired the professionalism of its siting.

'From what we hear there's no contact between the Soviets and the Border Guards, they don't have anything to do with each other, and that includes a quite separate communications system. A few years back a Soviet squaddie came over the wire just beside a manned tower and nobody dared challenge him because he was in Ruskie uniform . . .'

Across from the dark homes and mine workings of Weferlingen they stood on a raised viewing platform, and the white-cased SM 70s were identified on the fence.

'An SS officer designed them during the last war for use on the concentration camp fences, a way to reduce the number of guards required. They have a scatter range of about twenty-five metres, and they set them five metres apart. They're at different heights . . . face, balls and feet. Wicked buggers. This SS man was carted off to Russia after the surrender and they glossed them up there before this lot had the use of them. It's a charge of steel slivers, doesn't make a pretty sight afterwards . . .'

As they pushed on the troops became used to the presence of Carter, and he concocted a tale that he was Foreign and Commonwealth Officer and had a day to spare from his visit to Bonn, and wasn't everything most interesting, and Mr Davies was doing him a real favour by letting him come along.

Another viewing point, where a mud track was close to the fence and marker posts.

'See that down there, that culvert drain, not very wide, right? Not wide enough for any of us, but a kiddie could get through. There was a hell of a shambles some months back down on the Bundesgrenzschutz central sector, a 4 year old wriggled through. He was bawling his eyes out on one side, his mother raising Cain on the other. Should have stuffed him back where he came from, but no-one thought of that. Took bloody hours to get the protocol sorted out and a gate opened by them so he could be sent through. He'd have had a hell of a belt from his mum, that kiddie . . .'

A patter of anecdotes and information.

There was generally a bit of fun as the morning wore on, Charlie Davies warned, when the cameras came out. They reached a viewing platform in the woods south of Weferlingen sector and the Grenzaufklarer reconnaissance troops were waiting. Mud brown denims, rifles with magazines fitted, cameras with telephoto lenses. In front of the wire. Between the border post and the fence. Three of them and little more than a dozen paces away. No smile, no recognition, expressions humanised only by the contempt at their mouths. The Grenzaufklarer photographed the cavalry who photographed the Grenzaufklarer . . . And attention slipped to Carter, the one civilian, and the camera lens followed him, dogged him. Carter hated the man, wanted to shout at him, lob a rock at him. The camera spoiled the cheerfulness of the little party. These were the men who were waiting for Johnny. And the guns were armed.

'We call these the 150 percenters,' Charlie Davies boomed. 'They're a law to themselves, they can come through the wire whenever they want to, they can come right up to the frontier marker. In all my time I've only ever known one of them step the last yard over . . . Hey, Fritz, don't you go wasting film, do you want me to get the lads in a nice group for you, do you want me to do that? Look at the buggers, not a flicker. The day I get a wave out of that lot, I'll bloody drop dead . . .'

The convoy took a chipstone road that showed the wear of the forestry lorries. The car bumped and rolled. They passed a Bundesgrenzschutz van and Davies waved and was acknowledged and then they were alone again in the vastness of the woods. With the engines killed a quiet came on them. A lonely, green, leafy place till they walked up a soft mud path to within sight of the fence. The ground on either side of the close mesh wire had been cleared years earlier but now the bushes had sprouted and the grass grown and there was only the ploughed strip and the vehicle ditch and the patrol strip to show where the fence builders had tried to halt the encroachment of cover.

Carter was beside Charlie Davies. The troops had dropped behind. Just another stretch of border to them, and not much of a vantage point because the ground was flat, and they had been to better places and after the meeting with the Grenzaufklärer their interest had flagged.

'This was where he came on the second day, your lad, Johnny . . .'

'What attracted him?'

'Difficult to say. There's no permanent position here. No towers or bunkers, no mines either. That's the plus side . . .'

'And the negative . . .?'

'There's a Hinterland fence . . . there's a fair concentration of company garrisons all along this stretch, there's vehicles patrolling through the night and less often by day, there's SM 70s on the fence.'

Carter gazed through the mesh into the scrub beyond.

'Where should he be now, if he's coming tonight?'

'Five hundred metres or so the wrong side of the Hinterland.'

'He'd be trying to sleep, I suppose,' Carter said, a private thought.

'If I were stumbling into that lot tonight, I'd not be sleeping . . .'

327

Carter heard the crack in Davies's voice, recognised the emotion, realised that Johnny had reached and touched another man. The low pitched voices of the troops did not break into Carter's closed concentration. Johnny out there with the scientist and his daughter.

'I'll have to be here tonight . . .'

'I'll bring you up, can't have you running around here on your own,' Charlie Davies said brusquely. 'But you'll have to appreciate one thing. Till he gets to where we're standing now there's nothing we can do to help him. Whatever happens out there, nothing . . .'

The morning had passed. The patrol expressed their gratitude. Davies and his driver dropped Carter at the Stettiner Hof. They agreed a rendezvous time for the evening.

The Trade Minister maintained a granite faced façade of interest as he walked with a covey of managers and shop stewards between the aisles of carburettor engines. His attention was far from the production figures and output quotas for the machinery it was hoped his government would buy. Before leaving the Midlands he had spoken to the First Secretary by telephone.

The new men, he had concluded, were a weaker and poorer breed than those of the Old Guard with whom he had come from Moscow on the last day of April, 1945, to set up the fledgeling civilian administration at Frankfurt-an-der-Oder behind the rolling advance of the Red Army. Pieck and Grotewohl and Ulbricht would have known their minds, accepted his advice that he should return to Berlin immediately in the face of the criminal violation of the DDR's sovereign territory. But the new men were cautious, subservient. When there was a prisoner, when the net had trapped the fugitive, then he should cut short his visit.

But he believed that he had noted in his conversation with the First Secretary a growing impatience in the offices of the Central Committee at the inability of the forces of the SSD and the Schutzpolizei to track their quarry.

Doctor Frommholtz marched at the head of his entourage towards the canteen.

The Deputy-Under-Secretary was shown into the Prime Minister's private office. He had requested a meeting at Downing Street within minutes of having received a digest of Henry Carter's communication with Century House. He had been told that the Prime Minister was holding back on a scheduled meeting.

'Thank you for making yourself available at such short notice, sir.'

The Prime Minister stared at him, fascinated by the wreckage of a proud man. 'Please take a seat.'

'I'd prefer to stand and I'll be brief. We have reason to believe that the DIPPER matter will be concluded during the hours of tonight. One way or the other. We think that our man will attempt to break out of the DDR, to cross the frontier into the Federal Republic.'

The Prime Minister shuddered. He had been told before he arrived at Downing Street that many of his predecessors had found the workings and mechanics of the Service to be a narcotic. 'Are you in contact with him?'

'The prognostication is based on contingency plans made before his departure for East Germany.'

A slight smile from the Prime Minister. 'So, you're going to wave a magic wand, Deputy-Under-Secretary, cover the silk hat with a handkerchief, and then, hey presto, you're going to produce the agent safe and well and we're all to fall down before you and exclaim that the Service is the finest in the world.'

'I thought you'd want to know, sir.'

'It will be no credit to the Service if we get out of this without disgrace. It will be because of my efforts with the East Germans.'

'If we get out of this,' said the Deputy-Under-Secretary icily, 'it will be because my man successfully crosses the Inner German Border.'

'What about Guttmann? Have you written him off?'

'With the border in its present security state, we accept it is inconceivable that Dr Guttmann can accompany our man.'

'I must say, the Service's finest hour.'

'I drafted my letter of resignation at lunch-time. It will be with PUS in the morning. I've asked for it to be effective from midnight tomorrow. Goodbye, sir.'

He had made more noise approaching the hide than he would have liked, but the poles were heavy and he lugged them with difficulty through the undergrowth. He would have left a trail, but it was close to dusk. Three larch poles, strong and straight, and an armful of young birch stems.

They sat with their arms around each other on the ground as Johnny broke cover, and their faces shone with relief at the sight of him. They would have been fearful at the sound of his approach, praying it was Johnny.

His admiration swelled for them.

'Everything's fine. Just as we wanted.'

Otto Guttmann stared in disbelief at the larch poles, noted that the ends were neatly axe chopped into tapering, sharpened points.

Johnny grinned. 'A woodman gave them to me . . .'

'Gave them?'

'I think he did. He left me a nice pile to choose from . . .'

He saw the tension evaporating, the slow smile of understanding.

'. . . If he didn't mean them as a gift, he can have them back in the morning.'

The old man laughed, and the girl chuckled.

Johnny felt in his anorak pocket, reached amongst the grenades and the pistol's shoulder stock, and produced a greaseproof paper bag. 'He's a decent chap, the woodman, he gave me these for you . . . well, he left them for someone when he put his bag down. I scattered the paper and ripped it a bit, the bag they were in . . . I suppose he'll think he gave them to a fox . . . generous of him, whether they were for me or a fox or whoever.'

He tossed the package in a gentle arc so that it fell on

Erica's lap. Her hands tore at the paper, exposed the rough bread, the protruding meat. She and her father ate ravenously, stopping only to pick at the dropped pieces that spilled to their legs.

Erica looked up sharply at him. 'You have had something, Johnny?'

'He gave me a steak . . . and some onion rings . . .'

She sprang to her feet, came fast at Johnny, clasped the sides of his head with her hands, kissed him on the lips. Cold, dry and cracked. Johnny blinked. As fast as she had come she was back on the ground, back beside her father.

Johnny grimaced. 'If that happened more often I'd come here every year.'

Otto Guttmann beamed. Erica dropped her eyes.

'We have much to thank you for,' the old man said through a mouth full of food.

'Keep the thanks for tomorrow.'

Keep the bloody thanks for tomorrow. For after the Hinterland fence and the vehicle ditch and the ploughed strip, for after the wire that was 3½ metres high. Keep the thanks for tomorrow.

'I'm sorry, I didn't mean that,' said Johnny.

'What do we do now?' Erica asked.

'We have to build the ladder, before it's dark.'

On their hands and knees, as the daylight ran from the woods, they fashioned the ladder from the wire flex and the birch stems and the larch poles.

Chapter Twenty-three

=

Johnny stood, Erica kneeled.

Otto Guttmann crouched with lowered head and eyes and spoke the words.

'. . . And forgive us our trespasses,
As we forgive them that trespass against us . . .'

The ladder lay on the ground between Johnny and Erica, two larch poles forming a steep triangle and four birch stems lashed with the flex to them to make the steps. An untidy contraption, but sturdy.

'. . . And lead us not into temptation,
But deliver us from evil . . .'

The two lengths of coiled rope strand were beside the ladder and the third larch pole. They had been measured for length and the knots had been pulled and found strong enough.

'. . . For Thine is the Kingdom,
The power and the Glory,
For ever and ever . . .'

'Amen,' said Johnny.

Time to be moving. Otto Guttmann had wanted the prayer, and Johnny had acquiesced and found something comforting in it.

Now he was anxious to be on the path. He had lectured them on the procedures, made them repeat aloud what he had told them, had drilled the programme for the night into their minds. He would lead, and they would obey his every command instantly. There would be no hesitation, no discussion. Only once had he faltered during his last briefing.

'If anything happens to me . . . anything at all, and I can't go forward, then you do not try to go on by yourselves. You stand your ground, absolutely still, your hands on your heads. Don't give the bastards the excuse . . .'

Johnny led them to the path.

He carried the single pole and the rope and the spare flex. Between them Otto Guttmann and Erica must take the ladder frame. They must wait while he went forward and covered the first hundred metres, then he would come back for them. Each hundred metres he would personally clear and vet. The slow way, excruciatingly slow, a painful pace, step by step along the path . . . but safe, and safety was the jewel. Only Johnny would speak, father and daughter were committed to silence.

Sometimes a twig cracked under his foot, sometimes a dried leaf rustled beneath his boot, sometimes a low branch clutched at his clothing.

Impossible to be truly quiet, to maintain absolute stealth. And all the time the throbbing thought that they would be waiting, listening and concealed, ready to spring, hands on the flashlights, fingers on the rifle triggers. All the time they could be there, and the only way for him was forward.

In the daylight, during his foraging exercise for food and timber, he had rediscovered the trip wire that last night's boy and girl had skirted. He had paced out the distance between the wire and the hide: 224 paces, and then the diversion into the trees for the bypassing of the danger strand, and Otto Guttmann and Erica followed him blindly and would not know why at this particular place his muffled counting stopped and they must stumble on rough ground for a few yards before returning to the ease of the path.

Johnny ahead of them again, ahead and alone . . .

There was an explosion of movement not five yards from him.

Johnny froze.

The crashing roar of escape away from him, and pigeons in the high branches clattered into flight. The sounds of desperate, clumsy escape, echoing into the dark distance of the woods. All the bloody world would hear it . . . Johnny's heart pounding, his breathing petrified. The hand that did not hold the pole was clasped on the butt of the Stechkin.

Bloody pig. The woods were packed tight with them. Not hunted here. Too close to the frontier. Fucking game reserve . . . A full minute Johnny stood rock still and as the fear slipped so came a sprinkling of confidence. If the pig had been browsing in the leaf-mould for young roots and had been disturbed by him then there was no other interloper in its territory. The immediate path was clear.

Six times Johnny ventured forward, retraced his steps to Otto Guttmann and Erica, advanced with them, and then set off again on his own. He had known it would be slow, but there was no call for hurry and he must stifle the desire to rush.

An hour and a quarter after they had set out, Johnny saw in front of him the shadow of the woodman's hut and the clear ground beyond and the silvery brightness of the Hinterland fence.

Charlie Davies collected Carter from the Stettiner Hof. The lights lit the Holzberg Square, shone on the leaning and timbered facades of the houses, on the cobbles. Noise and laughter spilled from the bars and cafés, a carefree accordion wheezed at the night. A cheerful community that was soon behind them as they took the road north.

'My wife did a flask of coffee and I put a half of Scotch on the NAAFI slate, and there's some sandwiches . . .' said Davies as he drove. 'There's a groundsheet in the back, too, and a torch. We could be out there all night . . .'

'Signals said again this afternoon that the radio traffic over there is still lumping Johnny with Guttmann and his daughter.'

'Not my business, but they're important, are they?'

'They're what Johnny's there for.'

'And he's an old man, this Guttmann?'

'In his seventieth year.'

'Jesus . . . Who's this caper down to?'

'The high and the mighty, and they've had sod-all luck.'

'Luck doesn't get you far on the wire,' Davies said gently. The mood was oppressive and he sought to change the tempo. 'I can't take the car that close. We'll have to walk the last mile, and death quiet then, no lights, no talking. Right?'

The car was off the main road, coughing along a rough track between the trees. Carter was subdued. A thousand miles from home. A thousand miles from Century House. A thousand miles from the 'Green Dragon' and the snug bar. A thousand miles from everything that was real and dear to him. A thousand miles from Johnny who was across the wire and coming.

Charlie Davies parked the car, ran it off the track and under the trees.

'I think we'll have a last fag here,' he said. 'And maybe we'd better break open the bottle for a quickie.'

He stripped the cap off the small whisky bottle and passed it to Carter.

Johnny looked at his watch. For forty-five minutes they had been in the cover at the back of the woodman's hut. The pattern of the jeep patrol had developed in front of him. Ten minutes after they had come to the hut the vehicle had crawled along the makeshift track on the south to north run. Fifteen minutes later it had returned, chugging in low gear; its headlights sharp and glinting on the fence. Another fifteen minutes and again south to north and Johnny had seen the silhouettes of the two men through the doorway space of the jeep.

All hinging on the watch face, because Johnny had sneered that he was exact, that he had a plan. All dependent on the moving minute hand.

Five more minutes and the jeep should return and with the heading away of its winking tail lights they would go for the Hinterland fence. If there was a concealed surveillance position, occupied since the previous evening, then he believed he would have seen a sign, heard a greeting from the jeep.

No moon, only a wind that drifted the clouds, curled the upper branches, shivered in the leaves.

'After the next run, we go . . .'

One hand in Otto Guttmann's, the other in Erica's.

Johnny felt them grasping at him, trying to borrow from him the strength for their survival.

'Just do as I said, exactly as I said. There aren't going to be any problems.'

He loosed the old man's hand, but Erica's hand he held longer, and her fingers were slipped between his. Afterwards, Johnny, afterwards is the time for thanks. Her fingers played on the palm of his hand.

The jeep was coming.

Johnny snatched his hand away, sank to a crouch, pulled them down beside him, was aware of the slow, stiff movements of Otto Guttmann. God knows how you managed to get this far, old man.

First the twin beams of the head lights, then the following shadow of the jeep. Fifteen miles an hour. In its own time. Johnny covered his eyes to save his vision. The jeep passed within thirty yards of them and there was a murmur of voices beside the engine noise. It sank away out of their sight and the arc of light was lost, and they were left in the crowding darkness with only the fading lurch of the motor.

Johnny ran forward with the single larch pole. Thirty-five strides to the fence. A yard short he stopped, panted, caught at himself for control. Behind him he heard Otto Guttmann and Erica, coming more slowly because the burden of the ladder was greater. Johnny raised the pole to the level of the second wire. He couldn't reach over the very highest. He edged the pole forward inch by inch between the wires. A fraction to spare top and bottom. The muscles of his back rippled and shook with the weight of it. His wrists ached in pain. At last he reached the fence with his hands. The pole was clear through. He let the far end down as slowly as he could. As it dropped the last two feet to the ground his hands jumped, brushed, tickled the wire ... not enough, you bastard, the pressure only of a sparrow. Reaching through the strands he manoeuvred the pole against the cement post. Erica took his place and held the pole firm. He turned to bring the ladder. She began to bind the larch pole in two places to the post. With Otto Guttmann Johnny lifted the ladder and they carried it upright to the fence and with infinite care lowered it against the single pole. The angle above the bound join of the ladder slipped tight against the pole tied to the fence post. Johnny rocked the frame lightly at first, then more fiercely, allowed it to slip, then find its hold.

Clear of those bastard wires, free of them, because a scientist had worked the calculations. A small, friendly, fragile gap between the bark of the larch wood and the taut length of the upper wire beneath.

Johnny went first. He spread his feet lightly on the supports, pivoted at the join high above the untouched wire, dropped easily to the ground, fell and rolled in the style they'd taught him as a young recruit.

Otto Guttmann next. He would climb more slowly. Erica came under the ladder, prepared to take its weight against her shoulders, to protect from the depths of her strength the wires above. He climbed and once the smooth leather of his shoe slipped on the birch wood and the ladder danced and Erica gasped and Johnny cursed, and the wire remained untouched. At the highest support of the ladder Otto Guttmann swung a stiff, unsupple leg over into the void above Johnny's shoulder. It was caught, guided down and Johnny's hands reached up and clasped him about the waist.

'Let go . . .' the hissed command.

Johnny swung Otto Guttmann to the ground, as a man lifts down a child, and they tumbled together on the grass.

Then Erica. Easier for Johnny. And his hands caught at the softness above her hips, and she was down.

Johnny's eyes darted at the watch face.

Onto Erica's shoulders. His shoes cutting into the material of her coat, his ears hearing her struggle, his legs feeling the steadying hands of Otto Guttmann. The pole bound to the cement post supported him as he heaved the ladder up from the far ground, hoisted it over the wire, threw it to the grass below him.

337

One over you, little bastard, one you didn't bloody trap, and the wire was still and the demi-light winked on its cold, untouchable surface.

Johnny jumped. Erica fingered open the knots at the post. Otto Guttmann dragged the ladder to the cover of the tree line.

Johnny on his feet, holding the pole, waiting for Erica to finish with the knots and at last lifting it back and free.

Indistinct as yet, far from them, the sound of the jeep engine.

He caught her by the arm, dragged her without ceremony away from the fence, trailing the last pole.

All on the ground, all married to the wet night grass, they watched the spreading halo of the jeep's lights. Its pace was constant, its progress uninterrupted. They watched its coming and its going.

Otto Guttmann chuckled. 'It was perfect . . . brilliant . . .'

'Well done, Johnny,' whispered Erica, and her hand rested easily, naturally, on Johnny's.

'I said there had to be silence . . . you've seen damn all yet.' But he allowed himself one sharp snigger of pleasure. Hadn't been a bad effort.

In front of them was a quarter of a mile of woodland, and then the final barricade, and the guns and the high fence. In front of them was what Charlie Davies, just one week ago, had breezily called 'the Chopping zone'.

At company headquarters in Walbeck village the new day's first shift had drawn their rifles from the armoury, signed for their ammunition and filed into the briefing room.

Heini Schalke stood at the front, close to the Politoffizier who had publicly congratulated him, close to the major who had praised him grudgingly, close to the sergeant who had queried his need to shoot and not spoken to him since. The other men with whom he messed had avoided him. He was not shunned, not ignored, only left in no doubt that his company was not wanted.

They never knew where they would be placed until the briefing. That was the way of the border. No man could take for granted that he would patrol the outer perimeter of the Restricted Zone, or the Hinterland fence, or lie up in a hide, or climb a watchtower, or ride in a jeep.

Many times in the day Heini Schalke had seen the fair sweeping hair that rolled in the headlights, and the young dead face of the girl. Ulf Becker was in his thoughts, too . . . Becker, who in the manacles of the captive met his eyes without fear. It was not possible for Heini Schalke to understand why the man who had slept four beds from him in the dormitory at Weferlingen would have come with his girl to the Hinterland fence.

'Corporal Schalke, you are with Brandt. The jeep run on the forward road from the Walbeck Strasse tower to two kilometres north.'

Two kilometres, backwards and forwards for two kilometres, four minutes up and four minutes down, and in between the pull off the patrol road and only Brandt, who was from the farm country of Mecklenburg in the north, to talk with. He looked behind him, saw Brandt, saw the grim resignation on the boy's face.

'A car has been found at Bischofswald, between here and Haldensleben. The car was stolen from near Magdeburg yesterday morning. It is believed that three persons are attempting an illegal crossing of the frontier. There are two males and one female. Battalion have called for especial vigilance from all personnel. I know you will do your duty if confronted by these criminals. I know the company will not be found wanting in the fulfilment of its responsibilities.'

Johnny held the stick that was stripped of leaves and their stems as a blind man walks with a wand. He held it loosely between forefinger and thumb and rocked it forward and back with a great gentleness in front of his legs.

By his estimate they were half way between the Hinterland fence and the final cleared cutting in the forest.

It had been cripplingly slow along the path, torture to their nerves, and now the stick's swing was blocked. The impediment was at knee height. Three times he had swung the stick. To the right of his legs, to the left of them, to his front. Each time the thin stick stumbled against the obstruction. He had allowed Otto Guttmann and Erica to be with him for the last push, had reckoned there was a greater terror for them if they were behind and cut off from him. They wanted to be with him, close to the source spring of encouragement. He pushed Otto Guttmann softly back to avoid being crowded into error.

The stick was his guide in the darkness and his fingers found the contact point where it met the trip wire. They were not so sensitive, these wires, not like those on the Hinterland. A man's whole weight would activate the alarm, but not the impact of a running hare or a wandering fox. The wire was tight stretched, there for the unwary, there for the fool.

He reached out and coaxed Otto Guttmann forward and lifted him over the single wire, and Erica after him.

It pleased Johnny to have found the trip. If there was a wire on the path then there could be no foot patrols.

The wind played at his face because the tall trees were no longer around them. They were into the space that had been cleared and where only intermittent waist-high undergrowth had come to replace the pines. He remembered the place as he had seen it from the far side, remembered the cover that stretched to the dull grey of the patrol road and the sandy earth of the ploughed strip.

Close to midnight, a good time for them to be coming. The time of the change of the Border Guard details. The time when some were cold and hungry and tired for their beds, when others had not accustomed their eyes to the night.

They had eaten the sandwiches, they had drained half the bottle, they had broached the coffee flask. The groundsheet was spread across the track that ran parallel to the line of the

340

border. A desperate, lonely place, Carter reckoned, the Roteriede at night. No life here . . . except when the moon passed beyond the wire and threw colours of light between the bushes. Not a job for Carter, not his end of the business, not here wet and half frozen. Should have been someone half his age.

There was an owl somewhere in the tree above. Could have been a tawny from its call, *Strix aluco* and fifteen inch wingspan. An awkward, cussed creature, for ever stamping at its perch. Each time it shouted, Carter flinched. Lucky bugger, with its night sight, and elevation. Carter could see damn all from the level of the groundsheet.

'If he comes, do you know where it will be, how far either side of us?' Carter whispered in Charlie Davies's ear.

'Right here.'

'Where we are now?'

'Where we're lying is where he stood, right here, there's something of a path that comes out opposite us . . .'

Nothing more to be said, and Davies offering no encouragement for conversation. Only the waiting and the straining for a sound of the coming of Johnny.

Why did the bastard jeep come so often?

Johnny had clocked it, watched the pattern. When it passed them going north it returned in two minutes, when it passed them going south it was with them again in six minutes. Shit, that was tight time. Six minutes, but that took no account of the speed with which it would return once the automatic guns were detonated. Then it would be racing, accelerator down, roaring forward on the patrol road. So much to bloody do. The run to the fence, the fastening of the ropes, the exploding of the SM 70s, the climbing of the wire. And the jeep could never be more than three minutes from the firing of the SM 70s, never more and always less. Not a yard of cover from where they knelt in the undergrowth beside the patrol road to the wire.

He could do it on his own, no sweat, he was not alone. One old man and one girl to go first. Johnny was down the order. Otto Guttmann, scientist from Padolsk, had first priority on the fence.

Should they lie up another night and hope the patrol pattern tailed off?

But when daylight came and the foot patrols were out by the Hinterland then there would be the trampled grass, the disturbed earth from the sharpened poles. The dogs would come, heaving their handlers along Johnny's trail.

Has to be tonight, Johnny. What's the problem, Johnny? Frightened? Scared witless, what else.

It's a hell of a way to the fence. I can bloody see, every time the bloody jeep goes by.

The guns are set close here. They're set close every bloody place.

Johnny reached out, felt Erica's shoulder, slid his fingers down the sleeve of her coat, found her hand and held it. There would be another time for them, wouldn't there? Somewhere removed from this bastard evil place.

The jeep went past, the regular throb of its engine, the regular speed of its wheels.

There had to be another bloody chance, for Johnny and Erica, somewhere as comforting as the hand that held his own. Somewhere, anywhere; any time, all the time. Over the other side of that bastard fence.

'Doctor Guttmann. It's the last time I say it, I promise, but you have to listen . . .' Johnny whispered and a nervous smile flickered at his lips. 'The patrolling is very thorough, so it won't be easy but we *can* manage. Nothing to spare but we can manage. When we go, then you and Erica run straight for the ditch, down on your faces, take all the cover the ditch gives you. I go first to the fence with the ropes, then I come back to you and we fire the guns. I can't over-emphasise it, but we have very little time after the guns go. Very, very little. We stop for nothing, we wait for nothing. Doctor Guttmann goes first, then Erica. There are no guns, no mines on the other side, but you must run straight for the trees, at least fifteen metres and you must make a hiding

342

place. Don't call out, don't shout . . . or you'll be fired on. Can you do it?'

'You ask me to do nothing,' Otto Guttmann said. 'You take everything on yourself. You are a fine boy. Both of us think that.'

Johnny let go of Erica's hand, took the long loops of rope.

'As soon as the jeep is past, we go.'

'We are ready.'

'Remember your hands on the top of the wire . . . Pull your cuffs right into the palms of your hands.'

'Yes.'

'You too, Erica.'

'Yes, Johnny . . .'

The engine sounds of the jeep. Johnny saw the glow of the driver's cigarette. No door on the jeep, because on the border a door could mean delay. He closed his eyes.

The jeep was ten yards gone. Johnny was on his feet and running forward, hunched and fast and stretched. Slower steps behind him, he did not look back. Go, Johnny, go. All the way, darling. All the way, you crazy bugger. Off the patrol road and into the ploughed strip his feet sinking and slipping into the loose earth, over the ditch his fingers clawing at the top rim of cement blocks and he pulled himself up. Only the fence now.

Calm, Johnny, calm for God's sake. You have to take time to find the wires, find the rope ends, tie the loose knots. Twenty-five yards killing range the bastard guns have, and there's one that's white and protected in its shield and it's five bloody feet from your guts. They rip your insides out, Johnny, it'll spread you back over the ploughed zone. They're razor sharp, the bits inside, Johnny. Cut your face, your bones, your veins, gouge your eyes, strip your skin. Two firing wires you have to find. You have to take time, you have to be right.

There's no bloody time.

The ropes were looped over the upper two of the three firing wires, the knots tied with leaping, fumbling fingers.

343

Johnny turned, played out the twin ropes, stumbled back, plunged into the ditch, fell on Otto Guttmann's legs. He looked at his watch, found the second hand. Give it a little while, darling, let the jeep run to its extremity.

Carter had surged to his knees.

Charlie Davies's fist was embedded in Carter's coat, wrenching him down.

'Someone was there . . . at the fence.'

'Get down.'

'It'll be Johnny . . .'

'Or the aufklarer, or the NVA . . . or Johnny.'

Carter fell back. 'It has to be Johnny.'

'And if it is, how do you help him? I told you before there's nothing . . .'

The twin explosions raked the night. Two sheets of flame streaming from the separated posts. A fraction of time before the third detonation. The singing howl of the shrapnel in the air, the whine of ricochets from the fence. Brilliant, echoing noise cascading through the trees.

Johnny jumped from the cover of the ditch, slid at its rim, scrabbled for support, found it, felt the stench of the explosive charge at his nostrils, twisted back with his arm outstretched. He grappled for a hand to seize, found none, swept his fingers through the darkness. He touched the coat of Otto Guttmann, pulled it, dragged it. God, he was heavy. And stiff too, rigid, unhelping, an old man and disorientated and confused, cringing back from the smoke and the noise.

A Very light burst in the sky, showered the tree tops with slow falling stars.

Can't move him, Johnny, can you? Can't lift him if he won't help. He has to help, the bloody fool, he has to help if he's to go over. It's four feet above your eye level, the top of the wire. He has to respond. He has to want to climb.

'Erica . . . you have to help me . . .' Johnny desperate, Johnny in panic. All of them stumbling in the darkness and

344

the chaos rampant and contagious.

The howl of the first siren. The powered roar of a jeep engine. Closing on you, Johnny, and the sand's running, the time's spilling. The second hand's spinning on the watch face. The jeep's eating the yards.

Johnny circled his arm round Otto Guttmann's waist. Gently, darling. Cut the fluster. Gently because that's the only way, because otherwise it's catastrophe.

'All the guns have gone, Doctor,' Johnny said quietly. 'There's only the fence now. As I lift you, put your hands on the top and pull yourself and roll off the top and let yourself drop . . .' He'll have no hands left, they'll be shredded, they'll be slashed. 'I'm going to lift you now, Doctor . . .'

He forced Otto Guttmann up and his feet kicked and slipped on the smoothness of the mesh, and the old man's hands reached up, naked and white, for the top of the wire and grasped at it, and he screamed and the blood drops spattered on Johnny's head.

'You have to go over,' Johnny shouted. 'You have to find the courage . . .'

The jeep lights broke on the fence, dawn with day running behind, clearing the blur of movement from the shadow edges, sharpening the images of confusion. Johnny on his toes and stretching, and the strength was fleeing him. He thrust Otto Guttmann's legs onto the summit of the wire, saw a shoe balance at the top, an ankle catch, he heard the tearing of the clothing.

'Help me, Erica . . .'

'I can't . . . I can't reach him.'

'We have to.'

'I can't. I can't . . . I can't reach him.'

There was a long, rippling burst of automatic fire.

Above Johnny's head, Otto Guttmann lurched and rolled and gasped as the bullets struck home.

The crack of the gun, the thud of the impact. Sounds that were together and inseparable. Only the clothing held him, and the hand that was bloodied and had gripped the wire. One single shot to follow and Otto Guttmann toppled back

345

from the wire, shaken clear by the force of the blow, landing at Johnny's feet.

Erica on the ground beside him, Erica with the keening cry and the hands that were loving at her father's face. Johnny spun away from the wire.

The jeep on the patrol road with its lights turned on them, and in front of the lights the outline of the soldier.

Johnny dropped, reached for the Stechkin, rolled and aimed. The range at Aldershot, just as the Para sergeant had told him. Half a clip he fired. Three shots to fell the rifleman. Three shots to stagger, twist and drop him. Three shots for the windscreen of the jeep, the cry of fear, the pain.

New Very lights in the sky, more sirens in the wind.

'We have to go, Erica,' said Johnny.

'I won't leave him.'

Johnny's arm was round her, he felt the convulsions of her misery. 'You can't help him . . . we *must go now*.'

'There is nothing for me there.'

'You have to come, Erica.'

She looked into his face. He saw the sorrow and the obstinate calm. 'If I were to come, then who would bury him? . . . You go, Johnny. You have done what you were sent to do.'

She turned away and pulled her father's head closer to her, she rocked him, a mother that has a lullaby for her child. He did not see her face again.

'Go, Johnny,' he heard her murmur.

Johnny flung the Stechkin out towards the jeep, the dismissal of Excalibur, heard it clatter on the concrete, then threw the grenades, unarmed, after the pistol.

The engines of the jeeps were closing in, the sirens bleating through his mind. He tugged his hands into the cuffs of his anorak and launched himself at the top of the wire. His hands gripped and clasped, and he bit at the pain, and swung his body easily over and dropped to the ground on the far side.

Charlie Davies held Carter's arm, restrained him, and they

waited for Johnny to reach them.

They could not see his face under the shadow of the trees, and he never turned to look back at the jeeps and their parade of lights, and the men in uniform who sprinted towards the wire, and the old man who must be buried, and the girl who stood tall and heroic with her hands held high.

Charlie Davies and Johnny ran, bent double through the trees, out of range, and Carter trailed behind them until they slowed to a walk when they were close to the car.

'Take me home, please,' Johnny said.

Gerald Seymour

writes internationally best-selling thrillers

'Not since Le Carré has the emergence of an international suspense writer been as stunning as that of Gerald Seymour.' *Los Angeles Times*

HARRY'S GAME
KINGFISHER
RED FOX
THE CONTRACT
ARCHANGEL
IN HONOUR BOUND
FIELD OF BLOOD

FONTANA PAPERBACKS

Duncan Kyle

'One of the modern masters of the high adventure story.' *Daily Telegraph*

GREEN RIVER HIGH
BLACK CAMELOT
A CAGE OF ICE
FLIGHT INTO FEAR
TERROR'S CRADLE
A RAFT OF SWORDS
WHITEOUT!
STALKING POINT
THE SEMONOV IMPULSE

FONTANA PAPERBACKS

Desmond Bagley

– a master of suspense –

'I've read all Bagley's books and he's marvellous, the best.' *Alistair MacLean*

THE ENEMY
FLYAWAY
THE FREEDOM TRAP
THE GOLDEN KEEL
LANDSLIDE
RUNNING BLIND
THE TIGHTROPE MEN
THE VIVERO LETTER
WYATT'S HURRICANE
BAHAMA CRISIS
WINDFALL
NIGHT OF ERROR
JUGGERNAUT
THE SNOW TIGER
THE SPOILERS

FONTANA PAPERBACKS

Fontana Paperbacks: Fiction

Fontana is a leading paperback publisher of both non-fiction, popular and academic, and fiction. Below are some recent fiction titles.

☐ THE ROSE STONE Teresa Crane £2.95
☐ THE DANCING MEN Duncan Kyle £2.50
☐ AN EXCESS OF LOVE Cathy Cash Spellman £3.50
☐ THE ANVIL CHORUS Shane Stevens £2.95
☐ A SONG TWICE OVER Brenda Jagger £3.50
☐ SHELL GAME Douglas Terman £2.95
☐ FAMILY TRUTHS Syrell Leahy £2.95
☐ ROUGH JUSTICE Jerry Oster £2.50
☐ ANOTHER DOOR OPENS Lee Mackenzie £2.25
☐ THE MONEY STONES Ian St James £2.95
☐ THE BAD AND THE BEAUTIFUL Vera Cowie £2.95
☐ RAMAGE'S CHALLENGE Dudley Pope £2.95
☐ THE ROAD TO UNDERFALL Mike Jefferies £2.95

You can buy Fontana paperbacks at your local bookshop or newsagent. Or you can order them from Fontana Paperbacks, Cash Sales Department, Box 29, Douglas, Isle of Man. Please send a cheque, postal or money order (not currency) worth the purchase price plus 15p per book for postage (maximum postage required is £3.00 for orders within the UK).

NAME (Block letters) _____

ADDRESS _____

_____

_____